Praise for Barbara Cleverly

'The historical background of Barbara Cleverly's novel is as fascinating as the murder. Stiff upper lip soldiers, American heiresses, handsome Afghan tribesmen – they are all here in spades. A great blood and guts blockbuster.'
—*Guardian*

∽

'A well-plotted novel . . . The atmosphere of the dying days of the Raj is colourfully captured.'
—Suasanna Yager, *Sunday Telegraph*

∽

'Spectacular and dashing. Spellbinding.'
—*The New York Times Book Review*

∽

'Smashing . . . marvelously evoked.'
—*Chicago Tribune*

∽

'An historical mystery that has just about everything.'
—*Denver Post*

∽

'Maintains the high standards set by earlier Sandilands tales, blending a sophisticated whodunit with full-blooded characters and a revealing look at her chosen time and place.'
—*Publishers Weekly* (starred review)

Also by Barbara Cleverly

The Last Kashmiri Rose

The Last Kashmiri Rose

BARBARA CLEVERLY

First published in the UK by Constable,
an imprint of Constable & Robinson Ltd, 2001

Published in the US in 2011 by
Soho Press, Inc.
853 Broadway
New York, NY 10003

Library of Congress Cataloging-in-Publication Data
Cleverly, Barbara
The last Kashmiri rose / Barbara Cleverly.

1. Sandilands, Joe (Fictitious character)—Fiction.
2. Police—India—Bengal—Fiction 3. India—History—
British occupation, 1765-1947—Fiction I. Title
PR6103.L48 L37 2002

ISBN: 978-1-61695-002-6
eISBN: 978-1-61695-003-3

Printed in the United States of America

10 9 8 7 6 5 4 3 2 1

BARBARA CLEVERLY lives in Cambridge, England, surrounded by ancient buildings and bookshops. She was born and educated in the north of England at a Yorkshire grammar school and then at Durham University.

The Last Kashmiri Rose was Barbara's first book, which she was inspired to write following a successful outline sent to the Crime Writers' Association/*Sunday Times* Debut Dagger Competition. A shortlisting and warm reception by the judging panel led to its writing in full. It was a *New York Times* Notable Book of 2002, and Barbara has written a further eight Joe Sandilands novels.

The Last Kashmiri Rose

Chapter One

BENGAL 1910

THE NIGHT BEFORE her sixth birthday Midge Prentice woke under her mosquito net and breathed the familiar smells of a hot Indian night. There was the smell of wet khaskhas mats hanging across the doors and windows to keep out the heat of early summer, sweet and musty; there was the smell of the jasmine which grew over the bungalow; there was the bass accompaniment inseparable from India of drains and of dung. But tonight there was something else.

Sharp and acrid, it was the smell of smoke. Midge sat up and looked about her. Running across the ceiling of her room there was a flickering reflection of flames. She struggled out of her mosquito net and, barefoot, stood down on the floor. She called for her father and then remembered he was away in Calcutta. She called for her mother but it was Ayah who answered her call.

'Come with Ayah, now, Missy Baba,' she said urgently. 'Come swiftly. Be silent!'

Ayah gathered her up. 'Put your arms round me and hold tight. Very tight. Put your feet on mine and we'll walk together as we used to when you were a baby and then the bad, bad men won't see my Missy Baba. If I hide you under my sari they'll just think that Ayah has another baby on the way.'

She swept silky folds over Midge's head and they set off to waddle together towards safety. They had often done this

before; it had been a game of her infancy. It was called 'elephant walk backwards' and now this clumsy game was to save
her life. Midge caught brief glimpses of Ayah's sandalled feet
and was aware of others milling protectively about them and
then they were in the open air. They were free of the bungalow. Men's voices – Indian voices – shouted harshly, shots rang
out, a woman's scream was abruptly cut short and then the
roar of the fire as it took hold of the thatch grew deafening.

But then, gravel was crunching under Ayah's feet and she
stopped. 'Sit here,' she said. 'Sit here and keep quiet. Don't
move. Be hidden.' And she tucked Midge away amongst the
rank of tall earthenware pots overflowing with bougainvillea
and zinnia.

In the mess, half a mile away, Jonno crossed and uncrossed his
legs under the table and with a slightly unsteady hand poured
himself a glass of port and passed the decanter. He was thinking – he was often thinking – of Dolly Prentice, or, more formally, Mrs Major Prentice. He was sure he hadn't imagined
that, as he had helped her into her wrap after the gymkhana
dance, she had leant back against him, not obviously but perceptibly. Yes, surely perceptibly. And his hands had rested on
her shoulders, slightly moist because it had been a hot night,
and there had been a warm female scent. What was it she had
said when, greatly daring, he had admired? 'Chypre.' Yes, that
was it – 'Chypre.'

And that wasn't all. They had danced close. Not difficult
when doing a two-step and she had said, almost out of the
blue, 'You're getting to be quite a big boy now.' It might have
meant anything; it might have meant nothing. But he didn't
think so. In memory he held that slender figure in its red chif-
fon dress as close as he dared.

The young subaltern on Jonno's left was also thinking of
Dolly Prentice. He knew she'd only been joking but she had

said, 'Just bring your problems to me, young man, and I'll see what I can do.' Had she meant it? He thought probably not. But it had been accompanied by a steady and speaking glance and, after his third glass of port, he decided, nevertheless, to take her at her word.

That bloody pony! Fifty pounds! He hadn't got fifty pounds! Why had he fallen for it? He knew only too well why. He'd been goaded into it by Prentice. 'Take it or leave it. Pony's yours for fifty pounds but be warned – he takes a bit of riding!' And the clear implication – 'Too much of a handful for you!' He thought if he threw himself on Dolly's mercy, she might intercede for him – get him off his bargain. Perhaps she could persuade her husband not to take advantage of a young and inexperienced officer? He didn't like appearing in the role of innocent naughty boy but still less did he like having to borrow yet again.

Then, by God! The pony! In his secret heart he was aware that he couldn't manage it. The pony was vicious. He had made a mess of Prentice's syce. Put him on his back for a week, they said. 'Oh, what the hell!' he thought. 'Damnation to you, Major Prentice!' And he drained his glass.

The regimental doctor sitting opposite watched him guardedly. He always felt out of place in the elegant company of Bateman's Horse. He tried not to, but could not help contrasting the splendour of their grey and silver mess dress with his own Indian Medical Service dark blue. He was not, in fact, thinking about Dolly Prentice. He was thinking about Prentice. He remembered (would he ever forget?) the public shame that had followed his first greeting at the hands of Major Prentice.

'Tell me, doctor,' he had said, '– we are all so eager to know – from what barrow in Petticoat Lane did you buy those boots?'

It was true that his boots did not come from a fashionable boot-maker. They had come from a saddler in Maidstone and they had looked good enough when he had first tried them on. He was painfully aware that, by comparison with the officers of Bateman's Horse, the 'Bengal Greys', he lacked the skintight precision supplied by Lobb of St James's, the skin-tight precision which forbade anything more substantial inside than a cut-down ladies' silk stocking.

His thoughts turned to Dolly. Dolly with her large eyes and her ready sympathy. How could she bear life with that devil? How could she put up with him close to her? And a vision of Dolly in the arms of Giles Prentice rose, not for the first time, to trouble him. He imagined the heat of an Indian night. He imagined the close confines of a mosquito net. He tried but did not succeed in keeping at bay the vision of Prentice's slim brown hands exploring the surface anatomy which his fervid imagination and medical experience con-jured up. Too easily.

The senior officer present, Major Harry, looked up and down the table. Over-bright eyes, mottled faces, desultory and slurred speech – there was no doubt about it, when Prentice was away conversation ebbed and the drink flowed to fill the gaps. And Prentice was away. He had gone to Calcutta for an interview for promotion to the senior branch. 'But why Giles? Why not me?' There could only be one of them this time and that one was Prentice. This had been the moment when he might have broken through and God knew when there might be another one.

His career really needed the step. He needed the money. Very soon there would be children to be sent home to school in England. Already his wife was complaining and he was sick of the endless litany – 'Nothing to wear . . . only one carriage horse . . . when can we buy our own furniture?' He had des-perately needed this step and now Prentice had it. Pretentious Prentice!

Dickie Templar likewise surveyed the company. On attach-ment and waiting to join a Gurkha regiment on the north-west frontier, he was glad that he was not to be gazetted into

Bateman's Horse. He felt that though they had a glowing past (they had been golden heroes of the Mutiny) they had for too long rested on their laurels and their promotion prospects were not good. And the officers – they bored him. Further than that, they even repelled him. Sick of their company, he rose from the table and made his way to the ghulskhana where, with difficulty, unbuttoning the flap of his tight mess trousers, he stood for a moment aiming largely by memory in the darkness.

It was a fetid little enclosure and with his spare hand he pushed open the window through which instantly there came a murmur of unfamiliar sound. An unfamiliar sound in a crescendo and – there – what was that? A shot. And another shot. Buttoning himself up, he stood on tiptoe and gazed out of the window. There was a yellow leaping flame beginning to spring from one of the bungalows, about half a mile away, he judged. A fire? Yes, there was a fire and now there was a smell of smoke. A fire in the lines? Probably nothing. No one else seemed aware of it as he hurried back to the dining-room.

'There's a fire!' he said. And then again, 'There's a fire in the lines!'

In line abreast, the five Greys officers cantered on down towards the disturbance. They clattered into the compound and surveyed with dismay the ruin of Prentice's house. And here they were challenged by a figure in a scarlet mess jacket, his white shirt front blackened. The Braganza Lamb in silver thread on his lapel identified the Queen's duty officer. Four British soldiers, presumably the Queen's fire picket, were hauling on the handle of the fire engine and two more were directing a jet of water into the ruin. Others, faces bound in cloth, made useless attempts to approach. Riflemen stood by.

'What the hell's been going on here?' said Major Harry.

'Disaster! Total disaster!' came the reply. 'We did our best but we were too late. Bloody fire engine! About as much good as a water pistol! We organised a bucket chain but we were too few and too late.'

'Too late to save the bungalow?'

'To hell with the bungalow! Too late to save Dolly and Midge Prentice.'

'But they're in Calcutta with Giles! He always takes them with him!'

'Not this time, he didn't! It's Midge's birthday tomorrow – Dolly stayed at home with her for her party. Good God! My girls were going!' He wiped a blackened and bleeding hand across his face. 'My girls were to be there,' he said again. 'No, there's no sign of Midge or her mother . . . must be still in there . . . what's left of the poor devils . . . The minute this lot cools down enough to get men in we'll look for the bodies. Jesus! And Prentice away! I say – a disaster!'

'But who the hell . . .?'

'Dacoits . . . we think it was dacoits. Doped up, no doubt – drugged-up courage. In a mood to stop at nothing. It happens. Prentice had been routing them out of village after village and they came for him. Didn't know he was away, I suppose . . . Or perhaps they knew only too well! They've chased all the servants off or they've fled. No sign of them anyway. Come crawling back in the morning I dare say and then we'll find out more.'

Dickie Templar had heard enough. He turned aside and blundered into the darkness to hide his distress. He stopped dead. He had heard a faint cry.

From a stack of tall flowerpots there emerged a ghostlike figure: Midge Prentice, white face a mask of terror, her bunched nightie gripped convulsively in a small hot hand. Dickie fell on his knees and gathered her in his arms, sobbing, kissing her face and holding her to him, murmuring childish endearments. 'You got out!' he said at last. 'You got out!' And then, 'Where's Mummy?'

For reply, the child pointed dumbly to the smouldering ruin of the house.

Chapter Two

CALCUTTA 1922

COMMANDER JOSEPH SANDILANDS of the Metropolitan Police was delighted to be going home. Delighted that his six months' secondment from the Met to the Bengal Police should, at last, be at an end.

He'd had enough India. He'd had enough heat. He'd had enough smells.

Though no stranger to the midden that was the East End of London he'd not, by a long way, been able to accept the poverty that surrounded him. And he still resented the social formalities of Calcutta. As a London policeman, his social status had been, at the least, equivocal in the precedent-conscious atmosphere of the capital of Bengal. He had counted the days until he could pack, say his farewells and go, but even that pleasure was denied him; inevitably, the bearer who had been assigned to him had done his packing for him. But, by whatever means, it was at last done and tomorrow he'd be gone.

For the last time – he sincerely hoped it was the last time – he made his way into the office that had been allocated to him. For the last time he cursed the electric fan that didn't work. For the last time he was embarrassed by the patient presence of the punkha-wallah manipulating the sweeping fan that disturbed but did not disperse the heavy air. There was,

however, a neat envelope lying on his desk. Stamped across
the flap were the words: 'The Office of the Governor'.

With anxious hand he tore open the envelope and read:

> *Dear Sandilands,*
>   *I hope you can make it convenient to call in and see*
> *me this morning. Something has cropped up which we*
> *should discuss. I have sent a rickshaw.*
>   *Yours sincerely,*

And an indecipherable signature followed with the words
'Sir George Jardine, Acting Governor of Bengal'.

Joe didn't like the sound of this. Could he pretend he'd
never received it and just leave? No, they'd catch him in the
act and what could be more embarrassing than being brought
back from the docks under police escort? Better not chance
it! He looked angrily out of the window and there were,
indeed, two liveried rickshaw men waiting to deliver him to
the Governor. He'd met George Jardine on one or two formal
occasions during his secondment and formed a good impression of the distinguished old pro-consul who had come out of
retirement to bridge the gap between two incumbents.

The appointment seemed to be a formal one and he
paused in the vestibule to check his appearance. 'God! You
look tired, Sandilands,' he muttered at his reflection. He still
half expected to see the eager youth who had set off for the
war with the Scots Fusiliers but, though the hair was still black
and plentiful, after four years in France and four years with
the police his expression was watchful now and cynical. An old
wound on his forehead – badly stitched – had pulled up the
corner of one eyebrow so that, even in repose, his face looked
perpetually enquiring. Six months of Indian sun appeared to
have bleached his grey eyes as it had darkened his skin. But at
least in India everything he possessed was polished without
any word from him. He adjusted his black Sam Browne belt

shining like glass, his silver rank badges and his medal ribbons, the blue of the police medal almost edged out by the red
and blue DSO and his three war medals. He'd do.

The rickshaw set off without a word, the rickshaw men trotting steadily ahead through the heavy press of traffic. Seeing
the Governor's livery, people made way for him. 'Another six
months,' he thought, 'and I believe I could get used to this.
It's certainly time I was home!'

'Morning, Sandilands,' said the Governor, as though greeting
an old friend. 'Not too early for a peg, I hope? Whisky-soda?'

'Yes,' thought Joe, 'far too early but what can one do?'

He watched as Jardine poured out two generous glasses.

'I have your chit, sir,' he said, hoping he didn't sound as
resentful as he felt.

'Yes, well . . .' the Governor began. 'Funny business. I've
wired your chaps in London, and hope you don't mind my
having done so, over your head, as you might say. But – your
lecture the other night – I was very impressed . . . Everybody
was. Opened our eyes to a lot of things! Don't want to cut down
our chaps here – they do a wonderful job – but they're up to
their ears and it has come to me that maybe we need a little bit
extra. May be nothing in it, of course. Once the women start
gossiping you never know quite where it's going to end and . . .'
He paused and sipped his drink. 'Do help yourself. But the fact
is that I telegraphed your chief to ask if we could borrow you
for a bit longer. Everyone here would be delighted – but the
problem isn't here, it's in a place called Panikhat about fifty
miles south of here. It's on the railway. Not a bad journey and
they'll put you up in splendour and state, no doubt. Pretty
good fellows down there. It's a civil and military station.'

Joe Sandilands was hardly listening. 'I could have been sail-
ing down the Hooghly River by now! Why the hell didn't I go
last night?'

The Governor resumed, 'I don't suppose this is what you wanted for a moment but if you'll take this on it couldn't do your career any harm, I think. As I say, there are some very good fellows down there – Bateman's Horse. We call them the Bengal Greys – grey horses – the Indian equivalent of the Scots Greys, don't you know . . . But I won't waste any more time chatting.'

He held up a letter by its corner. 'It's all here but there's somebody I would like you to meet.' He seemed for a moment reluctant to come to the point, finally concluding, 'It's my niece, you see. She's about the place somewhere . . . Her husband is the Collector of Panikhat and they're stationed down there. Between you and me and strictly between you and me – he's a peaceful sort of chap . . . anything for a quiet life. Not much go about him. Perhaps Nancy's only taken this up because she was bored. But, I don't know – they seem happy enough together. Anyway, Nancy's as bright as a new rupee and ah! Nancy, my dear, there you are! This is Commander Sandilands. Sandilands, my niece, Nancy Drummond.'

For the first time since this terrible news broke for Joe, he woke to the possibility that there might be compensations in this so unwelcome interruption to his life. Mention of the Collector's wife had instantly produced a vision of Anglo-Indian respectability at its most oppressive but the figure before him was quite a surprise.

For one thing, she was younger by twenty years than he had been expecting and for another, she was smartly – even fashionably – dressed. White silk blouse, well-cut jodhpurs, broad-brimmed hat in one hand, fly whisk in the other and an enquiring – if slightly suspicious – face. He tried not to be too obviously appraising her. He was aware that she was fairly obviously appraising him. This could just be rather fun.

'Now, Nancy,' said the Governor, 'sit down and tell Sandilands what you told me. I've warned him that there may be nothing whatever in it but you've interested me at least and we'll do our best to interest him.'

Nancy sat down in a chair opposite Joe and looked at him seriously and for a long time before speaking. Now she was closer he saw that the pretty face was pale and strained. She made no attempt at a smile but went straight into her narrative. Her voice was low and clear, her tone urgent. She'd obviously prepared and prepared again what she was going to say.

'A week ago a ghastly thing happened on the station. Peggy Somersham, the wife of William Somersham, Captain in the Greys, was found dead in her bath with her wrists cut. Of course, everybody said "Suicide" but, really, there was absolutely no reason. They weren't very long married. Quite a difference in age – that's often the way in India – people wait to get hitched till their career is established and an officer does not in fact qualify for a marriage allowance until he is thirty. One can't always tell, of course, but they seemed not only happy, but very happy together. People often said – "Ideal marriage".

'I know that funny things happen in India but just the facts by themselves, to my mind at any rate, were suspicious and Bulstrode, the Police Superintendent, didn't seem able to explain anything to anyone's satisfaction. We all thought for one moment he was about to take the easy way out and arrest poor Billy Somersham . . .'

'Now Nancy,' said the Governor, 'tell it straight.'

'Sorry, Uncle! And look here . . .' She took an envelope from her uncle's desk, slid out two photographs and handed them to Joe.

His mouth tightened with distaste.

'Who took these?'

'Well, actually, I did . . .'

'My niece served as a nurse on the Western Front for three years,' said the Governor and sat back, apologetic but happy with this explanation.

'Mr Sandilands, sadly, a bathful of blood in my experience is nothing. And I have first-hand knowledge of wounds. Even cut wrists . . .' She paused, disturbed momentarily by her memories. 'I suppose you think it rather shocking that I should be able to stand there in front of this appalling scene and take photographs?'

Not wishing to stop the flow of her story Joe merely nodded. He did find it shocking but realised that a conventional denial would not deceive this determined woman. His professional curiosity was eager for details of how she had managed under those difficult circumstances to take photographs of such clarity but he remained silent and looked at her with what he hoped was a suitable blend of sympathy and encouragement.

'Yes, well, I was pretty much shocked myself. She was my friend, Mr Sandilands, and this was not easily done. But this is the hot season. There was little else I could do to preserve the scene of the death as it was. Bulstrode was giving orders for the body to be taken away and buried at once and he authorised the khitmutgar to arrange for the bathroom to be cleaned up. I'm afraid I stepped in and insisted that Andrew – that's my husband, the Collector – called him off. Of course the body had to be buried, after a quick post-mortem done by the station doctor, but we managed to get the servants to leave as much as possible of the bathroom untouched. I don't want to interfere, of course . . .' (The Governor smiled ironically.) '. . . but a word with the doctor mightn't be out of place. His name is Halloran. I don't know him very well. Irish. A lot of army doctors are. He seems nice enough.'

'You preserved the scene of crime – if crime it was – Mrs Drummond, and with the skill, apparently, of a seasoned officer of the Met. But I'm wondering why it should have occurred to you to take these steps . . .?'

'My uncle had spoken about you and the work you were doing here in Calcutta when I was last here some weeks ago. I popped into one of your lectures and I was very impressed with what you had to say. I tried to wangle a meeting there and then but you were besieged by a phalanx of earnest young Bengali Police Force officers and I had to drift away. But then, when this happened, I rang Uncle at once and he made a few telephone calls, worked his magic and here we are.'

She smiled for the first time since they had met and her face lit up with mischief. 'And I don't suppose you're at all pleased!'

Joe smiled back. He had an idea that there was not much he would be able to conceal from the Collector's wife.

'It's difficult to make out but if you will look at the second photograph . . .' she said, drawing his attention back to the horror he still held in his hand.

Joe concentrated on the close-up of the dead girl's wrists and saw at once where she was leading but he let her go on.

'You see it, don't you? She couldn't have done that herself, don't you agree?'

Joe nodded and she went on, 'But that's not all of it, nor perhaps even the worst of it, Commander. After Peggy's death the gossip started. I've only been on the station for three years and I hadn't heard the stories . . . in any case, I think people thought it was all over . . . like a nightmare. It stops and you lull yourself into thinking it's never going to happen again. And then it does. And it's worse than before.

'Everyone who had been there since before the war was eager to tell me the stories.' She leaned forward in her chair to emphasise her point. 'Mr Sandilands, every year before the war and going back to 1910, the wife of a Greys officer has been killed. In March.

'The first to die was Mrs Major Prentice – Dorothy. In a fire. Tragic, of course, but no one paid all that much attention as it was quite clearly due to an act of dacoity – banditry. The forests and some of the villages too used to be infested with bandits before the war. They are still to be found but it's nothing like so bad as it was thanks to Prentice and others. The following March in 1911, Joan Carmichael, the wife of Colonel

Carmichael, was fatally bitten by a snake. And there's nothing strange about that in India, you're going to say – but in this case there was an oddity . . . The next March, Sheila Forbes fell over a precipice while out riding and in 1913 Alicia Simms-Warburton was drowned.'

'And then came the war.'

'Yes. People were moved around. The series was broken and – goodness knows! – there were enough deaths to worry about in the next few years . . . people forgot. But this fifth death revived memories. It began to be said that marrying an officer in the Greys was a high-risk occupation! Gossip and speculation are meat and drink to officers' wives and they live in a very restricted circle. They can and do talk each other into a high state of panic about the slightest thing – you can imagine what this is doing to their nerves! One of the wives is talking, quite seriously I believe, about returning to England. And some of the younger ones are running a sweep-stake on which one of them is to be the next victim! Just a piece of bravado but I think it's a sign that the tension is becoming unbearable. Commander, we need you to come to Panikhat and get to the bottom of this. Either we investigate the whole thing, decide there's no foundation for any of these wild theories and reassure the ladies or . . .' She paused for a moment and her expression grew grim,'. . . or we find the . . . the . . . *bastard* – sorry, Uncle! – who's killed my friend and make absolutely sure he's in no position ever to do it again!'

Chapter Three

ANGLO-INDIA GOES TO bed early. By ten o'clock the rattle of trotting hooves had died away. Sweet and haunting, the strains of the Last Post played by the buglers of the Shropshire Light Infantry, sharing the station with the Bengal Greys, had died away and Joe Sandilands, glad of the peace that had descended, set himself to write up the notes of the day.

A very long day! A day that had started in the Governor's office at ten o'clock that morning and had extended onwards through the railway journey to Panikhat in the company of Nancy Drummond.

Half his mind was on the flood of information and speculation, gossip and rumour she had poured out and half was on her. He remembered her reclining, her feet on the opposite seat, fanning herself as her narrative unfolded, pausing occasionally to pass an order in enviably fluent Hindustani to her bearer, organising the day, ensuring that the ice block which sat melting in its tin tray between them on the floor of their first-class carriage was duly renewed as the train drew into one station after another. He recalled listening to the staccato whine of the extractor fan and gazing through the window as the lush, grey-green landscape unfolded.

And he remembered the surprise with which, as she had searched her hand luggage, his eye had been taken by a pistol. Nancy had caught his interested look. 'Andrew makes me carry it. It's only a Smith and Wesson .22 target pistol and it would take me hours to dig it out, slip the safety catch and "load, present, fire!" but it makes him happy. Mind you – I'm a pretty fair shot.'

Joe believed her.

'It's nice to be locked away from prying eyes for an hour or so,' she said, finding her cigarette case. 'Even in 1922 a Collector's wife can't be seen smoking in public! You're a bit surprising, Commander,' she added.

'Surprising? How so?'

'When Uncle George first suggested I go to hear you speak I was expecting a London bobby. Inspector Lestrade at best, perhaps.'

'Well, you're a bit surprising too! I was expecting an iron-grey mountain of rectitude, a one-woman Deed That Won the Empire, if you like. Instead of which . . .'

She laughed. 'Instead of which – what?'

'Now how can I answer that?' he thought. 'If I said what I was thinking – young, beautiful, clever, energetic, talented – what would she think of me?'

He drew a deep breath. Oh, the hell with it!

'Instead of which, you're young, beautiful, clever, energetic and talented,' he said.

'Great heavens!' she said. 'I was just about to say the same to you! But, tell me, Uncle George is taking all this very seriously – are you?'

'Yes, I am. I don't see how one could do otherwise. We're considering five deaths. "Once is happenstance, twice is coincidence, three times is enemy action," as they say in America. What does that make five times, I wonder? Come on – begin at the beginning and take me through it again.'

'Well, I'll begin at the beginning . . . No, come to think of it, I'll begin at the end because that's the bit I'm clearest about. That horrible thing that happened last week. We were looking at the photographs. On the advice of Bulstrode the

coroner brought in a verdict of suicide but I saw the cuts, now
you've seen the cuts and so has Uncle George and I think we
can start from a point where we all agree that they could not
have been self-inflicted. How we can just sit here and talk
about it so dispassionately is more than I can imagine. But, it's
just run-of-the-mill stuff for you, I suppose?'

'Well you do acquire a modicum of detachment, but, come
to think of it, I've never investigated the death of anyone I
knew. Certainly not the death of anyone I was fond of. Perhaps
the old detachment would wear a bit thin if ever I did.'

'But I knew Peggy Somersham very well. We hadn't known
each other long but I suppose you could say she was my best
friend.' She paused and ruminated a bit and then said, 'In this
funny world of India friendships brew up very quickly. Peggy
and I had the same background, we knew the same jokes, we'd
both suffered an English education – well you get very fond of
each other when you have so much in common. And, besides,
she was a bright and amusing girl.'

She looked bleakly at him for a moment. 'I was shattered. I
was nursing in France for three years in circumstances where
one corpse more or less is hardly stop-press news. But I know
what you mean – when it's someone you know . . .

'When it came to us that all was not perhaps what it seemed,
I discovered quite by chance what had happened before the war.
I think it was Ronny Bennett who said, "Poor old Bengal Greys!
They don't have much luck with the memsahibs!" I asked him
what he meant and he said, "But wasn't there a bit of a scandal
before the war? Weren't there one or two sudden deaths?"

'And then I started enquiring and I found that Alicia, the
wife of Captain Simms-Warburton, was drowned crossing the
river on the ferry. They all used the ferry then and they all use
it now. Since the accident, though, the bullock-hide contrap-
tion has been replaced with a less terrifying and much more
solid boat.'

'Bullock-hide?'

'Mmm. Ingenious arrangement and obviously effective because I've never heard of another accident using one, but, as I say, totally terrifying! Four bullock hides are inflated (legs still attached and sticking up into the air, can you imagine!) and a little platform bridges the central two. That's where the passenger sits. And then you have two native ferrymen lying stretched out like outriggers one on either side and they propel the thing along with their feet. On this occasion though there was only one.'

'And it capsized?'

'Yes. Two of the hides burst at the same moment and the whole thing tipped over shooting Alicia into the river.'

'Any odd circumstances?' Joe asked. 'Were there any other passengers? Spectators? Was the raft inspected?'

'Plenty of spectators. The whole thing was witnessed from both sides of the river. No other passengers – they can only carry two persons at the most and she was crossing by herself that day. But the ferryman gave a clear account of what happened.'

'The ferryman?'

'Yes. He was interviewed afterwards, of course. I've got copies of the coroner's notes at the station. You can examine them. He was a brave man. The coroner commended him for his courage. He could have just swum to shore but he saw Alicia struggling in the water – sinking under the weight of her long skirts I should think, and there's some doubt as to whether she could even swim – and he dived under and tried to rescue her. He nearly made it. They were seen struggling together but by the time one or two bystanders had jumped in and swum out to help it was too late.

'But it was a long time ago – 1913. Quite difficult to beat up any fresh evidence now.' She broke off and shouted, 'Koi-hai!' to the bearer in his little cabin and issued an order, resuming her story with the words, 'I thought we could do with a cup of coffee – unless you'd like something stronger? I've got some whisky somewhere.'

'No. No whisky for me. Anglo-Indians start rather too early in the day for me. Don't forget I spent some time fending off Uncle George's hospitality this morning!'

'Well, to continue my trip down Memory Lane, we turn back now to 1912 and Sheila Forbes. There's a favourite ride in Panikhat. Everybody does it all the time. You go across the river at the ford and then you go up a very narrow little track up the side of the mountain.'

'Mountain?' asked Joe with a glance through the window at the endless stretch of low-lying paddy fields they were passing through.

'Don't worry, the hills will be coming up soon on the starboard bow. Of course it's not a real mountain, more an outcrop of reddish, rocky high land. It's not a dangerous track but you have to be careful what you're doing. It seems that Sheila's horse shied at something and threw her off. She was riding side-saddle and when you're riding side-saddle you can only depend on balance so, at best, it's a bit precarious. They all rode like that in those days and even now you'll find an old jungle salt who will look sideways at the Collector's wife for riding astride. Men! But that's not fair – the women are just as bad!'

Joe asked again, 'So much for the basic story. Were there witnesses?'

'No. Not really. The party she was with were ahead and had gone on round the corner. There was a beggar on the path and he saw it happen. His evidence was just what you'd expect – Sheila's horse had shied and poor old Sheila went over the cliff – it's quite a height – and didn't stand a chance. The horse survived, incidentally. Bold as brass. But . . . the only unusual thing was that she was not a regimental wife – her husband was in the IAMC. Still, in everyone's mind it counted as another death on the station.'

The bearer came into the carriage with a copper tray on which stood a coffee pot and tiny china cups. He set it down beside Nancy and she resumed her story.

'Now we go back to Joan Carmichael, wife of Colonel Car-michael. A bitter man. Didn't do quite as well out of the war as he thought he ought to have and got stuck at Lieutenant-Colonel. I knew him very slightly from my distant childhood; he was the worst the Indian army had to offer – all moustache and bluster, not kind to the young officers, not popular with the men. I don't think he and Joan had much of a life together.'

Joe sipped his coffee, his mind more distracted than he would have liked by the story-teller. So she was presumably born and brought up in India; he would have guessed that from her easy manner and knowledge of the language.

'Tell me what happened to Joan.'

'Ah, this really makes my blood run cold! She was killed by a cobra. Not unknown in India though actually less common than people back home seem to think. They've all read *The Jungle Book*! They all expect a cobra to pop up out of the plug hole every time someone takes a bath!'

'I always travel with a mongoose,' he said seriously.

She laughed and carried on with her tale. 'Well, it's a pity Joan didn't have hers with her that day. She always rode out every morning – most of us do – and she always went the same way.'

'Does anyone know exactly what happened?'

'Well, the police work seems, for once, to have been quite good. Again, I've read the reports. There were evidences that she – er . . .' She seemed suddenly embarrassed and finished with a rush, 'that she had dismounted to answer a call of nature. Can you imagine anything more appalling? Being bit-ten by a cobra with your knickers down? I'm not trying to make a joke of it but there's something awful about people . . . it's just the kind of thing that makes us laugh until we think about how terrible it must have been.'

'It's a very human reaction,' said Joe easily. 'You must have encountered it a lot when you were nursing. We certainly did

in the trenches. Laughing was sometimes the only thing that
kept us sane. In the beginning. It made the unspeakable something we could handle.'

They were both silent for a moment, thoughts on the death
and final painful indignity of the Colonel's wife.

'But how did they know it was a cobra?' Joe asked. 'I have
never been to India before and perhaps there are things obvious to an old Koi-hai that would be a mystery to me . . .'

She leaned forward, suddenly intense.

'They knew it was a cobra because it was still there! At the
scene. This sounds really extraordinary and there may be a
simple explanation but – it makes me shiver to talk about it –
but, someone had killed the cobra – chopped its head off –
and left it lying there right beside Joan's body.'

'But that means . . .?'

'Yes, that someone passing by had seen Joan lying dead.
Someone passing very soon after the attack. Or even witness-
ing the attack? Soon enough after to have caught the cobra
and have killed it. But why? In revenge for Joan? It's macabre!
Now, Mr Policeman, what do you make of that?'

'Did the police at the time form a theory?'

'As far as they were able to discover there were no witnesses
to this death, not even a passing beggar. They thought, as I
suggested, that perhaps a woodsman – a charcoal burner perhaps – may have tried to save her from the snake, killed it and
then realising it was a hopeless case just cleared off and kept
his head down.'

Joe sat in silence for a moment, suddenly grieving for Joan
Carmichael. Lonely Anglo-Indian wife, unsatisfactory marriage, unkind husband, seeking what relief from boredom she
could find by riding out in the early mornings, suffering the
while from a bladder complaint, it really was a bleak and
pathetic story.

Following his sorrowful thoughts, he turned to Nancy. 'Had
she friends?'

'I don't really know. It didn't occur to me to find out. Acquaintances, obviously. You couldn't live in a place like this without acquaintances, but close friends, no, I wouldn't know. Is it important?'

'No, I don't think so. It's just that I was getting such a sad picture. I'd like to have thought she had some nice chum she could call in on, on her way back from her ride.'

She arched her eyebrows. 'A sentimental policeman? But I know what you mean . . . We can ask about. There are quite a few officers and their wives on the station who were there before the war. They haven't been there all the time, of course. They move around. Everyone in India moves around! They may have been posted to several other stations in the meantime but they will remember. If they were here, they will remember. You can count on that.'

'And you say the first death occurred in 1910?'

'Dolly Prentice. Twelve years on – and that's a lifetime in India – but people still remember Dolly! Half the regiment were in love with her from what I hear. Even the memsahibs liked her and that's unusual because she was young and quite lovely. There are photographs. They salvaged almost nothing after the fire but a tin trunk with the family valuables in it wasn't too badly damaged and it contained, among other things, two photograph albums. She was a real English rose, Dolly – all fair hair and huge blue eyes. The sort of fluffy, feminine creature that turns men's heads . . . all the charm of a twelve-week-old kitten . . .'

Joe smiled. He looked at the rather sharp profile being offered to him, the tilt of the chin, the straight, determined nose and the knowing, mischievous smile, and thought that Nancy Drummond would not have had a great deal in common with Dolly Prentice.

'She was married to . . .?'

'Major Prentice as he was then. Giles Prentice. He's now Colonel Prentice and commands the Bengal Greys on the station. You will meet him, of course.'

'Was their marriage a happy one?'

'I can't tell you for certain. I've heard stories. Some say he worshipped Dolly and certainly there is evidence that he was completely undone emotionally by her death. Some say he was indifferent to her. He's a rather . . . well, you will decide for yourself . . . but I think he's a bit odd. A difficult man to understand or like. But whatever his faults he clearly wasn't responsible in any way for Dolly's death.'

'Can you be certain?'

'Oh, yes. Beyond any doubt. He was in Calcutta dining at the Bengal Club with the selection board at the time of the fire. He was apparently truly devastated when he got back and they told him about it. The officers had left the bodies in the place where they found them in the wreckage of the bungalow and . . .'

'Bodies? Did you say bodies?'

'Oh, yes. There were two. In the bedroom. There was Dolly's body still lying on the bed and there was another . . .'

Her voice faltered and she looked uncomfortable as she frowned, considering how to go on.

'Another?' he prompted.

'Yes, another. Holding Dolly in his arms. It was Chedi Khan. Prentice's Pathan bearer.'

Chapter Four

ANGLO-INDIA GOES TO bed early. Anglo-India wakes up early too. Joe Sandilands was awoken at six o'clock by the insistent clamour of a bugle. The Reveille. And as his mind fitted the words which British soldiers had taken to singing to this jaunty call:

> 'Wake up Charlie, Wake up and wash yourself.
> Wake up Charlie, Get up and pee!'

Joe, half awake, thought himself back in France. Back in the army. Back in the war. It was a moment before he realised that the bugle was sounding in the hot awakening of an Indian summer day and not echoing flatly across the muddy fields of Flanders. He fought his way out of his mosquito net and stepped down to feel the welcome coolness of the tiled floor.

He had had a troubled night. His brain had coursed with a mass of undigested and uncorrelated information. His attempt the night before to write up his notes had not been entirely successful. His damp wrists had blotted the page. Ink had run on the soft foolscap paper with which Nancy had supplied him. Paper stamped 'The Office of the Collector of Panikhat'.

He pulled up the blind and opened up the window and leant out. Feeling the promise of another hot day and, mindful of the formidable list Nancy had given him of people he ought to see, he was aware that these might be the only hours during the day that he could have to himself. He decided to set off on a voyage of exploration before it got too hot. He armed himself with a small notebook stamped 'The Metropolitan Police. New Scotland Yard W1. Telephone, Whitehall 1212.'

The heat struck him as he stepped from his verandah on to a corner of the parade ground and reminded him that he should be wearing a hat. To his right a tree-lined road opened before him and, glad of the shade, he set off down this. It was evidently called Victoria Road (what else?) and a quick reference to his notebook reminded him that William and Peggy Somersham had lived at number 9 (a house which John and Alicia Simms-Warburton had occupied before the war) and, further, that Sheila and Philip Forbes, the doctor, had lived at number 30.

Although the bungalows were of many different periods evidently, they all conformed to the same pattern. They each had a passionately tended garden within a dusty compound, thatched roofs, tiled roofs, even corrugated iron roofs, wide eaves and, on all sides, a wide verandah. Views into the interior as he went on his way revealed pyjama-clad men beginning their day, women in early morning deshabille, here and there children being got ready for the day or playing in the sun with attentive servants. In most gardens a water carrier was seeing to the avenues of pot plants that lined every entrance drive. Further reference to his notebook revealed that Dolly and Giles Prentice had lived at number 5 Curzon Street.

Walking on, a branch road set off to the right identified itself as Curzon Street. In 1910 there had been a substantial house at number 5 but now there was nothing. The plot was set apart from its neighbours at the end of the cul de sac, its rear open to cultivated fields and, Joe calculated, eventually to the river. And wide open to a night attack by dacoits, he thought. He made his way on to the abandoned site but his progress was hindered by the dense scrub and weeds which struggled across the place where Dorothy Prentice had died in the fire and where Chedi Khan had died holding her in his arms. Joe stood for a moment, feeling his way back to that disastrous night. He was not surprised that Prentice had chosen not to rebuild. Consulting his notes again, he discovered that Prentice, however, had not gone far away. The neighbouring property was now his, a large bungalow whose garden adjoined the scene of the old disaster.

But disaster seemed to be all around him. As he pressed on down the street, he peered more closely at little plaques attached to the gates of some of the older bungalows and shivered in spite of the warm morning when he understood what he was reading.

'In this bungalow on Sunday the 17th of May 1857 died Mrs Major Minter and her three children, cut down by mutineers and their bodies thrown down the well' read the plaque on number 1 Clive Street. At number 9, Captain Hallett of Bateman's Horse had died 'gallantly defending his wife and son from an attack by mutinous Sepoys. All were hacked to death.'

Who was it who had called India 'The Land of Regrets'? He walked on and a turning led him once more back to the parade ground where the full heat hit him. He decided it was time to turn back. Two young officers trotted past, eyeing him curiously until, with a flash of recognition, one called out derisively, 'If you want to know the time, ask a policeman!'

Joe was not in the mood to be patronised and favoured them with a repressive police stare, a stare he had perfected in dealing with recalcitrant fusiliers during the war and London's criminal classes and even disrespectful police constables. He was pleased to note that it did not seem to have lost its force; under his level regard, both seemed abashed.

Resolving never again to step out into Indian sunshine without a hat, Joe turned back in the direction of his dak bungalow. By the time he reached it, military Panikhat had awoken to full and raucous life. Nailed boots marching formed a clashing foreground to the softer noises of the town and marching orders, familiar to Joe, were heard in an almost continuous stream.

'Move to the right in fours! Form fours! *Right!*'

And, from a distance, 'At the halt! On the right! Form close column of platoon!'

'Good old army,' thought Joe, 'though what relevance this has to infantry action on the north-west frontier which is probably what's waiting for these men, I can't imagine. Probably pretty useful for Wellington's army in the Peninsula and here they are, still at it! I've been out of the army for four years but I could step back in and form fours!'

He returned to the care of the bearer assigned to look after him. His bearer had decided that, on this his first public appearance in Panikhat, he should be in uniform. Pressed, folded and neat, his khaki drill lay on the bed. In the ghulskhana his bath was full, his towel folded over a towel horse.

The bearer appointed to him, his palms pressed together, greeted him. 'Egg, bacon, sahib. Coffee. Jildi.'

Joe thanked him in English and, deciding it would be churlish not to wear the uniform put out for him, stepped thankfully into the bath which was neither hot nor cold and washed away his sticky night and his no less sticky walk. Breakfast appeared at astonishing speed and, assuming that someone would tidy his room, empty his bath, empty the large top hat-like contrivance in the corner which did duty for a closet, he decided it was not too early to embark on his course of obligatory calling.

He thought that the Police Superintendent should come first followed by the doctor, the Collector and, not least, the CO of the Bengal Greys who, by a small note on his table, had elected him an honorary member of their mess. A second note from the Panikhat Club told him he had been elected a member ('for the duration of your stay') of the Club. In both of these he detected the hand of Nancy Drummond.

Armoured against the growing heat by a standard issue British army pith helmet that some thoughtful soul had left in his bungalow, he set off to walk to the office of the Police Superintendent.

The Police Superintendent was cold, the Police Superintendent was resentful and far from pleased to see him. He was pleased enough not to have to deal with what he clearly believed to be a nonsensical mare's nest uncovered – as he put it – 'by the women', though relieved to find, after a quick look at the medal ribbons on Joe's chest, that he was dealing with, if not a soldier, at least someone who had been a soldier.

He looked Joe over, his sharp blue eyes cold and suspicious. 'Don't know what on earth you'll make of this, Sandilands! And please don't think it was any idea of mine to waste your time with it!' he began almost without preamble. 'Don't want to pre-empt anything you may find out for yourself but, in my opinion, this is a lot of nonsense and even if it wasn't a lot of nonsense, we're looking at a cold trail. A very cold trail. If there's the slightest thing I can do to help – though I can't imagine what – let me know. For a start, we're chronically short-handed here. The Governor blandly suggests I put an officer at your disposal. Easy for him! I've assigned a police havildar to you. Naurung Singh. His English is quite good, you'll find, if you don't rush him. He served for a year as interpreter to a British unit and – well –' he gave a chilly smile, 'we haven't got anybody else. He's very ambitious and I wouldn't recommend you believe everything he tells you. Tries hard to please, if you understand what I'm saying. I'll call him in in a minute but in the meantime – where do you want to begin?'

Without giving Joe a chance to reply he went on, 'Rather expect you'll want to begin with the Somersham bungalow.' He threw a key on to the table between them. 'Take Naurung with you – he'll show you around. Not that there's much to see. It had pretty much been trampled over by the time I got there. I was out myself in the native town when it happened . . .' He cleared his throat and stirred uncomfortably.

Joe waited in silence for him to carry on.

'Bit of petty thieving going on. In the bazaar. By the time I got word of the unfortunate occurrence the world and his wife and his bearer had traipsed through. At least three people had handled the razor . . . Somersham himself was covered in blood, the whole household scurrying about yelling and in the middle of it all Mrs Drummond, cool as you like, taking photographs!'

'Exactly how much cleaning was done?' asked Joe.

'Hot country, India,' said Bulstrode, 'as I'm sure I don't need to remind you. No refrigerated units here for storing . . . er . . . cadavers. And you can't just let blood lie indefinitely. To cut it short – I had to order the cleaning of every surface that had blood on it. Apart from that everything's as I found it when I entered.'

Joe's heart sank. A cold trail and a clean one. Deliberately cleaned? Nancy's suspicions were beginning to chip at his objectivity.

'I suggest you have a look at these,' said Bulstrode, depositing a wad of papers on the table. 'I haven't had time to copy them – we can't call on the squad of clerks I expect you're accustomed to at the Yard – so for heaven's sake don't lose them. Documents relating to the other deaths the women are getting worked up about. I've put aside all the transcripts of all the police interviews in each case. Pretty formidable file, I'm afraid! And that's something Naurung won't be able to help you with – he doesn't read English all that well. (He'll have to improve if he's going to get where he wants to in the force.) Ask him anything though – where to go, who to speak to, who to salute and who not to salute and so forth. Still, at least when you've read through these, you'll be able to set the ladies' minds at rest. Quell the clucking in the moorghi-khana . . .'

'The . . .?'

'The hen coop. That's what we call the room the mems use at the Club. Humph! If they closed that down half our problems would disappear. Make life a lot easier. Anyway, Sandilands, they won't listen to me, perhaps they'll listen to someone who knows bugger all about it as long as he's from London. Put your medals on, parade before them and tell them not to worry their pretty little heads – that's all you need do.'

He realised his tone was degenerating into bitterness and added crisply, 'I've put an office by for you, unless you can think of something better. Poky little place, I'm afraid. It used to be the stationery store. I've cleared it out for you a bit. There's a desk, two chairs and a window. No telephone, but you can always use mine. Now, let me offer you a peg.'

Joe had resolved not to drink before midday but suddenly, insidiously, the idea of a whisky and soda was an attractive one and he accepted.

The Police Superintendent poured out two whiskies and handed a glass to Joe. He jangled a little bell and the door opened to admit Naurung Singh. Naurung was tall and commanding. Despite luxuriant whiskers, Joe guessed that his age was not much more than twenty-five. His police uniform was topped with a blue turban. He bowed without much subservience and smiled a smile discreet but friendly.

The Superintendent rose to his feet and spoke rapidly in Hindustani and said, 'I'm going to leave you, Sandilands. Give you a chance to read your way through all this bumf. I'll leave Naurung here so ask him anything you want to know. Oh, and by the way, you'll be expected by the Greys for tiffin. One o'clock. Naurung will show you the way.'

Joe drew the bundle of papers towards him and gestured at Naurung to take a seat. The Sikh hesitated. He perched for a moment at the extreme edge of his chair, rose, unnecessarily, to adjust the blind and did not sit down again.

'I shall have to find out who to salute and who not to salute,' thought Joe, 'but I shall also have to find out who to offer a chair to and who not to offer a chair to. Obviously, Sikh policemen do not get a chair. In the Met I can think of a number of officers who wouldn't let a constable sit in their presence . . . Suppose it's all one world.'

He settled himself to turn over the bundle of papers before him. They were of all sorts and sizes, written on all sorts of paper, some on privately headed writing paper, some on lined foolscap sheets with a government watermark. Some were in an educated English hand by men accustomed to the Greek alphabet, others were in the flowing and elaborate copperplate of Indian clerks.

'Naurung,' he said, 'have you read these?'

'I have tried, sahib, but I do not read English easily.'

'Do you know the stories?'

'I have heard them.'

'Now, you're a policeman with experience. The Superintendent thinks there is nothing suspicious, only a series of . . .' He had been going to say 'coincidences' but he changed this and continued, 'a series of chance happenings . . . a series of things that happened at the same time by chance. What do you think?'

'I do not think it is coincidental, sahib.'

Their eyes met for a moment.

'I'm going to like this man,' thought Joe.

'Tell me,' he said. 'We're looking at five – possibly more – mysterious deaths over a long period. At least, there's nothing particularly mysterious about the deaths – the only mystery is that they all occurred in the same month of the year. I can't believe that Mrs Drummond is the only one who's noticed this. Others must have said the same thing. Now, tell me, Naurung, what is being said?'

Collecting his thoughts while Joe was speaking, he said slowly, 'They do not think it is a coincidence.'

'Well, if we dismiss the chance of coincidence, what alternatives have we?'

'What is left is what you would call foul play.'

'So they are saying openly that it was foul play?'

'Sahib, you ask me what people are saying and I tell you what people are saying. But there is a third explanation which many people whisper. I do not want to appear an ignorant black man – "natives are so superstitious" – I think that is sometimes said?'

'Yes, I've no doubt that is sometimes said. But remember, I'm an ignorant London policeman – you can say what you want to me.'

Naurung looked acutely embarrassed and it was some time before he replied, saying finally, 'Sahib, do you know what I mean by a Churel? No? A Churel is the ghost of a woman who died in childbirth. She haunts rivers and fords. Her feet are turned backwards so that she can lead men to their destruction. I say this but I do not believe it. They are vengeful spirits. People will say that a Churel seeks to be revenged on the mems of the Bengal Greys because of something – perhaps a long time ago – that happened. Because of a grievance she carried to the grave. A grievance that has not yet worked itself out. I tell you this because you ask. Me, I dismiss it as idle gossip. If you listen to all the gossip you will never find your way to anything.'

'Listen,' said Joe, 'I'll tell you straight away – I don't believe in your Churel.'

'I tell you, sahib, neither do I. But all the same, there is a link to the Churel through water.'

'Water?'

'May I remind you, sahib, that Mrs Somersham died in her bath, Mrs Simms-Warburton was drowned crossing the river and Mrs Forbes fell over a precipice and died on a river bank. It is not much but is there another connection?'

Joe riffled through the bundle of yellowing papers on the table between them.

'A connection. Yes, Naurung. A connection is what we have to find. If there is a thread, any thread at all connecting these five deaths, then I think we will have an idea of why the mem-sahibs died. We know how they died – though we are far from knowing how the deaths might have been brought about – but we do not know why. I was taught that if you know "how" and "why" you will soon know "who".'

'Yes,' said Naurung, 'my father also has said that.'

Joe reflected for a moment and said, 'We must study the reports and find what these ladies had in common. How closely have you been involved with these cases?'

'With the death last week of Mrs Somersham I was involved. I was here at the station and helped the Police Chief Bulstrode Sahib with the investigation. I was not allowed to witness the scene of the death . . . Later . . .' Naurung hesitated.

'I understand. Go on.'

Joe read his unspoken thoughts and cut short the explanation which Naurung would have found embarrassing to give. The sight of a naked Englishwoman in a bath full of blood would have been kept from native eyes.

'You've seen the photographs? And come to your own con-clusion?' he pursued.

'It was I who had them developed for Mrs Drummond. There is a sergeant in the Signals who can do this. Yes, I saw the photographs, sahib,' Naurung muttered and looked uneasily away.

'I would have shown them to you anyway,' said Joe. 'Here, look again. Tell me what strikes you as odd.'

Naurung approached the table and glanced diffidently at the black and white photographs. Joe stared, seeing more than his first cursory and polite glance in the Governor's office had revealed.

'I see much to make me unhappy, sahib. But perhaps you would like to tell me what an experienced London policeman sees?'

Pushing back his feelings of revulsion and his pity for the girl who lolled naked in her bath, full white breasts buoyed up and outlined by the blood-blackened water in which she lay, Joe tried to keep his mind on the even more disturbing elements in the hideous scene.

'Firstly, Naurung, a few details to put me in the picture before we go to look at the bungalow. Tell me who discovered the body, at what time and so on.'

'Somersham Sahib found her body. Poor man – he was at first crazy. His screaming brought his servants running. At seven in the evening. They were preparing to go out to dinner with friends and then to a dramatic performance. She had gone to have her bath at six. The bheesties who carried in the water and her ayah who poured the water confirm this. Somersham Sahib had been working in his study waiting until she had finished and he suddenly thought it was taking an unusually long time and went to the bathroom where he found her dead.'

'What efforts did he make to seek help?'

'Oh sir, he sent servants running everywhere. To the Collector, to Bulstrode Sahib, to Dr Halloran of course. But it was Memsahib Drummond who was the first to arrive.'

'Did anyone apart from the ayah confirm when Mrs Somersham went to her bath?'

'Memsahib Drummond took the temperature of the water – you will see this in your notes – and agrees that it would have been poured an hour before the body was discovered. The doctor, who arrived just before eight, confirms that she had been dead for less than two hours.'

'And the knife wounds? What do you make of the knife wounds?'

'Ah, sahib, I have discussed this with my uncle . . .'

'Your uncle?'

'He is a butcher, sahib, and his opinion is worth hearing.'

'Yes, I expect it would be. Go on.'

'As Memsahib Drummond says, and she has nursing experience I understand, these wounds could not have been both made by Mrs Somersham.'

He pointed to the cut wrists on the photograph and made explicit slashing movements with each hand in turn. 'This is how it happened, you see. She could not have made these wounds herself. And if she did not, there is only one other explanation.'

'And the weapon? I presume it was found at the scene?'

'It was a razor. It was found at the bottom of the bath. Nothing unusual about the razor – the usual three and a half inch hollow ground blade that all the sahibs use. Bone handle.'

'Was it identified?'

'Oh yes. It belonged to Somersham Sahib. It was part of his shaving set. He keeps his razors in the bathroom in a mahogany box on his shaving stand.'

'Could Somersham himself have done this?'

'Of course. Apart from the servants he was the only person in the house. But, sahib, I interviewed all the servants and they swear he was in his study the whole time. His bearer was called several times by Somersham to bring tea and then pink gin and to tidy the room. He says the sahib was working at his desk and never left the room. So the ayah was the last person to see her alive and Mrs Somersham dismissed her at six.'

'At six? How can she be so precise?'

'The bugle from the infantry lines was blowing "Cookhouse". It calls the men at six o'clock every evening.'

'And did the ayah notice anything unusual in her mistress's mood? Behaviour?'

'She says the memsahib was happy, chattering and looking forward to her evening.'

'I think it's time we went to look at the scene of the death, Naurung.'

Joe picked up the key, the photographs and the folder of papers and they set off together, Naurung at times following three paces behind and at times hurrying ahead to point the way.

On arrival at the Somersham bungalow Naurung set the key in the lock and stood back. Across the door a careful hand had pinned a notice in three languages – 'Crime Scene. No Entry.' Naurung clicked his tongue disapprovingly. 'This is not accurate. There is no proof that this is a crime scene.'

'It'll do,' said Joe. 'Suicide is a crime, after all.'

In two places there was a blob of sealing wax and as Joe looked round the outside of the bungalow, he noticed similar blobs on each window. 'Good,' said Joe. 'A proper arrangement. Yours?'

'Thank you, yes, it was my arrangement. I think Bulstrode Sahib thought it was fussy.'

'Not at all,' said Joe. 'Procedurally correct.'

The two men smiled at each other briefly and stepped into the bungalow. The atmosphere was stale. Stale and unbreathed and smelling of nothing more strongly than disinfectant. Joe stood in the hall and looked about him. One by one he stepped into the rooms leading from the hallway where an air of casual everyday activity suddenly interrupted reigned. Somersham's clothes were laid out in the bedroom as were also those of Peggy. Someone had stuck a list of things to do on the dressing-table mirror:

Ring J.B. before lunch, Saturday.
Pay Merrick's bill.
Order refill flit-gun.

And then, in a different hand:

Write to your mother before Friday!

The evidence of life continuing was everywhere to be seen. There was no evidence of life about to be deliberately extinguished.

He wandered from room to room checking their use and looking out for anything that struck him as unusual. With a sigh of irritation on entering the drawing-room he realised that nearly everything about the bungalow was foreign to him. The strange mix of lightweight rattan furniture and heavy Victorian pieces was disconcerting and even the use to which the rooms were put was alien to him.

The study at the front of the bungalow at least was a familiar blend of library and office and Joe took in the mahogany desk where Somersham had been working while his wife had gone to her bath. The desk top had been cleared and Joe assumed that he had taken his records with him. A check through the drawers told the same story.

'Captain Somersham has moved his effects out of the bungalow?'

'Yes, sahib. He is located now at the Club in one of the guest rooms until such time as Bulstrode or your good self say he may return. He would not, in any case, wish to be in this sad place.'

A picture of William Somersham bleakly alone in an anonymous club bedroom, haunted by what he had seen and haunted by memory, aware that somewhere suspicion still attached to him, came into Joe's mind. He shook himself and returned to his search.

He concluded that life was mainly lived on the verandah. Now shadowed by the lowered rattan blinds and abuzz with flies, it must have been a pleasant space here on the cooler side of the house with the doors standing open and a draught of air blowing through. Joe put his heavy file down on a small table and sat on the chair beside it preparing to leaf through in search of Bulstrode's report. He grimaced as he put his weight on a solid shape underneath the cushion which went some way towards easing the uncomfortable stiffness of the rattan. He fumbled under the cushion and took out a leather writing case with a fountain pen slipped into the spine. The initials MES in gold on the front told Joe what Margaret Elizabeth Somersham had been doing before she went to her bath. And she had hidden it with that automatic gesture that comes to people who live in a busy household with many servants coming and going. Particularly when they have things they wish to conceal.

Without hesitation, Joe picked up the case, opened it and took out the half-finished letter it contained. Peggy had been writing to her parents. He read through an account of her week's activities. An ordinary life full of routine things but the girl's sparkle shone through. She was doing her best to entertain her parents with exaggerated pictures of station characters, and her lively description of a polo match which Panikhat had lost to a visiting team would have made Joe smile if an oppressive sadness had not smothered the reaction. He noted the pride and affection with which she described her husband's prowess on the field. But Peggy had saved her real news for the end of the letter.

Joe's shoulders sagged. He turned abruptly away from Naurung, swiped roughly at his eyes with his handkerchief and blew his nose noisily. Turning back to the sergeant he said, 'Naurung, remind me. This Churel of yours – a ghost, you said? The ghost of whom?'

'She is the spirit – the vengeful spirit – of a woman who died in childbirth, sahib.'

Chapter Five

JOE WAVED THE letter at Naurung, waiting patiently but puzzled. 'We'll take this away with us as evidence of Peggy Somersham's state of mind. It should have been discovered earlier.'

'Her state of mind, sahib?'

'Yes. This letter was written to her mother and father in England. It tells us quite clearly that she was happy, that she loved her husband and that she had much to look forward to. She was expecting a baby in the autumn.'

Naurung for once was at a loss for words and answered with a hissing breath of surprise and something else – satisfaction?

'Come on then, let's take a look at the bathroom. I think I've seen everything I need to see in the rest of the house.'

The bathroom door was splintered at the lock, presumably from Somersham's desperate forced entry. The bathroom was exactly as it had been described to Joe and exactly as he had expected to find it. The bath had been cleaned and washed out but he found traces of dried blood under the rim. On one wall was a small mirror on a shaving stand carrying a mahogany box, its lid wide open, and a razor-strop. At the bath's side was a tall wall mirror with, in front of this, a rickety bamboo table laden with toiletries.

Joe surveyed them. 'Good Lord! Enough stuff here to stock the Coty shop! Look here, Naurung! Loofah, tin of talcum powder, eau de cologne, manicure set, Pears soap . . .'

'That is so sad! The memsahib was obviously preparing to be a beautiful lady,' murmured Naurung.

Not for the first time, it came to Joe that Bulstrode – perhaps deliberately – undervalued Naurung.

'Exactly! And look – this is interesting.' Joe pointed to an elegantly sculpted scent bottle. 'It's a perfume by Guerlain of Paris – Mitsouko. All the go at the moment for bright young things and costs the earth. Bought a bottle or two myself in my time,' he added in response to what he imagined to be a slightly raised eyebrow. 'This is very significant, don't you think?'

'I had thought so too, sahib. She was not preparing to die. She was expecting to go out for a pleasant evening. My wife also when she bathes sets out her bath things. And she keeps her special perfume locked away from the servants and takes it with her to prepare herself for a special occasion. A perfume so precious would not, I believe, have been put there as a matter of course by the memsahib's maidservant.'

Joe's attention went next to the open box on the shaving stand. 'Somersham's razors. Would it be usual for him to keep them in the bathroom? Didn't he use a barber? Would you know this, Naurung?'

'It is known, sahib. I have talked to his bearer. Somersham kept his razors here always in this box. He always shaved himself and never used a barber. He was careful with his blades. He kept them well stropped and always put them back in order in the box.'

Joe peered into the box. Lined with velvet, there were seven spaces, one for each day of the week. The third space from the right was empty. Joe took out the razor on the extreme left and examined it. London-made and expensive. He admired the fine bone handle and tested the sharpness of the blade against his thumb. Inscribed along the metal blade was the word 'Monday'. Joe counted along the row to the empty space. Friday.

'Naurung,' he said slowly, 'remind me. When exactly was Memsahib Somersham killed?'

'Just after six o'clock on the 3rd of March last week, sahib. It was a Friday.'

'If you were an intruder intent on killing Mrs Somersham, with little time to spare, which razor would you take from the box?'

'I would take this one, sahib,' said Naurung pointing to the nearest, 'the Sunday razor.'

'So would I. Tell me what happened to the Friday razor.'

'It was taken away by Bulstrode Sahib. We have no way of taking fingerprints and it was said that so many people had handled it anyway there was no evidence to be taken from it. It was found at the bottom of the bath by the ayah who came to help with the body. She screamed and passed it to Somersham Sahib who gave it to another servant and he took it to Bulstrode. I think it remains locked in a drawer in his office. Would you like to examine it?'

'Not now, Naurung. Much too late.'

Joe sighed. If only he'd been first on the scene how different the outcome might have been. He made no comment. There was nothing to be gained by criticising police procedure. No good would come from antagonising Bulstrode though a word to the Collector might not be out of place. He sensed that Naurung understood the shortcomings and though in no way accountable for them he was feeling embarrassed at the continual admissions of failure he was having to make. Joe began to see exactly why Bulstrode had put his havildar in the firing line.

'At least we have a fresh and unbiased account of the scene in Mrs Drummond's photographs. Let's have another look while we're here on the spot.'

Joe took out the photographs Nancy had taken, held them up and compared them with the scene before him. He produced, with the slight air of theatricality he always felt, a magnifying glass and began to examine them. No quips and jibes were forthcoming from Naurung who looked at the glass with appreciation.

He shuffled his feet slightly and said carefully, 'While you have that device in your hand, sahib, perhaps you might find it worth your while to examine the marks on the lady's shoulder. I have not had the benefit of such a glass but I am quite certain that there were marks of some kind there.'

Joe moved his glass to the white shoulders. 'Yes, you're right. And I think you have already guessed what these are? Impossible to say for certain and we will need to check this with Bulstrode if it's not in the report – and as you question it, I take it that it is not?'

Naurung nodded, continuing to look uncomfortable.

Again Joe got the clear impression – and one which he was convinced was being subtly signalled by the havildar – that he found much to criticise in the professional performance of Bulstrode Sahib. He indicated by a slight pause that he had received Naurung's unspoken message and went on, 'Well, perhaps we should wait until I've spoken to the doctor but I think we'd both say that these are finger marks. Someone has forcibly held her down in the water while she bled to death. And the water was warm – the blood would flow.'

Again Naurung nodded then he asked, 'But she would have screamed, would she not, sahib? Somersham has said that he heard her singing in the bathroom. He would surely have heard her screaming?'

'Certainly. But no one has reported hearing any unusual sounds let alone a scream. He must have taken her by surprise and stopped her from shouting by putting a hand over her mouth, which would make it pretty difficult to subdue her and cut her wrists at the same time . . . I think he got into the room before she entered, hid somewhere, then slipped out and caught her unawares and gagged her with something – that sponge over there? A flannel? I don't think so. I think our friend is too well organised to leave such details to chance – I think he probably brought a gag with him and took it away with him. On the same principle, he could have brought his own weapon too and used the razor on the spur of the moment. But why? A taunt? Some sort of appalling joke?

'So what have we got? A happy young woman going to her bath at six o'clock. By seven she is dead. Her husband goes nowhere near the bathroom. So how did the killer get in?'

He looked around the room. In the corner of the room was a tall cupboard, locked and with the key still in the lock. At high level on the outer wall there was a small window. The top-hung casement was shut but not secured. Beneath this little window there was a stool.

'Hold the stool for me, Naurung, I want to look at that window.'

When Joe climbed on to the stool the window sill was at his waist height. Peering through it he saw a narrow alley.

'Where does this alleyway lead?'

'It leads to the infantry lines and then on to the village.'

'The village?'

'Town perhaps. The native town. That is where I live.'

Magnifying glass in hand he examined the sill of the window with great care. Without question there were small smears of blood which, being above eye level, had avoided the cleaner's cloth. He steadied himself on Naurung's shoulder and jumped on to the ground. 'Have a look,' he said, handing him the glass. 'What do you find? Paint? Chilli sauce? Lipstick?'

'No, sahib, it is blood.'

'Now let's have a look in that cupboard.'

The cupboard had evidently been used as a box room. There were two suitcases, there were files of correspondence, a cricket bat, a hockey stick and a tan canvas shikar helmet hung on a peg. At first sight the cupboard seemed dusty and it seemed the dust was undisturbed but, on a closer look, it was clear that there had been recent disturbance. Joe took a

flashlight from his pocket and examined the floor. The dust
was scuffed and stirred up but there were no clear footprints
to be seen. He turned the beam on to the walls and looked
carefully at every square inch of the wooden partition. On the
point of giving up his search he remembered to check the
back of the door and, as he pulled it towards him, the light
reflected on something white about a foot from the bottom
edge. Bending nearer Joe saw that a tiny scrap of white fabric
had been caught up on a splinter of the rough wood and delicately he detached it and held it up for Naurung's
inspection.

'Indian cotton, sahib. Rough cotton. It is not a fabric a
lady's dress would be made from. And catching so low down
on the door it must be from a man's trousers – an Indian
man's trousers.'

Joe took a small paper evidence bag from his back pocket
and popped the fabric into it, sealed it and put the date, time
and his initials on it. Passing his pen to Naurung he asked him
to add his own signature.

'And would anyone have noticed someone climbing out of
a high window? Someone bloodstained perhaps?'

'Anyone bloodstained would have been noticed. Though
when the crime is committed in a bathroom . . . it is not
difficult to clean the blood away. And there was a blood-
covered towel found by the bath. He could have used it as
protection or cleaned himself on it afterwards. As for being
noticed – a sahib climbing out of a bungalow and using the
alleyway would certainly have been noticed, covered in blood
or not, but an Indian walking in the alleyway would not have
been commented on necessarily. It is commonly used by servants on their way to the town.'

'Was there anybody nearby?'

'You will find this problem in India – there is always somebody nearby. There are servants in the compound, strangers
come and go.'

'Did anyone come forward to be interviewed?'

'No one wants to get into trouble, you understand.'

'So, suddenly this popular pathway is deserted?'

'Almost deserted. You will see in Bulstrode Sahib's notes – a witness did come forward. A merchant. A representative of Vallijee Raja. Spice merchants in Calcutta. He was on his way to the kitchens at the Club where he was going to try to sell spices to the cook and was taking this short cut from the village. It was being said in the bazaar that such a man had been seen leaving the alley and then he came forward willingly to make a statement. He said that he had reached the Club shortly after "Cookhouse" sounded and must have been in the alleyway about ten minutes earlier. He saw nothing suspicious and heard no unusual noises.'

'Bloody hell!' said Joe, exasperated. 'I'd give a lot to interview him!'

'It would be difficult. Bulstrode Sahib did not detain him. He did not appear to be lying, according to the Superintendent. If he had anything to hide he would have lied about the time he was in the alley. He called at the kitchens at the time he says he did and the cook confirms that he placed an order with him for spices. He could be anywhere in India by now. These box-wallahs travel many miles in a week. Sometimes by train.' He shrugged his shoulders.

Joe was aware of a sense of helplessness. He was not short of evidence. In many ways there was too much evidence, too many witnesses. He would need to settle down for a quiet half-hour and go through Bulstrode's notes, however imperfect, and dredge out the important material.

He walked with Naurung back into Somersham's study, unconsciously choosing to be as far away from the murder room as possible. Joe turned to Naurung. 'Here are five deaths spread over twelve years. Were there other deaths of English-women during the same period? It must be a matter of record. Can you find out?'

'Sahib,' said Naurung, 'I have a list here. It was perhaps the first thing I thought of.'

From the back of the packet of papers he extracted a handwritten list which he put on the desk in front of Joe. It was headed 'The Demise of English Ladies. Panikhat 1910–1922.'

There were thirteen. Of these, two had died of cholera in the hot weather season, two had died together in a car smash in Calcutta in January 1918, one had died in childbirth and one of pneumonia whilst on leave and attempting to climb a peak in the Himalayas. These were all married to officers in the infantry regiments stationed at Panikhat. The second group were all wives of cavalry officers of Bateman's Horse. Two had died of fever and the remaining five had all died unnaturally and in the month of March.

Joe sighed. Nancy Drummond and the chattering memsahibs had it right, he feared. Dolly, Joan, Sheila, Alicia and Peggy. Five ladies violently done to death.

Naurung took a fat gunmetal watch from the breast pocket of his tunic. 'It is now a quarter to one, sahib. It is about ten minutes' walk to the mess where you are expected for tiffin. I think we should start out now.'

They set off to walk together. Although Joe declared himself quite capable of finding the way Naurung obviously thought it would be inappropriate if he was left to do so by himself.

'Tell me,' said Joe as they walked, 'Bulstrode – he said to me, and I think I quote his words correctly, "I was out myself in the native town when it happened." I don't suppose it's relevant but it was some time before he could be located. I would be interested to know what took him to the native town at that exact time of day. Is it known? Was he on police work?'

'Bulstrode Sahib is always on police work, I do believe . . . but he was not in the old town officially as far as I know. Although he spends much time there, it is said.'

There was a very long pause and Naurung seemed to be wrestling with himself. To say more or to let Joe's question go unanswered?

Joe prompted him. 'I know very little about Bulstrode. I don't know where he lives. I don't even know if he's married. Is he married?'

'He is married but the memsahib is in England. I know this because my father was havildar before me. It is no secret. This happened when I was nine years old and beginning to be a help to my father. The Memsahib Bulstrode came out from England to marry him. I think it was not a happy marriage, sahib. She discovered that he had already an Indian woman though she had been sent away as was the custom. One day the memsahib took her little boy who was no more than a baby at the time and went back to England. She said it was not healthy for a child to be brought up in India and that is the last any-one saw of her or the boy. Bulstrode Sahib was very upset by such an act of betrayal and everyone was very sorry for him.'

'So Bulstrode's all alone, then?'

Again Naurung looked acutely embarrassed saying finally, 'Not exactly alone and not exactly all the time.'

'So, would you like to make a guess as to why he was down in the old town?'

'There are ladies. Not ladies it is good to be with, you will understand.'

Joe pondered this piece of oblique information.

'Can't blame the poor bastard,' he thought. 'Lonely work at the best of times being a policeman, but I really have to pursue this.'

'Many men do the same,' he said consolingly, 'but tell me, Naurung, if you think you can, does it weaken his position? There must be people who know things he would rather the world at large did not know.'

'If there are such things I do not know them, sahib, but it is said that he has been seen in the company of very small girls . . . This is India and even in Panikhat such things can be arranged. For a fee. Or an exchange.'

'An exchange?'

'I do not want to say any more, sahib. It is all, at the best, speculation.'

It occurred to Joe that a Police Superintendent who had arranged at times to be supplied with underage girls was a vulnerable man. A colleague not to be entirely relied on. And then, he himself had an ethical problem. Should he be discussing these things with Bulstrode's inferior officer? For the time being he decided to let it go and they resumed their walk.

A few yards from the mess Naurung stopped.

'I will wait for you here and we will continue our work afterwards. But the sahib need not lose any time. He can go on working even over tiffin.'

'Working?'

'You may meet one or two bereaved husbands there. As one officer to another, they may confide things which they would not reveal to an Indian Police Sergeant, sahib.'

Joe paused for a moment in front of the mess and looked at it without much favour. To all outward appearances the Officers' Mess was bleak and functional, its walls painted a public works department grey and its corrugated iron roof painted public works department red. Window boxes with flower pots were meticulously cared for but the general impression was one of utility. Externally that is. Internally, the visitor stepped back in time to the nineties or beyond. Here was the extreme of opulence that mahogany, turkey carpeting and regimental silver could provide. A host of whiskered officers looked down from the walls from posed Victorian portraits and stiff Victorian groups. Their disapproving faces were interspersed with the no less disapproving and no less whiskered faces of tiger, leopard and wild pig. A ferociously moustached and stiffly posed

figure stared out from a dark portrait. Presumably Bateman
himself, the founding father of the Bengal Greys. There was a
spirited oil painting occupying the whole of one wall showing
Bateman's Horse charging with Havelock to the first relief of
Lucknow. Loyal, turbaned troopers, their dripping lances at
rest, led a battalion of kilted Highlanders. It kept the memory
of that celebrated episode alive and well since the regiment
had hardly been in action between the Mutiny and the blood-
bath of Flanders.

Joe was unsure of his welcome with the Bengal Greys. A
London policeman, appointed by the Lieutenant-Governor to
investigate and possibly uncover a scandal in the closed ranks
of a fashionable regiment, was likely to be given a frosty reception. Anglo-India was caste-conscious. There was a rigid order
of precedence. The Indian Civil Service were at the top of the
pile, the British army below and the Indian army below that,
cavalry regiments taking precedence over infantry regiments
and, as Joe rather suspected, all taking precedence over visiting policemen. There was even a condescension for which he
was sure he ought to be grateful in his invitation to lunch in
this exclusive cavalry mess.

He was a sociable man on the whole and on the whole – as
he was aware – it was his tendency with strangers to talk too
much. He decided to don a mask of formal severity but this
did not survive his encounter with the adjutant who, with
hand outstretched, came congenially to greet him.

'So glad to welcome you, sir! Station's buzzing with
rumours. Half of us expected Sherlock Holmes, the other half
expected a red-necked London bobby!'

'I think I'm something between the two,' said Joe.

'Let me give you a glass of sherry and let me introduce
you . . .'

And he led him round the circle. John this, Bonzo that,
Harry something else, the names meant nothing to him
with the exception of William Somersham. Tall, with a

cavalryman's stoop and balding, the husband of the girl whose body he had so recently been inspecting was the only one of the company of officers who did not smile when he shook his hand. His grip was firm and he gave a not unfriendly nod but his eyes on Joe were wary, his expression concealed.

The adjutant resumed his hospitable burble. 'If there's anything in the world we can do to help, please do tell us. Make full use of the mess, of course. Life can be a bit spartan in the dak bungalow, I know, and – something to ride? We'll find you a syce. Talk to Neddy. He'll fit you out with something. Neddy! What about Bamboo for the Commander? Good pony. Nice manners. He'll look after you. Even got a turn of speed if required. Not working this afternoon, are you, Neddy? No? There we are then. That's decided.'

Joe settled down to clear soup, a lamb stew and a prune mould. It reminded him of staying with his grandparents and he presumed that the menus had evolved over the same period.

Refusing a glass of port, he went out with the obliging Neddy, embarrassed to find Naurung seated on the ground outside the door waiting. He said as much to Neddy.

'I said that once,' said Neddy. 'Doesn't last. You do get used to it.'

They set off for the stables, Naurung, to Joe's irritation, a respectful three paces behind.

India was evidently still horse-drawn though a model T Ford in a haze of carbon monoxide rattled its way with a grinding of gears across the parade ground and a syce was to be seen applying the starting handle to the polished brass nose of a Morris Cowley. Officers changed for polo cantered by in twos and threes, all acknowledging Neddy with a wave, all looking with curiosity at Joe. A carriage and pair in the charge of a smart groom trotted past bearing an opulent Indian lady under a fringed parasol. A solid, monolithic Englishwoman in her sixties, Joe guessed, in a veil and solar topee drove a smart gig up from the lines and went on her way.

'Now,' said Neddy, 'that's who you ought to be talking to.'

'Why? Who is she?' To Joe she looked as if she'd stepped straight out of the pages of Kipling. *Plain Tales from the Hills*, perhaps.

'Oh, that's Kitty. Mrs Kitson-Masters. She's the widow of the last Collector and the daughter of the Collector before that. I suppose at some time she must have gone home to England for school but, really, apart from that she's spent her whole life here and what she doesn't know about the station isn't worth knowing. Her information isn't always entirely reliable but at least it's pretty spicy! She can even make me blush sometimes! You'd enjoy her. She may not be able to help your enquiry but you'll get a burra peg at any hour of the day or night. She keeps late hours, Kitty.'

They arrived at the stabling and Neddy had Bamboo led out for Joe's inspection. Rangy, chestnut, white blaze, three white stockings, old – distinctly past mark of mouth – but with the wise face that seems to go with age in a polo pony.

'I couldn't ask for anything better,' said Joe sincerely.

'Now,' said Neddy, 'if you'll excuse me, I'm playing squash at three. Naurung'll look after you.' And he was gone.

'Can you get a horse?' said Joe. 'I mean, can you get a police horse?'

'Oh, yes, sahib, there are always police horses.'

'Why don't you get one and meet me back here in about a quarter of an hour. I'm tired of talking to the soldiery – I'd like to look round at the geography.'

'Geography?'

'I mean the lie of the land. Take me round and show me things. Show me the ford where Mrs Simms-Warburton was drowned. Show me the precipice from which Mrs Forbes fell, and the place where Joan Carmichael met her snake – I'd like to take a closer look at that.'

Naurung soon returned on a ponderous waler, an import from Australia and the established workhorse of Anglo-India. Joe mounted and they set off together heading towards the ford but, as they rode, Joe heard the soft drum of cantering hooves coming up behind them and paused to meet the anguished gaze of William Somersham.

'Sandilands,' he said. 'I fear I interrupt you. If you will spare me a few minutes? I was hoping to catch you. There's one thing – they say – that you can't buy in India however rich you are and that is privacy. What I have to say to you needs privacy.'

He glanced round at Naurung who had tactfully fallen back once more and he resumed, 'You're here, I believe, to investigate the . . . the death . . . of my wife. Is that so?'

Joe hesitated to reply, not quite sure how far he wanted to take this complete stranger into his confidence, finally saying, 'I'm here to investigate the death of your wife but I'm here, likewise, to enquire into what we are beginning to believe may be the linked deaths of other women, other wives, that is, in the Bengal Greys, stretching back over a number of years. Stretching back, indeed, to a time before the war.'

'You think they may be linked?'

'I don't know what I think but it is a suspicion, even a sup-position that comes to mind. Note this – they were all the wives of Greys officers and they all died in March.'

'All died in March! I hadn't appreciated that.'

'It may be insignificant but I, for one, do not believe so. Further than that, honestly – and remember that I have only been here five minutes – I am not prepared to go. But that much is public knowledge.'

'You will be aware of the suicide verdict. May I ask you – are you satisfied with that?'

Joe hesitated again. 'I will be quite candid,' he said. 'No, I am not.'

'Neither am I,' said William Somersham. 'I have more rea-son to know than anybody that such an act would have been

entirely out of character. Entirely. It was horrifying and astonishing to me but, initially, with everybody else, I accepted it.
For a moment perhaps, but there is too much . . .'

'Too much? You were going to say . . .?'

'Too much that is not consistent. To begin with I was con-
fused. I was stupid. Perhaps I was self-regarding but the incon-
trovertible fact is this – that if we are not discussing suicide,
then we are discussing murder. You wouldn't presumably
deny or dispute that?'

'No,' said Joe, 'I wouldn't.'

'And who, in those circumstances, is the prime suspect?
Oh, all right, you don't have to feel embarrassed with me – I
know who the prime suspect is. Quite obviously myself. When
this horrible thing happened, to my shame, I was concerned
as much as anything to divert suspicion from myself. God
knows why! Perhaps I'm not a very courageous character. I was
even anxious that a suicide verdict should be upheld but only
then did I realise how disloyal I was being to Peggy.'

'Let us for a moment,' said Joe, 'let the alternative murder
verdict stand between us. Let me ask you a few routine police
questions.'

William Somersham laughed shortly, '"Purely routine you
understand . . .only anxious to exclude you from our enquiries" – do I get the words right?'

'Yes, if you like. Tell me – had your wife any enemies? Was
there anyone who might have a grievance against her? Real or
fancied?'

'No. Emphatically not. Never. She was the gentlest creature.' His voice choked. 'People often say this after a death but
in her case it's true – she hadn't an enemy in the world. She
was really, I believe, beloved by all.' And he concluded, 'And
she was beloved by me. I think you should understand that.'

'Take me through that evening again. Or rather tell me if
I've got this right – you had gone to your study to work and you
were under observation from the compound throughout the

period in question. Your door was shut but the window was open. Correct so far? Your wife had gone to have a bath. A bath had been filled for her. You were getting ready to go out, to dinner and then on to a play? Correct? Pick it up from there.'

'I listened for a while to Peggy giving instructions to her ayah – she was telling her which dress to lay out – and then she went off, singing, to her bath. Sandilands, she was singing! I was trying to get my quarterly returns in before the weekend – it's always a problem and I always leave things till the last minute.' A bleak smile. 'After a while I suddenly realised I hadn't heard her for a long time, a very long time. I began to get cross. I needed to have a shave, get ready for the evening. When you've been a bachelor for years, sharing a bathroom even with someone you love can be a bit of an irritation.

'I went and tried the bathroom door. It was locked. Most unusual. We almost never locked the door. I banged and said something like – "Hurry up, Peg, we haven't got all evening." Something like that. There was no reply and I got worried. I thought perhaps she'd fainted. They always fill the baths too hot. And then I remembered that she, that she . . .' Somersham was unable to go on.

'Look, Somersham, you don't have to spell it out for me. I know that she was pregnant.'

Somersham looked at him in surprise but then appeared to take the omniscience of the Law at face value and blundered on. 'Ah, yes, well, can't say I know much about the condition myself but it did come into my head that she might have swooned or whatever women do because of it. And then I got frantic. We had both wanted this baby so much. I couldn't bear to think that something might have gone wrong. I yelled and pounded on the door and when there was still no reply I kicked it open.

'The first thing I saw was that the window was open. It's quite high – I suppose the sill must be five feet from the floor and the stool we use in the bathroom . . .'

Joe felt that tears were not far away. He reached out a consoling hand and patted the other on the knee. 'Take your time,' he said.

'Sorry. But, dash it! Peggy used to sit on that stool when she was drying herself. And there it was under the window and even before I saw Peggy I saw there was blood on the stool and there was a smear of blood on the window sill. And then I saw Peggy dead in a bath full of blood. Terrible, terrible sight! I'll never get it out of my mind. Whenever I close my eyes I see her lying there . . . Her wrists were cut to the bone. They say she'd probably been dead for almost an hour.'

'Your servants saw nothing? Heard nothing?'

'No.'

'Tell me, Somersham – if you think back to the hours before six o'clock, to the period before she must have died, perhaps well before – were there any visitors to the house? Indian or English?'

'Oh, good Lord! I was not at home until about three that afternoon. Peggy said that the padre had called in the morning. She went out to have lunch with one or two of her friends. No one in the afternoon, I think. But Indian? Look, you'd better have a word with my khitmutgar. There are natives in and out of the kitchen quarters all day. Delivering things, selling things, taking the washing away. Peggy and I wouldn't necessarily have seen them.'

'And when you began to see you were looking at a murder didn't your suspicions light on some member of your staff?'

'No, they didn't. How can I explain this to you? It isn't an *Indian* crime. People have a sort of picture of India – lustful black men seeking to do harm to virtuous white women. Oh, yes, I know it happened in the Mutiny but the Mutiny was a madness. An Indian once said to me, "An evil wind blew through the land." Peggy's death was an elaborate act. It wasn't an impulse. It was carried out by someone who wanted to hurt her. To hurt her in a very personal way. And again, I say, I do not think this would be the Indian way.

'My servants, so far as I have discussed it with them which is hardly at all, I might say, believe this act was not of this world . . .'

'Yes, I've heard that,' said Joe. 'But look, we are agreed that it was murder, that it was not the act of a native – we are left with a European murderer. Would you accept that?'

'What else can I accept?'

'One more question, Somersham, and believe me when I say we have to ask these things – were you happy together?'

'Happy? Yes, we were. I was nearly twenty years older than she but I think she loved me. She was thrilled that we were to have a child. We both were. We had both decided just that day to announce the news. She was going to write to her parents.'

Unchecked, the tears began to flow, 'It wouldn't be too much to say she was all the world to me. It'll sound like a lot of twaddle to you, I dare say, but I used to sing "Annie Laurie" to her. "Oh like winds of summer sighing, her voice was low and sweet. She was all the world tae me. And for bonnie Annie Laurie, I'd lay me doon and dee."'

It occurred to Joe that this was probably the first time since his wife's death that William Somersham had felt able to share his feelings with anyone and, in spite of his determination to remain detached, his heart and his sympathy went out to him. Joe had seen much suffering and bereavement – had become an unwilling expert – and he would have bet a year's pay at that moment that the pain he was being shown was genuine. He waited for his companion to gain control of his emotions before continuing gently, 'Somersham, I hope I don't insult her and I hope I don't offend you but I have to ask this question – was there anybody else in her life? Had there ever been?'

'I was anticipating the question and I'll tell you roundly – no. Ask anybody. I think they'd all say the same.'

While they had been speaking the horses had ambled on but now William Somersham pulled his horse to a halt and, turning to look seriously at Joe, he said, 'Another thing, Sandilands, a deuced peculiar thing and one I haven't yet mentioned to anyone else. Not sure they would have taken any notice. Fact is, Peggy was horrified by blood. Couldn't bear the tiniest cut on a finger and a nose bleed – well, one of the children had a nose bleed at a fancy dress party she was helping to give – only the usual childish thing – but it was too much for Peggy. She screamed and ran from the room! There is no way in this world that, if she wanted to take her life, this is the way she would have chosen. And if someone killed her by slitting her wrists and holding her there while the bath filled with her blood, then it was the most cruel, calculated death they could have devised! Why, Sandilands? Why?'

Chapter Six

THERE WAS A long pause, broken at last by Somersham. 'For God's sake, Sandilands – do what you can!' And he swung his pony about and cantered away without a further word.

Naurung drew up beside Joe. 'The sahib is very distressed by his wife's death. We must perhaps think that he certainly did not kill her . . .' Naurung left the sentence trailing so that it turned into a question.

'We must think no such thing! I've interviewed many bereaved husbands in tears and storms of emotion and calling on the police for retribution only to find their fingerprints all over the knife or bludgeon. And the strange thing is, Naurung, that the tears and the distress are genuine. No – William Somersham must remain a strong suspect for the time being.'

Naurung pondered this for a moment but then nodded his approval and they resumed their tour.

Turning into Plassey Street, Naurung pointed to a card on a gatepost. 'Terence Halloran. IAMC.' The station doctor. 'You are expected, sahib.'

Joe handed his card to a servant who came out to greet him and was shown instantly into the doctor's office where he sat surrounded by the debris of lunch. Jovial and Irish, he greeted Joe as an old friend, shouting orders for the remains of his meal to be cleared away and coffee served.

'I was hoping we'd meet sooner or later,' he said. 'Very interested to help in any possible way with your enquiry. I expect you've come to talk about Peggy Somersham? Not much I can tell you that's not in my report, though, and I take it you've seen that?'

'I've had time to do no more than glance through it,' said Joe, selecting the document from the pile. 'So, if you wouldn't mind going through it with me while I check the facts it would be a great help. Especially now I've familiarised myself with the scene of the death.'

'Of course. Fire away. Though I should say at the outset that you must understand that I'm not a pathologist – I'm an army doctor, no more than that. Autopsies are not something I'm ever called on to perform. Stitching people up is more my line, not taking them apart!'

'Yes, I understand that,' said Joe. 'Now you say in your statement that you were fetched to the Somersham bungalow by your bearer?'

'Yes. I have a telephone here and the Collector rang with the news. My bearer took the message. I was out in the lines at number 12 Victoria Road – suspected measles – and he came running over to find me. It was about a quarter to eight by the time I got there.'

'Can you tell me what state the corpse was in when you arrived?'

'As I said, any initial cadaveric rigidity had passed so death had not occurred immediately preceding my arrival. But there was no sign of rigor mortis either so I would place the death at less than two hours before.'

'The time given by the ayah of her last sighting of Mrs Somersham alive was six o'clock.'

'Yes. I believe she died very soon after that. Impossible to calculate from the evidence of the blood clotting because the temperature of the water would distort it. It was still very liquid when I saw her.'

'Did you see anything odd about the wounds which caused her death?'

'Yes, of course I did!' said Halloran. 'But, as Bulstrode pointed out to me on more than one occasion, it's no part of my job to do more than indicate the cause of death and the cause of death was obvious enough – loss of blood. Poor girl bled to death.'

'But did you notice anything unusual in the direction of the cuts?' Joe persisted. 'There is no mention of the actual wounds here in the report.'

'I most certainly did notice something unusual. And so did Mrs Drummond. It's not in the report because Bulstrode told me not to waste time theorising but if you're ready to listen, then I'll tell you. There were three anomalies. Firstly, there were no trial wounds.'

Joe looked questioningly at him and he elaborated, 'If someone's going to cut his wrists he usually makes a few trial slashes on one wrist – just to get the feel of it, to estimate how much force he's going to need to do the job. And I say "he" because it's a male sort of method. Can't think of another woman who's done it . . . Secondly, the direction and strength of the cuts was odd. You find that one cut is weaker than the other. Peggy was right-handed. I would have expected her to cut the left wrist first then transfer the blade to her weaker hand and have a go at her right wrist. This second cut would normally be much more hesitant with the shock of the blood flowing. Also the direction was not right. Show me how you'd do it – go on, cut your wrists with this,' he said, offering Joe a paper knife.

Joe made two slashes across his wrists.

'That's right. Outside edge to inside on each. With Peggy's wounds it was outside to inside on the left and inside to outside on the right. Try that. Impossible, isn't it? Well, not impossible perhaps but bloody unlikely if you're killing yourself. A bit of fancy knife-work is going to be the last thing on your mind if you're doing away with yourself, I would have thought.'

'And the third thing?' asked Joe.

'The force used. Now Peggy was a strapping lass but I have strong doubts that she could have exerted the degree of strength that was shown. Her wrists weren't just *slashed* – her hands were damn nearly severed.'

'Thank you, Halloran,' said Joe, scribbling in his notebook. 'And lastly, can you tell me anything about the marks on her neck? They were even visible on the photographs Mrs Drummond took.'

'Finger and thumb marks. I did manage to get a reference to that into the report, you'll see. When I insisted that it couldn't be suicide, Bulstrode interpreted the marks as evidence that Somersham had tried to strangle her before cutting her wrists.'

'Are they consistent with a strangulation attempt in your estimation?'

Halloran shrugged. 'Not unless Somersham is deformed and has his hands on back to front. Look here,' he said, getting to his feet and walking behind Joe. 'There were thumb marks (pre-mortem) here on the back of the shoulders and finger marks here at the front at the base of her throat.' He demonstrated the hold used. 'That's not how you'd go about strangling your wife.'

'But it is exactly how you'd hold a wriggling woman down in a bath of water until she bled to death.'

'Quite. Tell you something else, Sandilands. If you've seen the room you'll have noticed the stains?'

Joe nodded.

'You should have seen them before they were cleaned! Sprayed all over the walls. She'd obviously thrashed around and waved her arms about in agony. You don't do that if you're killing yourself according to the Roman tradition. You sit quietly and wait for the end, thinking noble thoughts.'

'But if you're being killed surely you scream? If the murderer has both his hands on your shoulders, you are free to scream? And your servants and husband come running.'

'Not if the person unknown has already gagged you,' said Halloran. 'Not something you could have made out on the photographs, however sharp Mrs Drummond's Kodak lens! There were abrasions at the corners of her mouth, abrasions consistent with the application of a gag. Removed after the act because it was never found.'

'One last question,' said Joe. 'You didn't do a full post-mortem investigation, I see – I wonder whether you were aware that Peggy Somersham was pregnant?'

Halloran sat back in his chair, his surprise evident. 'Good Lord, no!' he said. 'Oh, no! How bloody! No, she hadn't been to consult me. Not unusual . . . they normally wait until they're absolutely certain. This is terrible news, Sandilands! Bulstrode was pushing for burial – we don't get the thirty hours before decomposition you get in London and the cause was very obvious . . .' His voice trailed away and he looked uncomfortably through the window, lost in thought.

'I think she had told no one but her husband, so no surprise,' said Joe equably. 'And I think it might be a good idea to keep it between ourselves at this stage.'

'Certainly. Quite see why,' agreed Halloran quickly. 'And look here, Sandilands, off the record and stepping outside my job – the poor girl was murdered, we both know that – and I'm overjoyed that, belatedly, someone has picked this up. Rumour has it that we owe this to Nancy Drummond. Am I right? Determined girl! She's got the ear of the Governor and now she's got your ear too. And come to that, she's got mine, begod!'

Thanking him for his time and mutually expressing the hope that 'we should meet at the Club one of these evenings . . . always glad to pick up the gossip from London . . .' Joe resumed his ride.

Naurung took him first along the dangerous mountain pass on which Sheila Forbes' horse had shied. He dismounted at the place where the accident had happened and, lying down, peered over the edge into the void below. A dizzying drop, he noted, with no cushioning scree slope down which a well-clad memsahib might bounce between the precipice rim and the river bank many yards below. The river curled on its way between its dusty banks like a fat brown adder and Joe shivered as he conjured up the scene ten years ago when Mrs Forbes had fallen screaming into this abyss. He pictured her wearing a cumbersome pre-war riding habit, being suddenly ejected from her side-saddle and falling head first to her death.

The place itself was full of ancient terror. Hard-nosed policeman he might be but Joe admitted to himself that he was sweating with fear. He wriggled carefully backwards on to the path and rose to his feet.

Naurung eyed him for a moment and said, 'This is a bad, bad place. The horses do not like it.'

'Can't say I'd stop for a picnic here myself. Let's look about, shall we?'

He turned and looked back the way they had come from the station. 'Well-used track apparently but here, about fifty yards back, it narrows and a group of riders would have to split up and ride along in file.' He looked in the northern direction. 'And after this bend where the path runs right along the precipice between the edge and that large rock is another hundred yards – would you say a hundred? – before there's a chance of bunching up again with your friends. Naurung, pass me the records, would you? It would be interesting to see where exactly in the file of horses Sheila Forbes was riding. Did Bulstrode record that?'

'No, sahib, but I believe one of the witnesses mentions it.'

Joe found the place and sat in the shelter of the rock to read the accounts of the accident given by the friends she had been riding with.

'This is interesting, Naurung. Mrs Major Richardson – Emma – has this to say: "Sheila was riding her own pony, Rowan – she never rode any other – and began to fall behind almost at once. She called to us that Rowan was going short on his near hind and she was going to dismount to look at it. She signalled to us to go on without her. It must have been a stone or something lodged in the hoof because she got back into the saddle and carried on. By this time she was about a quarter of a mile behind. We waved to her and rode on, expecting her to catch us up. We were getting to the slow bit anyway, the bit where the path narrows and you have to go single file, and we lost sight of her when we wound around the rocks. We'd all passed the tight place and gathered together to wait for Sheila to come round the bend. She never did. The next thing was the most appalling scream. The horse was neighing and we realised something dreadful must have happened. We rode back and there was just the horse, Rowan, by the side of the path, shivering. No sign of Sheila. Cathy Brownlow looked over the edge and shouted, 'There she is! I can see her!'

'"Two of the party rode back to the station for help while the other three looked for a way down to the river bank. While we were casting about we came upon a saddhu by the road side . . ." A saddhu?' Joe queried.

'Yes. They are wandering holy men and I will say that I do not like them. For all their ritual washings they are dirty people. Some, I suppose, truly seek enlightenment and many stand on one leg for hours, perhaps days, on end. But I and others like me see them as dirty scoundrels who get what they can from foolish people – mostly from women – and what they get they spend on opium or on bhang. They daub their faces with wood ash and saffron. They wear a little pouch on a string and nothing else. They are really a naked people – very disgusting. I would chase them away and my father often did. They cover their bodies with ash and yellow paint and they are not polite to women. Oh, there are bad stories but they are holy people and must be allowed to behave as they have always behaved.'

Joe resumed his reading. '"He told us how we could get down to the river. He didn't speak any English but luckily Cathy can manage a bit of Hindustani and that seemed to work. We gave him a four anna piece and asked him if he'd seen anything. He said he'd seen the whole thing. The horse had shied at something in the path – a snake possibly – and had unseated Sheila.

'"At the time it never occurred to us that he could have been responsible. He made no attempt to hide which he could easily have done in that terrain – I mean, you could hide a whole division in those rocks – and was really very helpful. For a saddhu. We offered him another four annas and he agreed to come back with us to the station and make a statement."'

'And so on . . . I notice that there's no statement from the beggar! Not surprised. He must have taken his annas and run.' Joe shook his head and smiled at the credulity of women. 'Still – good witness, Emma. Brave girl too. She managed to scramble down to the river with her friends and they found Sheila or rather Sheila's body. It seems she had died instantly from a broken neck. I think this tells us almost everything we need to know. I would just like to have a talk with Sheila's husband to round things off.'

'Do you agree, sahib, that this was an unfortunate accident? Now that you have seen the dangers of the place . . .'

'No, Naurung. Nor do I believe that an evil spirit exacted a sacrifice, though it's tempting in this place to imagine it. No – Mrs Forbes was murdered. With deliberation, with calculation and in very cold blood!'

They remounted and followed the trail for a further five miles until it arrived at the junction with one of the main roads to the station, a road which stopped abruptly at the river bank and continued across the other side north towards Calcutta.

'This can't be the main road north, can it?' Joe asked, taking in the single small boat which made up the ferry service and which was just casting off on the further bank to make the crossing.

'Oh no. Ten miles downstream there is a bigger road and there is a bridge. This is the road used by people going to the village of Jhalpani, two miles beyond the river.'

Joe watched as the boat came steadily towards them, rowed along by one Indian pulling on the pair of oars. His back was towards them but they could easily make out the two faces of the Indian ladies he was ferrying. Joe's gaze intensified as the boat reached the middle of the river.

'Now that's about where the ox-hide ferry was when it went under?'

'Yes, sahib. At the centre. About forty yards from where we are standing.'

'Do Englishwomen from the station often use this crossing?'

'No. Very rarely. They would normally have no reason to cross the river here. They would have no business in Jhalpani. If they came out riding they would have broken off at the place I showed you five miles south where there is a road branching back to the station, sahib.'

'Then what on earth was Mrs Captain Simms-Warburton doing risking her neck on an ox-hide raft?'

Joe sighed. The heat was beginning to tire him and so much concentrated death was becoming unnerving. The slaughter on the Western Front which he had never expected to survive had disgusted and degraded him like every other man who had been involved but this digging up of dead memsahibs affected him quite differently. These were not soldiers expecting death at any moment; these were perfectly ordinary ladies, some happy, some dull, none outstanding apparently, and all being snuffed out in bizarre ways. Were they no more than random victims of their surroundings? People kept telling him, 'Of course, India is a dangerous place, Joe. Watch out for . . .'

But no one had mentioned ox-hide ferries.

'There's a cool spot under that tree over there, Naurung. Let's have another look at the notes on Alicia Simms-Warburton, shall we? Here we are – coroner's verdict: accidental death by drowning.

'Now first things first, why was she going over? Here's an account from her husband, written to the coroner whom he apparently seems to know as he addresses him as "Dear Wilfred". This seems to be leading up to it:

'"I curse the day when somebody told her there was a hatch of Camberwell Beauty butterflies over there. 'The Mourning Cloak' they call it. Ironic, don't you think?

'"As you know, Alicia was a keen lepidopterist. But – for the record – I mean really keen. She had thousands of butterflies in her collection. And she didn't do it like most of the mems – just a way of passing the time by finding something pretty and sticking it in an album. No, she really knew about them. Have a look at her collection! All carefully pinned out and labelled. Good God, she even collected samples of their eggs, chrysalides and caterpillars – what have you – and stuck them in alongside. A really professional job. Up to museum standards. The servants were always bringing her samples of butterflies and insects but what she really liked to do was to go herself to examine what she called their habitat. There was one specimen that had long eluded her. This Camberwell Beauty thing. 'Can't you get one in England?' I asked her. Apparently not. They're even rarer back home than they are in India. And anyway I think it was the thrill of the chase that appealed, you know.

'"Anyhow, word got to her that a Camberwell Beauty had been spotted on the other side of the river south of Jhalpani and that was it. She was off the very next day. Couldn't wait for me to come home and escort her. I was away on tour in the mofussil and didn't find out what had happened for a week. I hear it was through Prentice that she found out about the wretched thing. One of his bearers or somebody had spotted one. You'd better ask him. I know about all this because she'd rushed off and left an unfinished letter to her sister who's as mad as she is . . . was . . . on her desk. I think you should probably see this but I'd like to have it back when you've finished with it."'

It was signed 'John Simms-Warburton'.

'And where, I wonder, is Captain Simms-Warburton now? Is he still on the station? Would you know, Naurung?'

'Alas, sahib, he is dead. He was killed in the war.'

'Pity. Well, let's hear what the lady herself has to say.'

The attached copy of an unfinished letter confirmed all that Captain Simms-Warburton had to say about his wife. Joe winced at the innocent enthusiasm with which Alicia communicated her coming coup to her sister Anne in Surrey.

'". . . news to make you turn positively green with envy, Anne! I have in my sights no less than – a Camber-well Beauty!! I heard just this morning from Colonel Prentice that they are to be found in a clump of willows on the river bank near a small native village just a few miles north of the station. What luck! His mali – that's his gardener (see how I'm picking up the phrases!) – came to him and asked him to tell the memsahib who loves butterflies that there was a rare one near his own village. He described it and Colonel Prentice looked it up and there it was! And there shall I be very soon. The only problem will be crossing the river. You know how I feel about rivers! And John is not here to go with me – he's off gashting round the countryside with ten other like-minded, pig-sticking shikari . . ."'

Here the letter had broken off.

'Well, this gets her to the scene. She came here, presumably on horseback, tethered it where we have left ours and climbed aboard the ferry. And look, over there, that's where she was going – those willow trees! So she wouldn't have needed transport on the other side, not even her horse. Now I think we have an account by an eyewitness here . . . yes . . . here it is. Signed by Gopal who was the ferryman involved on that day. Translated from the local native language by . . .'

'By my father, sahib. He too was a sergeant in the police force at that time,' said Naurung with pride.

'He says, "I was the ferryman working on Friday the 12th of March 1913. Before noon an English lady arrived on horseback and asked me to take her across the river. She was alone. The ferry would only carry one lady in English skirts so the three people who arrived shortly after seeking to cross to the village waited on the bank for our return. Yes, sahib, there were also people waiting on the opposite bank. I started to paddle across when suddenly the two hides on the downstream side collapsed. The air came out of them with a rush and the ferry capsized. The lady screamed and fell into the river. I think she could not swim. She struggled and sank under. I dived under to help her but the water is so dark I could not at first see her. I found her and pulled her to the surface but by then she was no longer conscious. I tried to swim with her to the bank but she was too heavy. Two of the men who had been waiting to cross jumped in to help me and between us we managed to get her to shore."

'And here is what one of the bystanders had to say: "The memsahib did not look at ease as she climbed on to the ferry. She was shouting a lot of instructions to the ferryman and took a long time to settle down. When they reached the middle of the river the left side of the raft sank under the water and the platform on which the memsahib was sitting tilted over, throwing her into the water. She was screaming and thrashing around in the water and then she sank under. The ferryman swam after the memsahib and dived under to find her. They were both under water for a very long time and we were watching, wondering what to do. Then they came to the surface again and my brother and I jumped in and swam out to help them. She was weighed down by water in her skirts and it was a struggle to get her back to land although we are both good swimmers. The ferryman was exhausted but the lady was dead."

'Mmm . . . Anything known about the hide boat, I wonder? Was it even examined?'

Joe riffled through the documents relating to the drowning with disappointment. 'Doesn't seem to be anything here.'

'It was never found,' said Naurung confidently.

'How do you know this?' asked Joe.

'I was twelve at that time and very interested in police work. I was a great help to my father. I could go to places as a village boy that my father could not have visited in his uniform without attracting attention. I overheard many useful things which my father was pleased to use in his enquiries. He was very concerned that the boat should be found. He very much wanted to examine it. My little brothers and I were sent to search the river for it. We went for ten miles along each bank in the direction of the current and we could find no trace of it. No one had found it, no one had even seen it. I talked to the old man who ran the ferry about the accident. He enjoyed talking about it. He said he did not know the ferryman who was working that day. His own men had been taken ill three days before and he had been desperate for help. Usually there are two swimmers to take these rafts across. It would have been a most difficult and tiring job for one man. Most difficult. It is not a job, you understand, sahib, that most men would want to do or would be able to do. A man appeared in the village at the right moment, he blessed Shiva for his good luck, and set him to work. He was very happy with him. And then the accident happened. The man who tried to save the memsahib came forward. But after the enquiry he told the old man he no longer wished to do the work and he left. The old man says he was a local man, judging by his accent, but not from the village, and he told him he was on his way to find work on the station. Is this helpful, sahib?'

'Yes, Naurung. But I'm afraid what you have to say raises as many questions as it answers!'

'It answers a question, sahib?'

'Oh, yes, Naurung. The question, was Alicia Simms-Warburton murdered? And the answer is yes, decidedly yes.'

Chapter Seven

THEY MOUNTED THEIR horses and swung away from the river and back towards the station. As the day declined they parted and went their separate ways, Naurung to his wife and the welcome of his family and Joe to the austere comforts of his guest bungalow. He was casting about for a scheme to help him while away the dead hours, wondering whether his reception would be more congenial in the mess or at the Club when, on the road down to his bungalow, his eye was taken by a notice. A notice of a dance at the Club. 'Saturday, March the 11th at 7.30. Last of the Season.'

'Tonight!' An impulse came over him to attend. He would surely see Nancy Drummond there, he thought with a spurt of excitement. He had been made an honorary member of the Club – so why not? He looked again at the notice and read 'Black tie'. Somewhere in his luggage there was a dinner jacket, probably by now crumpled, but 'This is, after all, Anglo-India – presumably all I have to do is clap my hands and call for someone to come and press it for me.'

On entering his bungalow he called, as to the manner born, 'Koi hai!' With a gesture he indicated to his bearer the dinner jacket, a boiled shirt, butterfly collar, dress studs – no cummerbund, he would have to make do with an evening waistcoat – but he really needn't have bothered. He was obviously not the first person for whom his bearer had had to put out evening clothes. With a further gesture he indicated his bath.

At seven o'clock, duly bathed, shaven and starched, he set off for the Club. 'Protective colouring,' he thought. 'I think I have it!'

The clubhouse and its gardens occupied the best part of one side of the maidan. Dating from the spacious days of the East India Company, it was a building which, though it had seen better days, was luxuriously designed. Somewhat in the Italian manner, somewhat in the Islamic manner and owing not a little to Hindu architecture, it made a very confident statement. A fitting residence for its first owner, a Calicut nabob whose summer residence it had been. If the stucco was perhaps beginning to peel, the swarming bougainvillea and jasmine and the embracing spray of climbing roses concealed most of the effects of time. The Club employed five full-time gardeners and the lawns were watered and immaculate, the flower beds ablaze with English flowers.

There was a press of buggies, horses, men in dinner jackets, women in evening dresses gathering round the door of the Club and Joe lost himself in this crowd, making himself briefly known to the servant on the door before walking past the long bar on to the verandah to get his bearings.

Internally, the 'large ballroom' had been converted by a vandal hand into squash courts but the smaller ballroom remained. The dining-room, lit through a series of french windows opening on to the all-embracing verandah, was furnished in the heaviest possible Victorian style with furniture from Maples in the Tottenham Court Road. But the life of the Club, Joe guessed, was lived on the verandah and the tennis court and even on the croquet lawn. In more recent years a single-storey extension surrounding a courtyard had been added at the rear with spare bedrooms for the use of visitors, for the use of bachelors from up-country, for the use of the bereaved such as William Somersham whose grief and despair had taken refuge here.

The verandah was supplied with an endless array of bamboo planters' chairs with their long foot rests, with sockets thoughtfully provided in the arms safely to contain a tumbler. Here was the social life of Panikhat while the punkhas creaked overhead, the click of croquet balls came in through the windows as one late party drew to a noisy close with shouts and laughter, while, in the charge of attendant syces, horses kicked and fretted in the shade.

Joe became aware of two men, invisible behind the high backs of their long chairs, both, he judged, in spite of the early hour, somewhat drunk and both prepared to be indiscreet with each other.

He overheard: 'It's all the fault of the Greys, I hear. Can't imagine why Prentice was so keen to elect the feller an honorary member of the mess and, of course, if they made him an honorary member the Club had to follow suit. Damned embarrassing, if you ask me!'

His companion rejoined, 'Damned embarrassing! Quite agree! I suppose we should be grateful we've only been visited with one blue locust! Hear they usually go about in swarms! Damned chap's come down here to investigate – spy on us, you might say. Can't believe anybody that's been involved wants any of this raked up again.'

There was a laugh from the other. 'What do we have to put up with? Magnifying glass and fingerprint kit? "Where were you on the night of the 11th of March 1910?" I mean, scent's a bit cold, wouldn't you say? Anyway, not very keen on the idea of a London policeman prancing round the dance floor! Are you?'

'Mind your toes, girls! Here comes a pair of regulation police boots!'

There was a chink of glasses and a laugh from both as they scrambled to their feet. 'Nancy!' he heard. 'Good evening, my dear. How are you? We were just talking about your policeman.'

'Joseph Sandilands?' He heard Nancy's voice. 'Have you met him? I was hoping he might be here somewhere . . .'

Joe decided the time had come to step forward.

'Mrs Drummond!' he said. 'I was hoping to hear a friendly voice!'

He was well satisfied with the confusion his sudden appearance had created.

'Commander!' said Nancy Drummond. 'I'm so pleased to see you! Come and meet my husband, if these two sots will excuse us.' And, to the two sots, 'See you in a minute or two.'

She took Joe's arm and led him away.

'Well,' she said, 'tell me everything! Tell me what you've been doing. Give me the benefit of the razor-sharp accuracy with which you have cut to the heart of our problems! And, by the way, take no notice of those two.'

'I wasn't going to,' said Joe, 'but I've been quite amused to hear what's being said.'

They walked together through the thickening crowd, attracting many curious glances as they went. Joe was aware that they made a striking couple and he didn't wonder that Nancy should draw so many admiring gazes. He watched her covertly as she stepped aside to exchange a brief greeting with a middle-aged pair. Her slender shape in yellow silk was all energy and grace. The dress was the height of London fashion, floating a discreet inch below the knee, the clinging and diaphanous top held up by narrow straps over her shoulders. Where most of the ladies were wearing their long hair up in tormented chignons, Nancy's shiny, dark chestnut bob swung free about her neat head and Joe was aware that every man she spoke to would have liked to run his hands through it. He decided that he would do just that. When the occasion offered itself.

She led him to a table and two chairs. 'Let's sit for a moment. You never get more than a moment for private conversation on a barrampta of this sort! Sit down. Buy me a drink.'

She waved a hand and a waiter came to her side. 'We don't seem to drink anything but gimlets these days. Gin and lime? That suit you?' And she held up two fingers. 'Now, let's look about us. First, that's my husband over there waving to us. He's very eager to meet you but he appears to be rather affair´e at the moment. I'll introduce you to him in a minute. And that's Giles Prentice over there of whom you will have heard a great deal, I dare say. I think he's outside our enquiry – I hope you don't mind my saying "our" enquiry, do you? – but he's probably the most interesting man on the station, or anywhere else for that matter. His father was British Resident at Gilgit in the North-West Frontier Province and he was brought up there as a child. He's a fantastic linguist and that, no doubt, is where it all started. He spoke Pushtu before he spoke English and was practically brought up by Pathans. He speaks Hindustani, Bengali when required, Persian they tell me and not only that – half a dozen dialects as well. He never went home for schooling. You've probably already gathered that poor little European children get sent home when they're about six. An iniquitous system! But instead of going to a smart public school in England he went to a Catholic school in Calcutta and from there to Sandhurst.

'When he came back to India the Indian regiments were queuing to get him. He had a family connection of some sort with the Greys and that's where he ended up but he hadn't been in India five minutes before he got himself attached to a Scouts Unit, the Gilgit Scouts, I think . . .'

'Scouts?'

'Oh yes. The Scouts. Regular or semi-regular forces on the north-west frontier with Afghanistan. Toughest men in the world. English officers, Pathan other ranks. Giles Prentice joined them on attachment and spent five years back on the frontier where he was born. I don't think he would have ever come away but his regiment insisted on his doing a little regimental duty. I'll call him over. Hey! Giles! Come and meet the police!'

Joe saw a dark face, a commanding nose, hair unfashionably long and a searching eye. So this was Colonel Prentice.
Now commanding the Bengal Greys. This was the man who'd
come home to find his bungalow destroyed, his wife burned
to death and his little girl hysterical and terrified. This was a
man who had taken the Bengal Greys to France in 1914, had
led the charge of the regiment at Neuve Chapelle, who had
won a DSO and bar and now, austere and aloof, ascetic and
seemingly dedicated, commanded the regiment in
peacetime.

He looked at Joe with guarded friendship. 'Glad you're
here,' he said. 'Too many mysteries! Having this in common,
each with other – no mystery at all! Distressing, even horrifying, but all susceptible to explanation and the only mystery is
that they should have happened in the same month. I expect
you're a clever man – wouldn't be here if you weren't – but I
think you're on a loser considered purely . . .' He hesitated for
a moment and continued, 'considered purely as a matter of
forensic detection. I'll give you my explanation if you like
which is "This is India". India is not Seven Dials. Still less are
we investigating a country house mystery – roast beef for lunch
on Sunday, vicar coming round for a glass of sherry after matins, body on the library carpet and a domestic search for the
truth through a cast of predictable characters. This is India, I
say again, where the strangest things happen. I've lived for
years on the north-west frontier where any Pathan would
merely acknowledge the presence of a malignant spirit. They
exist, you know.'

'A Churel, perhaps,' said Joe, remembering the word with
difficulty.

'A Churel, certainly,' said Prentice, surprised. 'And I could
think of half a dozen phenomena the existence of which is
widely believed to put beside your Churel. This is the country
of Kali, the Destroyer, as well as of Vishnu, the Benevolent.'
He paused and Joe sensed that, though there was much more

Prentice had to say, was even keen to say, he was about to obey the code of the Club which forbade that anyone should talk shop and was preparing to close down the conversation.

'Keep it light, don't dance with the same girl more than three times and don't monopolise anyone's time. Be like a butterfly and pass from flower to flower, that's the drill for a Club Dance,' Joe silently reminded himself. At that moment, the dance band of the Shropshire Light Infantry went into a foxtrot. He smiled, nodded and got to his feet, going through the ritual distancing gestures. Then, 'Oh, one thing before dance floor duty calls, sir . . . Hardly like to ask but two minutes now will save us an interview at a later stage which would probably waste time for both of us . . .'

'Carry on, Sandilands,' said Prentice equably. 'These are unusual circumstances and, if I understand the women's concerns correctly, time is of the essence.'

'Then I won't apologise for asking you to go back to 1913, to the death of Alicia Simms-Warburton. The report mentions a piece of information which triggered her dash to the river and thence to her death . . .'

'You mean the butterfly. The Camberwell Beauty.' Prentice sighed. 'I've always held myself in some way responsible for Alicia's death. Indirectly, of course, but I am aware that if I hadn't passed on the information she would never have been crossing the river that day. Though when the significance of the butterfly strikes you, you might begin to agree with me that I was used. Fate's instrument. No more than that.'

'The significance of the butterfly?'

'Yes, the Camberwell Beauty. That's quite odd. They're very rare in India but almost unknown in England. No wonder she was excited! Don't suppose you've ever seen one? It's large with black, drooping wings. Sinister-looking object, if you ask me. The local Indians call it something like Harbinger of Kali – in other words, precursor of death.'

He paused for a moment, assessing Joe's response.

'And the man who brought you the information? Was he known to you?'

'I'd better explain. Everybody knew about Alicia's passion for collecting. It was quite a joke, you might say, but everyone, English and Indian, indulged her. Brought her specimens, told her where they'd spotted something interesting, that sort of thing. I'm afraid she used to tip the Indians far too heavily. Simms-Warburton had to speak to her about it – she was spending half the housekeeping on creepy-crawlies, he used to complain. Well, one day an Indian came asking to speak to me. I took him for one of the gardeners (though I was to find later he was no such thing – chap just disappeared). He had no English and only spoke his village dialect. He came to me because he knew no one else would be able to make any sense of what he had to say. Could hardly make it out myself. And what he had to communicate was a request that I should tell the lady who collects butterflies that there had been a hatch of a very rare one in the willow trees along the river by the ferry on the far bank. I thought he was just another chap try-ing to get money out of Alicia and was on the point of sending him away. Then he launched into a vivid description of the creature and told me its name, Harbinger of Kali, and, I must say, I began to be intrigued. Looked the thing up in a book and checked he knew what he was talking about of course. I gave him a tip – a reasonable amount, he'd have done better with Alicia – and passed the information on. Straight away. Butterflies wait for no man or even memsahib. Never set eyes on the fellow again.'

'Another tool of Fate?' murmured Joe.

'Very probably. We must continue this conversation another time. I think there is much more you want to know. Now, are you dancing, Sandilands? I'm sure Nancy would let you pilot her round the floor.' And, with a bow to the return-ing Nancy, he turned and walked away.

'Well,' said Nancy, 'what did you make of that?'

'Formidable man,' said Joe, reflectively. 'I've met one or two but I think he tops my list. What can I guess? Faithful friend, implacable enemy, devious schemer – am I getting it right? I think he'd usually get his way.'

'That's not bad,' said Nancy. 'Not bad at all. That's very much Giles as I understand him. The only thing you leave out is that his men are devoted to him. Some touching and remarkable stories came back from France. Servants too. They're very loyal and you never hear gossip spreading from the Prentice bungalow. The bearer who was killed in the fire they say never left Giles' side so the fire was a double disaster for him, poor chap.'

'Lucky not to have lost his daughter. She was smuggled out by her ayah, I understand.'

'Yes. And she's back in India, they tell me. She must be eighteen now. She's been away at school in Switzerland and sailed into Bombay last week under the sketchy chaperonage of Millie Bracegirdle! She's spending a few days to recover from the voyage with an aunt and then coming on back to her father here at the station. Giles doesn't show many emotions but he loves his daughter and if he were capable of showing excitement, I'd say he was excited at the thought of her coming back into his life again. He's got plans for a party to welcome her back to the regiment so perhaps he isn't such an icicle after all. Now, come and dance with me! Let's give the gossips something to gossip about!'

The band went into a slow waltz and Joe gathered her to him. 'The Destiny Waltz'. His mind went back at once to France. This had been one of the few gramophone records they owned and he had last heard the tune being played on a wheezy accordion in an estaminet not many miles behind the lines. And here it was again. 'Police boots!' thought Joe and, with a quick glance down at Nancy's silk stockings and delicate, high-heeled kid shoes, he said, 'Can you do a reverse turn?'

'I don't know,' said Nancy. 'I don't think I've ever tried.'

'Come on, then,' said Joe, with a quick glance around which told him that, satisfactorily, every eye in the room was following them. 'Hold tight! Now!'

'That was good!' said Nancy. 'Let's do it again!'

Under the proximity engendered by this complicated manoeuvre, Joe let his cheek brush hers.

'What shall we do next?' said Nancy.

Joe raised an eyebrow.

'No! I wasn't talking about a hot, squashy time behind the potted palms in the kala juggah! What over-heated stories have you been listening to about memsahibs? I was talking about the investigation, for goodness sake! Just remember I'm the Collector's lady! The Governor's niece! Caesar's wife!'

'Seriously,' said Joe, 'you may not think so but I'm working through my list and I want to see Forbes, the husband of the girl who went over the precipice, to find out if he's got anything to add. But, more importantly, Carmichael, the snake girl's husband. Neither is on the station still. Is it known where they are?'

'More or less, but not exactly. Carmichael sent in his papers just before the war. He wasn't particularly happy with Joan as I think I told you but all the same, he was pretty shattered by her death. Who wouldn't have been? But she left him quite a lot of money and, as I say, he left the army and went into business in Calcutta. Wine imports or something of that sort. He went into partnership with some box-wallahs, Gujeratis from Bombay, I think. They didn't get on. Not surprised about that – not many people found they could get on with Harold Carmichael. He was very bitter. He was passed over once or twice and when the war began he didn't rejoin the regiment so he didn't go to France with them. He was very much criticised for having stayed safe. Perhaps I'm being unfair. He wasn't very fit and – as I say – he was very knocked about by Joan's death. They say demon drink took its toll too. I suppose he still lives in Calcutta.'

'And Sheila Forbes' husband?'

'The regimental doctor and a good one by all accounts. He went out to France with the regiment but got a job in the Hospitals Inspectorate after the war and he's based in Calcutta too though I expect he spends most of the year on tour.'

'So, in other words, if we wearily tracked our way back to Calcutta we could perhaps see both of these gents? True?'

Nancy nodded and said, 'Leave it to me. I'll do a little telephoning tomorrow,' and added, 'I wonder what everybody thinks we're talking about so earnestly? I bet nobody suspects that we're at the throbbing heart of a police enquiry.'

'Throbbing?' said Joe. 'Maybe, but not at the heart of a police enquiry. I ought to be saying, "I say, old girl, you look jolly fetching, I must say, in that get up. And, I say, when am I going to scc you? I mean see you properly?"' And, his voice dropping to a seductive growl, '"I want to see more of you!" Am I getting it right?'

'Certainly,' said Nancy. 'Jane Fortescue certainly thought so!'

'Jane Fortescue? Who on earth's she?'

'She was just beside us when you made that remark. And don't imagine that won't be echoing round the bridge tables and the mah jong sessions tomorrow!' And she went into her own imitation, '"My dear, *who* was that man, *plastered* to Nancy Drummond?"'

'Not all *that* plastered,' said Joe sadly.

With a riff of drums, the band fell silent and the voice of the comp`ere was heard. 'Ladies and gentlemen, please take your partners for a gentlemen's excuse-me.'

The Shropshire Light Infantry went dreamily into 'If You Were the Only Girl in the World'.

Joe led Nancy away from the other dancers to the edge of the room and they stood for a moment together, Joe's protective arm still unnecessarily close about her waist. A laughing thick-set young man tugging an unwilling girl in his wake bumped into Joe and excused himself. 'Andrew! So sorry, old man! Oh! Good Lord! Sorry again . . . not Andrew . . . er, oh, I say!'

Nancy cut short his embarrassment. 'Harry! You find me in the hands of the police! This is the Commander Sandilands I was telling you about. Joe, this is Harry Featherstone, our Deputy Collector.'

They shook hands and, muttering further apologies, Harry hauled his partner on to the floor.

'Do you mind if we don't attempt a gentlemen's excuse-me?' he said. 'But I could do with a drink.'

'Come along, then,' said Nancy. 'It's about time I introduced you to my husband. He'll give you a drink. I'm booked for this one, though I can't see my partner.' And she took him to a corner of the room where a middle-aged man sat with one long leg awkwardly askew on a stool and with two pretty girls sharing his foot rest. 'That's my husband,' she said. 'He may be lame and he may even perhaps be old but I can't help noticing he's never alone!'

Joe looked and liked what he saw. Nancy leant across and kissed the top of his head. 'Andrew,' she said, 'this is Commander Sandilands – Sandilands of the Met as they call him.'

'I hope they don't,' said Joe.

Drummond extended a hand. 'Excuse my not getting up,' he said. 'Wasn't there a book by Edgar Wallace called *Sandilands of the River*?'

'*Sanders of the River*, I think,' said Joe. 'But a book called *Bulldog Drummond* did come out at Christmas.'

'And this,' Nancy continued, 'is my husband, the distinguished Collector of Panikhat.'

They shook hands and as the two girls were led away by partners, Joe sat down beside the Collector who snapped his fingers at a passing waiter for a drink. 'Pink gin do you? That's what I'm drinking. I'm so glad you're here. Rumours abound, I know. Nancy, bless her heart, has got the bit completely

between her teeth – seems to have Uncle on her side, in the
presence of whom, of course, a humble Collector takes back
seat! I really admire her, you know. She doesn't let things drop
but . . .' He paused for a long time and gave Joe a level glance.
'Tell me, Sandilands,' he said, 'speaking confidentially – is she
on the point of making a fool of herself? Digging all this up
after all these years? Could be, you know. Not trying to force
a confidence, of course, but give me a lead if you can. Is this a
lot of nonsense?'

Joe decided to trust his instincts. He judged that Andrew
Drummond was a man in whom he could – and must – confide
and said carefully, 'It's early days for me, you do realise that,
I'm sure. I've only been here two days. But I'm bound to say,
as far as first impressions go . . . I think the whole thing stinks!
How easy it is to criticise, and I've no idea what facilities were
available to the police or the coroner at the time, but – looking at it now from the perspective of 1922 – very sloppy police
work. Witnesses not interviewed, statements taken on trust, no
fingerprinting or blood typing done and more of the same.
I'm speaking without prejudice but you did ask me and that's
my impression.'

'Well, I'll tell you something, my boy,' said the Collector,
'that's been my bloody impression too! I wasn't here before
the war and I wasn't here during the war and perhaps I have
no right to speak and, God knows, I don't want a scandal to
sweep through the station but if we're really talking about
murder, more than one murder, we have a duty, I have a
duty, you have a duty. Police giving you facilities, are they?
Oh, you've got Naurung in your corner, have you? Now
there's one that'll go far! Spotted him a long time ago!
With Indianisation going at the pace it is, I wouldn't be
surprised if we were looking at the next Superintendent of
Police but two.'

'Not, I fear, if his advancement depends to any degree on
Superintendent Bulstrode.'

Andrew gave him a shrewd look. 'It doesn't – but I note your concern. I gather our local law enforcer has failed to impress?'

'I haven't time – we haven't time – for niceties, Drummond. We learned not to wrap things up in the war so I hope you'll understand if I say plainly – the man's an incompetent fool or else he's cleverer than I at first gave him credit for and is up to something I shall have to get to the bottom of. How well do you know him?'

'Not well. He's been here on the station for years but, funnily, there's not many who would say they know him well, I think. He doesn't find policing the civil lines, the cantonment, particularly onerous, of course – hardly any crime to speak of. No, his value and, Sandilands, it is a value, is in policing the native town. Not an easy task. It's heavily overcrowded, many different races and castes living on top of each other in the most squalid conditions. It could be a nightmare but Bulstrode seems able to keep the lid on with surprising efficiency. Not what you expect to hear, no doubt, but in fact, I have to say, he makes my life very easy.'

Joe considered this. 'He speaks Hindustani well? That must be a help.'

'Hindustani, yes, and fluent Bengali which is what most of the natives speak. Many of us who've lived here all our lives do, as a matter of course.'

A girl paused beside him to sip from his drink, extended her cheek for a kiss and went on her way.

'Briefly then,' Joe began, 'this is where I've got to.' And slowly his discoveries and suspicions began to unfold. Andrew Drummond listened with the closest attention, asked sensible questions from time to time and, as Joe's account drifted to its close, he said:

'Only one of the "incidents" took place in my time. We have the evidence of the photographs that Nancy took. The girl's wrists! I'm not Sherlock Holmes, still less Sir Bernard

Spilsbury the distinguished pathologist, but even I could see she could never have inflicted the wounds herself. Now, if we're accepting the alternative, that is to say it wasn't suicide but murder, we're looking at a very clever fellow. A very clever murderer. He'd set this up with such care! He's not going to make the foolish mistake of cutting the right wrist left to right and it occurs to my suspicious mind that this may be a mistake made deliberately to keep the police on their toes. To make sure that notice was taken. To draw attention to what he'd been up to. Keeping his head well below the parapet but there's no doubt in my mind – he wants us to know he's there! For some reason it's important to him to announce his presence. What do you think? Could be so, couldn't it? And, if I'm right, we could be dealing with an outstandingly nasty customer! Sandilands! Catch him for us! You catch him and I'll shoot him!'

Chapter Eight

SUNDAY MORNING AND Joe settled down to breakfast. A pot of coffee (excellent), two boiled eggs (perfect), chappatis (leathery), butter (tinned, he suspected, and slightly off) and the most solid, uncompromising pot of Cooper's Oxford marmalade he'd ever seen. 'Good old India,' he thought.

As he finished dressing he heard the tinny clamour of a church bell. 'Sunday, of course. Church parade, I suppose. That's what I'm going to do this morning – set a good example for the honour of the Met. And, anyway, I might pick up some gossip. What was that woman's name? – Kitty something or other, the doyenne of Panikhat? Perhaps I'll make a formal call.'

As he buckled his Sam Browne about him, he checked his pocket to make sure he was equipped with calling cards and set off, swagger stick under his arm, towards the distant church.

Thunderously in step with a rhythmic clash of nailed boots and marching rigidly to attention, the second battalion of the Shropshire Light Infantry overtook him and preceded him into the whitewashed garrison church. They took their places, noisily securing their rifles in the racks provided. Joe remembered that since the Mutiny, where a very large number of people had been caught unarmed in church and massacred, British troops now paraded each with twenty rounds of ball, each with his side-arm.

A rather sanctimonious-looking sergeant in the Royal Corps of Signals, acting as sidesman, looked him up and down and showed him to an appropriate pew, probably accurately gauging Joe's social consequence in doing so. If it wasn't for the troops, if it wasn't for the heat, if it wasn't for the punkha beating overhead, he really might be in any suburban church in England. Automatically, he looked at the hymn board, read off the numbers and checked through the hymn book provided to see if he knew any of them.

'All Hail the Power of Jesus' Name', 'There Is a Green Hill Far Away' and – wouldn't you know? – 'Onward Christian Soldiers'. His customary churchgoing ritual complete, he looked round, seeing the haggard face of William Somersham, gazing at the dutiful faces of Greys officers, taking in the mutinous faces of British Other Ranks in serried rows and alighting with pleasure on the dark head of the Collector and, with an unseemly lurch of the heart, on Nancy at his side. The Collector also was scanning the scene and, as his eye lighted on Joe, he gently nudged Nancy and raised a stately but genial hand in greeting.

The chaplain preached inaudibly, the Shropshire Light Infantry sang uproariously, the assembled mems added their fluted accompaniment and Joe was out in the sunshine once more. His attention fixed at once on a recognisable and formidable female figure – Kitty, Mrs Kitson-Masters, conveniently standing talking to Nancy and Andrew Drummond.

'Oh, Nancy!' he thought. 'Could we get a couple of horses, ride out into the country, take a picnic with us, find somewhere to swim? Dash it, it could be work! We could discuss the case, we could pool our thoughts . . .'

Settling his cap on his head, he made his way over to them and saluted. 'Good morning, Collector,' he said formally. 'Good morning, Mrs Drummond. Did you hear me singing in harmony in "There Is a Green Hill Far Away"?'

'Oh, it was you, was it?' said Kitty. 'I heard it! Haven't heard that since I was at school! You should come more often. We're short of male voices in the choir. There, I know who you are, or I would know who you are if the Collector would condescend to introduce us.'

'I was,' said Joe, 'thinking I might do myself the honour of calling . . .'

She eyed him with a calculating and seeing eye, standing stiff as a ramrod, as would befit the widow of the Collector. A bearer stood beside her, parasol in one hand, hymn book, prayer book and service sheet and what Joe guessed was a bottle of smelling salts in the other.

'Yes,' she said in a decisive voice, 'do that, Commander. Perhaps you would do me the honour of walking back with me? We must leave the Collector and his wife to do the polite. It's usual after matins. Nancy, my dear, I declare, you get more the burra mem by the minute! I've always seen myself as the senior lady on this station but I'm going to have to watch out! You'll never be as good as I was but you'll always be a great deal prettier! Right, then, come with me, Commander!'

They set off together through the heat and dust. As they walked the call for sick parade rang out and Joe found himself automatically fitting the words to it:

> Sixty-four, ninety-four,
> He'll never go sick no more.
> The poor bugger's dead!

And as they walked, they passed two British Other Ranks, by their pale faces obviously new recruits, hands on hips, disparagingly surveying Panikhat.

'Panikhat?' they heard one say. 'Phanikhat . . . Phanicunt if you ask me!'

'Could do with a bit of that,' said the other.

'Yer, a nice dog an' duck! S'what we all need!'

Joe's face remained impassive as they passed by in earshot. He wondered if Kitty had understood this and from the increased rigidity of her spine as she walked, he guessed that she had and liked her the better for it.

On arrival at her spacious bungalow, surrounded by the best gardens Joe had yet seen in Panikhat, a cascade of servants tumbled out of the door to greet them. A maidservant took Kitty's hat and veil, her bearer handed over her church-going gear to another servant, a third set drinks out on the verandah and a fourth abjured a punkha-wallah to speed it up.

Kitty led him to a long chair. 'I know why you're here, of course,' she began without preamble. 'The station is divided, you know. Did you know that? Divided into those who think you're wasting your time and wish you'd leave sleeping dogs to lie – this faction is headed by Superintendent Bulstrode, but I suppose he would think that. Anything you might turn up reflects unkindly on police procedures – and then there's the other faction that thinks there's been dirty work at the crossroads and this is headed by Nancy, under the benevolent eye of Andrew, of course. His eye is always benevolent where Nancy's concerned as I dare say you've already found. He lets her do pretty much what she likes. Wouldn't have done in my day! But there . . . He was very badly wounded in the war. His game leg is a legacy of the second Battle of the Marne. I respect and admire him and I wouldn't like anything sad to happen to him. He didn't have to go off to the war. The Indian Civil Service was a reserved occupation but he'd served for a year or so with the Rajputana Rifles and was on the reserve of officers and they were glad enough to lure him away. With the wartime expansions they needed all the linguists they could recruit so Andrew went off to France and only just made it back again. He always says he owes his life to Nancy's nursing.'

After the slightest pause she continued, 'Now tell me who you've met, where you've been, what you've seen, what you're thinking. For example – have you met Prentice yet? The Pathans have a name for him. I can't speak Pushtu so I can't tell you what it is but – translated it means "never asleep" or something like that. He spent many years on the frontier, you know. Had a second tour with the Gilgit Scouts and only came away because his regiment insisted. Just in time to take them to France. By then he was more Pathan than the Pathan! What he didn't know about Pukhtunwali . . .'

'Pukhtunwali?

'Yes, the Pathan code of honour. Giles pretty well lived by it. Still does, I've no doubt. Ready to avenge an insult to the third and fourth generation if necessary, ready to defend the stranger within his gates to the same degree. It's logical, it's consistent and no doubt essential for existence on the north-west frontier but it can be a frightful nuisance in Bengal. And an intelligent Pathan – if that's not a contradiction in terms – would be the first to admit that it leads to some wild and ludicrous events. Drink up and have another one – must keep up the fluids in this country!'

'And Dolly Prentice? What about her?'

'Oh, she was wonderful! She's been dead twelve years and she was at least twenty years younger than me but I still miss her. She was my friend, she was everybody's friend. There was a quality about her that all admired. She could light up a room just by walking into it and if she was talking to you, you felt honoured and all the better for her conversation. I know it sounds sentimental and absurd but ask anyone who knew her and they'll all say the same. Wait a moment.'

Kitty clapped her hands and called for the bearer. She spoke briefly to him and he bowed and left the room to return carrying two dusty and ragged, leather-covered books.

'The Prentice family albums,' said Kitty. 'I don't know that Giles would approve of my showing you these but I shan't inform him of my intentions. It comes under the heading of helping the police with their enquiries, wouldn't you say?'

She waved for the servant to place them on a table between them and began carefully to turn the pages. 'Now, these

escaped the fire. About the only things that did. They were
kept in a metal trunk in Giles' office at the end of the bungalow with the family papers. When they were salvaged, of course
they were brought to me. Giles and Midge both know I've got
them in safe keeping but they have never asked to have them
back and, somehow, it never seemed the right moment to
return them. Midge comes over to look through them and
hear me tell stories of her mother but Giles has never shown
any desire to have them returned. Too painful.'

She found the photograph she was looking for and pushed
it towards him. 'There, you can see something of her style. She
was beautiful. There was an elfin quality about her that
appealed to everybody.'

Joe looked with admiration and sadness at the bright, mischievous face raised to the camera. Yes, Dolly would have
enslaved him too, he thought.

'And her reputation remained intact?' he asked
delicately.

'Well, she could have said, with Queen Elizabeth:

> '"Much suspected of me,
> Nothing proved can be."

'And so it was. I would suspect there was a string of affairs
or at least flirtations and if I was minded to do so I could name
names.'

'And Prentice? Was he aware of all this? Did he mind? Was
he very devoted?'

'What can I say? He had a reputation for devotion and it's
true that when he had to leave the station he took her with him
whenever he could. And that's unusual. Most of the officers are
only too glad to leave domestic bliss behind for a few days, I'd
say. But devoted? Truly I'd say he wasn't. I'd almost be prepared to say he was indifferent to her, though you wouldn't
find many to agree with me. Fond of her perhaps and he never

mistreated or neglected her certainly but, compared to all the other men on the station, indifferent.'

'How did he come to marry Dolly? On the surface they don't seem to have a great deal in common.'

'Dolly had an Indian background. Rather like Nancy and dozens of other girls – if you want to have a place in India there's only one way to achieve it – you have to marry a man who is making his career here. After school, Dolly came out on the fishing fleet and never was likely to be a "returned empty" as we rudely used to call the poor plain girls who went back home without a husband. She had her pick of the eligible men that year 1902, was it? Of course, by far the best catch is a three hundred pounds a year dead or alive man . . .'

'Dead or alive?' asked Joe puzzled.

'A civil servant, like the one Nancy's got for herself, the best paid and having the advantage that if he dies, you go on drawing your husband's salary in full for as long as you live. Not a bad bargain, I think you'd agree?'

'It beats police arrangements, certainly,' said Joe.

'And Dolly had her offers from that quarter but – and to many people's surprise – she chose Prentice. And here they are on their wedding day.'

'He was a handsome man,' Joe commented.

'Oh, yes. Physically an outstanding man. And he still is. Fiendishly handsome, don't you think? But there was something about him which did not appeal to most girls. He didn't flirt. All those years in the hills were no preparation for the trivialities of polite society. He had no idea, I think, of making himself attractive to women. It's my opinion that he had been sent back to the regiment here in Bengal with advice from his senior officers to make a serious push for promotion and there is a point beyond which it is difficult to proceed if you do not have a wife. There's a saying in the Indian army: "Subalterns may not marry. Captains may marry. Majors should marry. Colonels must marry." Prentice was determined to make colonel. He got Dolly in his sights and carried off the prize of the season.'

The album with its melancholy parade of singed and stained but evocative images was entrancing Joe. 'May I?' he asked.

'Certainly,' said Kitty. 'Take your time.'

She waved a hand again to her bearer who interpreted her gesture without a word and presented a cigarette box at her elbow and a lighted match. At her invitation, Joe helped himself to a cigarette.

'And this is Midge?' he asked, pointing to a tiny child being supported on a pony by a smiling syce.

'Yes, that's Midge. Very dark, you see. Takes her colouring from her father.'

Joe was silent for a moment as he gazed at another portrait. A tall, dark young man dressed in the baggy white trousers, loose white shirt and tight waistcoat of a Pathan tribesman smiled in a confident and swaggering way at the camera.

'Ah, I see you've found Prentice's bearer.'

'Chedi Khan?'

'Yes. Now how do you know that? Am I going to have to respect your detective abilities after all? Chedi Khan. That's the name. Haven't heard it for years. But I would never forget the man! No one who saw him ever would. I can still remember the flutterings he made in the hen coop when he appeared on the station with Prentice for the first time! The women swooned! Discreetly, of course!'

'He has a strong look of Rudolph Valentino in *The Sheik*.'

'We haven't yet had the pleasure of moving pictures in Panikhat, so I am not able to comment. But Chedi Khan certainly cut a most romantic figure about the station. He was about six foot two and, as you see, handsome as the devil. He moved like a panther – stalked through the station looking neither to left nor right and he was subservient to no one but Prentice. His hair was black and he wore it long on his

shoulders . . . sometimes he would twine a red rose through it.
That was surprising enough but the most amazing thing about
him was his eyes. They were blue. Yes, turquoise blue and he
would ring them with kohl which made the effect even more
devastating. Apparently some of these northern tribesmen do
have light skins and blue eyes. They say the colouring goes
right back to the invading armies of Alexander the Great.
Extraordinary.'

'But where did Prentice acquire such a servant? If servant
is what he was . . .'

'He certainly didn't behave like one. He was a law unto
himself. The story is that he was committed to Prentice's care
when he was a boy after some flare up on the frontier. Where
Prentice went, Chedi Khan followed.'

'And what were his relations with Prentice's family? Is it
known?'

'I wouldn't say known for certain. That was a very tightly
knit household by Indian standards. He seemed to be devoted
to Dolly and to Midge. Of course, there were wagging tongues
to hint that in the face of Prentice's indifference, Dolly found
special comfort in her husband's bearer. And perhaps she
did . . . No, Commander, it would not be unknown,' she
finished in response to Joe's enquiring glance. 'And when the
two bodies were discovered entwined together in the wreckage
of the bed in Dolly's room, well, you can imagine that the station biddies had all their suspicions confirmed!'

'It puzzles me that anyone should have been still in their
beds in those circumstances,' said Joe. 'According to the
report there was a lot of noise – servants screaming, fire roar-
ing . . . there were even shots. Loud enough to attract the
attention of officers half a mile away in the mess . . .'

'It was no puzzle to anyone who knew Dolly,' said Kitty
thoughtfully and she was silent for a moment while she
decided how far she might confide in Joe. 'Look here, Commander, you haven't seen much of station life but perhaps

enough to judge that for many women it's a boring and lonely life. It's rarely necessary for a memsahib to lift a finger for herself and when her morning task of supervising the servants is complete, there is little else to occupy her time and certainly not her mind. Dolly was bored. She drank. She'd been drinking a bit for months before the fire. It's an old story. I would guess that when the dacoits set fire to the bungalow she was lying dead to the world already.'

'But Chedi Khan?'

'A Muslim so he certainly wasn't under the influence of alcohol. Who knows? The bodies were trapped under a beam. Perhaps he'd been trying to wake her up . . . make her move . . . left it just too late. Chedi Khan was devoted to Prentice and what would he do but spend his life defending the memsahib? Well, that's always been *my* version of the story anyway.' She looked at him with the trace of a challenge. 'And I would be obliged if you would accept it as the authorised version, Commander. There are the living to consider and to me they are more important than the dead. And perhaps even more important than the truth.'

Joe nodded his acquiescence and understanding. He would leave it there – for the moment.

It occurred to him that a proper autopsy would have revealed the contents of Dolly's stomach. Drunk? Drugged? The fire started to conceal evidence? He couldn't recall a medical report on Dolly's body and made a note to himself that he would need to enquire further. His mind automatically sped down a widening avenue of speculation.

'Can you remember how Giles Prentice reacted when he heard what had happened?'

'He was devastated. He didn't utter or move for a week. He was in no fit state to care for Midge, of course, and she, poor dear, was out of her mind with panic and distress. My husband and I scooped her up and brought her over here and cared for her. She lived with us for nearly a year. Too disturbed to

be sent away to school so I taught her her lessons myself.
Bright little thing! But terribly highly strung and who shall
wonder?'

Her face clouded at an unwelcome memory. 'She was sitting at my feet one day while I was sewing, reading her way
through my children's old books and she came across an old
Victorian volume – *India Told to the Children* I think it was
called. Suddenly Midge pointed to a page, screamed and
began to sob. It was a long time before we could calm her
down. In fact, we had to fetch Giles to reason with her.'

'What on earth had she seen?'

'A depiction of the ritual of suttee. A beautiful young
Indian lady, dressed in her finest clothes and her jewels, was
lying on a blazing funeral pyre by the side of her husband's
dead body. Just the thing for a children's book, I think you'll
agree!'

'And Prentice took her back to live with him again?'

'Eventually. She stayed with us until their new bungalow
was built.'

'At number 3, Curzon Street?'

'That's right. Next door to the ruins of the old bungalow.
Very odd of Giles, I thought, to build so close to the old site
– it must have brought back bad memories every day. But then
he already owned the land. He was always an unpredictable
fellow! Though in military ways, perfectly predictable. When
he came back to his senses after the disaster the Pathan in him
took over. He gathered up a troop of Greys – at the express
request of the Collector because there was much public sympathy and outrage, as you can imagine – and he rode off. They
came back after ten days. No one has ever seen troops so
exhausted. Not one of them has ever spoken about that
sortie.'

She shivered. 'But I think the dacoits learned the meaning
of the word "Pukhtunwali".'

Chapter Nine

THERE WAS A silence filled only by the rhythmic creaking of the punkha. Kitty was lost in the horrors of the past.

While Joe gave her the time to order her thoughts and emotions, his own mind was busy absorbing the details and weighing the importance to his enquiry of the bloodstained events of that March twelve years before. He was forming no theories, making no judgements yet; he was simply taking in as much as he could of this series of alien and macabre events. This was often the way in cases that he had worked on. In the initial stages, a voracious acquisition of facts and impressions characterised his approach. He made no predictions, advanced no theories until he was certain that he had learned as much as there was to be learned about the crime. He knew the danger of constructing a neat explanation which could then be shot to ribbons by the late entry of a new piece of information.

And there was something about this, the first death of a memsahib, which tugged at his attention. He had devised his own theory, drawing on evidence from the rash of multiple murders which had shocked the population of Europe over the last fifty years, that it was the first killing of any series and the latest which were the most likely to give away the identity of the killer. The first murder, being the first, was inevitably the most amateur, the most sloppy, the most nervously executed of the crimes. If the killer went on to survive this undiscovered, he would improve his technique, take fewer chances, cover his tracks more expertly the second and third and fourth times. If his career continued to flourish he might become overconfident, feeling himself immune to detection, and by the time the police were investigating his fifth or sixth offerings, their acquired skill might just be the equal of his.

The killing of Dolly Prentice, being the first and by far the most convincingly accidental, was, Joe considered, the most significant. The pattern was like and yet not like the pattern of the subsequent killings. As in the other four cases there was the probably lethal presence of a native – in this the supposed dacoits. It occurred to Joe that not one witness mentioned actually having set eyes on a dacoit, though there were reports that the servants had seen them and been herded roughly out of the building by a gang of four or five armed men. Could someone – Prentice? – have hired them, lured them or tricked them into an attack on the bungalow? During his absence? And then have pursued them and got rid of the living evidence against him? Joe decided to rein in his imagination; no man would put at risk his wife, his daughter, his bearer and his household of devoted servants indiscriminately.

He turned back the pages of the album and looked again at the wedding photograph. Even from the sepia-tinted paper, Dolly sparkled with happiness and some other quality . . . satisfaction? Pride, perhaps? Was there a touch of the same emotion he had caught in the eye of an old tiger hunter in a painting in the mess – 'See what a fine beast I have conquered'?

Joe looked at her conquest. Colonel, then Major, Prentice. Tall, athletic, commanding. Yes, a tiger. But he doubted that Dolly had her graceful foot on his neck. He remembered Kitty's saying about marriage in the army – 'Colonels must marry'. Was the man merely doing his duty for the sake of promotion? And Dolly, had she chosen the man or the station commander he would become? Had she been aware of his background, aware of his essential wildness?

'You're saying that Prentice, um, reverted to the code he was familiar with from his early youth . . . this Pukhtunwali . . . to exact retribution from the bandits who were responsible for his wife's death? Would it still have such significance for him, after so long?'

Kitty lit another cigarette and considered his question. 'Oh, yes, I think so. On the surface Giles Prentice is the pukka cavalry officer, punctilious, cold, arrogant, but I've always thought there was another layer to his character, something more volatile bubbling beneath the austere surface. And the Pathan code, well, it's very – what shall I say? – very seductive in its simplistic, masculine way.'

'Is there more to it than a duty of revenge?'

'Yes. But not much. There is the duty of melmastia – that's hospitality. It is expected that a Pathan will offer food, lodging, protection, even lay down his life to protect anyone who seeks shelter with him. Many British officers "take safe conduct" as the saying is. And come to admire the Pathan way of life while doing so. And secondly there's the right of nanawati which means "coming in". A Pathan has to offer protection to anyone who asks him for it, even his worst enemy. If a man comes to him with a tuft of grass in his mouth to indicate that he is subservient like the animals and with the Koran on his head, Pathans may not refuse nanawati. But the first and most important duty is badal – vengeance. Vengeance must be exacted for any injury done to the Pathan or to his family or tribe. He may wait many years before he accomplishes it – may even have forgotten the reason for it – but avenged he must be. There is a story – quite a recent one and I know it's true because the incident was investigated by my cousin – that a perfectly innocent English officer was shot dead on the frontier by a tribesman. When he was asked why he had shot the officer who was unknown to him, the Pathan replied that his great-grandfather had been killed by an Englishman and he was taking revenge. "But after one hundred years?" my cousin asked, disbelieving. "One hundred years . . . yes . . ." said the Pathan, "perhaps I have been a little hasty." And there are stories which tell of leathery old villains who have killed their own offspring when the code demanded it!'

'So, in pursuing the dacoits, Prentice was avenging the death of Dolly?'

'Yes. I'd rather not think about it but I would guess that's exactly what he did. There was something so chilling in the intensity, the implacability of the man. He had a face of gran- ite, an expression as fierce as all three Furies combined when he rode off on his punitive raid. But, then, you don't have to be Pathan in your way of thinking to insist on your revenge. There were many British officers to encourage him. A burning bungalow, a burning memsahib, a terrified child, these woke fearful memories, you can imagine.'

'Memories of the Mutiny?'

'Yes. I was completely overwhelmed myself by the sight of a bungalow burning and I expect others of my age were too. I was what they used to call a Mutiny Baby. Born in 1857, actu- ally in the residence at Lucknow. I knew all about the Mutiny. Our friends talked about it a lot of course and the destruction of the Prentice bungalow gave me quite a turn. I wasn't the only person who said, "It's all starting again". There is always, just below the ordered surface of army life, the fear that it could all happen again. And remember, Mr Sandilands, that it was Englishwomen, army wives, who were the first victims of the butchery.

'I had no bad feeling after the war until Peggy Somersham's alleged suicide brought back memories, and the bad feeling returned with a vengeance when I counted up and realised that there had been five deaths on the station in March in suc- ceeding years and I don't think it had occurred to anybody else until Nancy started to question everything. And now here you are ferreting about like a stoat or should I say stoating about like a ferret? What's your next move?'

'I'm going to Calcutta,' said Joe. 'Next week. To see Harold Carmichael and Philip Forbes. With Nancy.'

'Oh, yes?'

'All right,' said Joe, 'I know what "Oh, yes?" means! Perhaps I should say we're going in the Collector's official car, driven by none other than Naurung!'

'Impeccable chaperonage!' said Kitty and she extracted a small gold watch pinned amongst the drapery of her bosom and studied it in a marked manner.

Joe laughed. 'One thing we learn in the police is to take a hint! Thank you very much for many things and I'll see you again soon, I hope.'

'Sooner than you expect, perhaps, Commander. This afternoon if you like. People come to tea with me on Sunday. You could say I am "at home". If it were known that the mysterious and handsome police sahib was amongst the cucumber sandwiches, part of the menu, you'd see a good turn-out. Anyway, that's what you're here for – or so I understood – to calm things down . . . to reassure the hysterical women that Scotland Yard has everything in control. You'd better be here. Bring your smelling salts! Five o'clock. Don't forget!'

'I shall be delighted.' Joe rose to his feet, bowed, resumed his cap, saluted and turned on his heel.

'Oh, Commander, there is just one more thing . . .' Kitty called after him. 'It probably is not of the slightest interest or importance but there is one rather odd thing I've noticed . . .'

Joe smiled encouragingly and waited for her to go on.

'It's the roses. They've appeared again. Oh, I know, you'll tell me that every garden in the station is ablaze with roses and so they are but I'm talking about the ones in the graveyard. The crimson Kashmiri roses – well, that's what I call them. I believe they're actually a wild China rose that's made its way through Nepal and Kashmir and down here to Bengal, *Rosa indica minima,* but I first saw them in Kashmir and that's what they'll always be for me – Kashmiri roses. They aren't all that common. Dolly used to have one growing over her bungalow but, of course, that's gone. There's a good specimen in the Clubhouse gardens and I know Nancy has one or two but that's about all. Most people are keener on growing the bigger, showier blooms, you know. Well, a bunch of them appeared on Joan's grave and has done every year since her death. Nothing strange there but – can I be the only one who's noticed this? – a bunch appears regularly, every March, on Joan's grave, on Sheila's, and on Alicia's although there's no longer anyone on the station who would remember them in that way. And, this morning at church, I saw that someone had put some on Peggy's grave too. Now what do you make of that, Commander?'

The Bengal Greys' idea of an appropriate Sunday lunch in summer was, inevitably, mulligatawny soup followed by jam roly-poly. Joe found this anaesthetic in the extreme although he had refused the jug of claret which appeared at his elbow, contenting himself with a glass of India Pale Ale. He feared that if he gave way and slept for the afternoon as every instinct prompted him he would never wake in time for Kitty's tea party at five. He supposed that, conscientiously, he should be there. On an impulse he decided briefly to get away from the station and, calling for his pony, he went back to his bungalow and changed into jodhpurs and a shirt. He would take a distant view of the station in the hope that it might clear his mind.

He set off to follow again the mountain path that had been so fatal to Sheila Forbes. The sure-footed Bamboo made light of the crooked track, cantering easily upwards to follow the turns and finally arriving, as Joe thought of it, at the fatal corner. 'How would I manage,' he wondered, 'if a naked saddhu bounced out from amongst the rocks?' He was riding with a bitless bridle and would not have had much control but

decided on the whole that Bamboo would be undaunted. And
Joe had the advantage of two strong legs one on either side of
the horse, perfect balance and years of riding experience. He
glowered at the concealing rocks and fingered his crop, passionately wishing his enemy would make an appearance.

The path wound on and finally debouched in a little enclosure amongst the rocks, shaded by trees and watered by a
stream. He could quite see why this was a favourite picnic
place and made up in his mind an alternative ending to that
unfortunate ride. In his mind he saw Sheila Forbes arrive
breathless and triumphant, catching up the others and dis-
mounting to join them on the grass in a sandwich and cool
drink. Something to put in her next letter home.

Joe found himself consumed with rage, with a healthy
hatred of the man who had persecuted and decimated this
innocent group, who had plotted and planned and set up an
ingenious series of cover stories and remorselessly watched
while each of his victims had died before his eyes. He dismounted and looped his reins round a hitching-post obviously
set there for the convenience of picnic parties and walked to
the edge of the cliff looking down on Panikhat. 'There's my
problem. Somewhere down there is my problem. Down there
is a problem man. Perhaps he's even looking up and wondering what I'm doing. Perhaps he's afraid of me. I'd like to think
he's afraid of me.

'" 'I am Nag,' said the cobra, but at the bottom of his black
heart he was afraid."

'Oh, for God's sake, let me be the bloody mongoose! Be
afraid, whoever you are, you bastard! Make a mistake! Show
your hand! Bring me some evidence, for Christ's sake! Any
little scrap will do. Something to hang an accusation on.'

He found that he had come to identify his adversary as a
cobra. Not the common Indian cobra but a King Cobra, a
Hamadryad, sometimes twelve feet long and who could strike
from the bushes and kill unseen. He made for a rock and,

feeling foolish as he did so, he thrashed the ground around it, not wishing to be the second to be bitten by a snake basking in the sun, and sat down, lit a cigarette and began to search the distant rooftops below, trying to identify Nancy's house. His eye moved on to the large expanse of Kitty's roof and he wondered what on earth he was going to say to Kitty's assembled flock of nervous ladies. His task, it seemed, was to reassure but, far from reassured himself, he couldn't for the life of him imagine how this was to be done.

A seasoned lecturer, he was accustomed to leading committees, forming opinion, getting his own way and, above all, moving things forward. People of all ranks listened to him, liked him and generally did what he asked them to do or believed what he was telling them. But he had to admit that he was at a loss as to what he was to say to this small group of women. Well-bred, polite and struggling to force down their panic, they would be only too ready to absorb any word of wisdom or comfort he had to offer. Joe sighed. He would far rather face a hundred sceptical and bloody-minded bobbies! But he had a part to play and though it was not one he had chosen he would give it his best attention and make sure he was prepared.

He sat on for a long while, rehearsing phrases, deciding the line he was going to take. 'Naurung!' he thought. 'I'm going to need his help.'

⁂

As the tinkling sounds of Kitty's clock chiming five faded, Joe was ushered on to the verandah by the khitmutgar. Cool from his second bath that day and comfortably dressed in a pair of box cloth trousers, white shirt and riding jacket, he strode forward to kiss Kitty's hand.

'My dear Commander,' she said laughing at him, 'how fresh you look! And how charmingly informal. Now, do I regret the passing of the wing collar, the lavender gloves, the pearl tie pin? Perhaps not. But you must come and meet the lady wives of the officers – the "Bengal Mares" as my father used to call them.'

Joe turned to face the rest of the company. Nancy and six other women had been standing chattering in a tight group when he entered and now they broke up and approached in order of seniority to be introduced to him.

'Nancy of course you know,' said Kitty proceeding down the line. 'Now, Mary, may I present Commander Joseph Sandilands of the Metropolitan Police? Commander, this is Mary Crawford, the wife of Major Crawford . . .'

There followed Biddy Kemp, Jane Fortescue, Lucy Meadows, Phoebe Carter the MO's wife and the wife of the veterinary officer, Joyce Wainwright. He tried to form an impression of each as she passed in front of him but ended with a blurred vision of bright colours, floating fabrics, scented hands, shy smiles, teasing smiles and, above all, of clever and calculating eyes. What he did not see a trace of was panic.

Colonial wives had a reputation for being dowdy but the selection before him brought to mind an English herbaceous border at its midsummer best. Kitty and Mary Crawford were dressed with the utmost correctness in ankle-length crepe tea gowns. Hemlines rose, he noted, in inverse proportion to age and the youngest, little Lucy Meadows, was wearing a rose pink day frock which barely covered her knees. The youngest three wives all, like Nancy, wore their hair short, their figures uncorseted and their expression direct.

Kitty waved a hand towards a table laid out with a lace cloth on which stood two silver teapots, one with a red ribbon attached to its handle, the other with a yellow ribbon. There was a Coalport china tea service, plates of sandwiches and a cake stand laden with slices of Dundee cake and iced sponge cake. The khitmutgar presided, smiling, over the table as Kitty invited everyone to choose their tea – red ribbon for Indian, yellow for China.

Joe chose Indian tea and an anchovy paste sandwich and chatted with each of the ladies in turn. They compared the weather in London with that of Panikhat, they told him of their plans for the coming hot weather season when the traditional exodus to the hill stations of the Himalayan foothills took place and Jane Fortescue offered flirtatiously to show him the delights of Simla should he care to make the journey. The teapots were refilled from a spirit kettle and Joe sipped his third cup of tea, beginning uneasily to wonder exactly why he had been asked to come. He cast a furtive glance at Kitty's clock and was surprised to find he had only been there for forty minutes.

At last Kitty called the tea party to attention. 'And now, ladies, if you would make yourselves comfortable, the time has come to ask Commander Sandilands to sing for his cup of tea.'

Cups and plates were laid down on tables and the chattering company fell silent. They began to exchange sideways glances and Jane Fortescue stepped forward. 'Oh, no, Kitty! It is not the Commander who shall sing! We shall! Come on, girls!'

To Joe's amazement she seated herself at the piano and the other girls grouped themselves around her. After an opening chord from Jane they began to sing.

> 'Watch your back! Be ready!
> For no one will heed your cry.
> There are five of us dead already;
> Under six feet of earth we lie.
>
> Hold the line, girls! Steady!
> And wipe the tears from your eyes.
> Here's a toast to the dead already,
> And here's to the next girl that dies!'

They broke up, laughing, and settled into chairs watching for his reaction.

Joe knew the tune. It always brought a shudder of horror with it. He had last heard it sung in tones of bright despair by a quartet of young Flying Corps officers before they took off for the last time over the German lines. The women had just treated him to a bastardised version of the old 'Calcutta Cholera Song'. Challenging him? Telling him they weren't afraid? Hiding their fear under a flourish?

He waited for a moment then hummed the first line reflectively. 'Yes, I thought I recognised it! "The Panikhat Panic Song"! We used to sing the same tune in the trenches but if I were to tell you the words *we* used Kitty would have me ejected.'

Some of them smiled and out of the corner of his eye he noticed Nancy begin to relax. The khitmutgar began silently to clear away the tea things and Joe went into his talk. He moved forward and sat facing them on the edge of a table. He had decided that these bold and lively women deserved nothing less than the truth as he now saw it, however unpalatable.

'I know about fear. I know about death. And I'm not going to tell you not to worry your pretty little heads about the deaths that have been occurring on the station. I am going to tell you that you may have good cause to be afraid. You are members of a group which for a reason I have not yet ascertained is the target of a killer. And a very particular type of killer . . .'

Soft-footed, Naurung entered the room. He was wearing, not his usual police uniform, but the loose white outfit of a house servant, a red waistcoat and a blue turban. Joe went on talking, the women's attention riveted on him. Naurung began to help the khitmutgar with the clearing of the table. Suddenly he dropped a plate which crashed to the ground and broke. Naurung exclaimed loudly and began to sweep the remains together. The khitmutgar advanced on him and

Naurung, hissing invective at him, was hurried from the room. The women, who had all turned to stare at Naurung on hearing the noise, averted their eyes in embarrassment or distaste at the extraordinary scene and fixed their attention once more on Joe.

He continued to talk to them, concisely setting out the dates and details of the pre-war deaths and summarising his suspicions. Suddenly he broke off and reached into his pocket. He took out some sheets of paper and pencils and passed one to each lady.

'Before we go on – and believe me there is a point to what I'm about to ask you to do – I want you to think back to what happened in this room five minutes ago. Take your pencil and write down a description of the Indian who came in to assist the khitmutgar. What was he wearing? What were his features like? What language was he speaking? What did he do?'

Puzzled looks were exchanged, pencil ends were chewed and short notes were written down. Joe collected the papers in and put them on the table by his side.

'Coming now to someone you all knew,' he went on, '– Peggy Somersham who died last week. I know you have been told that she committed suicide but I have to tell you that, like the others who preceded her, I fear she was murdered. Murdered and not by her husband. It is my intention to have the coroner's verdict of suicide overruled.'

There was a murmur and a nodding of heads in approval of this.

He went carefully over the evidence he had collected and concluded, 'There was one witness, a vital witness who unfortunately was allowed to go free after giving his statement . . .'

'Bulstrode!' someone interrupted. 'The man's an incompetent idiot! He should have locked him up and thrown the key away!'

'The witness was an Indian. We do not have a good description of him although he was seen by several people and even interviewed by the officials. From the accounts I've given you, you will have noted that at or near each murder scene an Indian of one sort or another was noticed. Where are they? Who are they? One man or several? How can they, or he, just have slipped into the sand? I'll tell you how. People are very bad observers. Ask any group of six onlookers to describe a man who has just knifed another in a London street and you will be given six different (and possibly all incorrect) descriptions. Let's take this group of six. I asked you to write a description of the Indian servant who created a disturbance a few minutes ago.'

Joe leafed though the notes, discarding one that said, 'It was Naurung, you fool! Nancy' and read out a sample:

'"It was an Indian. He was wearing Indian clothes and he shouted in Indian. He broke something. A teacup?'

'"It was Kitty's bearer Ahmed. Tall, dark, blue jacket, beard, yellow turban. Broke a teacup. Kitty won't be pleased! Spoke Hindustani.'

'"Vicious-looking. Elderly. Red turban. Medium height. Struck the khitmutgar and swore in Hindu.'

'"Young. Short. Shifty-looking with a large moustache. Red turban, green jacket. Spilled a cup of tea on Khit's foot. He spoke Bengali.'

'These descriptions reflect well on your imagination, ladies, but less well on your powers of observation! Come in, Naurung!' Joe called.

Naurung appeared smiling and bowing to the ladies who gasped when they recognised him, laughed and turned to each other pointing out that it was Naurung Singh the policeman in disguise.

'Not in disguise. Merely wearing clothes you are not expecting to see him wear and appearing in a context in which you would not expect to see him. He has no connection with Kitty's household in your experience so you did not recognise him. Thank you, Naurung,' said Joe, and he left exchanging a joke with the khitmutgar who had obviously enjoyed the whole performance.

'Well, you didn't get many details right, did you? By the way – he broke a plate – an old one, with Kitty's permission! He was speaking Hindustani and he said something unrepeatable about the khitmutgar's parentage. And your descriptions of the man himself were far from accurate. Although you all in fact have seen him on many occasions. The reason for this? Because he is Indian. You simply do not register brown faces with any interest or accuracy. And this is precisely the failing that enables our killer to get close to his victim unnoticed and then get away.'

'So what are you suggesting, Commander?' piped up Lucy Meadows. 'That we should all sleep with a hockey stick under our bed and avoid all brown faces? Pretty jolly difficult in India, you know!'

'I think the Commander is trying to tell us,' drawled Phoebe Carter, 'that we should give up and go home to England next March. Can you guarantee that the streets of London are any safer, Mr Sandilands? Have you caught Jack the Ripper yet?'

Her jibe earned a ripple of laughter.

'Mrs Carter,' said Joe seriously, 'you would, I can tell you, be at far less risk of your life in Whitechapel where the murder rate is less than one per year among a population of many thousands, than here in Panikhat where one out of six of you could well die next March. And the drawing-rooms of the home counties, I believe, are still reckoned to be entirely safe . . . though there is the ever present danger of an attack of terminal boredom . . . and, seriously, this is an option, should our man still be at large next year.

'But I wanted to say, in conclusion, this: I believe no one here is in danger *before* next March. The man I'm looking for is not a deranged killer. He is following a plan – I am tempted to say, a sacrificial ritual. I'm going to work out what scheme or

compulsion lies behind the killings and bring the man to justice. It's my opinion that there is some religious or quasi-
religious motive at the bottom of all this, a motive which as
Westerners we may be hard pushed to understand. We have all
heard of the religion and despicable (to us) habits of the Thugs
who infested this part of India until quite recent times . . .'

Again the girls nodded in understanding. Thuggee. The
word still had the power to terrify. The thousands of innocent
travellers, garotted and buried in mass graves in the last cen-
tury and all in the name of sacrifice to the blood-thirsty goddess Kali, were not forgotten.

'. . . it is quite possible that our man is acting under the
same kind of compulsion.'

'So what can you do, Commander, to get hold of this man
before he strikes at another one of us? You're only here for a
short while and you say Bulstrode's let him go!' said Jane
indignantly. 'How can you get him back? He could be anywhere in India by now!'

With a confidence he didn't feel, Joe set out to reassure
them. 'These are the days of the telegraph and the telephone
and the train. If *he* can move about the country easily, how
much more easily can the forces of Law and Order! I am going
to Calcutta to check on this man's story and I'll inform the
Governor. Wherever he's fled, we'll follow and we'll stay on his
trail until we've caught him.'

He looked around his audience, catching each woman's
eye and said quietly, as though making a promise to each indi-
vidually, 'And I'm going to get him. If it takes another week,
another month or another year!'

Chapter Ten

AFTER BREAKFAST ON Monday Joe put on his topee and set off to catch Bulstrode before he started out on his rounds. Presenting himself at his office building he was politely asked by a young Sikh officer to wait for a few moments. The few moments turned into several minutes of waiting time, carefully calculated to annoy, Joe guessed. He sighed and set himself to wait patiently, using the time to leaf though his notes. Eventually the door to Bulstrode's office opened.

'Sandilands!' said Bulstrode with bonhomie. 'Glad you could spare the time. Come in. Take a seat? Had coffee, have you? You've been turning the Somersham bungalow over, I hear. Up-to-date forensic methods hot from the press in Scotland Yard. Manage to turn up anything?'

The tone was friendly in the extreme but the eyes were suspicious.

Joe felt his professional detachment slipping. He desperately wanted to punch Bulstrode on his arrogant nose. Instead he said easily, 'Nothing of any great consequence . . . Only perhaps two facts you might like to consider. One, that Peggy Somersham was certainly murdered and secondly that she was expecting a baby.'

Bulstrode stopped dead and turned to face him.

'Good Lord! You don't say! But that is certainly of consequence. That could well supply a motive!'

'A motive?'

'Yes. Certainly. A motive for suicide. I mean if the poor girl was preggers, maybe perhaps not Somersham's – he was after all much older than she was . . . not exactly love's young dream, you know, and the station's not short of good-looking young fellers. It happens. The women are at it all the time. Can't turn your back! In some marriages there's a pregnancy not easily explained. Think about it. Don't judge India by the standards of – well, what shall I say? – Wimbledon!'

'Peggy Somersham did not kill herself,' said Joe mildly.

'Then Somersham killed her,' went on Bulstrode unabashed. 'Stands to reason. He found out she was playing away from home, doesn't want to bring up a child that's not his and takes the quick way out. Snip, snip!'

'I will bear what you say in mind,' said Joe without emphasis.

Bulstrode fell silent for a moment, confounded perhaps by Joe's calm replies. He began to arrange and rearrange the piles of papers on his desk.

'So where are you now, Sandilands? You demolish the suicide theory and overset the conclusion of the coroner. You declare that this is a murder investigation and yet as far as I can see you dismiss the prime and obvious suspect – Somersham – without any examination. So where are you left? Murder by person or persons unknown? A person who insinuated himself – or, if we are exploring all avenues, herself – through a high window about seven feet above street level. Doesn't look too good to me! Who could have got in that way? An acrobat?'

After a moment's hesitation Joe decided to go all the way and treat him as a colleague and without hostility.

'I'm not,' he said carefully, 'looking for someone who came in through that window. I'm looking for someone who went out through that window. From inside the bungalow the sill level is only five feet above the floor and there was a stool to hand . . .'

'But really, Sandilands, your murderer – what does he do? Ring the front doorbell and say, "Is Mrs Somersham at home?"'

'We're dealing with a clever man, Bulstrode. As clever as you, as clever as me. Someone, I suspect, familiar with the habits of the house. Someone, it would seem, who knew that the Somershams were going out for the evening: it wouldn't take a tour de force of deduction to assume that Peggy Somersham would have preceded such an occasion by having a bath. The man I'm looking for entered the house perhaps hours before the murder was committed and concealed himself in the bathroom cupboard. It wouldn't be difficult and there is evidence that someone was lurking in there.'

There was a snort of derision from Bulstrode but Joe resumed, 'This would not be difficult. There are always people coming and going – in the kitchen, buying and selling at the door, delivering and collecting. You know this better than I do. And such a one, I say, entered the house, concealed himself, perpetrated the murder and escaped through the window, choosing a moment when no one was passing in the alley. It would need a level head and it would need a measure of calculation that really freezes the blood. But you know that such things happen.'

'Sometimes. Not often. Hardly ever. And your attacker would need a surprisingly intimate knowledge of European habits.'

'If he were a European himself he would have that knowledge,' said Joe.

'Oh, come on, Sandilands, for God's sake! You're not suggesting . . .'

'Yes I am suggesting,' said Joe, 'and perhaps while we're on the subject you can tell me where you were at the relevant time on that evening? Let's say between four o'clock and seven?'

Bulstrode leapt to his feet and stood glowering down at Joe. 'I really resent that! Who the hell do you think you are? Not in bloody Scotland Yard now, you know! This is my bloody district! I've a good mind to ask the Collector to have you taken off the case. Know what a quagga-quagga bird is? If you don't – I'll tell you. It's a bird that flies round in ever-decreasing circles until it finally disappears up its own arse! And that, I suspect, is what you're busy doing.'

'Well,' said Joe, 'perhaps you could tell me what you were doing at the relevant time?'

'I was in the lower town,' said Bulstrode, 'as I think I've already told you.'

'Dealing with petty theft in the bazaar, you said. I remember well. And if I asked to see your report on the incident . . .?'

Bulstrode's face flushed with rage. 'I'd tell you to mind your own bloody business!'

In the face of Joe's expression of continued polite enquiry, after a moment, spluttering in disgust, he flung himself over to a shelf piled high with papers. He snatched up a battered file with 'Shala-mar Bagh' written across the spine.

'I repeat, I *was* in the lower town, though not in the bazaar exactly. To be precise, I was *here.*'

'And what is Shala-mar Bagh?'

'It's a tea house. It's a sort of dance hall, I suppose you'd say.'

'What does it mean – Shala-mar Bagh?' Jo persisted.

Bulstrode looked uncomfortable. 'It means, The Garden of Cupid. Had some trouble. Put it out of bounds to BOR's. There was a fight and two stupid privates from the Shropshires got themselves cut up. I went down to see that the rules were being obeyed.'

'And is this documented? Did you bring a case against the management?'

'I didn't need to. I cautioned them. Very easy-going sort of establishment. Get anything you want there. Perhaps you're interested?' he concluded venomously.

'The alarm was given when, according to medical evidence, Peggy Somersham had been dead for an hour. It was some time before you could be located, er, digging in Cupid's Garden, and you arrived at the crime scene three hours after the body was discovered. Presumably there are people in this dance hall who would vouch for your presence there over the period in question?'

'Of course there bloody well are!' said Bulstrode.

Joe's mind was racing ahead. What was it Naurung had said? 'An exchange.' Drop charges against the establishment in exchange for an alibi? But could Bulstrode have entered the house unobserved? In disguise? Joe resolved to take Naurung into his confidence: to find out when – and truly when – Bulstrode had entered Shala-mar Bagh and when he had left.

'We'll leave it there for the moment,' he said.

'Leave it there for ever, you bloody fool!' and the Superintendent strode from the room.

Hardly had he left when Naurung entered.

'Ah, good morning, Naurung,' Joe said cheerfully. 'You've just missed Bulstrode Sahib but you arrive in time to escort me to my next interview. Colonel Prentice's bungalow? Can you take me there?'

On the way to the bungalow Joe briefed Naurung on his superior officer's alibi and asked him to discreetly check on his movements on the day of the murder. Naurung listened with expressionless discretion but there was a gleam in his eye which said, 'Give me a bit of routine policework and I'll know just where I am.' In front of Prentice's bungalow Joe dismissed him and began to walk down the drive unaccompanied.

He was hailed by a voice behind him and turned to see Prentice handing his horse over to a syce.

'Looking for me?' Prentice asked.

'Yes, I am. I was hoping I might be able to talk to you. Away from sharp ears and wagging tongues.'

'When would you like to do that?' said Prentice without much interest.

'Well, I rather thought now . . . the sooner the better . . . no time like the present . . .'

Prentice laughed. 'That alone would mark you out as a European,' he said. 'No Indian would say, "No time like the present." For them *any* time would be better than the present. But there we are, you've said it. Come in and I'll give you a cup of tea.'

'An early ride?' asked Joe as he walked down the gravelled drive alongside Prentice.

'Regimental exercise. Try to get in one a month and this month's was today. I like to start them early at this time of year – get them over before the heat.'

He led the way on to a verandah, called out 'Koi hai!' and sat down on a stool. A servant appeared and took his hat and whip, a second performed the same service for Joe. A third hurried forward to pull off Prentice's boots. He stood up again and padded forward in his socks. 'Shall we go through to the north verandah? It's much cooler on that side at this time of day.'

They passed through the house and looked down at the garden, neat, tidy and totally unimaginative. The adjoining garden, however, was almost theatrically overgrown. Mar´echal Niel roses had run rampant and there were rose bushes as big as cottages. Seeing Joe's attention taken by this wilderness, Prentice stopped, smiled and said, 'That is the garden of what used to be my house. Destroyed in a fire, as you may have heard. Big garden. It goes all the way down to the river.'

'And the pretty little building down there at the end?' Joe asked.

'Garden pavilion. Terribly overgrown now. It's older than the British Raj – it's older than John Company. It's a Mogul building. I've often thought of selling the site but to do so would mean selling the pavilion and that I really can't do. It's been such a refuge to me. There are times when you want to get away from the demands of matrimony; there are times when you want to get away from the cares of parenthood, to say nothing of the demands of the regiment. When I go and work there it's understood that I'm not to be disturbed. I don't think I could run my life without it! But, come on now, let's see if I can find you a drink or a cup of tea.'

To all outward appearance, Prentice's bungalow was a fair example of the Raj public works department as they developed such things in Edwardian times. Four rooms of identical size surrounded an open sitting area and the whole within a wide verandah. There the resemblance to a typical Anglo-Indian house finished because Prentice had furnished exclusively with Indian furniture. No nostalgic glance towards the English home counties here. No framed hunting scenes by G.D. Armour or Lionel Edwards, not even a copy of the ubiquitous 'Midnight Steeplechase'. In their place Indian illuminated paintings, many on silk, many on rollers, small jade, ivory and soapstone figures, Kashmir embroidered hangings on the walls, Bokhara and Afghani rugs on the floor.

Joe paused beside a large painting of an elephant bearing a small jewelled figure.

'The Emperor Akhbar, riding an elephant,' Prentice explained. 'I oughtn't to keep it hanging like this. It ought to be kept on a roll but I really enjoy it so much, this room would seem unfurnished without it. Now, come with me.'

They walked through the house together and Prentice opened a door leading off from the central hall, pointing as he did. 'Getting this room ready for my daughter. She'll be home soon. Haven't seen her for four years.'

Joe was amused to see the array of spindly bamboo furniture, the paintings and the fabrics that the surprising Prentice had thought suitable for an eighteen-year-old fresh from the sophistications of Europe. The centrepiece of the room was a light wood-framed Indian charpoy bed whose simplicity had been relieved by silver decorations which twined their way up the legs. Above it, at the head, had been tacked a delicate embroidered hanging depicting the goddess of the night. Against a background of midnight blue, she threw a protective fold of her silver-starred sari around the dimly seen shape of a child, naked but for the two silver bangles around its ankles. Joe compared this with the iron bedstead, the neatly folded rug, striped in the school colours, the steel engraving of the 'Light of the World' that Midge would have grown accustomed to in Europe and thought that Prentice probably had it right.

Prentice led the way out on to a cool verandah and tea appeared.

'One concession to the home counties,' said Joe appreciatively, viewing an English teaset.

'Darjeeling,' said Prentice. 'I hope you can drink it. But now – what can I do? What can I tell you? I told you my theory at the dance but I don't suppose you would accept that unscientific idea of a malign spirit?'

Joe smiled. 'I'd love to,' he said. 'It would really appeal to me. But if I was caught dismissing the matter in that way it might be held that I was not really doing my job. But if you could clear up one or two small things for me . . . We'll go back to the beginning.'

'To Joan Carmichael.'

'Well no,' said Joe, surprised. 'Back beyond that. Back – if you'll forgive me – to the death of your wife.'

'Of course,' said Prentice hurriedly. 'Of course. But I don't think of them as being the same. After all, in that case the perpetrators were identified and executed.'

'Perhaps we can start there? "Executed" you say. Can you tell me about that?' 'Very little to tell. I knew who they were. I knew where they came from. I knew most of them by name.

They were vengeful – they were courageous with hash. They were not men of much judgement. It took me a day or two to recover from the shock and then I collected a troop of Sowars from the regiment, boys I'd had my eye on for some time and who were delighted to be involved in this foray. Not short of volunteers, I might say. I went after them. Executed them. Of course I should have done nothing of the sort and they should have been brought to trial in the proper way. I even had to face a court of enquiry. But by then the deed was done and everybody, Indian and English, was on my side. All saw it as a very proper act of retribution and, if you'll allow me to say, Sandilands – so it was!'

'You have no doubt in your mind,' said Joe carefully, 'that they had come to kill you and only incidentally your wife?'

'And Chedi Khan.'

'Yes, Chedi Khan. Does he come into the equation?'

Prentice paused a long time before replying. 'He was a very fine man,' he said at last. 'The finest the Pathan nation has to offer. Loyal, courageous, persevering and, like many Pathans, artistic, poetic and ingenious but the whole salted with a cynical and ribald sense of humour.'

'How did he come to be in your service?' Joe enquired.

Prentice poured them both out a cup of tea and lay back for a moment in his chair saying at last, 'Long story. Know what I mean by proscription? No? It's a system on the frontier. Tribes will raid their neighbours, they will pursue blood feuds, come raiding down into India and steal things. Anything they can lay their hands on, particularly rifles. Girls too. It's their way of life. Of course we criticise but any nation that sells girls into prostitution is in no position to criticise those who merely steal girls for themselves. But a time comes when it has to be stopped and offending villages are proscribed. A punitive raid is mounted, fortifications are dismantled, watch towers demolished, crops burned, hostages taken. They're called barramptas, these raids. It was – and still is – an accepted part of life.

They know the rules. I conducted many such raids when I was serving with the Scouts on the frontier.

'I led my first barrampta – a green young officer fresh from Sandhurst, though not new to the country – against a village called Lashtar. It was occupied by a small though extremely warlike tribe, always at odds with their neighbours, always at odds with the government. Never, it seemed, able to learn. The chief man – the Malik – was a ferocious old devil with a very bad reputation. He decided to defend the village and there was quite a scrap. He was killed. His two sons were killed and some of his neighbours and the village was set on fire. By mistake. We were not fire-raisers.

'I rode up to supervise the conclusion of this operation and was sitting looking on when out of the smoke there blundered a slight figure. A Pathan boy aged about thirteen. Under his arm he had a brass-bound jezail.'

'Jezail?'

'Yes, an old musket. It could have been a hundred years old. Loaded with God knows what – nails, bits of glass, shot even. As soon as he saw me he dropped on one knee and was about to blow me to perdition. One of my troopers galloped up, sword in hand, and knocked it out of his arms. He was about to lop the boy's head off with his talwar . . .' Prentice pointed to a trophy of arms on the wall of the adjoining room. 'There's a talwar.'

Joe glanced at the curved blade as long as a man's arm with its single slicing edge.

'I yelled at the trooper to stop and put his talwar away and then I shouted in Pushtu to the boy. I told him to stay still where he was and no harm would come to him. I got off my horse and went over to talk to him. Sad tale – he was an orphan but distantly related to and living in the household of the old devil we'd just killed. As the man's sons had been killed this boy, who told me his name was Chedi Khan, had taken it upon himself to kill as many English soldiers as he could, starting with the commanding officer – me. Honour of the tribe. I think he was very surprised to see that I wasn't more than a few years older than he was.

'Difficult to know what to do with him. He had no remaining ties with that village and it was quite plain that if he stayed on there – one day sooner rather than later probably – he was going to take a successful pot shot at an English officer and get himself killed into the bargain. We discussed his options. Man to man, sitting side by side on a rock. I gave him a cigarette. He seemed very intelligent. I pointed out that his future looked bleak if he stayed on and that I could order him to be taken away with us and kept as a hostage for the good behaviour of the tribe which was a usual procedure or, and I offered him a third and pretty unusual choice, he could come with us voluntarily, giving his word of honour for his good behaviour, and when he reached the appropriate age he could train as a Scout.

'I saw by the gleam in his eye when I mentioned this third option that the soldier's life was the one that appealed to him and decided to take a chance. There was no way this boy was going to agree meekly to ride away with us in full view of his village. The Pathan are impressed by the grand gesture so I staged one. I kicked his musket far out of reach with a derogatory comment and handed him a Lee-Metford rifle. "This is yours," I said. Then I got up, turned my back on him and walked away towards my troop.'

'Good Lord! Was it loaded?'

'Oh, yes, no use being caught with an unloaded rifle in a place like that. Subadur Amir Shah was covering him, I'd already taken that in so perhaps I wasn't risking much. All the same, I don't think I'd have the nerve nowadays.'

'What did the boy do?'

'He got to his feet, aimed the rifle straight between my shoulder blades and tracked me for several yards. He never attempted to shoot the bolt. Enjoying his power, I think. Then, when he was sure the whole tribe had witnessed this, he slung the rifle over his shoulder and marched up to the company. They unloaded his rifle, mounted him behind someone and off we went.'

'And did he join the army?'

'Not then and there. He was too young to start with. Badly nourished as well. Scrawny little thing with conjunctivitis. And there were signs that he'd been ill-treated for some time. We had to feed him up and doctor his wounds – cuts and burns mainly – when we got him back to camp. One of my men said, "You'll never get rid of him. He'll follow you to the ends of the earth and one day, watch out, he'll decide to be revenged. That boy's just biding his time."'

'And did he try?'

'In no way. It didn't work out like that at all. I've told you he was clever, he was ingenious and extremely amusing. I saw a great future for him. There was a movement – has been for many years and still is – towards the foundation of an independent Pathan state – Pukhtunistan – and in my romantic way I saw this child perhaps one day as the first president of such an independent state. Just a dream really but I played with it in my mind. Then the question arose of what on earth to do with this boy.'

'What did you do with him?'

Prentice grinned. 'What any Englishman would do – I sent him to school. There's a little community of Anglican Fathers who run a mission school in the hills. In addition to other things they were medical missionaries. Good people. I knew them well. They said they'd look after him. He didn't want to go but I insisted. I delivered him there and left him in tears. Six months later he ran away and came back to me. I ticked him off properly, even beat him and sent him back again. Three months later he was back! It wasn't what I'd planned but it seemed I'd got him for life. I recruited him into the Scouts and appointed him my bearer and so he remained. Till the day of his death.'

'And the manner of his death? Was that surprising to you?'

'Not in the least. He died trying to save Dorothy. It's exactly what he would do. I'd left him in charge, you see.'

'That's a fine story,' said Joe.

'He was a fine man,' said Prentice. 'It was sad. Tragic even, but there's no mystery about it. None whatever.'

Joe had been carried away by the man's story. Once the icebergs of military brevity and understatement had melted and the narrative began to flow, time had passed unnoticed. He collected himself, recognising the ploy for what it was. By talking at length on a subject peripheral to the main investigation, Prentice was presenting himself as a co-operative and genial interviewee, a charming man with nothing to hide. Joe admired his skilful piece of deception and went along with it, writing notes at intervals and posing interested questions. But, at the mention of Chedi Khan's death, he decided that the time had come to perform his own bluff.

It was his successful technique when conducting an interview to make notes assiduously on topics he was aware were not very relevant to the case. This appeared always to reassure the person he was questioning. People, even villains, he found, enjoyed telling the truth to a copper especially when they thought they were leading him by the nose. He made a point of asking a series of questions to which he knew accurate if misleading answers could freely be given. Then, at a juncture, he would smile agreeably, snap shut his notebook and put away his fountain pen. Sometimes he would let his victim get half-way to the door before, with no change in his tone, he put a further question, almost as an afterthought. In a surprisingly large number of cases he got better information from that one last question than from a previous hour's interrogation.

He tried a variation on this technique now, never forgetting that he was dealing with a highly intelligent and ruthless man. He scribbled one last note, stretched his legs and closed his notebook. Leaning forward and lowering his voice he managed to give the impression that his next question or comment was not being recorded and was a simple exchange between two gentlemen.

'Tell me, Prentice, did you know your wife was drinking heavily?'

'Of course,' Prentice replied without hesitating. 'Though I would say moderately. By station standards. That is why I usually took her with me whenever I had to be away from the station. She got lonely, as most of the wives do, when she was left alone. I accept that it may well have been a contributory factor in her death.'

'Speaking of the deaths, Prentice, and you understand how much I dislike having to bring up the subject at all, I must ask you – because I have already asked or intend to ask in due course the other bereaved Greys husbands – do you know of anyone who had reason to kill your wife?'

'Of course not! Everybody loved Dorothy. She was an easy woman to like.'

'She would have made a good colonel's wife?'

'Excellent. She'd listen to anybody's problems, enjoyed solving them however tedious. People like that. She was used to life in India – it was the life she'd chosen. She was very sociable. She may have had the occasional glass of gin too many but she was no Emma Bovary. I'm luckily not dependent on my army pay and she had good clothes and fine jewellery, better looks than any of the other women and her prospects – which is to say my prospects – were all that she wished. Dorothy was a contented woman. I used to think of her as a mountain pool, clear, inviting and always reflecting the sunshine.'

'And shallow, perhaps?' Joe wondered silently.

Aloud he said, 'You must have found your daughter a great consolation . . .?'

Prentice's face became a degree less stiff. 'Yes. Certainly. No children of your own, Sandilands?'

'No. But I can imagine the joy. And the pain,' said Joe seriously.

A bearer appeared discreetly in the doorway, trying to catch Prentice's attention.

'Have to cut this short now, Sandilands. I'm expected at the stables in twenty minutes and my bearer will insist I take a bath before I set foot outside again. Not that the horses will notice.' He rose to his feet and Joe walked with him from the room. 'How are you getting along with Bamboo? Good. I thought he'd suit you. Used to ride him myself. Now look – if there's anything I can do, anyone's arm I can twist, that sort of thing, let me know.'

They shook hands and Joe emerged into the blinding sunlight with a hundred other questions buzzing in his head and the strong feeling that Colonel Prentice had just given the professional policeman a sharp lesson in how to conduct an interview.

Chapter Eleven

JOE'S BREAKFAST ON Tuesday morning was interrupted by a squawk from the bulb horn of the Collector's 1910 Packard and, hurriedly assembling maps, notebooks, cigarette case and camera, he went out to find Naurung standing to attention and Nancy sitting in the back seat.

They greeted each other as old friends. She reached out to shake his hand and as he sank into the grey corduroy upholstery it was a moment or two before he remembered to release it.

'This is a very luxurious vehicle,' said Joe, taking in the appointments with a good deal of pleasure and satisfaction. 'Sliding plate glass window between us and the driver, comfortable seats . . .'

'Yes,' said Nancy, 'and there's even a little silver trumpet to put a flower in. Remind me to pick one if we see one. It's as well to arrive in style when you're visiting the Acting Governor.'

'Uncle Jardine? We are to see him again? The man who shot me into this vipers' nest!'

'See him? We're to stay with him! I've been busy on the telephone and I've fixed up everything. You don't need to worry.'

'That's exactly when I need to worry! Tell me our programme.'

'Well, to save time I've arranged for you to interview old Carmichael while I go to see Dr Forbes this afternoon. Then we meet up again at the Great Eastern Hotel for tea and then on to the Residence to spend the night with my uncle.'

'More impeccable chaperonage,' Joe muttered.

He opened the dividing window. 'Good morning, Naurung,' he said.

'Good morning, sahib.'

'You know where we're going?'

'Indeed,' said Naurung, 'but I thought it would be sensible if I took the same route as the Memsahib Carmichael in 1911. So we start from the Carmichael bungalow which is just down there,' he pointed, 'go to the end of the maidan and turn right.'

'What is this?' said Joe, surprised, as they followed a rough road some minutes out of the station. 'New road?'

'No, it is a fire break that the Forestry officer has cut through the jungle. It is a popular way for ladies to ride. It takes you up to the high ground where there is a fine view and the Memsahib Carmichael was a nervous lady, I have heard people say. She would have liked this open ride; forty yards wide, quite straight and no surprises.'

He pulled off the road and followed the bumpy ride onwards until he said, 'It was here that the memsahib was killed.'

He stopped the car and they all stepped out.

'Nothing whatever to see,' said Nancy.

'She was found just here,' said Naurung. 'There was a pile of brushwood here then and there is a pile of brushwood here now.'

Joe took a seat on the running board of the car and stared around, trying to recreate the scene of eleven years ago. 'Horrible story!' he said. 'It really haunts me . . . What's the matter, Naurung?'

Naurung was staring at the ground.

'What have you seen?'

'It's not what I've seen, sahib, it is what I've always thought. But I'll tell you. This is a very strange place to find a cobra.'

'Strange? How strange?'

'This was not a King Cobra, this was not a Hamadryad. They are sometimes found in jungle places like this but this was the common Indian cobra – *Naja naja.* They are not found in the open jungle. They are found where they can find what they like to eat which is rats and mice. And rats and mice live near human habitation in grain stores and gardens. Anywhere rats and mice can be found you may find a cobra – but not out here. You can find a cobra in every village. To some they are sacred. You will find a cobra in the village temple – the village priests put milk out for them . . .'

'So what are you saying, Naurung?'

'I am saying I have a different picture. I see this lady who is not well and she comes up here and she squats out of sight of everybody behind this brushwood pile because I'm sure there was always a brushwood pile here. Somebody comes out of the jungle with a cobra in his hand . . .'

'In his hand?' said Joe, horrified.

'Oh, yes,' said Naurung. 'I could not do it but there are many who can catch a cobra. If you catch it just behind its head it may writhe and wriggle but the catcher is quite safe if he keeps hold of its head and puts it in a sack. I know six, perhaps more, Indians who could do this. He approaches the memsahib. She is shocked, she is horrified, she is terrified. He holds the snake in his hand and he throws it at her. She was bitten here, sahib,' he said, pointing to his left buttock. 'From here to the heart is not far for the venom to travel. She would have died very quickly. It is terrible but I think that is what happened. And then, because he is a very bad man, he stands and watches her die and when the poor lady is dead he cuts the snake's head off and disappears into the jungle. I have seen it in my imagination so many times. Now I stand here I believe it is the truth.'

'Christ!' said Joe. 'I believe you're right! It sounds terribly true. I didn't know about cobras.'

'I did,' said Nancy, 'but I never connected it. Naurung, we must catch this man.'

'He is clever,' said Naurung. 'He is very clever. Now that we know he exists, we will find him.'

'One last thing, Naurung,' said Joe. 'Have you ever heard of a white man, a sahib, who would know how to catch and handle a cobra?'

Naurung dropped his eyes to his boots and replied slowly, 'No, I have never heard of such a man.'

Chastened, they climbed back into the car and made their way back on to the main trunk road through to Calcutta. Progress along the potholed road crowded with people and animals kicking up clouds of dust was slow in spite of Naurung's enthusiastic use of the horn and Joe discovered that on Indian highways even the Collector's Packard gives way to cows and elephants. Shaken and stiff in spite of the luxurious springing, it was well into the afternoon when they caught sight of the welcome green expanse of the maidan, the reassuring octagonal bulk of Fort William and the crowded masts and funnels on the river beyond. They drove north up the Chowringhee Road, their eyes dazzled by the glare of the whitened palaces along its route, and Joe was surprised, after his four days' absence in the country, that he was finding the familiarity of the city reassuring. Naurung stopped the car.

'Well, here you are,' said Nancy. 'This is where you get off. I think you know your way about? Carmichael's establishment is somewhere along this street – here, I've written out the address for you. Naurung is going to drop me off at the hospital where I'm to meet Forbes and we'll meet up again for tea. Just take a rickshaw to the Great Eastern when you've finished with Carmichael.'

Naurung seemed anxious to go off on his own business and asked if he might be excused when he had finally dropped them off at the Residence, announcing that he was staying the night with a member of his family. Joe waved them off as they set off back towards the hospital and fixed his mind on Harold Carmichael, formerly second-in-command of the Bengal Greys, formerly the husband of Joan.

British India does not walk very often, but distressed by the anguished face in his imagination of Joan Carmichael, Joe resolved to walk the length of Chowringhee to Carmichael's office. As he made his way past the once opulent villas of bygone nabobs – many of which ranked as palaces rather than villas – he noted that the further he walked from the centre, the more multiplex the subdivision of these great houses became.

Initially, brass plates discreetly announced the presence of banks, insurance companies, the Calcutta office of internationally known trading houses, engineers, architects and solicitors. But soon the brass plates got smaller as the number increased. Brass plates gave way to cards. The number of bell pushes multiplied. Names appeared on upper windows, front doors stood open. Kites circled the damp air and crows pecked crumbling cornices. Numbers grew into the hundreds.

After about twenty minutes' walk, keeping to the shade of the arcades whenever he could avoid being forced out into the road by the crowds, he found himself outside number 210. Number 210 had no fewer than twenty names at the door, some of these boasting new name plates, most boasting cards and amongst these – after quite a search – he identified Carmichael, Popatlal and Mandavia, Importers of Fine Wines, Beers, Spirits etc. There was an electric bell push which, without much hope, he duly pressed. An Indian emerged from the darkness within and spoke to him at length. Joe shrugged his shoulders and smiled, pointed to Carmichael's card and looked a question which only elicited a further flood of Hindustani but eventually a hand pointing helpfully up the dark staircase.

As he progressed, heads appeared in various doorways and eyed him with curiosity. A Metropolitan policeman in uniform was not often seen at this end of the Chowringhee.

He came at last to an open door through which he saw a white-clad figure seated at a desk and writing without much urgency on a pad in front of him. He was balding, he had a grey moustache which might once have been the standard moustache as issued to, or at any rate worn by, British cavalry officers. His collar, which had once been stiff, lay on the desk beside him and his shirt was open at the neck. A large copper ashtray was full of the butts of many cheroots. There were two empty whisky bottles in the waste paper basket and another about half full at his elbow. An Army and Navy Stores 'Colonial' refrigerator in a mahogany case stood against the wall but the door was open and the contents were gone.

The walls were lined with photographs, mostly, Joe noticed, of the Bengal Greys, but these were spotted and damp-stained and thunder flies had made their way in and perished behind the glass. There was not much about the figure before him to recall the dapper cavalry major.

Joe knocked tentatively on the door and then, getting no response, with more authority. He was greeted by an irascible 'Yes?' Putting his cap under his arm, he strode into the room.

'Major Carmichael?' he said. 'My name is Sandilands.'

Carmichael looked round. 'Sandilands! Good Lord! Is it three o'clock already? Oh, I am sorry! It's been rather a hectic day. One damn thing after another in this business . . . but now – come you in.' He rose to his feet and extended a damp and hairy hand. 'Funny time of day, this,' he said. 'Seems too early or too late to offer you a peg but I expect you won't say no. You'd think in this humidity you wouldn't necessarily need to keep up the fluids but everybody says you should so, here we are – a khushal ye.'

Joe knew the appropriate response but wondered whether in the light of what he saw it was entirely appropriate. 'Khwar mashe,' he said, the literal meaning of which he understood was 'May you not be poor.'

'Now,' said Carmichael, as two fairly full tumblers of whisky appeared on the desk, 'what can I do for Commander Sandilands? Of the Metropolitan Police, I understand? Rare bird in Calcutta!'

Joe went into a prepared speech, '. . . here at the invitation of the Governor . . . no particular anxiety to stir up old troubles or open old wounds . . . the Collector . . . some anxiety when – as you've probably heard – the death of Peggy Somersham last week awoke old rumours . . . thought it better to scotch these at the outset and reaffirm the finding of the coroner . . . not a good idea to let speculation grow . . .' And so on.

Carmichael eyed him bleakly and in silence for a moment or two. Joe remembered Nancy's words, 'A bitter man . . . the worst kind of Indian army officer . . . all moustache and bluster . . . not popular with the men . . .'

Moustache, yes, bluster no. Joe did not believe he had ever seen such a figure of defeat.

'If you're thinking about poor Joanie's death, I can certainly reassure you. Very clear case. Killed by a snake but I expect you know all that.'

'Was that usual – being bitten by a snake?' Joe asked. 'Remember I'm only an ignorant London bobby.'

'Don't know about usual . . . Not very common but by no means unknown. One or two a year, I suppose. If you're quick and medical attention is immediately available it doesn't have to be a fatality but Joanie was all on her ownsome and that's all there is to say about it.'

Something prompted Joe to say, 'You must have been very distressed?'

'Have been?' said Carmichael. 'Still am. Most distressing damn thing by a long way that ever happened to me. And, of course . . .' He paused for a long time and then resumed, '. . . I suppose this often happens in marriages. Something happens to one partner and all you can think of is the things you never said or did. Are you married? No. Then you probably wouldn't appreciate this but, every marriage is full of times when you could have been a bit kinder, more considerate. Give you an example – Joanie hated snakes. Terrified of them and at that time we were living in a thatched bungalow – one of the old pre-Mutiny ones. It had a canvas ceiling. One night we were sitting there and we saw a big snake crossing from side to side above the ceiling under the thatch. Looking for mice. I thought Joanie would have a catalepsy! She screamed and sobbed and cried . . . damned embarrassing! Servants came running from all directions! Nothing would please her but that we should move house. We couldn't at that time have sold the house without dropping quite a lot of money and I said, "Quite out of the question!" I didn't have to say that, you know. Not a kind thing to say. And then, of course, this cobra business. It seemed like a terrible fate. A judgement on me perhaps. I was just going to say it took me a long time to recover but I don't think I've ever recovered. Ah, well. You do your best at the time. It may not be very good but nobody can do better than their best, I'm always saying.'

With an unsteady hand he refilled his glass and Joe took him quickly through the other deaths. 'Sheila Forbes?'

'Nasty, dangerous place, that. Could happen to anybody.'

'Alicia Simms-Warburton?'

'Those bullock-skin rafts – damn dangerous, if you ask me.'

'Peggy Somersham?'

'Wouldn't know. Never met her. Sorry, I don't think I'm being much help.'

'If you're in the police it's sometimes just as helpful to know where not to look as to know where to look,' said Joe and it was not the first time he had said it.

'Yes,' said Carmichael, 'yes, I suppose that's true. Never thought of it like that. Know where not to look – eh?'

'Yes,' said Joe. 'Well, that's it, I'd say. Thank you very much for your patience. You'll think I'm an infernal nosy parker, I'm afraid.'

'No, no,' said Carmichael. 'Not at all. Come and see me again next time you're in Calcutta and choose not such a busy day, if you know what I mean. Excuse my coming down – I've got this, er, these, er, to put together before – tomorrow.'

Joe found himself back in the baking street. Very reluctant to walk all the way back up the Chowringhee, he hailed a passing rickshaw and, confident that he had not unmasked a subtle, devious and skilful multiple killer, he made his way back, calling at one or two shops on the way, to the Great Eastern.

Here, amidst the strangeness of Calcutta and following the depression of his interview with Carmichael, he was overjoyed to see Nancy presiding over a small tea table. He strode forward with outstretched hands and seized hers as she rose to greet him. A longing to kiss her was only overcome by the assumption that the room would be full of people she knew and he compromised by kissing her hand and then, after a minute hesitation, her other hand.

'Ah, my dear Watson,' he said, 'I hope you've spent your afternoon more profitably than I!'

With the fluent rapidity that he envied, she ordered him some tea and in due course a fresh pot, a plate of sandwiches and a substantial slice of fruit cake appeared.

'I don't know whether I've achieved much,' she said, taking out a notebook and setting it on the table, 'but he's quite a useful chap, Philip Forbes. After all, he was the MO from 1910 right through until the regiment came back from France. He did a post-mortem examination on Dolly Prentice and Prentice's bearer and the same for Joan Carmichael. Same, indeed, for his own wife. That was a sad case, Sheila. She was really terrified of heights, you know . . .'

Joe put down his slice of cake and said sharply, 'Say that again.'

'She was really terrified of heights, you know . . .' Nancy dutifully repeated and went on, 'So I said, "Well, why did she go up that path if she was terrified of heights? It's not the best place in the world for anyone with vertigo," and he said something so pathetic. As a member of the IAMC, he and Sheila were never really part of the regiment. They were tolerated rather than welcomed and when she was invited to ride out with these people to a picnic, Sheila was flattered and delighted. It was the social breakthrough she'd been waiting for. Poor kid, she was only twenty-three! So although she didn't fancy that track, she just gritted her teeth and went for it. Oh, snobbery! What crimes are committed in thy name, I sometimes wonder. He has no idea, you know, Forbes I mean, that Sheila may have been murdered. None at all. Just accepts it as a particularly grotesque joke on the part of Fate.'

She was silent for a moment then said hesitantly, 'Joe, do you think there's any chance we may have got this wrong? That it was no more than an appalling accident? Given that Sheila was a nervous horsewoman at the best of times, very anxious to do the right thing. Nervous and a bit scared. It communicates itself to the horse, you know.'

'I'm sure her death was arranged,' said Joe firmly. 'And that it was planned for some time before. Someone who had access to the stables and who knew her horse, knew even that she was about to ride out with her new friends, deliberately caused it. I think this someone put a stone under the frog in her horse's hoof at some time before they set out. You remember that she began to fall back almost at once and waved to the others to carry on without her and that she would catch them up. That delay was just enough to ensure that she was out of sight of the rest of the party at the time she was passing the precipice. I think that someone hiding in the rocks, perhaps the saddhu, leapt out and pushed her over. And her worst fears became a reality and her last thoughts were sheer panic.'

They sat together for a moment in silence. 'This,' said Joe, 'is a pretty bloody sad investigation, you know. Everywhere we turn there's sorrow and grief.' And he recounted what Carmichael had told him about Joan.

'Ah, yes, Joan,' said Nancy. 'I'll tell you something else – Philip Forbes was treating her for cystitis.'

'Cystitis?' said Joe. 'What's cystitis?'

'Can there be such ignorance? It's a bladder complaint. Makes you want to pee all the time. It all hangs together, doesn't it? Poor Joan, "squatting", as Naurung would say, in the brushwood and out leaps her very worst nightmare . . .'

Nancy gasped and dropped her teaspoon in shock and as a waiter hurried to replace it she stared at Joe, white-faced.

'Her nightmare?' she said again softly.

'Thought you'd get there in the end!' said Joe.

Nancy glared at him. 'I would guess I was precisely two minutes behind you and that's not bad for an amateur! But, Joe, if what I'm thinking is what you're thinking and we're both thinking correctly, this is pretty bloody disgusting, isn't it?' She shuddered and looked at him searchingly, appealing to him to contradict her awful suspicions.

'We said we were looking for a coincidence, something all these killings had in common, and then we would begin to be able to tease out a thread between them. And this is shaping up to be a pattern, wouldn't you say? Let's look at it backwards from here. Peggy: her husband said – volunteered the information – something like, "It was exactly the way she would not have wished to go . . . Peggy couldn't stand the sight of blood."'

'Oh, my God!' breathed Nancy. 'That's true. She used often to ask me how on earth I could have coped in the war with the blood and the wounds.'

'And Joan – her husband tells me she had an intense fear of snakes. Now you're saying that Sheila who fell to her death

had an unreasoning fear of heights. Alicia – we can't check
with her husband but – wasn't there something in her letter
to her sister . . .?'

'". . . I shall have to cross the river and you know how I feel
about rivers!"' Nancy supplied. 'I wondered about that when
we read it! I bet she was afraid of drowning! Don't you think?
Can we check? Who would remember? Kitty probably.'

'And that takes us back to the first – to Dolly. Death by fire?
Lots of people have a fear of fire. It won't be difficult to check
on that. But we're looking at three definite phobias out of a
possible five.'

'Joe, what sort of a man kills women in the way that holds
most terror for them?'

'It would be all too easy to say a disciple of le Marquis de
Sade but no, actually, I don't think that's what we've got here.
You see, there's no sexual aspect to any of these killings, is
there? Unless the doctor had other revelations?'

'No. And I don't think he was keeping any sordid details
from the mem. I told him I'd been a nurse and he paid me the
compliment of talking to me in medical terms and very openly.
I was very sad to hear from him though, and this was not generally known at the time, that Dolly Prentice was pregnant
when she died. Did you know that?'

'Good Lord! No. There was no autopsy report with the
papers I was given.'

'Sounds as though someone suppressed it because Dr Forbes
definitely did one. It must have been kept quiet out of respect
for Prentice. He finds sympathy hard to take, Forbes said. All
the same – one does feel sympathy and one begins to understand the ferocious revenge you say he took on the dacoits.
Losing your wife and your unborn child in one fell swoop – it's
unimaginably distressing! But apart from that piece of information, nothing at all salacious. I'm sure he would have told
me if anything – er – sexually driven had occurred.'

'Would that the doctor who examined your friend Peggy had been as thorough!'

Immediately Joe wished the words unsaid. Nancy stared at him in horror.

'Peggy? You don't mean . . . Oh, Joe what are you trying to say?'

'No, no – there was no sexual attack. I mean that the doctor failed to discover that she was pregnant. Not obviously so – I think she had only just found out for certain herself. She had been writing to her parents to tell them the good news. I found the letter. I gather she had not shared the news with you?'

Nancy was silent for a very long time, staring at her teacup. Tears began to flow down her cheeks and Joe, cursing himself out loud for his poor timing, passed her his handkerchief with a muttered apology.

'It's all right, Joe,' she said finally. 'There really isn't a good or a right time to give someone news like that, is there? I was going to be shattered by it whenever you chose to tell me. And at least I'm sitting down with a cup of hot sweet tea in front of me! Carry on. I'm ready. I'll mourn for Peggy and her child in my own good time . . . Now it's more important to find out who's responsible. What else does this tell us about him? Are you beginning to see further connections here?'

'Two of the women were pregnant,' Joe went on, taking her at her word. 'But I don't think we can count that as something in common because we have no evidence that the rest were. Unlikely, I should have thought. And just think – if you, her best friend, didn't know, and her doctor didn't know – there's no mention of it in his records – her killer would not have known of it either. Unless she was killed by Somersham himself. But there is something in common with all the victims. They were well known to the killer.'

'He knew them? Well? How well? How can you be sure?'

'He is close enough to them to know their phobias. Think for a moment, Nancy. Everybody has a phobia of some sort. I have a phobia which I am certainly not going to disclose to anybody in India so please don't ask me! Have you a phobia? And who in your circle would know that you had it?'

'Yes, I have. And – yes, you're right – everybody, I'm afraid.' Nancy sighed. 'But, really, I can't see Bill Bulstrode or Harry Featherstone creeping up behind me with a spider to make me jump out of my skin! But I understand what you're saying. If I were standing on the top of a ladder at the time it might be a different story. Anybody on the station with ears to hear that sort of gossip will hear it. The servants know everything and they talk amongst themselves. They talk to their sahibs and memsahibs. How do you suppose Kitty knows everything that goes on? That chaprassi of hers is a one man information bureau!'

'So anyone, Indian or British, could have known about the phobias.'

'Certainly. But why? If we knew why, we'd know who, wouldn't we? There could be no reason why anyone would want to kill these women at all, let alone in this cruel way! We're dealing with insanity!'

'I think so too. But insanity on our terms. Not in the murderer's mind. There is a pattern and a purpose to his crimes. These are not random killings for lust or robbery. They are cleverly planned and for quite some time ahead. They are planned by the kind of man who, on a Friday, selects the Friday razor to slit the wrists of his victim. A stranger or a native or someone hired to do the killing would have taken up the nearest. This man is European, I'm sure of that. I'm sure he knows his victims. I think he's playing some kind of game we haven't even guessed at and though he doesn't want to be caught, he wants something else – acknowledgement perhaps? I don't know. I'm still fumbling about in the dark! What I do know is that these killings are not the work of an Indian Jack the Ripper, an opportunist who prowls outdoors in a defined area and leaps on whatever prey comes to his knife. They are not the sequential killings for gain of a "Brides in the Bath" Smith. So two of the strongest motives for killing can be ruled out.'

'Goodness! Two! How many does that leave us to sift through?'

'Only four.'

'Suddenly I'm tired! Come on, Joe! Let's go and meet my uncle. I could do with a cold bath closely followed by an iced drink and an evening of conversation that doesn't include multiple murders!'

Chapter Twelve

THEY SAT FOR a moment in the car on the Governor's gravelled driveway as Naurung stepped out and opened the door.

'Beautiful!' said Joe. 'Beautiful garden!'

He looked with pleasure on lawns that would not have been
out of place in the Thames Valley, trees as old as the British
Raj, a broad walk with a double flower border leading to a
fountain. In the shade of a distant pavilion on a man-made
hillock irrigation channels gurgled.

They stepped out of the car and at once the khansama
came forward bowing and salaaming and offered a note on a
silver tray. He was known to Nancy who greeted him as an old
friend.

'A note from Uncle,' said Nancy in surprise and slit it open
with her thumb. She read aloud: '"Was so looking forward to
our evening together and now, instead of spending the evening with you, I'm spending the night in a train on my way
back from Delhi. Unable to get away any sooner. See you,
therefore, tomorrow morning (my train gets in at half-past
ten). '"I've told them to put a bottle of Niersteiner 1916 on
ice for you and there's a good Château Lafite to go with it. I
even made bold to order your dinner but as Bobagee seldom
takes any notice of what I say, I won't attempt to prophesy
what will actually appear on the table. But, anyway, have a
good evening and I'm sorry I can't share it with you. Your
affect. Uncle."'

They looked at each other. There was no question but that the same thoughts had occurred to both.

A liveried khitmutgar stood attentively at the head of the stairs and, salaaming from the shadows, the ayah emerged to take Nancy under her wing and bustle her off with much clucking sympathy while the khitmutgar led Joe up a flight of stairs. Out of the corner of his eye he saw Nancy disappear up a second flight of stairs and, with ironic amusement, wondered whether Uncle had deliberately sited them a decent distance apart.

To one accustomed to the dak bungalow at Panikhat, the room into which he was shown was a miracle of luxury. Marble floor, marble walls, fretted screen opening on to a wide balcony, a bed that would have slept four, a bath with actual running water and, in place of the top hat-like contrivance he had become used to, a genuine and unmistakable water closet with 'John Bolding, London' inscribed on it. The whole set within a mahogany seat in which was recessed an ivory handle inscribed with the words 'Lift to flush'. On his dressing-table he found a further note which said in a slightly uncertain hand, 'Dinner will be served at seven hours. This man will show you the way.' Joe bowed to 'this man' who stood in attendance and allowed him to run a bath.

In preparation for his dinner with the Governor, Joe had on his way back up the Chowringhee called into the Army and Navy Stores and bought himself a white mess jacket and a dark blue cummerbund. He hadn't the faintest idea what the appropriate colour for the Metropolitan Police would be but didn't think dark blue could be wrong.

Shaved and bathed, dressed with the assistance of his appointed bearer, he surveyed himself in the long cheval glass. He was alarmingly agitated and excited at the thought of an evening alone with Nancy. Alone, that is, apart from the attendance of six or more khitmutgars. To collect his thoughts he stepped out on to the balcony, enjoying the sudden descent of the dusk and the evening wind setting in from the Hooghly River in the south. And, from long habit tucking a handkerchief up his sleeve and putting his cigarette case in his pocket, he followed his guide through the labyrinth of the big house. Down a flight of stairs, across a broad landing, up a further small flight of stairs and to a verandah with a wide view of the city. Through this and on to a balcony, lamp-lit and cool, a table laid with starched white linen and silver at which candles were being lit.

Joe put his hands on the balustrade and gazed down into the dark garden, breathing the teasing night-time scents. Scents to which, suddenly, there was a sharper focus. He spun about and Nancy was standing in the door. She was wearing a silvery grey silk dinner dress which managed, to Joe's mystification, both to cling intriguingly to her top half and float flirtatiously around her knees. Slim and straight and eager, she had the grace and immediacy of a moonbeam, he thought fancifully. Forgetting the soft-footed servants, he held out his hands and when she approached he gathered her closer and kissed her cheek.

'Mmm . . . I'm holding the spirit of the garden in my arms,' he murmured, breathing deeply.

'Nonsense!' said Nancy, pulling away. 'It's as Parisian as you can get! Mademoiselle Chanel would be miffed if she could hear you describe her new scent as something out of an Eastern garden. It's meant to revive memories of Paris in the springtime and all that!'

'Well, I won't say you look wonderful,' said Joe, 'because I assume you know that already but, all the same, you enchant me. I notice that Uncle has put us at extreme ends of the palace. Just as well, I believe.'

Nancy laughed. 'If I've got it right, you went up a flight of stairs and turned right. You walked through an audience hall and turned left. Here you found your bedroom. What you don't realise is that I was doing the same thing in reverse and although it appears that we are at opposite ends and miles apart our rooms are actually very close together.'

'I'm overwhelmed!' said Joe.

'Well, get underwhelmed,' said Nancy, 'and let's sample Uncle's Niersteiner while we're waiting for dinner. And look – wouldn't you know – Uncle would never do anything so common as to serve wine in its bottle – the Niersteiner has been decanted as befits a gentleman's dining-table. Very old-fashioned man, Uncle!'

The wine was excellent, the dinner that followed was outstanding, comprising tinned (but delicious) turtle soup from Lusty of Covent Garden, hilsa fish in tamarind sauce, chicken served with many vegetable dishes and a platter of rice, and a towering sugary model of the Taj Mahal accompanied by a mango water ice.

'Say something appreciative on my behalf,' said Joe as this fabulous meal drew to its conclusion and Nancy turned to the waiters and spoke at length. Her praise was received with beaming smiles and many salaams from all present.

'God! I envy you,' said Joe. 'What I miss by not being able to speak and understand. How long would it take me, do you think?'

'I can't tell. When I was a child – when I was a baby – my parents were busy most of the time and I spoke more to the servants than I did to them. I spoke more Hindustani than I did English for the first five years of my life. When I was in England at school and even more when I was in France in the war I found myself dreaming in Hindustani. And I think I could say that for the first seven years of my life I was entirely happy all the time and when I was cut off from it I had only one thought in my head – "When can I get back to India?" I used to whisper "India" to myself when things got bad. I swore an infantile vow that it was only a matter of time before I'd be home again.'

'And they snatched you away from all that and sent you back to school in England? That's terrible!'

'Well, I certainly thought it was terrible. It happened to everybody. It never crossed anybody's mind to complain. And it still goes on. I was lucky though. I was sent home eventually to school in Cheltenham. To a school that specialised in Anglo-Indian exiles like myself. I travelled with two friends in exactly the same situation. Minnie da Souza and Kate Bromhead. I don't know where I'd have been in an English boarding school if it hadn't been for them. We must have been a pain in the neck! We were all in our different ways exiled and bereft. We got over it by making a little enclave. We spoke Hindustani to each other and, to the limited extent that we could, we wrote notes to each other in Hindustani. Sometimes one of us would pretend we couldn't understand what the teacher was saying and then another would translate it. It's a wonder we had any friends at all!'

'I should think they thought you were very exotic,' said Joe. In his mind a picture had formed of three sallow little girls, spindly legs and big eyes, doing their best in alien surroundings to set themselves apart under an Indian flag.

Nancy resumed, as coffee was put on the table beside them, 'I even made myself a tick-off calendar counting the months, weeks and days until I might be able to come home. But as the number of days to tick off diminished to manageable proportions a terrible blow struck us. The war. Everything suddenly was thrown into the melting pot. My parents were in England at the time on a year's long leave. My father scuttled back to India where his regiment awaited him. We – the three witches as we called ourselves – had a serious conference, I remember it so well, in the box room at school. We decided to train as nurses. You can't imagine the complications of that decision! But we persisted and we got our way and finally we became the three most innocent Red Cross nurses in the world.

'We had heard that there were Indian troops in France. We thought if we were clever we could get to where they were so we could nurse them. We wrote a letter to the War Office saying nurses who could speak Hindustani must be in short supply – what about it? Some old India hand at the War Office picked up our letter, apparently, because – the wheels ground slowly – there came a day when we found ourselves on a troop ship en route for St Omer. The British Forward Hospital. We thought we'd died and gone to heaven! We loved our uniforms, loved the respect the chaps paid us and we didn't mind the admiration of our fellow schoolgirls left behind. I had a letter from my father which said, "Jolly good show, old girl! Mummy and I are proud of you!" Poor old poppet! He didn't have long to be proud. There was cholera in Srinagar where he was and before he could write again, he and Mum were dead.

'I had never liked England, except when my parents were there. People had been very kind – to all three of us – and we were never short of invitations for the holidays but we welcomed France. It was the first station on the road back to India, you see. I thought of India as being white and gold. I thought of school as being red and brown and I came to see France as grey and grey and almost always raining. I suppose it wasn't; there must have been hot days but I don't remember them.

'I remember when we arrived at the hospital in St Omer, lying in bed on the first night. I heard somebody muttering and wondered who it was and then I realised that it wasn't a person at all – it was guns. Guns, always guns muttering. From then on for three more years.

'You really can't believe that anyone could be as ignorant or as innocent as we were. The training had been pretty perfunctory, you know – a few months in the Indian troops' convalescent hospital in the Brighton Pavilion, if you can believe! And that was all. We didn't really learn much more than how to tie a clean bandage out of a packet, how to carry a breakfast tray and how to stop the men getting too fresh! How to keep them at arm's length. Arm's length! How do you keep a man at arm's length when half his stomach has been blown away? They were desperately short-handed so we were thrown in,

virtually untrained, at the deep end. In my first week I saw five
men die. Little Cheltenham schoolgirls don't often see men
die but there we were in the middle of it. I doubt if any of us
schoolgirls had ever seen a naked man before – our only
knowledge of male anatomy was derived from the statuary in
the Louvre museum. But by the end of our first week we were
conducting bed pan parade without turning a hair!'

Joe took advantage of the lightening of her mood to ask a
question he had long wanted to ask. 'Were there ever affairs
between nurses and patients? I can tell you, amongst the common soldiery it was the subject of much speculation!'

'Rarely. And very discreetly.' She paused, wondering
whether to confide secrets and, after a calculating glance,
went on, 'Yes, it happened. Life is intense – concentrated and
very ephemeral under those conditions. Men were often
declared fit and sent off back into action again too soon. We
girls knew – we just knew – when a boy wasn't going to come
back from the front. And, you know, Joe, some of them, especially the ones who'd got close to a particular nurse, would
know it too and their regret, their main regret, would not be
the complete waste of their lives but that they were going to
die before they'd ever loved someone. And nurses are there
to give comfort. It's what they believe in and I'm not going to
criticise the ones who chose to follow their instincts.'

She looked at him directly and defiantly. Was she trying to
tell him something about herself? Why did she feel that was
necessary? There was some mystery here. The possible reason
made his heart thump with excitement.

'Wasn't it, I mean, couldn't it have been dangerous . . .
um . . . of uncertain outcome?'

'Of course. If we'd been discovered we could have been
dismissed and sent home. But no one was going to get rid of a
competent and experienced nurse. We were in short supply.
But I don't think that's what you were hinting at?'

Nancy's eyes crinkled in amusement as she remembered. 'Our matron was not the kind of matron you might envisage – all bosom, starched and rustling! She was slim, twenty-four years old and her mother, the Countess, was a director of the VAD! No, the only starchy thing about Madeleine was her apron. We all knew she wore eau de nil silk cami-knickers underneath her uniform. She used to say they reminded her of who she really was. She gave us a piece of advice on relationships with the men – "Girls, don't!!! But if you must, be sensible!! You'll find what you're looking for in the bottom drawer of my desk!"'

They fell silent as a side table, glasses and decanters, each with a silver label around its neck, were placed beside them. Joe selected a balloon glass and swirled a little brandy around quietly, anxious not to interrupt Nancy who was almost lost to him in the memories.

'I remember,' she said, 'in the spring of 1918 there were some American troops. They'd had a bloody awful time. They were so brave it broke your heart! There was one boy – he was dying. You soon get to know and I knew that he was dying. I'd gone to bed but couldn't sleep so I went down to see him in the ward. I didn't bother to put on my uniform, I just pulled my dress on over my head and went and sat beside him. Oh, God, Joe! Can you imagine this – he suddenly said, in a sort of little boy's voice, "Is that you, Mommy?" What could I say? I said, "Yes, it's all right, darling." And then he said, "Is John there?" And I said, "Yes, he's here – somewhere about." And he rambled on. I wanted to do something for him, something special. So I peeled off my dress and lay down on the bed beside him, put my arms round him. He stopped muttering, sighed and snuggled close. About two o'clock in the morning – it always happened at two in the morning – he died. It really was my darkest hour. I saw no hope for anyone and I had to be on duty again in four hours.

'I had seen others die and was to see more but, somehow, this really entered my heart. He had, in a way . . .' She paused for a long time and then resumed, 'Maybe you'll find this ridiculous but he had, in a way, become my baby. And his passing left a gap in my heart that the years have not filled. Dammit! I don't even remember his name!

'In tears I called for stretcher bearers and while I was waiting for them my attention was called to another man lying nearby. His service dress cap was on the bed beside him. Idly I picked it up. He was an officer – rather unusual on that ward. He was in the 23rd Rajputana Rifles, the Raj. Rif. as we used to call them. I thought he was dead or at the very least, dying. He looked up, reached out for my hand and said, "Well done!" Just that – "Well done."

'He was in pretty bad shape. He was my first Indian army casualty and as best I could, I made a tremendous fuss of him. His wound was terrible.' Nancy hesitated for a moment, her thoughts slowed by the weight of memory. 'His leg was practically shot to pieces. Multiple fractures and the flesh was cut to ribbons. We all thought it would have to be amputated but the young doctor who dealt with him had only just arrived and hadn't yet begun to bargain limbs against speed and efficiency. He made a heroic effort and the Raj. Rif. officer began to mend. Eventually – after about a month, I suppose – there was talk of moving him back to the base hospital in Rouen. I tried to keep him – very selfish of me. We used to talk about India and I told him the only thing in the world I wanted was to go home. He understood and we talked about it a lot.

'One day he had an official-looking sort of letter. He asked me to read it to him. He'd been in the ICS before the war and this was an offer. The Collectorship of Panikhat, can you believe it! He was quite upset. "This would have been just what I wanted," he said, "if I weren't a cripple." And I went for him! "Just what you wanted? Then take it! I haven't wasted six months patching you up to have you at the end of the day turning down an offer like this! You'll walk again. You'll ride a horse again. Take it!"

'He was very amused and then he said something so extraordinary, something that actually transformed my life. "Do you really want to go back to India?" and I said, "Yes, more than life." And he said, "Give you a first class, one-way ticket if you like." And I said, "What on earth do you mean?" He said, "Marry me. It's not much of an offer . . . you know the state I'm in . . . but marry me and be the Collector's lady."

'I couldn't believe it! Still can't sometimes.

'Shortly after that Raj. Rif. wounded began to come in and we found ourselves talking to them, writing letters for them, listening to them and all the time telling them they were going to be all right. And the Collector-Elect of Panikhat persuaded the authorities to allow him to stay in the forward hospital (quite irregular, of course). He said, "I can do more good here talking to the chaps than I would sitting on my bum in base hospital in Rouen playing bridge all day long."

'I really loved him, you know. And I still do.'

She fell silent, her eyes in the candlelight shimmering with tears, and Joe waited, finding no words to speak, sensing that she had almost got to the end of her story.

'The war was on its last legs by then, though we didn't know it. There were miles of red tape to unwind so it was two months before we could get married. As soon as we could we said our goodbyes and suddenly everybody was going home – all the Yankee boys, the British singing "Auld Lang Syne" and the Raj. Rif. just smiling. Quite a lot of us were crying including me and then we were off in a train to Paris for a honeymoon. From there to Marseilles, on to a P&O steamer to Bombay and all my dreams came true.'

'All your dreams?' asked Joe quietly.

Chapter Thirteen

'ALL MY DREAMS?'

Nancy repeated his question slowly and her eyes slid away from his to focus on the single orchid which stood in a slender silver vase between them. She was silent for a long while, gently stroking its silken petals and, from her silence, he understood that she was considering his deeper meaning.

'No. Not all my dreams. But most of them. Such as they were at the time. India was still white and gold and all that I had hoped for. The people smiled and the sun shone. The blood and the pus and the misery, the noise and the squalor, they were all far behind in France. I remember saying to myself, "I'll have clean clothes every day!" And, of course, in India you do have clean clothes every day. I was coming alive again. But then . . .'

Her face suddenly grew bleak as memory returned. 'Peggy Somersham, my best friend. There was I in India surrounded by the peace and comfort that I'd longed for and suddenly here was my friend lying dead in her bath. I knew that somebody had come into my paradise and murdered someone close to me for no reason I could think of. And why Peggy? Why not me? I was back with death. I was back with blood. And more than I have ever hated anybody or anything I have hated the man who was responsible for this!

'I imagined how he'd done it and tried to reconstruct it. I didn't get a scrap of co-operation from Bulstrode, condescending bastard that he is! If I tried to interest him or suggest he ought to look a bit further, he would just give me that irritating laugh, the laugh that said, "There, there! Don't you dirty your pretty little hands. This is man's talk. You wouldn't understand." So I rang Uncle George and we talked about you and about the forensic techniques and criminal character analyses we'd heard you lecturing on and we agreed – "That's the man for us!" And Uncle George – he's very good at that – pulled a few strings and here we are. He'd take it as a personal triumph I think if you could pull this off!'

She reached out and took Joe's hand in both of hers and said, 'It's transformed the world to have you here!'

Joe looked with tenderness into her excited face. '*Nous gagnerons parce que nous sommes les plus forts!*' he said.

'Who said that?'

'It's what the poor old frogs said at the beginning of the war. Never lacking in confidence! But then, in the end, I suppose they did win out.'

The khansama slid into the room, taper in hand, and proceeded to relight the candles. Nancy stayed him with a gesture and one by one they flickered and went out. The tiniest, discreetest shuffle in the corner of the room marked the appearance of ayah and, in a gentle voice, Nancy dismissed her. In moonlit silence with the mutter of the city drifting up from the street below, the bark of a dog, the call of a night bird, a sudden clamour from the market as suddenly cut short, seemed only to accentuate the silence that had fallen between them.

She looked up, at once both innocent and alert. Her innocence left Joe longing to hold her close, ruffle her hair and kiss the tip of her nose, to draw her down on to his lap, to sleep with her, to wake with her, but the air of alertness delivered an entirely different message. His mind went back to a bar in Abbeville and to an officer in the French Women's Army. She'd downed her second cognac and, staring closely into his eyes with that same concentrated alertness, had whispered a phrase whose crudity had left him breathless, '*Baise-moi, Tommy!*'

What would he say if Nancy had said the same? He knew exactly what he would do. In desperation, he made a half move towards her but she anticipated him and, falling to her knees beside him, she put her arms round his waist and buried her face in his lap. When she looked up her eyes were wet with tears but she was laughing at him.

'Joe,' she said, 'listen! I don't need to do any explaining, I think. You must have guessed I don't know much about this. Oh, God! You're so precious, you're so special and you're so absolutely my lifeline – I don't want to disappoint you and I know that happens sometimes.'

More moved than he could imagine, Joe lifted her face and turned it towards him. He kissed her gently and then kissed her open-mouthed. A small murmur, a small cry and they were standing.

'What do we do now?' Nancy asked awkwardly.

'Well, I've got a perfectly good bedroom over here some-where,' said Joe waving a hand vaguely.

'And I've got one over there. Shall we spin a coin?'

'No,' said Joe. 'Come with me.'

Chapter Fourteen

HE AWOKE IN a cocoon of disordered bedclothes. Not only disordered bedclothes – clearly the mosquito net had been in some way detached during the night as witnessed by a large number of bumps along his back. The bed beside him was warm from Nancy. His mind was a turmoil, remembering the innocence and the excitement with which Nancy had joined him in the night and remembering the smiles and gentle laughter, the tender clenching of her body as she lay with him.

He supposed that everyone in that large household would know exactly what had occurred. And if they knew, it was to be assumed that it would be no time before the Governor would know. He had tried to talk about this with Nancy but she had been unable to acknowledge that there might be social implications to their tempestuous night. What, he wondered, would be the reaction of the Governor? "Ship this bloody policeman home on the next boat!" He didn't think so. He thought her uncle was well aware of what would be the consequences of his so careful sleeping arrangements, to say nothing of his well-chosen wines. He even supposed that the Governor had brought this about for a purpose of his own. His mind ranged widely, seeking what may have been the purpose. He had, at their first meeting, spoken deprecatingly of Andrew Drummond. Feeling sorry for her, could he be putting a little distraction his niece's way, condoning adultery? Joe had heard the stories everyone had heard about the looseness of morals in tropical India and wondered whether he had been too quick to dismiss them as wishful nonsense. All the same, there was something here he did not understand.

Tired of appearing in uniform and duly bathed, he dressed in plain clothes and sat down to an enormous breakfast. Government House, clearly suspended in an Edwardian vision of what such things should be, had provided egg, bacon, coffee, a rack of toast and – to crown everything – a plate of well-made porridge. He might have been breakfasting in Oxford in the nineties.

When he had worked through this and, lighting a cigarette, had stepped out on to the balcony, the khitmutgar appeared, salaaming.

'The memsahib asks that you will visit her as soon as you are able to do so,' he said. 'And there is an individual downstairs to see you.'

'An individual? What sort of individual?'

'It is a Sikh havildar of police,' he replied, managing to convey that a Sikh havildar of police waits until he is sent for.

Joe's instinct was to say, 'Show him up,' but he decided that this would be a breach of protocol and asked that his visitor might be shown into an office where he could later come down and interview him after he had been announced to the memsahib.

Nancy greeted him with a beaming smile and, with a quick look round to assure herself that, for once, they were truly alone, advanced and put her arms round his neck. She kissed him firmly and said, 'Good morning, Holmes. I see that Mrs Hudson has served you with one of Baker Street's best as well as me. Now tell me – what are your plans for today?'

'Well,' said Joe, 'they were first to come and see how you are. No problem about that – you look absolutely blooming! How extraordinary! You're supposed to look pale and woebegone – "Now by my morning sickness I have lost my virtue to this rude and rammish clown." You know, all that sort of thing.'

'Can't be bothered,' said Nancy. 'You're quite conceited enough already so I'll merely say – you were wonderful! It was wonderful! I was wonderful – wasn't I?'

'Yes,' said Joe.

And there was a washed and dewy freshness about her face that he had never seen before.

'I'll answer your question though as to what we're doing today. Good Naurung awaits us downstairs.'

Suitably escorted they followed the khitmutgar down through the house, through the company rooms, through a discreet door into the offices at that early hour busy with Bengali clerks scribbling, chattering and bowing politely as they passed through.

Naurung greeted them with his usual self-sufficient deference. 'I had thought, sahib,' he began, 'that we should speak to my father. He doesn't have much to tell you but he was concerned – as a policeman, you understand – with the deaths of two of the ladies. Of Mrs Forbes and Mrs Simms-Warburton.'

'Can you bring him to us?' asked Joe.

'I can certainly bring him to you but better, perhaps, that we should go to him. It is not far. He works outside the Law Courts. He is a letter-writer now that he has retired from the police. The letter-writers all talk to each other. It is what I think you would call a trade union. They know a lot.'

Joe turned to Nancy. 'Shall we? Not too fatigued to attempt a little walk?'

Nancy gave him a repressive look and they set off into the mounting heat of the day to walk westwards along the Esplanade towards the red-brick gothic splendour of the Law Court building. line of scribbling or tapping figures seated under the arcade. A Sikh turban marked him out from the rest and, given only the disparity of years, Naurung senior looked exactly like his son. He was at work. Joe paused for a while and watched. The old man's client squatting on his heels in front of the smart new Remington typewriter leaned over and whispered urgently and volubly. Naurung listened and replied, obviously rephrasing what he had just heard, and then proceeded to tap out an agreed statement on his type-writer. Coming to the end of the letter, he wound the sheet out, read out what he had typed and handed it to his customer. Grateful thanks and a handful of coins were politely accepted and before the next client could shuffle forward, Naurung hailed his father and led them to him. He made the introductions in English and the old man turned to greet them in the same language.

'I am honoured.' he said, 'that the police sahib from the Scotland Yard visits me in my humble place of business.'

'I am honoured,' said Joe, 'that the renowned retired officer of police should set aside important concerns and spare a little time to illuminate the past for a London police-man but it has seemed to your son and it has seemed to me too that there may be thoughts that it would be sensible for us to share.'

'I am of that opinion. But this is not a seemly place for such a discussion. Will you allow me a few minutes and I will be at your service?'

Naurung senior closed and locked his typewriter. He turned to the man on his left and addressed him at length. 'He is an ignorant man and a humble man but he is honest and I will leave my typewriter and my place under his protection. Now, perhaps the sahib and the memsahib will follow me?'

Walking with Joe while Nancy and his son fell in behind, the old man led them north round two corners into a back-street and to a staircase above which there was an inscription in Hindustani. 'This,' he said, 'is a Sikh establishment and it is run by friends and relations of mine. Here we will be private.' And he led them up a narrow staircase to a wide room from which arcaded windows led to a balcony and in which tea and a dish of sweetmeats appeared. It was clear to Joe that they had been expected. He sat down with Nancy at a table and

Naurung's father sat down opposite. Naurung himself took up a sentry-like stance at his father's side and the old man listened with the closest attention to everything that Joe had to say but it was clear at intervals that he had lost the thread and when this happened Nancy intervened in translation and occasionally Naurung did the same. The conversation proceeded in English with intervals of Hindustani.

'My son has told me all he knows of your investigation and I add this to the knowledge of the affair I have derived from my own experience when working with Bulstrode Sahib at Panikhat,' the old man began. Joe thought he caught the ghost of an expression at the name Bulstrode, an expression he had seen many times on the face of the younger Naurung. Dislike? No – disdain. 'I am aware of a disturbing implication,' he said.

Nancy stumbled over the word and after a short debate Naurung supplied it.

'I will explain. I think, outwardly, in Bengal all is calm. Money was made during the war and people – though not all people – are prosperous but the burra sahib – your uncle – is not a fool. He looks under the surface. He did not invite the distinguished police commander . . .' He bowed to Joe. 'He did not invite you, sir, for nothing, or just – excuse me – just to humour his niece. He has a long memory. He thinks of the past and he also thinks of the future. The decision to move the capital of India from Calcutta to Delhi is resented by educated people in Bengal. And there is much resentment still about the war. The English talk always of the gallantry of Indian soldiers in France and there are gallant legends. What we know is that of the "gallant" band who set off to France a very great number did not return. Look, if you do not believe me, at the casualty returns amongst Bateman's Horse. It is believed that valuable Indian lives were squandered.'

He paused and looked a question at Joe.

'I was in France,' said Joe, 'and that same opinion was widely expressed by returning British soldiers including myself. The Germans described the British army as "an army of lions led by donkeys". I agree. But it is not of Indian troops alone that this could be said. I started the war with six cousins and now I have one.'

'Many Sikhs could say the same,' said the old man and went on, 'but it is our religion to die always with our faces to the enemy and serving our King. The Sikhs do do not complain but there is much ill feeling among others towards the British for involving the Indian people in a struggle that is not their own. But further . . .' He paused for a moment to emphasise the point he was about to make. '. . . it is believed that the British are subtle and clever and they are taking steps to separate Hindu and Muslim. I believe this myself. And it is being said openly that this move to divide Hindu and Muslim is motivated by the policy of "divide and rule".'

The last thing Joe wanted was to find himself stirring about in the snake pit of Indian politics but the Naurungs appeared so earnest in their desire to prevent a catastrophe which they could clearly see on the horizon that he made an effort to listen closely. Could the Naurungs be uncovering the undisclosed reason Uncle George had been so eager to involve him?

He accepted another sweet pastry and asked carefully, 'What are you saying? Where is this leading?'

'I am saying that, though apparently calm, the political situation is explosive and – if you will hear me – our affair of the memsahib murders may have a disastrous part to play. Remember that in 1858 it was in Bengal that the match was applied to the powder trail that so nearly blew British India to smithereens.' He produced the word with pride. 'And remember that then the powder keg was suspicion – unfounded perhaps but suspicion all the same – that the British were intent on forcibly converting the sepoy soldiers to Christianity. The fuse seemed a trivial enough matter to the British. They had issued to the soldiers cartridges which it was rumoured had been greased with pig and cow fat. To load his gun the soldier had to bite off the top of the cartridge thus polluting himself whether he were Muslim or Hindu. It was said that this was a cunning British means of destroying the caste of the Indian regiments. But the British were not cunning – careless perhaps and thoughtless, but the tragedy was that this was the fuse that was lit in Bengal in the hot weather when tempers grow short. Stations like Panikhat here in Bengal and Meerut near Delhi saw the first explosions.'

Joe remembered the pathetic plaques on the older bungalows. He remembered Kitty lost in a past which to her was only a touch away.

'Who will forget Memsahib Chambers, a young wife and pregnant, cut to pieces, the first victim. The first of hundreds of Englishwomen to die hideously at the hands of the mutineers. And because their women and their children had suffered so badly the English reprisals were equally hideous. The hangings, the sepoys tied to cannon and shot to bits . . . a dark time.

'And it would not need much to bring that horror back. Already we have the same pattern – many grievances, many suspicions. Let it be suggested in the bazaars that there is a movement, a movement to dislodge the British, and many – often ignorant – people would follow. The situation is once again extremely dangerous.'

'Again,' said Joe, 'I am asking where you are leading me?'

The room fell silent while they awaited his reply until at last he said, 'I think, Commander, you believe, as I do, that all these tragedies are linked? And looking at the evidence it would seem that in each case there was present a mysterious and disappearing figure. Consider the wife of Carmichael Sahib. Who was it who killed the cobra? People would assume a native. The wife of Forbes Sahib. Where now is the saddhu – a material witness if ever there was one? And the ferryman who made so gallant a rescue attempt when the wife of Simms-Warburton Sahib was drowned? And, most recently, the native box-wallah who came forward so helpfully to say that, though he had been in the alleyway by the bungalow of Memsahib Somersham at the time of her death, he had seen and heard nothing suspicious?'

Naurung cleared his throat deferentially, obviously with something to say but reluctant to interrupt his father who turned to him, however, in enquiry.

'I have made a small investigation, if you will pardon me, in respect of this death. Perhaps you will recall this disappearing witness – a merchant, a representative of Vallijee Raja. I have a friend who works for this firm and I asked him if he could find out who was the box-wallah in Panikhat who came a couple of weeks ago to sell the products of this firm. They have no record of any representative of the firm in Panikhat at that time or indeed at any time this year so this too is a figure of mystery.'

The silence which greeted this revelation was broken by Naurung senior. 'Now I will tell you something which is not generally known. That is to say it is no secret but it is not widely spoken of. Six weeks ago at Bhalasore, that is twenty-five miles from here, the wife of a post office official was killed when she was out riding. It was thought that she had been kicked by her horse. Fractured skull. Three weeks ago the wife of a planter who lives ten miles from here was killed "accidentally" by misreading the label on a medicine bottle. Such things happen. They are not what you would call the "stop press news". But for those with eyes to see a connection between these things a connection can be found. I myself think that we are looking at no more than the kind of thing that happens in India. Probably the kind of thing that happens in London? But I am remembering that in 1858 connections were seen which were not there. Truth was ignored because a lie was more valuable.

'Sandilands Sahib, you know that I am a letter-writer. We letter-writers hear things spoken in confidence – secrets, policies, mysteries. We speak little but we know a great deal. When we are concerned we share our knowledge and our fears. And there is a fear, a great fear in the bazaars and in the corridors of Government House that the country is on the point of another and greater rebellion than the one sixty years ago. Then the Sikhs stood with the British against the mutineers. If terrible times should come again, the Sikhs would stand with you once more. It is their way. But many fear the powder keg is in place.'

'And the spark that could ignite it?' asked Joe, already knowing the answer.

'A fuse. A trail of murdered memsahibs. Already it is spoken of. One thing is lacking, sahib. The match. And that you hold in your own hand.'

'Joe Sandilands holds it?' Nancy said sharply. 'What do you mean, Naurung?'

'He means,' said Joe, 'that when the great detective from Scotland Yard finishes his investigations and declares to the Governor of Bengal that five English ladies, wives of officers in a smart cavalry regiment, have each been murdered with much malice aforethought by Indians or even a single Indian, there will be reprisals. There will be token arrests, there may even be executions. And with a dedicated and implacable Colonel like Prentice in command of the regiment, who knows how far it will go? We all know what his reputation is for exacting revenge.'

'And then there will be retaliation and overreaction from native groups,' said Nancy, white-faced. 'The Congress wallahs could seize on this and use it! Just what they need as a battle flag to wave in our faces! Oh, Joe . . .'

Naurung, who had stood in almost total silence throughout the exchange, now spoke quietly.

'Sandilands Sahib says *when* he makes his revelation. May we know if it is indeed his decision to incriminate Indians in the deaths?'

Joe looked at the three strained faces around him and shook his head, smiling bleakly. 'You must think that so far I have done very little to justify my professional status and the confidence the Governor has shown in me. You may well even be recalling the title the press frequently gives us at Scotland Yard – the Defective Force. It is difficult to take over cases years old, badly managed from the outset, cases in which I cannot use any of the new forensic methods I have been so proudly demonstrating to the Bengal Police for the last six months.'

Naurung nodded in understanding.

'No fingerprinting, no blood-typing, no door-to-door enquiries, no string of informants. I've been forced back on to a dependence on reason and common sense . . . but something more.'

He paused for a moment, wondering how receptive his audience would be to what he had to say next, and then plunged on.

'I was billeted in the war with a very clever man – a well-read man. He'd brought two books to the war with him – the works of an Austrian psychologist, Sigmund Freud, and a Swiss called Carl Jung. I had snatched up the works of Shakespeare and *Kim*. When war isn't being instant noisy death whizzing past your ears it's being a boring longueur and my companion and I whiled away the waiting between pushes by reading each other's books. I don't know which of us had the better bargain! I learned much about the science of psychology of the unconscious mind, about psychoanalysis and the development of character. My friend didn't believe in the existence of evil and he laughed at the policeman's idea of the "criminal type". He believed that a man's character was set for life – moulded if you like – by circumstances in the first seven or so years of his existence. If he is born into poverty and crime, he is likely to grow up poor and a criminal, through no fault of his own.'

The Naurungs looked at him alertly and nodded. Naurung senior said, 'We have a saying in Bengal – "The Rajah's son does not exchange shoes with the cobbler's son."'

'Just so,' said Joe a little deflated. 'I have also made a study of a phenomenon in the history of crime in Europe and America which began with the slaying of five ladies of the night – five prostitutes – in the East End of London fifty years ago.'

Naurung senior listened with heightened attention and his son nodded eagerly. It was clear they were both aware of the case.

'Jack the Ripper?' said Nancy. 'Are you talking about the Whitechapel murders? The police never solved those crimes, did they?'

'No,' said Joe. 'But, with the help of my friend in the trenches, I do believe I have worked out Jack's identity. The motive, I think, is very different in the sequence of murders we're investigating but there are aspects in common. We're not looking here at a frenzied attack carried out through an overriding sexual motive but at a carefully executed pattern of killings. The victims have been *selected*. They didn't just happen to stray into range of the killer when he was experiencing a maniacal urge to destroy. Their habits were well known to him. He could follow them, even into their bathroom in the case of Peggy Somersham, murder them and instantly disappear. Like Jack, he could disappear with ease *because he was at home.*

'When I was doing some research into the Ripper murders a couple of years ago I came on a paper – or letter rather – addressed to the head of the CID in 1888 by a Dr Thomas Bond who was much concerned with the Ripper investigation. I was fascinated. What I had in my hands was a portrait of the murderer in words. The good doctor, as if by some magic it seemed at first reading, was sketching an outline of the man – his height, his weight, his disposition, his job, the place where he was to be found and the make-up of his family. Had I been on the strength in 1888 I could, on reading that letter, have walked down the Whitechapel Road and felt his collar! On second reading I was impressed for quite a different reason. The doctor was using nothing but sound common sense and inspired reasoning, drawing on information from the scenes of crime. And I could do the same.'

'You're about to tell us that you've solved our problem?' Nancy asked.

Joe grimaced. 'Your problem, I'm afraid, is a lot more complex than the Ripper case! There we had the same modus operandi – the same knife was used, the killings were done in the same framework of time and place and the motive was blatantly obvious. The killer experienced an ungovernable and psychotic rage against women – women of a certain type, that is.'

'You mean he was trying to clean up the streets? Get rid of the prostitutes?' said Nancy.

'No. I'm certain there was no element of crusade in what he did. I think it was an outburst of sexually inspired fury against a class of women he had good cause to hate. I believe he had personal reasons, springing from his own early days perhaps, for hacking to death and obliterating these women. He was possibly the son of a prostitute, reared by a prostitute – certainly the man was a client of and probably actually knew the women he murdered. It's my theory that he actually lived with one of them.'

'But none of the ladies in this case was molested, sahib, and all were killed by different methods,' said Naurung.

'And that is what makes it almost impossible to explain,' said Joe. 'Let's look for a moment at motivation. We have already ruled out the two most common ones – lust and financial gain. Not even the ladies' husbands gained in the slightest by their deaths. So we are left with four: jealousy, elimination, revenge and conviction.'

'Well, we can rule out jealousy, I think,' said Nancy. 'None of the wives had given cause for suspicion . . . At least I'm not quite certain about Dolly Prentice . . . There are stories that she was, well, a bit of a flirt . . . But about the rest there was no gossip at all. You'd say that all the men loved their wives and were quite devastated when they died. None has remarried and I think that's very significant, don't you?'

'Yes, and that in a sense rules out the next motive of elimination. You know – "I will kill off my wife because I want to marry someone else or because she is in possession of a hideous secret concerning me." Dr Crippen, for example, needed to eliminate his wife in order to marry his lover. But, no, the facts don't support this explanation in any of the cases. None of our husbands would appear to have profited and flourished as a result.'

'No. I agree,' said Nancy. 'Colonel Prentice, as witnesses claim, was horrified by his wife's death and out of his mind for a fortnight. There are rumours that all was not well with that pair but, according to Kitty, he took it very badly.'

'And yesterday I interviewed a wreck of a man. The husband of Joan Carmichael. You'd say he never smiled again after her death. He had some money from Joan but, as her husband, he could probably have had access to it at any time and he didn't make use of it until two years after her death.'

'And Dr Forbes whom I saw at the hospital yesterday. He's thrown himself totally into his work which is his whole life now. His distress at Sheila's death was still evident.'

'Simms-Warburton, well, we'll never know. He went straight into the war and never came home again but certainly there was no whirlwind remarriage, no instant elopement with the daughter of a subhadur-major!'

'And lastly Billy Somersham. You've met him. I know him. He gained nothing but heartache from Peggy's death. No, he had absolutely no reason to "eliminate" her. So that leaves only two motives – revenge and conviction, whatever you mean by that!'

'Revenge? Would anyone, seriously, have cause to be revenged on these women?' Joe asked. 'What had they done? All perfectly innocent creatures who had annoyed nobody, not even their husbands. I really can't see this as a convincing motive.'

'So – you're going to have to explain what you mean by your last motive, conviction.'

'Conviction.' Joe sighed. 'This could take us into the realms of madness. If a person is convinced, for example, that he has a God-given right to kill for religious motives, I would call that a conviction killing.'

Naurung could not wait for the end of Joe's explanation. 'Suttee!' he said. 'As in suttee! The disgusting Hindu custom of burning alive a man's widow on his funeral pyre! The British have tried to stamp it out but it goes on, oh, yes, it still goes on in the villages! Sometimes the lady goes willingly to her death as it brings great honour to her family but often her relatives force her. There was a case, in my father's memory, where the widow escaped from the fire and ran away. She was found hiding by her own son who dragged her back and threw her once more into the flames.'

'Yes, that would be, as far as an Eastern mind could encompass it, an example of killing for religious conviction.'

Nancy said angrily, 'Not necessarily religious! I think that's too convenient an excuse for such a revolting custom. Social, perhaps. A strong social reason – after all, who in a family wants to be saddled with a useless widow to support for the rest of her unproductive life? She cannot remarry and is bound to be a burden to her family if the problem isn't solved by means of the funeral pyre and excused by the notion of religious observance!'

'Which brings us to the second strand of "conviction". The social strand. If our killer had an unshakeable belief that he was ridding society of an undesirable element – a belief so strong that he felt his actions were above all laws – he might kill off a series of similar victims. Prostitutes? Priests?'

'Money-lenders?' suggested Naurung.

'Certainly money-lenders! But officers' wives?' Nancy exclaimed with derision. 'We've all been irritated or bored out

of our minds by them but hardly to the point of taking a knife
or a cobra to finish them off!'

Joe smiled. 'I agree. And this is where it all begins to get a
little unreal. They are not just a series of officers' wives. They are
a very particular group of officers' wives, chosen according to
some obscure pattern. There are things they had in common,
there are things they did not have in common. There are things
a proportion of the group had in common – both Dolly Prentice
and Peggy Somersham were pregnant. Is this significant or is it
misleading? But there is one thing which I think is very
significant. Naurung – Mrs Drummond and I have discovered
that the ladies all had this in common – they had a phobia.'

Translations of the word rattled back and forward over
Joe's head until the satisfied nods of the two Naurungs encour-
aged him to go on. Nancy supplied the details of each victim's
special horror, linking it with the means of her death and the
faces of father and son grew grim.

Finally, Naurung said seriously, 'This is the work of a devil,
sahib. I fear we have worked our way back to our first conversation if the sahib remembers?'

'The Churel? Kali the Destroyer? I still do not accept this.
But you and your father have added today another element to
the motive of conviction killing and that is – political. To murder, not soldiers but soldiers' wives and by subtle and repulsive
means might be a calculated way of sowing terror and suspicion in the ranks of the British army. A way which would lead
to the reprisals and overreaction we have discussed. But I
don't think the answer lies here either. For two apparently
insignificant reasons. The murders have all occurred in
March. On the grave of each victim has been placed a bunch
of Kashmiri roses – all in March. This is a *ritual* aspect which
rules out every one of the motives we have so far examined.'

Joe frowned. 'And so I am reduced to working out this
whole problem from what any decent policeman would

consider the wrong end. I have built up a picture of the person who must have committed these crimes . . .'

'Very well, Sandilands,' said Nancy with a hint of challenge in her voice, 'prove that you're not a defective! Tell us who's responsible.'

'He is male. He is European. He is middle-aged, strong and agile in body and mind. He is very close to Indians and either has employed them to do these killings or is sufficiently confident to have tricked himself out as an Indian to get close enough to do the murders himself without arousing suspicion. He lives on the station at Panikhat. If you passed him walking on the maidan you would greet him by name.'

There was a deep silence as names crowded into everyone's mind. Nancy shook her head and muttered, 'No. That's not possible.'

The young Naurung was more positive and Joe even wondered whether he had arrived at this point before he had himself. 'Sandilands Sahib, I think you know and I too can guess who has done these dreadful things,' he said, 'but why? My father,' with a short bow to Naurung senior, 'will always say, "Know how and why and you will know who," but what you are saying is quite the reverse.'

'I know,' said Joe, 'and to fill in the picture I must go back to Panikhat. That's where it started and that's where the answers lie.'

'One thing, Sandilands Sahib,' said Naurung's father diffidently. 'I worked with Bulstrode Sahib on the case of Memsahib Simms-Warburton who was drowned. It was I who interviewed the ferryman who nearly drowned with her. I suspected him. He could, unseen by the bystanders, have secreted a knife about the raft and slit the hides when they were in the middle of the river. He dived under water to help the poor lady but they were both under the surface for a long time. It occurred to me that he could have been holding her down until he was sure she was dead. I spoke to him afterwards and took a statement which unfortunately did not attract the interest of Bulstrode Sahib but I remember it well.

'Commander, Englishmen are brown down to their neck and pink below that. This man was naked apart from his turban and loin cloth. I saw his body. And he was Indian-skinned from head to soles of his feet.'

Chapter Fifteen

JOE AND NANCY rose to take their leave of the Naurungs, who accompanied them to the foot of the stairs with what Joe supposed to be an exchange of formal compliments.

'Well, Naurung senior rather exploded your theory, didn't he?'

'Not necessarily,' said Joe slowly. 'In fact what he had to say may answer other questions I still have.' He looked at his watch and said, 'Uncle George will be home by now. Perhaps we should report to him?'

'Oh, Uncle! There will be things he wants to know.' She gave Joe a searching look. 'And things perhaps we ought to explain. And I think I've got something I ought to explain.'

She took hold of Joe's arm and squeezed it to her. 'I don't know much, perhaps I don't have to tell you that, but at the outset – and it seems a very long time ago – I said that when I got back to India all my dreams came true and you asked me – I don't suppose you remember asking – whether *all* my dreams came true. Well, the plain answer is no. But last night you took me somewhere I hadn't been before. It was probably obvious to you – I don't know how these things work – but now I have to say that I am a trustee – a trustee for Andrew. He rescued me from France and in exchange I, and others of course, brought him back to life. I'm not going to do that and leave him stranded. You do understand that, don't you?' She looked earnestly at Joe. 'It's important to me that you should.'

'I understood,' said Joe.

'Well, go on understanding. That's all you have to do.'

As they drew into Government House, dazzling in the sunshine, a Daimler with a flag on the bonnet pulled in ahead of them.

'Uncle George,' said Nancy. 'Just beaten us to it.'

There seemed to be a heightened efficiency, a heightened formality associated no doubt with the return of the Governor. As they entered, George's European staff seemed much more in evidence. Their return was greeted on all sides and they were shown with rapidity into the presence.

'How do I play this?' Joe thought. 'Do I say, "I'm afraid I spent last night in bed with your niece? I hope you don't mind. Oh, and, incidentally, the next Mutiny may be about to break out".'

But with dexterity Uncle George went straight to the heart of the matter. 'Morning, Nancy, my dear! And good morning, Sandilands! Hope you got a good dinner last night? Sleep all right, did you? Can be damned hot in Calcutta. Now, been to see the Naurungs, I hear.'

'Now how the hell did he know that?' Joe wondered but the Governor read his question.

'How did I know? You can't do this job unless you've got eyes in the back of your head and whatever else I may have I have a very good information system. Good idea, though! I find old Naurung is very worth hearing. Perhaps you'll tell me what passed?'

Deeply relieved to be speaking in English without the necessity to pause for translation, Joe set to work to explain the scope of their enquiries, the fears of the Naurungs and the direction in which their deductions were moving. The Governor looked from one to the other, saying at last, 'I asked you to discover whether these deaths were linked. I asked you to discover whether a suspicion of foul play could seriously be entertained. That now seems a long time ago. The answer to both questions is yes and I grieve to hear it. A dark and mysterious affair and I would say "No light, but only darkness visible." Eh? What? And now you tell me you're looking for a European murderer? I never thought otherwise.'

'Yes,' said Joe, 'I think that fairly describes where we've got to. We have a strong suspicion as to who but we are no nearer the why and sketchy as to the how.'

'Starting at the wrong end, you might say?'

'Exactly. There must be a connection but we – or at any rate I – am too thick to see it.'

'Don't belittle yourself,' said George politely. 'Considering the cold trail you've been following, I think you've done very well. Now – leave it at that. Keep me posted. Come and see me whenever you want to. Hang on to the Naurungs. But continue to suspect everybody so don't exclude the Naurungs.

'But now I have another and purely domestic matter to discuss with you. You're going back to Panikhat today. Correct? In Andrew's car, I presume? Well you've got a passenger! Big enough to seat three, I assume? I have a very charming little guest (with a very great deal of luggage!) and perhaps you can guess who? No? Well, it's Midge or perhaps I should say more formally that it's Minette Prentice, Giles Prentice's daughter. She was going back with Molly Bracegirdle but now Molly's down with a gastric thing – Delhi belly as we sometimes call it, the Indian answer to Gippy tummy. Midge was here a little while ago but she's gone down to the town to do a bit of shopping belatedly having decided she ought to have a present for her father. No money, of course! Spent it all! Had to finance her! Oh, my goodness – it's Dolly Prentice all over again! Just like Dolly – of a, oh, er, a wheedling disposition, you'll find.'

'Where's the child been?' Joe asked.

'Finishing school. Finishing school in Switzerland. Why on earth it's called a finishing school I've no idea. Starting

school more like, if you ask me! Now, I've got work to do but
stay and have tiffin with me. In about half an hour? Nancy,
my dear, go and organise your packing. Ought to leave as
soon as we've eaten. You've a long way to travel and you
don't want to be motoring in the dark. And you, Sandilands?
I expect you can amuse yourself for a while and we'll meet
back here?'

Joe spent his time wandering in the rose gardens and duly
made his way back into the house in time for lunch. Walking
across the wide landing to the Governor's apartments, he
heard the voice of Midge Prentice long before he saw her.

A cheerful unending babble of reminiscence. Joe paused
outside the door and listened, curiously attracted by that little
voice and even more by the reality when he opened the door.
Recognisably the daughter of Dolly Prentice, recognisable
from that old and faded photograph. Though Midge had her
father's dark colouring she had the same upswept eyes, the
same pretty face and the same quality that Kitty had described
as 'elfin'.

The Governor made the introductions and Midge said at
once, 'I'm so glad you're here, Commander. Now you can tell
me what you think! I think it's beautiful! I think it's just what
he will like. What do you think?'

She produced from a box and from its tissue paper wrap-
pings a small ivory statuette. A figurine of an outstandingly
erotic subject. Conventionally, two figures, their eyes half
closed in bliss, were carved in convolute embrace and twisted
ingeniously through 180 degrees at the waist.

'There,' said Midge once more. 'What do you think?'

'I think he will be absolutely charmed,' said Joe, aware that
he was only saying that he would himself be absolutely
charmed. What the austere Prentice would make of it Joe
could only speculate.

'It must have cost a lot of money,' said Uncle George with
resignation.

'Oh, it wasn't too bad,' said Midge. 'I worked it out in pounds as best I could. I think it cost about thirty shillings. They were so nice about it when they saw I was with you from the flag on the car – they just let me sign for it.'

Uncle George began to look a little strained.

They sat down to lunch and Midge's account ran on. She was now describing a fancy dress dance. 'There we were,' she said, 'Betty Bracegirdle and me. She went as a Red Indian and I went as a cowboy. We won the prize easily and we did a lap of honour round the room and everybody cheered!'

'And have you,' asked Joe, 'left a train of broken hearts behind all across Europe?'

'No,' said Midge morosely. 'Not a train. Only one.'

'Tell us about him,' said Nancy as was no doubt expected of her.

'Oh,' said Midge, 'it wasn't a him, it was a her.'

'A her?'

'Yes.' And, with a fluttering of downcast eyelids and a hand theatrically on the heart, 'It was me. My heart was broken. Oh, he was so nice! He taught me to play piquet. If you're on a boat, everybody plays cards in the morning – mostly boring bridge or double boring poker but he taught me to play piquet. We taught other people and after a bit all the best people were playing piquet with us. It was – the fashionable thing to do!' And, to Joe, 'Do you play piquet?'

'Yes,' said Joe, 'as a matter of fact, I do.'

'We must play some time,' said Midge. 'I'm used to dancing on most nights but now he's gone off back to his regiment, leaving me forlorn, eating my heart out. No wonder I look so pale!'

'He's gone back to his regiment? After a tearful parting, no doubt,' said Nancy.

'Oh yes,' said Midge. 'Was there ever such a tearful parting!'

'And this Paladin,' said Uncle George, 'this hero, this maritime Lothario, has he a name?'

'This knight in shining armour!' Midge giggled. 'Oh, he's got a name all right. And if he comes down to see me all will be revealed. He's tall, dark and handsome . . . absolute blissikins! You've no idea! Oh, goodness, I do hope Dad likes him! He ought to!'

Her audience fell silent. All in their different ways were speculating as to how Giles Prentice would receive this unknown officer who seemed to have found his way into the doubtless inflammable heart of Midge Prentice. Midge Prentice, Dolly's daughter. With Dolly's looks and, it would seem, with Dolly's propensities.

After several hours sitting together in Andrew's car, to Nancy and Joe's relief Midge finally fell silent and fell asleep, her head companionably resting on Nancy's shoulder. It was dark when they arrived in Panikhat and when they drew up outside Prentice's bungalow.

A tall and slender figure, Prentice stood illuminated by the advancing headlights with the air of one who had been patiently waiting. Midge fell out of the car and ran towards him. Prentice dropped on one knee with his arms outstretched. Silently Nancy and Joe agreed to stay in the car. They waited until Midge's voluminous luggage had been taken out and transferred to the house then, on a word from Nancy, Naurung slipped in the clutch and the big car stole silently out of the compound leaving Midge and Prentice on the verandah, each with an arm round the other, Midge, predictably, doing all the talking, Prentice all the listening.

'Well,' said Nancy, 'what did you make of that? What did you make of Midge?'

'I thought she was an absolute poppet,' said Joe sentimentally.

'You would!' said Nancy. 'I thought she was an absolute menace! Not Dolly's daughter for nothing!'

'I wonder,' said Joe, 'what Prentice will do to launch her in Panikhat society?'

'I think I can guess! It's Manoli Day for the regiment on Friday. It's always held on the third Friday in March. Silly sort of thing really but in the Sikh War the regiment were, I must think, caught with their pants down and had to turn out in the middle of the night mounted any old how in their pyjamas – a sort of midnight steeplechase. It was, in fact, quite a gallant episode and they did whatever it was they were called upon to do (I don't know the details) and ever since then they've given a ragtime dance on the anniversary of Manoli Day. And the proceedings are followed by a sort of ragtime steeplechase. It used to be quite a dangerous ride – still is, I suppose – and someone got dreadfully injured one year. Since then they've restricted the numbers – six or eight or something. Names picked from a hat by the Colonel.

'Tell you what – I'll invite Prentice and Midge to dinner before the dance. I'll invite you too. Young Easton and Smythe seem quite jolly – I'll ask them. Young company for Midge. Perhaps I'll ask Kitty to balance the numbers. She'll certainly be intrigued to see Dolly Prentice mark two! I'll see what I can fix. Yes, come to the dinner and come to the dance.'

Joe sighed. 'And what must I wear for this horrible entertainment of yours? Pyjamas?'

'No, no! Mess dress. Your white jacket, blue cummerbund, black tie, mess trousers over boots with box spurs – just the usual. Don't worry – we'll provide the pyjamas!'

Chapter Sixteen

JOE HAD NOT slept well. The journey to Calcutta had tired his body but it was the evidence he had turned up and the new theories beginning to bubble in his mind that kept him awake. And there was something unidentifiably alarming in the figure of Midge Prentice. Something she had done or said had, at a subconscious level, left him in dread for her. Or was it something Kitty had said?

He plodded his way through the night, irritated to an equal degree by his thoughts and by the mosquito bites from Calcutta. In a despairing effort to cool himself he thought about his flat in Chelsea, its large windows open and a chill March breeze blowing through. There would be a thick mist over the Thames, there might even be the remains of snow clinging to the rooftops and, for a moment before he drifted into sleep, he heard the familiar hooting of a river barge.

But he had awakened to the usual bugle sounds and the noises of the station coming to life. He moved from his warm damp bed into a lukewarm bath and on to breakfast. For once the copious Panikhat breakfast served with clockwork precision at seven o'clock had lost its charm. So it was that, in his mood of indecision, he was glad to receive a chit handed in by a bearer from the office of the Collector and with a disproportionate spurt of excitement he recognised Nancy's handwriting. He read:

Good morning! I have a small – and probably
inconsequential – lead. Want to come and follow
it? If so, parade (mounted) here, as soon as possible. Send acknowledgement by the bearer saying
yes or no. ND.

He scribbled 'Yes' and handed the chit back to the bearer
for return to Nancy. He finished dressing and sent for his
horse. 'Sent for his horse'! How easy it was and how
beguiling!

He rattled his way through Panikhat, familiarly acknowledging several people as he passed, and dismounted at the
Drummonds' bungalow. A syce was walking a grey pony up
and down in the drive. Nancy appeared with a wave on the
verandah.

'Morning, Joe!' she said. 'The burra sahib is in the kutcherry.'

'Indeed? And I am here,' said Joe. 'For me, to hear is to obey.'

Nancy sat down on the step of the verandah and gestured
to Joe to join her. 'There may be nothing in this,' she said,
'and in the back of my mind is the thought that there isn't
anything in it so don't be too hopeful. But it's Naurung. He
never stops! He's located one of the ferrymen, one of the witnesses of the death of Alicia. He's long retired from the ferries
and is farming. It's not far away, at a little place called Lasra
Kot. It's about ten miles away and has the advantage of being
rather a nice ride. Are you on?'

'Truly,' said Joe, and he meant it, 'I can't think of any way
I'd rather spend the day. Time we got away from this place for
a few minutes.'

'Well, as I say, there may be nothing in it, but . . .' She gave
him a level and considering look. 'I don't suppose we'll waste
the day, do you?'

She called over her shoulder and a bearer appeared with a
small square basket on a strap.

'What on earth's that?' said Joe.

'Oh, very British! We're having a picnic lunch. No Lyons Corner House where we're going! Come on and say hello to Andrew.'

They made their way into the Collector's office where they found him in shirt-sleeves with clerks taking dictation in attendance, each simultaneously, one in Hindustani, one in English. Joe was impressed. 'That's very clever,' he said. 'I couldn't do that!'

Andrew greeted him warmly. 'Joe! Good morning! If you're really lazy – and I am – you don't write letters, you dictate them and if you're clever – and I am – you dictate two at once. I've even been known to dictate three! Actually, we've been doing this for so long, I just stammer a bit and these chaps put it into embarrassingly Augustan prose. So – you're off into the mofussil, are you? I've already said this to Nancy and I'll repeat it to you – don't sit on a snake, don't fall over a cliff, don't cross a river, don't have a bath – and you oughtn't to come to, er, serious harm. If you're not back in a fortnight I'll send a search party.' And to Nancy, 'Where did you say you were going?'

Nancy told him.

'Worse places to be,' said the Collector comfortably. 'Wish I could come with you.' He took Nancy's hand in his, kissed it, patted her affectionately on the bottom as she stood beside him. Not for the first time, Joe's heart turned over as he saw them so friendly, so humorous and so attuned.

'I really loved him,' Nancy had said.

'And she still does,' Joe finished to himself.

They turned north together and rode up the muddy river bank until they encountered a tributary to the main river where they splashed through a shallow ford. On all sides people working in the fields getting in the rice harvest stopped with smiling faces to acknowledge them as they rode by. On every hand, bullock-drawn ploughs were at work across the fields to which millet and barley and rice contributed each a different shade of green in a timeless patchwork.

'You can see why they call it the Land of Rivers. This is the India I love,' said Nancy. 'Do you wonder I wanted to get back to it from France?'

'It certainly isn't Calcutta,' said Joe.

'No. This is where we can really do some good. We stand between the farmer and his landlord, and, all the time, see that justice is done, you know. Keep the beady-eyed money-lender at arm's length with a government-managed loan scheme. Andrew introduced that. And later today you'll see the beginnings of his irrigation system. And you're right – it isn't Calcutta. I love it. I really do. I dream sometimes that I'm going to be taken away again. And wake up in a sweat. Oh, Joe – if only we could lift this shadow! If only!'

As usual when Nancy began with shining eyes to talk about India, Joe's natural contrariness was roused. He opened his mouth to challenge what she said about the beneficent British attitude to the tenant farmers by remind-ing her that the hugely rich zamindars had been granted their enormous estates by the British themselves. If they were now struggling to rectify a state of affairs which had got out of hand they had none to blame but themselves and the peasant farmers were their luckless victims. If there was any crime in Bengal, it had its roots in social injustice of this kind. But he remained silent. What right had he, a six months' expert, to challenge the views of someone born and brought up here, someone who was dealing with the reali-ties of life from day to day?

The road narrowed and began to climb and the heat of the day began to build. Nancy led the way with confidence and Joe fell in behind. Looking at her from the crown of her wide-brimmed hat, following the line of her slender back, its silk shirt beginning to cling in the heat, her soft and slender bottom outlined rather than concealed by well-cut jodhpurs, 'Love,' thought Joe.

'I could fall in love. Perhaps I have. But this is love for a day and if I was very lucky perhaps, love for two days. And anyway, she could be my sister. We don't need to say much to each other. She could be – and indeed she is – my lover. If everything were different, if all the cards were dealt again, if this and if that and if the other, for God's sake, she could be my wife.'

A stab of desire swept through him and his hands tightened. Indignant at this rough handling, Bamboo skittered aside and even humped his back.

Nancy looked back over her shoulder. 'Can't the squire from Scotland Yard keep his seat?' she asked derisively.

The scrub-covered hillside gave way to occasional stands of trees, thickening as their way led on until they were riding, side by side now, down a jungle path, the alternate shade and sunshine illuminating Nancy's face and casting it into darkness. Flights of raucous green parrots flashed across their path, mercifully ignored by patient Bamboo. Monkeys gibbered a strident warning of their approach, fleeing showily through the tree canopy overhead, and at times Joe fancied he could make out larger, darker shapes dimly imagined in the shadowy foliage at the foot of the trees but decided that if Nancy was not prepared to give them her attention, nor should he.

Topping a jungle-clad ridge, their road turned downwards towards a village presided over by a rhythmically creaking water wheel, turning and turning and lifting buckets to send a flush of water down the many irrigation channels. Thirty or so mud-walled houses with thatched roofs huddled companionably together, set out to no obvious plan and with no eye for drainage or ventilation as far as Joe could make out, but scattered, it seemed, haphazardly about a central square in

which stood a venerable peepul tree. In the windless day spires
of smoke rose from many households, bringing with them the
sharp smell of dung fires and cooking.

Chickens ran noisily about, occasionally being ejected force-
fully through the low, dark doorways. A fat brown child staggered on short legs to the edge of the village and squatted with
complete unconcern in the dust. As they reined in their horses
and stood waiting, a cascade of children poured out to greet
them and then, overcome with shyness, stopped dead. But they
were quick to respond to Nancy's greeting and soon surrounded them in a chattering group. One of them broke off a
stalk of sugar cane and offered it to Bamboo, others ran back to
the nearest house, to emerge proudly with a tray of sweet cakes,
and after a while a woman came forward with a bowl of milk.

'If this was all there was to it,' Joe thought, 'I could be
happy here.'

'Is this Lasra Kot?' he asked. 'Is this where we're to meet the
ferryman?'

'It's Lasra Kot, yes, but we're not here to meet a ferryman.'

'But didn't your note say . . .?'

'I did but it wasn't true about Naurung's message. There
was no message. I made it up.'

'But why?'

'I thought we had deserved a day off from police work. I
wanted you to see India as it really is. I know you have no time
for it and are rather desperate to go home but I just didn't
want you to disappear with Calcutta and the station as your
lasting, your *only*, impressions of the country. The station is
unreal. It's more British than Britain, an invention, a parade.
Calcutta is unreal – two extremes of wealth and poverty, both
disgusting to a man I am beginning to think of as seeing as I
do in spite of his being a policeman.'

A young girl in a bright red-bordered sari came hurrying
from one of the houses and spoke to Nancy in what Joe
guessed to be Bengali.

'This is my friend Supriya,' said Nancy. 'And there are other people here I ought to see. Why don't you tie the horses and take a seat? I shan't be very long.'

She indicated a small temple, little bigger than a summer house. 'Take a seat over there.' She unpacked some small parcels from her saddle bag and Joe led the ponies away to stand in the shade.

Gladly he went over to the temple to sit in the shade himself. He lit a cigarette and watched as a girl in an azure sari emerged from one of the houses and spread a carpet under the peepul tree and invited Nancy to sit.

At once a shy procession began to form up. Mothers – themselves little older than schoolgirls – with babies in hand or babies at the breast, infants tugging at their skirts, began to gather round Nancy. Each child in turn was led up for her inspection. She looked at eyes, she looked at ears, she felt limbs, lifted draperies and ran an exploring hand over fat brown stomachs, the whole operation accompanied by gales of giggles from the children and laughter from their mothers. From time to time she took a tin of ointment from her pack and gently spread it over an affected part; she applied drops to sore eyes; with a skilled hand and a tight cotton noose, watched by the interested Supriya, she dealt with the ticks that she explained were endemic in the valley.

'Conjunctivitis and diarrhoea,' said Nancy over their heads to Joe in a businesslike voice, 'those are our main problems. You can't teach these people anything about "personal hygiene" – they're probably the cleanest people in the world – but, oh boy! are there things they should learn about culinary hygiene and if only I could teach the children not to do their tuppences all over the place we'd be half-way to solving their problems. Still, I think I'm making progress and Supriya here is becoming my valuable assistant.'

She turned and spoke to Supriya who blushed and wriggled, bowed and salaamed with much gratification. Joe watched her with tenderness as, after each inspection, Nancy planted an affectionate kiss on each brown cheek which was immediately proffered to her. Briefly Joe remembered her speaking of the American soldier: 'He had, in a way, become my baby.' Were these small brown children elected to fill that gap?

As her inspection drew to a close, Nancy was obviously subjected to a barrage of questions most of which seemed to relate to Joe himself.

'They assume,' said Nancy, 'that you are my husband. And look, Joe – seriously now – for the purposes of this conversation we have to be married. The idea of an unmarried lady in the deep jungle with an unmarried gentleman would be incomprehensible and impossible.'

'Isn't that rather awkward?' said Joe. 'Supposing the Collector should call?'

'Oh, he often does. They assume he's my father so that doesn't present a problem. But the fact that we have no children does. That they can't understand, and perhaps you'd like to know that they assume that it's all your fault!' She turned and, speaking in Bengali, obviously had this confirmed in a shrill chorus.

'One of their problems,' she said, 'is that they've never seen such a *white* sahib before. It's all right though – they guess that you come from the far north. They assume the scar on your forehead is the mark of a wild animal, a panther perhaps. Oh, no – there's going to be a legend about this!' And judging by the flood of questions which ensued and the peals of laughter which Nancy's responses elicited, the legend was growing.

'I don't mind,' thought Joe.

'Aspirin and quinine,' Nancy said in an aside to Joe as she handed packages to Supriya. 'I've taught her how to administer them. They're beginning to trust me. They call me in now for eye problems, ticks and tapeworms and for childbirth. It was difficult at first to make them understand that it's not wise to wait for four days when a girl is in labour. Trouble is, they think it'll turn out all right if they say enough spells. The first baby I delivered here was four days overdue, it was the girl's first baby and it was *my* first baby if you see what I mean. Terrifying! I added my prayers to their spells and got busy. They worked on the top end, combing her hair and plaiting charms into it, and I worked on what you might call the business end. It was a boy and they both survived. And now they think I'm very good at delivering boys and if they call me in it's likely to be a boy. Supriya is able to help me now and her little sister, Malobika, is keen to learn too. So maybe I'm having a beneficent impact, or something of the sort.'

More sticky cakes were produced from one of the huts and another bowl of milk. Nancy explained that as a child she would not have been allowed cakes or sweets. 'What a lot of nonsense!' she said. 'Mind you, if they'd been lying open in the bazaar with all the flies in Bengal on them it would be a different story, but up here what harm can it do?'

They took their farewells at last, remounted and, accompanied by a contingent of children to the edge of the village, they turned their ponies to follow a track which led to the stream that fed the village water wheel.

'Well, what did you think of the real India?'

'I thought Lasra Kot was charming. But I wouldn't call it the real India.'

'No?' she asked in surprise. 'Then what is?'

He shook his head, wishing he had not so casually introduced a false note into their day, but Nancy waited for him to go on. 'I've been spending my lonely evenings in Calcutta reading, trying to understand this strange place where I've fetched up. I came across an Indian writer called Sri Aurobindo . . .'

The tightening of Nancy's lips gave away her opinion of Joe's reading matter.

'Yes, I know he was imprisoned by the British – all the best people are at some time or other! – and he's generally

considered a trouble maker, an insurgent, whatever word
you're using at the moment, but he had something to say
which has stayed with me – "We do not belong to past dawns
but to the noon of the future." Naurung, his father, their
friends, they are the noon of the future, if you like. Not a
romantic vision perhaps and certainly not a reassuring one
but, for me, that's where the real India lies.'

He instantly regretted having spoken the truth. Her look of
shining confidence was for a moment dimmed by foreboding
and he feared that he might have spoiled their day. But she
recovered her good humour quickly and said cheerfully,
'Then I haven't shown you enough. Come this way. We'll take
the road into the hills.'

They went on to climb beside a rushing stream. The track
became more stony and led between great creeper-clad boul-
ders until it ended by a pool and a waterfall.

The tension between them was by now extreme.

Nancy threw her leg over the horse's head and slid to the
ground, leading him to the water to drink.

'I'm hot,' said Joe and, feeling gently round the back of
Nancy's neck, 'you're hot too. Can you think of any reason
why we shouldn't swim – I mean – is it safe?'

'Safe?' said Nancy, breathlessly. 'Oh, I think so. As high as
this it's very cold and surely safe to drink.'

'I didn't mean that,' said Joe. 'What about water snakes?'

'Well, if you get in first and splash about a bit it ought to be
safe for me.'

She turned about and stood very close to Joe, her hands on
his shoulders. 'I have never swum alone with a man in my life
and, come to think of it, I've never undressed in broad daylight with a man either. Perhaps this hasn't meant much to
you – I've no idea of your private life – but I'll tell you, it's
meant a very great deal to me. More I expect than you could
conceivably imagine. And we aren't within miles of the end of
our investigation but I can see that there will be an end and

then you'll go back to your London flat and I'll go back – I've never been away – to my life as the Collector's wife. And happy enough to be that. But something important will have happened to me. Tell me, if you can, will you be sad when we have to say goodbye to each other? Because goodbye is what we're going to have to say. I shan't die but I shall be sad and I'd like you to be a bit sad too.'

'Nancy, you don't know the half of it!' said Joe. 'The moment hasn't come but I know it's coming fast and I shall be very sad. This is the Land of Regrets all right! And I think you're wonderful . . . I think you're very beautiful. But much more than that, I think you're bright and clever and brave and . . .' There was a long pause. 'I'd trust you with anything. I'd trust you with my life.'

'That's a very nice thing to say. I shall treasure it – when it came to the point, you'd trust me with anything. What more could anyone expect to hear? And I'd say exactly the same thing to you.'

For reply, Joe kissed her for a very long time, clumsily trying to unbutton her shirt as he did so.

'Come on, Joe! For a man with your savoir vivre you're a terrible unbuttoner! Let me do it. You could be unbuttoning yourself if you like,' she added and then, in a conversational tone, 'These have to be the least erotic clothes we could have chosen! And you haven't seen it all yet! Not knowing – or rather not being certain – how the day was going to turn out, I'm wearing the most sensible pair of knickers I possess! Just the thing for riding but . . .' her voice trailed away while they kissed each other some more, and she finally concluded in a slightly strangled voice, '. . . but not what I'd choose for dalliance.'

'And I'm not dressed for dalliance either,' said Joe. 'In the best of circumstances, it takes me a very long time to get out of these jodhpurs!'

They emerged at last, naked, and hand in hand on the edge of the pool.

'Swim first?' said Joe.

'Yes,' said Nancy, glancing down at him in some embarrassment, 'but only if you can contain yourself.'

'All clear of snakes, are we?'

Nancy stepped off the edge of the rock they were standing on, straight into deep water, and Joe jumped after her. The water was surprisingly cold. Nancy looked down at him once more. 'Not such a big boy, after all,' she said. 'Does that always happen in cold water?'

He looked down with appreciation at Nancy, turned to jade green under the water. 'You look like a bronze statue,' he said. 'Do Indians have Naiads? If so, you will always be the Naiad of this pool and I will always leave a bit of my heart here.'

'Yes,' said Nancy, 'I believe you will.'

They swam the circuit of their pool; they stood for a moment under the waterfall.

'Bronze, ivory and coral,' said Joe. 'Bronze curls, ivory skin . . .'

'And coral?'

'Coral nipples,' said Joe, stooping to kiss them.

'The cold water shrinkage system doesn't seem to be working,' Nancy said. 'Time to be ashore.'

Joe made an untidy pile of their clothes and, hand in hand, they sank down on this. Nancy was, to Joe, exotic and familiar; exotic because strange, familiar from their night in Calcutta, tasting as he had remembered and smelling as sweet as he had remembered. They made love with much passion, punctuated by Nancy who squeaked an inconsequential question requiring no answer. At last they fell apart from each other and lay back, each wrapped in silent thought.

After a few minutes Nancy began to stir and abruptly sat up. 'Tell you something, Joe,' she said. 'I'm hungry!'

'Good Lord! That's right. So am I! I'd forgotten – we've got a perfectly good picnic.'

They settled together to lay out their picnic on a cool flat rock, with appreciative murmurs from Joe as he unpacked sandwiches, two bottles of the inevitable India Pale Ale and a mango each accompanied by a silver fruit knife and fork.

They ate in companionable silence, neither feeling the need to fill the gaps with inconsequential chatter, each lost in thoughts for the moment unsharable.

'No coffee, I'm afraid,' said Nancy at last.

'Who wants coffee?' said Joe, leaning over to lick an errant drop of mango juice from between her breasts.

'I do, actually,' she replied. 'But there's something I want more than coffee and that's you.' Flushing slightly at her own boldness, she added hurriedly, 'Look, I'm not sure how men . . . how you . . . work. Is this all right?'

'It depends who you're with,' said Joe. 'I'll tell you – with you it's abundantly all right!'

As they rode slowly back together Nancy said, 'Tell me, Joe – I don't know anything about you. Where do you come from? What's your world? What's your family?'

'I wondered when you'd get around to checking my pedigree!' he said easily. 'I'm from Selkirk, the River Etrick, a place called Drumaulbin on the Borders. My father has a place there. It's quite big – three farms really – but even so there isn't enough to support two sons in affluence and I left it to my older brother to take care of and went to read Law in Edinburgh. But then the war came along and I joined the Scots Fusiliers. I and half a dozen lads from Drumaulbin all joined up together and set off south. Blue bonnets over the border, you might say.'

'But you didn't go back to the Law after the war?'

'No. By that time I'd got so identified with the Fusilier Jocks I wanted to do something for them which I didn't think I could do as a douce Writer for the Signet, called to the Scottish bar, so, after a certain amount of thought, I joined the police.'

'Now why on earth should you do that? I mean, it's not the place where you'd expect to find a gentleman, is it?'

'Well, I thought, in general, boys like the ones I was fighting with have a pretty rotten deal one way or another. I thought I could do more good as a bobby than as a lawyer.'

'What nonsense! Men don't join the police to do good!'

'Don't judge us all by the example of Bulstrode! But you're partly right. I had another compulsion. I was wounded in the trenches – shot through the shoulder . . .'

'I noticed! Someone did a good repair.'

'But while I was away from the front recuperating they kept me busy. I was given intelligence work to do. Interrogation of prisoners. I found I was rather good at it and when I came out I wanted to do more. There's been a big shake-up in the police force since the war. Everyone has a picture of friendly but stern blue-caped bobbies ticking little boys off for stealing apples but it's not like that at all. There are so many changes, so many developments – fingerprinting, telegraph communication, the flying squad – and I want to be there in the forefront pushing the force in the right direction!'

'Goodness! I hadn't realised you were such a missionary!'

'Missionary?' Joe laughed. 'I believe it's time the police force stopped being a servant of the aristocracy and became the guardian of society and that sounds very pompous so I suppose you're right. I am a sort of social missionary.'

'You must have felt you were coming back through time being sent to Bengal?'

'I've loved working with the Bengal Police. They're clever, eager and effective. There's nothing I'd like more than a squad of Sikh officers to take back to London with me! Give me twenty Naurungs! That would shake up Whitehall!'

'So your time hasn't entirely been wasted here?'

'No. I suddenly found myself locked in the arms of a dusky charmer and minded never to return. I mean – you don't pick up a timeless houri on every corner in life's road. Make the most of your opportunities, I say,' said Joe lightly. 'Is there anything else I can tell you about Sandilands of Drumaulbin?'

Nancy gave him a searching look, smiled and shook her head in uncharacteristic confusion. She kicked her pony and drew ahead, leaving Joe to watch her slender figure through narrowed and speculative eyes.

Chapter Seventeen

As THEY RODE into Panikhat in the late afternoon the air grew still, the glow of the sky deepened as the sun burned its way westward and wreaths of smoke from cooking fires coiled and flattened over the native town.

Joe looked at Nancy, flushed, sunburned and dishevelled. 'Shall I,' he wondered, 'tell her that she's got two buttons undone and the label of her blouse is sticking out? This is a little bit embarrassing, I think. Andrew might well be the nicest man I know and I sometimes think he is but – unless he's a fool, which I think he isn't . . .'

He needn't have worried. As they drew into the Drummond compound, a syce ran up to take the horses and a bearer hurried to Nancy with a note on a silver tray. She read it quickly and said, 'Oh, what a shame. Andrew's been called away to Goshapur. There's a row brewing apparently between a landlord and some of his tenants. He won't be back before sunset. Can I offer you a drink, Joe?'

Joe courteously refused, limp with relief that he would not yet have to look Andrew Drummond in the eye, and started to make his way back to his bungalow. Carefully keeping to the shady side of the street, he walked on, leading Bamboo. His thoughts were interrupted by swiftly trotting hooves coming up behind him and by an authoritative female voice.

'Good afternoon, Commander. Or – as formality seems to have been thrown to the winds – good afternoon, Joe.'

Joe turned about to meet the calculating eye of Mrs Kitson-Masters. The last thing he wanted to do, having narrowly avoided an inspection by Andrew, was to find himself the subject of scrutiny by Kitty. He smiled and bowed.

'Kitty!' he said. 'Exactly the person I most wanted to see!'

'You look as though you've had an exhausting day,' she said.

'I have. Are you on your way home, Kitty? Good. If I may, I'll come with you.'

'Informality on informality! I will look forward to receiving you.'

She drove on and Joe followed her round the corner, into Curzon Street and down her front drive.

'Now, tell me how I can help with the investigation. At least I assume that this has to do with the investigation, though I would prefer to think you were seeking me out for the charm of my company.'

'Both,' said Joe, settling on the verandah while a jug of lemonade appeared on the table between them. 'It seems rather an odd question but – as far as you know – did Alicia Simms-Warburton suffer from a fear of water, a fear of drowning? I mean a deep-seated, out of the ordinary fear?'

Kitty looked at him in astonishment for a moment then replied slowly, 'Yes, as a matter of fact, she did. A week or so before she died it was Panikhat Week . . . the station puts on lots of entertainments to celebrate the end of the working year before people start to go off to the hills, visitors come from other stations – you've just missed it this year – and that year someone had organised a regatta on the river just beyond Giles' place. "Henley on the Hooghly" or something like that, they'd called it. The local villagers are superb boatmen. They'd provided the boats and decorated them with flowers and everyone had a wonderful time – apart from Alicia! She refused to have anything to do with it. Made rather a silly fuss, I remember. Wouldn't put a foot in a boat. Yes, you're right, Joe. A phobia, I think you'd call it.'

'That's exactly what I'd call it. And did Dolly Prentice suffer from a phobia and, in particular, did she have a phobia about fire? Was she frightened of fire? I mean to an unusual degree? It might be significant if she was.'

Kitty considered for a while.

'No. Sorry, Joe. She never spoke of it,' she said at last. 'Fire is a hazard of course and if you've got a thatched roof as many of us have it's a perpetual worry. We're all afraid of fire and nothing abnormal about that. But you're looking for more, aren't you? Something unreasonable? I don't remember Dolly ever mentioning . . . Let me think back . . . Oh! Of course! Yes! The buckets! We never spoke of it though some of us did think it rather strange at the time . . . The corridors in Dolly's bungalow were lined with buckets full of water, fire brooms and all that sort of thing. They even kept one behind the door in the drawing-room. Yes, that was surely extraordinary behaviour? I had thought it must have been one of *Giles'* eccentricities – he has enough of those, heaven knows! – and didn't comment. But, you know, he doesn't have buckets of water in his new home so perhaps you're right. Joe, why do you ask?'

'Five out of five,' said Joe grimly. Rather lamely he explained, thinking as he did so that his theories sounded somewhat absurd. But Kitty didn't think so.

Reflecting on this, she said, 'That *is* a sinister aspect. That does argue a bad mind behind this. A sick mind. An evil mind.' She hesitated. 'But whose mind? Joe, the whole of Panikhat must have known at the time – about the buckets, I mean. If I can remember it twelve years on, many people would have been aware of it at the time. I haven't been much help, have I?'

'Oh, I think so,' said Joe. 'Dolly's phobia places her firmly in the group of victims. Now I know that every one of the murdered memsahibs was killed, perhaps not because of, but according to, her own personal fear. It's a common factor but it's not *the* common factor I've been looking for. There's something more – something appalling lurking on the fringes . . .' The dark and dimly perceived jungle shapes of the morning, pacing along with the horses but remaining hidden, watchful, came back to him and he shuddered.

'Joe, it's time to go and have your bath,' said Kitty with a softer note in her voice. 'Then perhaps a good meal at the Club, a sound night's sleep and you may well wake up with the answer in your head.'

This had been the most mysterious day Joe could remember. Firstly, the magic of the ride through the forest and the indelible image of Nancy in a sea of laughing and expectant brown faces, and the unhesitating gift of herself, so sweet, so yielding, so ingenuous and fired by a primitive longing of such force that it was outside Joe's experience. As sleep descended on him he was aroused by a thought. A thought of such complexity that, encumbered by the folds of his mosquito net, he sat up with a jerk, suddenly wide awake.

There was something here that he didn't quite understand. Something, perhaps, that he had understood all along but had not been able to put into words or even into logical thoughts, but he remembered the care with which Uncle George had absented himself from their night in Calcutta; he remembered the grace with which Andrew had sent them off into the forest together, his convenient absence from home on their return, and he began to think, for the first time, of the equivocal role of Andrew in the love affair which was taking place under his eyes.

Andrew. Something struggled in his memory, trying to come to the surface. The Deputy Collector – what was the wretched man's name? – on the night of the dance – Harry Featherstone! – he had bumped into Joe, standing with Nancy, and had said, 'Sorry Andrew!' He had mistaken Joe for Andrew for the good reason that, from behind, they must look very alike. No one could confuse them when seen side by side but there was, he had to admit, a superficial resemblance. Both men were tall, broad-shouldered and of spare build. Both men had dark hair, though Andrew's was now more grey than black. Had Nancy and her uncle seen this similarity when they had set eyes on him in the lecture theatre in Calcutta? Had they discussed it? Had they decided that he would be the perfect man to complete Nancy's schemes? Joe decided that they would not have needed to exchange a word. But both, if his wild idea had any foundation, would have taken precisely the action they had taken.

With a rush of anger, Joe acknowledged that he had been duped. Used. And the anger was swiftly followed by shame and embarrassment. He had assumed that Nancy had found him irresistible and, in the context of her easy-going relationship with her elderly husband, had felt herself free to enjoy an affair with an attractive and vigorous man passing through her life.

On an impulse he kicked himself out of his mosquito net and, equipping himself with a cigarette to ward off marauding night-time mosquitoes, he made his way to his small office and with difficulty lit the kerosene lamp, reaching as he did so for his cipher book. The telegram he had in mind could not be sent from the station en clair.

After a sweaty half-hour he had encoded and despatched the following to a colleague at the Yard.

9291A JOHN STOP NEED TO KNOW EXTENT OF WAR-
TIME INJURY SUSTAINED BY CAPTAIN A J DRUMMOND
23RD RAJPUTANA RIFLES 1918 STOP SANDILANDS

It would be three o'clock in the afternoon at New Scotland Yard and Joe imagined John Moore in the middle of his day, cursing, ringing the War Office, ringing them again and wearily proceeding to encode his reply. Joe realised he probably couldn't expect to receive this for two or three days at the best and, feverishly, he returned to bed.

To his astonishment he awoke to find that, overnight, he had received a reply in cipher sent round to him by the Panikhat telegraph office at about five o'clock in the morning. Joe decoded it and read the short contents again and again.

> 9291B WARTIME INJURIES EXTENSIVE STOP QUOTE INTESTINAL CHAOS UNQUOTE STOP RIGHT LEG MULTIPLE FRACTURES STOP MOORE

What did 'intestinal chaos' mean? Very severe abdominal injuries amounting perhaps to mutilation? Unseeing, the buff telegram form in his hand, Joe stared out of the window. 'So that's it. There was an agenda. A design that didn't include me! Though, in truth, I suppose, I was central to the plot, though not a party to it. God, I've been naive! And what do I say now? Do I challenge them? Do I say, "Nancy, you're a scheming hussy! Jardine, you are a crafty old bastard! Andrew, you are a scandalous conniver!"? What *do* I do?'

The answer came easily to his mind. 'Nothing. You go with it. If this is what Nancy wants, this is what Nancy can have in so far as it's up to me. Perhaps I even ought to be flattered. Of course I ought to be flattered. And when the other emotions have rolled away flattered is what I'll feel. But for the moment, my self-esteem – my ego, as Freud would have it! – has taken a bruising . . . And maybe that's no bad thing!'

Chapter Eighteen

HAVING HALF AN hour to kill before Nancy's dinner party, Joe made his way over to the mess to fill his cigarette case from one of the many boxes always charged with the fat oval cigarettes bearing the regimental badge and supplied by Fribourg and Treyer of London. He found the table laid for four only; evidently all others were dining at the Manoli dinner or, like himself, with Nancy, and the dining-room was in darkness. He was greeted from the gloom by a friendly voice.

'Oh, Sandilands Sahib, sir. Good evening. May I help you in any particular?'

It was the voice of Suman Chatterjee, a Bengali babu and the regimental clerk. Also, it seemed, the mess steward, since he was seated at a table in a small office surrounded by mess chits in neat piles. Joe had met him once or twice in the mess. He liked his unswerving affability, he admired his monumental physique but, above all, he appreciated his pedantic, idiomatic and heavily accented English.

'Do you ever get any time off, Babu-ji?' he asked.

'Oh, sir, this is not work! This is fascination! I like to keep everything shipshape and Bristol fashion. I like to make sure that it all adds up and here I am adding.'

Feeling that something more than a polite interest was called for, Joe said, 'What's your system, Suman?'

'Oh, sir, it works like this, you see: the officers sign chits daily. Oh, what bloody awful handwriting! They come to me and I enter them in a book and send out the mess bills promptly on the first of every month. My predecessor was – dear me! – a very muddled citizen. It took me the deuce of a long time to sort out the mess he had left behind but now I can tell you exactly who had what, when and how many. See – here is yourself: Sandilands J. (H). H stands for honorary member of the mess and here you see Smythe Sahib was absent. I put (Abs.) next to his name. Oh, no, this is a good system.'

Joe admired the fluent copperplate handwriting and said sincerely, 'Suman, do you ever wish you could use your talents more widely? You should be in government – you are a monument of neatness and clearly a genius with figures.'

'I wouldn't,' said Suman with a big smile and a wide gesture, 'change my job for a lackh of rupees! I am after all a member of a proud regiment and indeed I am hoping to write a regimental history. Besides, who would keep everything in apple pie order if I retired? I hear everybody from greatest to least say – oh, ten times a day – "Ask Chatterjee, he's sure to know." And, mostly, I do!'

'How far back do the records go?' asked Joe with no particular interest.

'To 1898,' said Suman immediately, 'when Staverdale Sahib commanded the regiment. But in my care, for fifteen years.'

'So, if you wanted to tell who'd had two glasses of port after dinner on November the 18th 1899 you could tell me?'

'Not as good as that but since I have been running things, certainly!'

'Let me,' said Joe, 'pick a date at random. What about this day, March the 17th, let's say in 1910?'

'Oh, that is no problem. That was in my time.'

He rose to his feet and, lifting portly arms with difficulty above his head, he fetched down from a high shelf a tall account book on the spine of which there was a strip of sticking plaster with '1908–1910' written on it. He placed it on the table in front of Joe and began to leaf through the pages. To Joe's fanciful imagination it seemed that from the dry pages an aura of wine-soaked corks, brandy and Trichinopoly cigars arose.

'Here you are, you see,' said Suman proudly. 'Here we are . . . March . . . and the seventeenth. It was a Saturday. Ah. Oh. That night . . .You have not chosen a good night. There was hardly anybody in the mess that night. The others had all gone to some jollification. In March there are many jollifications – it is the end of the season when many memsahibs go away to the hills. And here they are, sir. Five diners that night.'

He pushed the book over to Joe's elbow.

'Not very many but drinking quite a considerable amount, you see, sir. Oh, you could say the port was flowing that night!'

Joe did not respond. He was looking at the mess record for the night twelve years ago when Dolly Prentice had been burned to death. Predictably Prentice's name was not there. He had been in Calcutta. But five other men had been present.

Their names drew his astonished gaze and fixed it on the page. He read again and muttered the list under his breath. Major Harold Carmichael, Dr Philip Forbes, Captain John Simms-Warburton, Subaltern William Somersham and, lastly, a name he did not recognise, a Subaltern Richard Templar.

'Is all well, sir? May I assist you further?' asked Suman, concerned at Joe's long silence.

'Yes. Oh, please. Help me to understand the shorthand, will you? This says "Carmichael 5-p"?'

'That would be five glasses of port, sir. And here we have Forbes Doctor Sahib three glasses of port and 1-b that is one glass of brandy. Somersham Sahib, 4-p, that is four glasses of port and Simms-Warburton Sahib three glasses of port and one of c.b. – cherry brandy.'

'It must have been quite a jolly evening,' said Joe.

'Oh yes, sir, very boozy, to be sure!'

'And here, what does (A) stand for?'

'Ah, yes, that would be the young sahib Templar, sir. It stands for "attached". I remember him well. He was spending some time on attachment here before being gazetted and going off to join his regiment on the frontier. Very nice young gentleman, sir, and, as you see, not at all boozy – just two glasses of port.'

'Very abstemious, not rich enough perhaps to keep up with Bateman's Horse?'

'Very likely, sir.'

A trickle of excitement was running along Joe's spine. He ran his eye down the list again. What he was looking at was a list, a list of soon-to-be-widowers. The first four men on the list had all lost their wives roughly on the anniversary of this night. The fifth was an unknown quantity. If the wild theory Joe was beginning to form was to be proven, this fifth man, this Richard Templar, might hold the key to the mystery. And Somersham? Surely he would be able to throw some light on this fateful grouping? Joe was struck by a shattering thought. This grisly party was held well before the war – Somersham was not married then, had in all likelihood not even met his future wife – Peggy must have been all of ten years old at the time.

His mind scurried over the information he had read and listened to over the last few days. On this particular day in 1910 Carmichael and Forbes only were married. Their wives had been the first on this list to die. Simms-Warburton had not married until the summer of 1912 and his wife had been drowned in the following March. And then came the gap. Not, as he – as everybody – had naturally supposed, because of the war but because there were no more wives left to this group! And then after a period of eight years, Somersham was promoted to Captain. Kitty's awful little adage came to mind – 'Captains may marry'. This one had taken up the privilege and, the following March, he too was a widower.

He had searched; Nancy had searched. The Naurungs, father and son, were searching their minds and searching physically to find a link – anything, anything in the world that would bind these victims together and to the bloody series of crimes. And could this be the link? A link which was not through the women at all but through their husbands? Could the fact that they had dined together on the night of the first tragedy seriously be held to be their common cause? Was their meeting casual? Was there some deeper, more sinister meaning behind their drunken dinner?

Joe recited the names to himself again, Suman looking on in puzzlement, acknowledging by his silence that he understood the entertaining enquiry had taken on a new and serious dimension.

'Carmichael, Forbes, Simms-Warburton, Somersham and young Templar,' he muttered. Nothing obviously in common; completely different in character and ages. Not at all an outwardly congenial grouping.

A devastating thought came to mind. Suppose all these men had been Dolly's lovers and Prentice was following some hideous Pathan custom by killing off their wives? No sooner had the idea formed than he dismissed it. Why would they all be dining together and on the very night Dolly died? And even his vivid imagination could not couple Dolly with the deeply unattractive Carmichael or the 'nice young gentleman' Templar.

And then there was the question of Prentice. The first to be bereaved, the rogue of the group, the one unaccounted for. Where did he fit in with these other fellows? If at all? He too was a March widower. Of the listed men, Somersham was on the station somewhere. He would interview him again in the morning. But, meanwhile, there was another witness, immediately available.

'Were you here on this night, Babu-ji?' Joe asked.

'Oh, yes. In humble capacity then. Assistant clerk only on the strength because of the muddle. But I was there and I remember the fire. The fire at Colonel Prentice's bungalow. It was very dreadful. I remember many things . . .' His voice trailed away.

'What do you principally remember?' Joe asked. 'In a sentence, if you can, what was important about that evening?'

'Sheer chaos, sir! Sheer bloody chaos! Templar Sahib and the RMO saying, "Come on you chaps!" Carmichael Sahib shouting, "Mind your business! Stay put!" Bugles calling, shouts and even shots if you can believe. And all the time the Greys were too tiddly to think. They were watching the fire from the verandah as though fireworks, sir. Simms-Warburton Sahib called for a cherry brandy to be served to him on the verandah while he watched. In the end the doctor Forbes Sahib broke ranks and called for his horse. They all went down to the bungalow but – too late. And Memsahib Prentice dead. A fairly disgraceful affair. But we do not say that because we are shoulder to shoulder, knee to knee as good comrades should be. I can say this to you because it was a long time ago and you are one of us, after all. But Carmichael came back and – I thought at the time – looking like a dead man and said not a word but went straight to his bungalow. And Templar Sahib (he was only a boy; shaving every third day his bearer told me) was crying in the night.'

More than anything, Joe wanted a quiet moment or, not so much a quiet moment, a quiet half-hour to digest what Suman had just told him. He wanted to talk to Nancy. He looked into Suman's face, smiling but concerned, and he wanted to go through the whole of the evening – March the 17th 1910 – in detail, but a glance at his watch told him that he was due – almost overdue – at Nancy's dinner party and with profuse and repeated expressions of mutual regard, they parted.

Deeply puzzled by all that he had heard, Joe turned away to walk to Nancy's bungalow but as he stepped across the maidan he was arrested by a thought. A disturbing thought, a terrifying thought. Templar! What about Templar? Where was he? Was he still alive? Above all, was he married? The only member of the fatal dinner party unaccounted for, the only member of that fatal dinner party who might have a wife and, if he had a wife, would she not now – to complete the pattern – be in danger? How the hell would you find out whether an obscure army officer was married or not at eight o'clock on a Saturday evening?

A happy thought came to him – Uncle George! The omniscient Uncle George with access to information of all sorts. Telephone? Where was the nearest telephone? There was a telephone in the dim little cubicle off the vestibule to the officers' mess. Did it work? Joe realised that he had never made a telephone call in India before.

He made his way to the cubicle and in the dimness located a small wooden box with a handle. Without much confidence he picked up the telephone and wound the handle. To his surprise and delight almost at once a clipped and efficient Eurasian voice said, 'Number please?'

'I don't know the number,' Joe began. 'I want to contact the Acting Governor of Bengal in Calcutta. Sir George Jardine.'

The reply came back at once, 'I have the number here, sir.'

Scotland Yard could not have been more efficient. After an interval a smooth English voice picked up. 'Calcutta Residence.'

'I want,' said Joe, 'to speak to the Governor. Commander Sandilands here. It could be urgent.'

'Sir George is just going into dinner,' said the voice coldly.

'Then,' said Joe firmly, 'you'll have to see what you can do. As quickly as possible, please.'

Joe overheard the ensuing conversation.

'Who?'

'A Commander Sandilands.'

'Oh! Oh? Put me through.'

And after a further series of clicks and purrings, the crackling voice of Uncle George. 'Sandilands! Is this important? Make it as quick as you can, will you? I'm just going in to dinner.'

'It might be important,' said Joe, 'and I will explain later why I want to know but – a subaltern, Richard Templar, was stationed in Panikhat in 1910. On attachment. He joined his regiment on the north-west frontier. I urgently need to know whether he is married.'

Uncle George laughed comfortably. 'This is your lucky evening, Sandilands! Hold on, will you?' And, in an aside, 'Freddy! Just a moment, Freddy! Tell me – an officer – Templar. Serving on the frontier. Do you know him? You do? Good. Serving with 10GR. You were brigaded with them? Tell me then – is he married? No. You're sure?'

Uncle George turned back to Joe. 'No, he's not married. I just managed to catch hold of a friend who's dining tonight and he seems to know him quite well. Evidently not married. He's not in the country at all at the moment – he's on home leave and not due back with his regiment until next month. Is this good news or bad?'

'Good news,' said Joe. 'It certainly takes the immediate pressure off.'

'Are you going to tell me what this is all about?' asked Uncle George.

'I could but it might take a bit of time. I'm dining with Nancy tonight and I'm late, you've got a dinner party forming up – perhaps we could talk about this tomorrow?'

'By all means,' said Uncle George, his gargling voice only just audible.

Nancy's bungalow was clearly *en fête* and Joe, wan with relief, made his way there. All the house rooms seemed to be lighted and there was a procession of night lights in glass jars lining the drive. There seemed to be an unaccustomed number of servants, many of whom, Joe realised, had been borrowed from other households for the evening. The same was true eventually when dinner was served. China, glass and plate had been assembled from other establishments in the sensible Indian fashion.

Leaning on a stick and arm in arm with Nancy, Andrew Drummond stood on the verandah, hospitable and expansive. No chance for a while of speaking privately to Nancy but it seemed the heat was off for the moment and he could surprise her with his news later in the evening.

'Sandilands, my dear fellow,' Andrew said with a wide gesture, 'very good to see you! We had begun to fear that you had got lost. But there you are! Who do you know and who don't you know? Let's get the order of precedence right. I must make the presentations. Kitty! I think you've met Commander Sandilands. And Prentice you know, of course, and I hardly need draw your attention to the belle of the ball . . .'

He had no need to draw Joe's attention to Midge Prentice. From the moment of his arrival, like all the men present, he could look at no other. Laughing and lively, her slim boyish figure set off by a flame-coloured crepe de chine dress, she seemed aflame herself. She came instantly to his side, taking both his hands in hers. 'Good evening, Commander or, since our jolly drive down from Calcutta, perhaps I could say, hello Joe! How's the investigation going? Perhaps we ought to drink a toast to you? Andrew . . .' and she waved a hand towards the Collector, 'Andrew says, "Here's to the hound with his nose upon the ground" so here's to you!'

She took a glass from a passing servant and, handing it to Joe, clinked glasses with him and favoured him with a look which seemed in the most natural way possible briefly to set them apart together as two old friends and fellow conspirators.

'What did you think of your present?' said Joe, turning to Prentice. 'Your little ivory figure?'

Prentice withdrew a slender cigar from between his lips and said, 'Beautiful! Really good and of a good period. Worth twice what she gave for it.'

'Do you think,' said Midge, gratified, 'that I could make a living as an expert on Indian egotica . . .' She stumbled over the word and tried again, 'erotica, I mean.'

'Just let me see you try!' said Prentice and there was a general laugh.

Two Greys subalterns closed in on Midge and Joe found himself in the company of Kitty.

'That wretched child gets more like her mother every minute,' she said. 'Dolly had an eye for all things Indian and, of course, people gave her things! Quite a collection she had. Destroyed in the fire, I suppose.' She looked critically once more at Midge. 'The looks, the taste, the animation and, unless I make a mistake, the same capacity for champagne! Dry-as-dust-Prentice is going to have his work cut out! All the unattached men on the station and probably quite a few of the attached will be at her feet! Damn it all, Commander, I've seen it all before. This takes me back twenty years and the charm and the fascination is still there. Heredity! Where *does* it come from? Now – tell me something about yourself. What have you been doing since our tea party – at which you fluttered a few hearts, I can tell you.'

'My heart was a bit fluttered, to tell you the truth, surrounded by so much allure,' said Joe.

'Oh, you! I was expecting you to say, "All my fancy dwells on Nancy, so I'll cry tally-ho."'

'Kitty!' said Joe boldly. 'You've got a tongue that would clip a hedge! Spare me your amatory speculation and remember – I'm a policeman on duty!'

'All work,' said Kitty, 'and no play make Joe a dull boy!'

And dinner was served.

Considering the short time that had been available to Nancy to arrange her dinner party, the dinner was surprisingly good. It opened with a flight of snipe on toast, followed by a curry that nearly took the roof off Joe's mouth, followed by a bombe surprise (it must have been a logistic miracle to bring that to the table!) and terminated with an unidentifiable fish on toast by way of a savoury. Claret with the entr´ee, champagne once more with the dessert and the ladies, gathered together by a look from Nancy, disappeared.

The gentlemen made their way into the garden, glowing cigars like a flight of fireflies in the darkness. They unbuttoned themselves as though by drill and stood in a row on the lawn's edge. Joe found himself next to Prentice.

'This,' said Prentice, 'is an Anglo-Indian custom. I suppose it's an English custom too but I can't get used to it. I'm too much of a Pathan. On the frontier this would be considered a very shocking display.'

Joe was damned if he was going to be patronised by Prentice. 'We all have our rituals,' he said pacifically. 'On the frontier too, I expect.'

Prentice looked sharply up. 'Yes, we all have our rituals, don't we?'

They rejoined the ladies and the solid figure of Kitty came to his side and took his arm. 'You can escort me to the Club,' she said. 'When I was a girl, no one would have dreamed of walking a hundred yards. Times change.'

They set off to walk, Midge arm in arm with Easton and Smythe, Joe arm in arm with Kitty, Nancy between Prentice and Andrew Drummond.

The Club when they reached it was likewise *en fête*. The Shropshire Light Infantry dance band was beating out a polka and to Joe's astonishment, the Greys officers were all wearing night-shirts over their mess dress.

'Manoli Night, you see,' said Prentice. 'You must excuse me for a moment while I garb myself like Wee Willie Winkie.'

He walked to a table where were laid out various items of night attire and selected a voluminous starched white shirt. With the twittering help of Midge he struggled into it and arranged it in folds over his mess jacket. The other officers had set out to look absurd but not Prentice. He wore his white shirt with the air of one deliberately robed for some priestly ceremony.

Joe danced a stately waltz with Kitty, paused to have a drink with Andrew and, hoping he was not being too obvious, seized the first opportunity to gather Midge into his arms for a second polka. 'One, two, three, hop,' said Midge cheerfully. 'You're pretty good, Joe!' And, as they circled the room, smiling, 'I like to be noticed!'

'Don't we all?' said Joe. 'I certainly do!'

As the dance drew to a close, Midge seized his arm. 'I've got something I want to tell you,' she said. 'And I want to tell Nancy too! Nancy! I want to tell you a secret! Come where I can talk to you!'

'Well,' said Nancy, 'nothing like the Manoli Dance for releasing inhibitions. But even this early in the evening the kala juggah appears to be occupied. If you really want to tell secrets we'd better step out on to the verandah.'

'Listen,' said Midge, looking around to make sure they were not overheard and linking her arms with theirs, 'I said – didn't I – there was *somebody*?'

'There was somebody in your life?' asked Nancy.

'Yes. Somebody in my life. If he can get here in time, you're going to meet him! He's driving down from Calcutta! All this way just to see me!'

'Tell us some more,' said Joe. 'Tell us about this lucky chap. All we know so far is that he plays piquet and he's your knight in shining armour!'

'Well, for a start,' said Midge, 'he's a Ghurka officer – I think I told you that – and to go on with, I met him on the boat. We both got on in Marseilles. You'll love him! I do! But that's not all. I'll tell you something very odd. He didn't tell me until we had got to know each other very well and then he did and I think you'll agree that this is the most romantic thing you've ever heard! On the night of the fire – you know what I mean by the night of the fire?'

They both nodded. 'We know what you mean by the fire.'

'Well, on the night of the fire he was there! Not only was he there but they'd hidden me among some flower pots . . .' She gave a deprecating laugh indicating how odd it was that any-one of her charm and sophistication should have been found in amongst a stack of flower pots. '. . . and he found me! He dug me out and looked after me. And he said on the boat – when we'd got to be very good friends of course – "That isn't the first time I've kissed you." Because when he dug me out he gave me a kiss and he'd never forgotten. "I knew I'd find you again one day," he said. Wasn't that a romantic thing to say? Oh, I do hope he gets here this evening! I know you'll like him. I hope Dad likes him too.'

'Are you saying,' Joe began carefully, 'that we're talking about Richard Templar, at present an officer with the Tenth Gurkhas? And that Richard Templar is coming here this eve-ning perhaps?'

'Yes,' said Midge happily, 'that's just exactly what I'm say-ing. Fancy your having heard of Dickie! And you must call him Dickie – everybody does.' She smiled at Nancy. 'It's a surprise for Dad but I really wanted you to know first, Nancy, then you can help me to make him feel welcome.'

'Oil the social wheels perhaps?' said Nancy drily.

'Exactly! Don't you think it's exciting? I do! I wonder what everybody will say? There! Now you know! I'm glad I've told somebody. I'm a bit of a flirt, I know. Everybody says so, I know they do. But there's something a bit different about Dickie. He's serious.'

'There you are!' came the cheerful voices of Easton and Smythe. 'Found you both!'

'Next dance is mine, Midge,' said Smythe.

'And the next dance is mine,' said Easton to Nancy. 'You'll have to excuse us, sir.'

'I'll excuse you,' said Joe, only too thankful to have a moment to digest the information he had just received and to calculate its possible consequences. He turned to stare through the window into the lighted room. In accordance, it would seem, with the traditions of the Manoli Dance, the band kept up both tempo and sound, in this case, 'The Blue Danube' played fortissimo.

Chapter Nineteen

JOE SET HIMSELF somewhat apart. 'What would you say if you just came into this room now? You'd say, "An animated scene!" "On with the dance!" You'd say, "Hearts at peace under an Indian heaven."'

'How wrong you would be.'

The dance band gave way to a not very well rehearsed jazz group led by an unpractised tenor saxophone and under the influence of this the pace warmed up. Joe saw Midge, flushed and excited, being passed from hand to hand, he saw Nancy dancing with considerable skill in the arms of an unknown officer of the Artillery. Over the heads of the dancers his eye took in Prentice, alone, observing, austere and in every particular correct.

'Are you my man, Prentice?' Joe wondered.

Andrew Drummond limped over to him and sat at his side. 'Baffled, Sandilands?' he said.

'Less baffled,' said Joe. 'In fact I think I'm almost certain I know who is responsible and why. There are just one or two more questions I have to ask. But the worst thing – and this is a characteristic of enquiries leading to the solution of a series of killings of this sort – is that the police can do no more than wait for and be ready for the next incident. The girls on the station have written a song – you may even have heard it. It's the "Calcutta Cholera Song" brought up to date as you might say, and some may think this is funny but I didn't. It concludes

– "Here's to the dead already, And here's to the next one that dies!" That gets a bit near the bone for me.'

'It's a British way of going on,' said Andrew.

'Not to me it isn't,' said Joe. 'It just could be a bloody stupid way of going on! And, Drummond, if I've got it right, we all have good reason to be afraid. There will be one more killing.'

'Ceaseless vigilance, Sandilands?' said Andrew.

'Ceaseless vigilance, Drummond!' Joe agreed.

As they spoke, the saxophonist gave way to a cavalry trumpeter in the flashy mess dress of the Bengal Greys.

'Take your partners,' shouted the comp`ere. 'Take your partners for the Post Horn Gallop!'

There was a loud cheer as the dancers opened up to take their places round the edge of the dance floor. Joe took his place beside Nancy and slipped his arm through hers. 'Not galloping, Mrs. Drummond?' he enquired.

'Not if I can avoid it,' said Nancy. 'What about you? Are you steeplechasing?'

'Not if I can avoid it,' said Joe firmly.

But he was wrong. As the Post Horn Gallop drew to its tumultuous conclusion Prentice took the stage and his dry voice came across. 'Ladies and gentlemen,' he said, 'in accordance with tradition I will now say – take your horses for the Manoli Steeplechase! And I ask Mrs Kitson-Masters to do the draw.'

He held up a Bengal Greys ceremonial turban and proffered it to Kitty who started to draw and read out the names. 'Smythe. Hibbert. Fortescue. Bulstrode.' An ironic cheer. 'Prentice.' Another ironic cheer. 'Sandilands.' Applause from his admirers. 'Easton. Forrester.'

Prentice continued, drawing, to Joe's dismay, a service revolver from his pocket, 'I will invite the Collector to start the race. As soon as you are ready, gentlemen.'

There was a clatter and a confusion as the horses were assembled at the verandah with white eyes and frothy muzzles. Joe turned to Nancy. 'Do I have to do this?' he said.

'Yes, or be forever disgraced,' said Nancy. 'It's a setup. You realise that, don't you? Come on, Joe. You've got one half of the women eating out of your hand already – you might as well gather up the other half. But for God's sake – watch your back!' Amongst the confusion Joe was glad to claim Bamboo from the line of horses.

'Gentlemen,' announced Andrew Drummond, 'we dispense with the formality of Epsom Downs and I shall say, "On your marks. Get set. Go." I give you a count of ten to get in line and get mounted. The course goes across the maidan, down to the ford, right at the river bank, right again round the church, across the paddy and back up Station Road finishing here.'

'This is the last thing in the world I want to do,' said Joe, 'at my age. Irresponsible, half-witted cavalry officers, full to the tonsils with the Club's champagne! This is the braves of the tribe flashing their manhood, spreading their tails. I didn't come out to India to get ridden into a waddi by some little half-wit half my age!'

Grumbling, he took his place amidst the laughter in the rough line-up. The Greys officers had discarded their jackets and were riding in night-shirts, many wearing night-caps.

'Here you are, Joe,' shouted Midge, throwing a nightcap up to him. 'Wear this for me!'

'This is how it gets done,' thought Joe. 'Probably since the beginning of time and men fall for it! Christ! I bloody well fell for it!'

'What do I get if I win?' he shouted back to Midge.

Kitty answered for her. 'A ravishing smile, a blown kiss and a cigarette, I should think. Don't count on more than that! As you often tell me, you are, after all, on duty.'

'On your marks!' shouted Andrew and a pistol shot started the Manoli Steeplechase amid deafening cheers.

'This shouldn't be too difficult,' thought Joe. 'There's a torch at every turn, good moonlight. I'll stay back. I'm not going to lead this drunken mob in the dark. Thank God for Bamboo! This would be a great moment to get run away with.'

Shouting and swearing, the cortège streamed away across the maidan.

Prentice was riding slightly ahead and to his right. Two unknown officers were noisily attempting to ride each other off to his left. Someone else he did not recognise was ahead, one or two behind him. Comfortably packed into the field, Joe galloped to the first turn and settled down to ride. Unseen by him a drainage ditch opened up across their path but the reliable Bamboo flew it and galloped on.

In the moonlight and by the flickering light of the torches Joe became aware of a drainage ditch to his left – something more than a drainage ditch – something more in the nature of a nullah. Deep. And widening. He also became aware of a horseman on his right, a horseman boring into him. His mount was a tall black waler, all of fifteen hands, Joe calculated, with a hogged mane and a banged tail. Big enough to eat Bamboo.

'Bugger off, Bulstrode!' he shouted. 'Get out of my pocket, you stupid sod! You'll have me in the fucking ditch!'

Joe didn't want to be in the ditch. It looked very dangerous. He pulled to his right and crashed into the encroaching Bulstrode and Bamboo staggered. He lurched away to the left towards the nullah and at the last minute, at the crumbling edge of this obstacle, the horse took off on neat feet, jumping obliquely. As a piece of trick riding it was impressive and any who saw it must have supposed that Joe was a considerable horseman but it was clever Bamboo. Taking the obstacle at a diagonal it was a jump of about twelve feet. The take-off was not good but, mercifully, the landing was sound and Joe found he had put the nullah between him and his pursuer.

Bulstrode slithered to a halt at the edge of the ditch and Joe galloped on, painfully aware that in order to rejoin the race he would have to jump the nullah once more. He rode on, unencumbered by other riders, keeping the next torch in sight. In some inexplicable way, the obstacle became shallower and wider and he was able at a point happily to splash across on to the other side and found himself, having cut off a wide corner, leading the field.

'So exactly,' he thought, 'where I don't want to be! Not with these drunken louts behind me!'

He touched Bamboo with a spur and the horse laid itself down to gallop. In a wide arc he took the last turn and with relief felt the solid ground of the maidan and with more relief saw the bobbing lights of the finish.

'All right, Midge,' he thought. 'Get the kiss ready! Here comes Sandilands!'

And by five or six lengths he cantered in ahead of the field.

One by one the runners returned. Gasping, panting, horses with flared nostrils and foaming muzzles, jingling curb chains, they milled about. Already they all had stories that would become part of legend.

'Look at that!' said Smythe, pointing to a gash in his boot. 'Know what that is? It's your bloody spur, Johnny!'

'Oh, it was you, was it? I'd have upset you if I could but I didn't realise it was you!'

'Who was that in the ditch?' Joe heard somebody ask.

'Bulstrode,' said Prentice.

'How the hell did he get there?' said Joe. 'He nearly had *me* in the ditch, blast him!'

'So I noticed,' said Prentice, accepting a light from a servant and drawing on a cigar.

'Obliged to you, Prentice,' said Joe.

'Can't have people putting guests of the mess in the ditch. The Greys have a certain responsibility of hospitality, after all.'

'Melmastia?' said Joe.

Prentice gave him a level glance. 'Yes, if you like,' he said.

Midge battled her way through the crowd to Joe's side and, hopping beside him, put one foot on his toe, jumped, swung herself into his arms and, sweeping the night-cap off his head, kissed him firmly.

'That'll do, Minette,' said Prentice and Midge slithered to the ground.

'Well done, Commander,' came the voice of Kitty. 'I hear from Easton you ride like a Cossack!'

'I had a very clever pony who got a very bad rider out of trouble!'

'Never had much time for false modesty,' said Kitty. 'You did very well. The other runners are not exactly inexperienced, you know.'

There was a riff of drums and a distant voice said, 'Supper is served, ladies and gentlemen!'

Joe was content to have upheld the honour of the Met. Glad to have carried Midge's favour to victory. Glad to be alive. He sat on Bamboo for a moment looking over the heads of the company as they made their way across the verandah and into the brightly lit room to the supper table. His eye was taken by a silent figure standing in the lamplight in the doorway, a silent figure in green. Rifle green. Black badges of rank, a tanned face with the white stripe of a chin strap faintly visible and the blue and white ribbon of the Military Cross.

In a flurry, Midge erupted from the crowd and ran to this stranger.

'Daddy!' she shouted as she ran. 'Daddy! There's someone I want you to meet!'

Prentice turned and stood, it seemed, aghast, his face a mask of dismay and indeed of disbelief.

The young man took Midge by the hand, approached him and said, 'You won't remember me, sir, but we have met. Here. In 1910.'

Prentice collected himself and with great control said, 'I remember you. I remember you very well, Templar.'

Chapter Twenty

ON THE MORNING following the Manoli Dance, Joe woke to the conviction that he was getting too old for race-riding in the middle of the night. Stiff and unaccustomed muscles were reluctant to obey his commands and he sat up painfully with a groan, testing each limb in turn. His thoughts ran back over the incidents of the previous night and centred on gallant Bamboo, remembering with affection his convulsive diagonal jump over the drainage ditch. 'If I'm aching,' he thought, 'what about Bamboo, I wonder? Not getting any younger either.'

He knew that the horse would have been in good hands but a temptation came over him to assure himself of this. Painfully he kicked himself out of bed, pulled on the first clothes that came to hand and stepped out into a silent Indian dawn. Silent, that is, except for distant sounds. A dog barked and the bark was picked up in faint chorus by others and died away into the distance. Somewhere a water wheel was turning with a rhythmic clank. A small child awoke with a cry, instantly hushed.

Joe stood for a moment savouring the calm of a windless day. As he watched, the first spiral of smoke from a cooking fire began to rise, melting into the morning mist which lay in parallel with the sleeping earth. The world was waiting for the day. Soon the cacophony of life in Panikhat would break out once more but, for now, in opalescent peace, Joe had the town to himself.

Pausing to collect a handful of sugar lumps from his breakfast table, he set off through the town to the stables. Enjoying as ever the breathing and the smell, the clicks, the rustle and the constant movement of the stables, he looked for Bamboo. On the one hand he saw the ponies – Bamboo was amongst them – and on the other, stretching seemingly into infinity, the greys of Bateman's Horse.

Bamboo greeted him with a flattering whicker of recognition and noisily accepted four lumps of sugar, bumping with his head to search Joe's pockets for more. Joe ran a hand over his legs and over his quarters, decided that his companion of the night before was no more the worse for wear than he was himself and at a sound turned to see the long figure and haunted face of William Somersham.

'Sandilands!' he said in surprise. 'You're an early bird! I usually have the place to myself at this time of day. Do the police always get up at this hour?'

'No. Not always. Not even often. I wanted to make sure my old friend and adviser –' He slapped Bamboo on the rump. '– was none the worse for our efforts yesterday.'

'Congratulations, by the way,' said Somersham, sitting down on a straw bale and offering a cigarette to Joe. 'Congratulations! I didn't witness your performance but by all I hear you did well, brilliantly even. There aren't many who can outride Prentice. To look at me now you wouldn't believe it but I nearly won the Manoli Steeplechase once. Though I wouldn't have confessed it at the time I don't mind telling you – I nearly won it because I was run away with! Bloody awful horse! Bought it from Prentice. It nearly killed me. I was young in those days. Should never have bought the animal. It was vicious and dangerous but when the charming Prentice sets his mind on something, the sort of diffident young man I was in those days just gets carried away.'

'Tell me,' said Joe. 'It was a long time ago and you may not remember but I've been thinking a good deal about the night

of the Prentice fire. It may be relevant to my enquiry – and it
may not – but even so, do you remember that evening?'

'Obviously. I shall never forget it. But I don't think there's
very much I can tell you.'

He appeared to wish not to continue the conversation and
stirred uncomfortably.

'You were one of five officers dining together in the mess
that night,' Joe persisted. 'Did you know each other well? Was
it by arrangement that you met?'

Somersham considered this for a moment. 'Five of us were
there? No, we didn't know each other particularly well so it
was by pure chance that we were there in the mess together
that evening. The other officers and their wives had all gone
off to a midnight picnic. So what you were left with in the
mess was, I suppose, the social misfits of the day. Carmichael's
wife was ill and had cried off. Forbes the MO stayed behind
on duty and the rest of us, all bachelors, couldn't be bothered. Funny sort of entertainment if you ask me. I suppose
Jonno – Simms-Warburton – would have gone like a shot if
Dolly Prentice had been going but everyone thought she was
in Calcutta with Giles.'

'Simms-Warburton was in love with Dolly?'

'Weren't we all to some extent! But Jonno more than most.
In our different ways we were all captivated by her. She
deserved better than Prentice. He was not liked.'

'Not liked?' Joe queried. 'Wouldn't you put it stronger than
that?'

'All right, Mr Policeman. He was cordially disliked. It
wouldn't be too much to say he was cordially detested. Many
were frightened of him. I wasn't of course, but many were.'

'And yet I've heard it said that he's much respected by the
men?'

'Oh, yes. Very popular with the men. And the natives, the
Indians, of all sorts, they eat out of his hand. But the officers
have never been able to get along with him. It's impossible to

be easy in his company. He deliberately sets out to offend. He had nicknames for all of us – I was Silly Billy Somersham – still am! But Forbes, the MO, was a special target. Bullied him, you could say. Seemed to think he wasn't quite up to the standards of the regiment and was always having a go at him. No cause to do that. Chap was a perfectly good doctor.'

'And what were his relations with Carmichael?'

'Carmichael hated him. They should have been at level pegging in their career but it was always Prentice who was one jump ahead. Hard to live with that.'

'So what we have here is an impromptu meeting of the Prentice Appreciation Society? But what about the fifth man? Dickie Templar. Did he have cause to hate Prentice?'

'Dickie Templar?' Somersham barely seemed to recall the name. 'Oh, Templar! Passing through on his way to the frontier. No. He'd been here all of two minutes. Shouldn't think he'd managed to work up a hatred in the time. Dickie. He was the one who spotted the fire.'

'Tell me what happened then.'

'Well, what do you expect happened? The fire was spotted. Our horses were right there. We got on them and rode out to Prentice's bungalow. We weren't on duty, you know. I mean, no reason for us to investigate . . . no reason at all. The Queen's were dealing with everything. Good fellows . . . did their best . . . but they couldn't save the bungalow. They go up in no time at all. Thatch, weeks of hot weather drying everything out. Go up like matchwood. Not a hope. Bandits did it. No doubt about that. Never has been. Dolly never stood a chance. The guilty men were caught and punished, as you probably know. No, Sandilands, it's no use raking about in the ashes of the Prentice fire to solve your mystery. It doesn't compare with the tragedy of Peggy's death. That I really do want to know about! Are you any nearer to knowing what happened to Peg?'

'Yes,' said Joe. 'Very much nearer.'

With a clatter a pony was led out and Somersham excused himself. 'I ride at this time every day,' he said without further explanation, mounted and was gone.

On return to his bungalow, Joe was glad to see Naurung deferentially in attendance and greeted him cheerfully.

'The sahib is about to eat his breakfast,' said Naurung. 'I will wait.'

'You'll do no such thing,' said Joe, 'and that is an order. I'll give you a cup of coffee and you'll come and talk to me while I have my breakfast.'

Reluctantly Naurung entered and, as gingerly as ever, took a seat on the edge of a chair while Joe lifted a cover to reveal two perfectly poached eggs on toast.

'Right. Now, tell me what you have turned up.'

'The sahib asked me to discover what Superintendent Bulstrode was doing on the night of Mrs Somersham's death.'

'Had he an alibi?'

'Yes, I have to tell you that he has an alibi.'

Something in his manner caused Joe to look up. It would have been impossible for the dignified Naurung to be wrestling with suppressed laughter, but that, it seemed, was what was happening.

'I have informers, police spies perhaps. They are everywhere. Men and women. I have a small fund and out of this I pay for useful information. I let it be known, indirectly of course, that I was interested in the doings of the Police Superintendent that evening. I started my enquiries among the women of the town. You will understand that they know everything. Bulstrode Sahib believes that he conceals his tracks but I will say that this is not so. It would be impossible to do so.'

He paused for a moment and Joe said in encouragement, 'Good, Naurung. Just what I would have done in London. What did you find?'

'Acting on information received, and pursuant to your instructions, I am having the Superintendent watched. It seems that he often visits the Shala-mar Bagh. This is a disreputable, oh very disreputable house. And my information is that he often spends long times there and that he was indeed there for three hours at the time of Mrs Somersham's death.'

'Three hours is a long time in the circumstances,' said Joe. 'Not visited many brothels myself and things may well be different in India but I would have thought that for the needs of most, an hour would be enough?'

'I thought so too,' said Naurung. 'And for that reason, on Thursday, I set off to follow the Superintendent myself.'

For a moment Joe was embarrassed as he compared Naurung's assiduous pursuit of his duty with the self-indulgent way he had gone off picnicking with Nancy. But Naurung was not aware of any uneasiness and carried on with enthusiasm.

'He looked at me. He didn't recognise me.' Naurung looked pleased with himself. 'You yourself have said it, sahib, Indians are invisible to English people. I took off my uniform and put on Indian clothes. He looked through me. I wasn't there. Bulstrode Sahib sees only a uniform, he does not see Naurung Singh.

'I entered Shala-mar Bagh where I have never been before and spoke to the doorman – a great big, warlike Rajput. But less warlike when I offered him a rupee to look the other way while I entered. Bulstrode was nowhere. He had disappeared. Then I noticed a small door ajar and I opened it. It led me to a passage at the back of the establishment. I followed it to a courtyard I did not know existed, a pretty courtyard where several small children were playing and, at the far end, I saw Bulstrode going towards a house built into the wall. Two beautiful young Bengali girls came hurrying out to greet him and take him by the hand and then a large lady also appeared and greeted him.'

'This begins to look bad,' said Joe, shaking his head.

'I thought so too, sahib, but then, when I was wondering what to do next, the small children who had been absorbed in their game heard the cries and looked up. They threw down their toys and ran to Bulstrode and jumped at him shouting, "Daddee!"'

'Good Lord! Are you saying . . .?'

'Yes, sahib! I had discovered his secret! You will remember that Bulstrode Sahib put aside his Bengali woman when he married an English lady?'

'Yes, you told me. And the memsahib went back to England, you say, with her baby?'

'And so, he took up his Indian wife again. If he had ever really put her aside.'

'Well, I'm blowed! Poor old bugger! Leading a double life all this time! How tiring! No wonder he looks so done in! And all the time dreading being found out, I suppose.'

'Oh, yes, it would have been harmful – perhaps fatal – to his career if the Collector of the time had known about Mrs Bengali Bulstrode.'

'And it begins to explain why he didn't want anyone making incursions into his territory asking awkward questions about disappearing natives. I think we can put his odd behaviour down to self-protection and – let's not forget this – sheer incompetence. He knew there was more to Peggy's death than met the eye and his answer was to close that eye. And bury the evidence. With a neat label.

'Ah, well. If we had anything so useful as a list of suspects, Naurung, we could cross off one name. But that was well done – very well done, indeed! And it is something we should, I expect, talk to the Collector about. I have other important things to tell him. Things I found out in the mess before that mad midnight ride. Things you must hear too, Naurung. Come on, we'll stroll over and have a conference with the Drummonds.'

～

On arrival at Nancy's bungalow they were shown on to the verandah, where Andrew and Nancy were sitting over a last cup of coffee in deep conversation with Dickie Templar.

'Joe! Good morning! Just the person we were hoping to see! Thought you might be having a lie-in after your heroic efforts last night!' Andrew greeted him and Naurung with much good humour.

'We have a house guest, you see,' said Nancy. 'I think you met Dickie last night, though you were so done in I'm not sure you will have remembered. We asked Dickie to stay with us . . . in all the circumstances,' she added mysteriously.

Templar shook Joe's hand warmly, spoke to Naurung in Hindustani and was about to say something to Joe when his attention was drawn – everyone's attention was drawn – to a figure flying down the drive. Midge Prentice, hatless, shining black hair bobbing as she ran and dressed, improbably, in an old painting smock smeared with many colours, caught sight of them and squealed, 'Nancy!'

'Oh, Lord! What now?' muttered Nancy and got up to greet her.

Midge ran up the steps and, ignoring everyone else, threw her arms round Nancy in a storm of weeping, her pretty face congested and wet with tears.

'Goodness me!' said Nancy placidly. 'What's happened to you?'

'Oh, Nancy! You won't believe! Something awful's happened! Oh, why did it have to be like this? I was so happy – everything was utter bliss – and now I'm miserable. Miserable! I'm very sensitive – everybody says so and a shock like this could kill me! Don't laugh! It could! A doctor once told me I was emotionally fragile. Fragile!'

'Well, I'm not sure I would pay too much attention to that diagnosis,' said Nancy, 'but why don't you tell us what's the matter?'

Andrew, composed, favoured Nancy with a broad wink. Dickie Templar, looking concerned but outwardly calm, eyed Midge with affection from which amusement was not absent. He went over to her, kissed her cheek, rubbed at a paint stain on her nose and said, 'Good morning.' Midge burst into further floods of tears.

Nancy sank down on to a long chair and Midge came and firmly sat on her lap.

'It's Daddy,' she said, 'and I hate him!'

'You don't hate him,' said Andrew.

'I do,' said Midge and, turning to Nancy, 'you'd hate him too if you were me. It all began when I told him that Dickie had asked me to marry him.'

'Has he?' asked Nancy, throwing a look at Dickie.

'Yes, yes,' said Midge impatiently. 'A long time ago. Coming through the Suez Canal . . .'

'What did you say?' Joe asked.

'Well, I said yes, of course,' said Midge. 'Didn't I, Dickie? Straight out. What else would you say – "Oh but this is so sudden"? It wasn't sudden at all – I'd known it was coming since Malta. But Daddy was horrid. Just as horrid as he possibly could be! "You're far too young . . . You've only just left school . . . You don't marry the first man you meet . . ." And then – what a beastly thing to say – "You're just like your mother." I *want* to be like my mother! She came to a sad end, I know, but that wasn't her fault. It sounds as if she had a lot of fun. I want to be like her and I want to marry Dickie! Nancy, you and Andrew are my guardians. I know Daddy's left me to you in his will, he told me so, so you've got to speak to him! It's your duty!'

Tears began again. Joe looked at Dickie Templar with interest and their eyes met. He was wearing stiff Gurkha shorts, bare feet thrust into nailed sandals and a white shirt open at the neck. He looked, Joe decided, strong, brown, handsome and just what any girl aged eighteen would want to marry.

Dickie said, 'Now come on, Midge, you took the poor man by surprise. I mean – for God's sake – give him a chance! He hadn't seen me for twelve years – I might be the biggest rogue in Christendom for all he knows and whether we like it or not, you are only eighteen and you have only been back in India five minutes. We must give him time. I love you. I won't go away. I won't say I don't mind waiting because I do but I can bear it. You can bear it. We can bear it. We'll be all right. I'm not daunted. "Faint heart never won fair lady", you know.'

'Oh, Midge,' said Nancy, tightening her arm about her, 'it sounds like the voice of sense to me. I've not had the chance to say it yet so I'll say it now – I think you've got a good chap there.'

'And I'll add – don't ruin everything by going off at half cock,' said Andrew. 'Diplomacy. That's the only way. You'll only alienate Giles if he thinks you've come telling tales to us. What's he doing at the moment?'

'He was showing me how to do silk painting. I was enjoying it. We were having a good time until he spoiled it.'

'Well, I suggest you go straight back as though nothing's happened, pick up your brush and start painting again. We, meanwhile,' he indicated everyone present with a wide gesture, 'will put our considerable skills to discussing your problem and finding a way to its solution.'

'That's an outstandingly good offer, Midge, when you look at the talent on show,' said Dickie. 'Go back, love, and reassure him. Listen to what he has to say. And, above all, don't go throwing down any gauntlets that someone else will have to pick up. After all, he's been waiting for his daughter to come home and she's hardly unpacked her bags before she announces her intention of marrying an unknown Gurkha. You must allow him time!'

'Oh, all right. I'll do what you say, Dickie. But I don't think he cares a button about me,' said Midge morosely.

Chapter Twenty-One

THEY ALL STOOD and watched Midge walk slowly back through the street, dragging her heels and pausing to cast a last reproachful glance back at Dickie before she turned the corner.

'Are you really the guardian of that bundle of trouble?' Joe asked.

'Not exactly,' said Andrew. 'Midge wouldn't understand the distinction but I am Prentice's executor and trustee. People in India die quite often and quite suddenly, especially the military. It's safer to name an official by his position and there's always a Collector of Panikhat. And, for the moment, I am he.'

The calm that followed the tornado of Midge's appearance was welcome to all. Andrew called for another pot of coffee and, as though by agreement, they settled themselves at the table on the verandah. Discreetly, Andrew took charge of the coffee and dismissed the servants.

'Joe,' he said, 'if I read your expression correctly, you have something to tell us.'

Dickie Templar stirred uncomfortably and started to get to his feet. 'Look, if you chaps are about to have a conference or something, I'll make myself scarce for a while . . .'

'No!' said Joe abruptly. 'It is important that you stay. What I have to say concerns you, your future and your past very closely.'

Dickie looked puzzled. Nancy and Andrew exchanged glances.

Joe produced his notebook. 'Templar, I have a list here of names which I copied from the mess records last night before the Manoli binge. They refer to the night of the 17th of March twelve years ago. It was a Saturday and it was the night the Prentice bungalow burned down. There were five officers of Bateman's Horse dining that night. Their names are: Carmichael, Forbes, Simms-Warburton, Somersham and Templar.'

Nancy sat up with a jerk and Andrew put down his coffee cup very carefully. Neither spoke.

'Take your time to remember and tell us exactly what happened that night. As I say, it is vitally important.'

Dickie was silent, his expression grave. Finally he said, 'Important for whom? For you?'

'For me, yes, certainly, but mostly for you yourself.'

'Well, this is all very mysterious. And, quite honestly, it's not something I have any pleasure in thinking back on. But if you have to know I'd better tell you, I suppose. . . . It's Prentice, isn't it? Has he been talking? Has he asked you to rake all this up again? Is he trying to use this as a wedge between me and Midge?'

Joe shook his head. 'Prentice has said nothing to me. As far as I am aware he has never spoken of it to anyone. Just try and recall the events of that evening if you can.'

Dickie paused for a moment, focusing on the past.

'There were five of us dining in the mess that night. Most of us had cried off going to some awful Panikhat Week event – a midnight picnic, I think.' He shuddered. 'Being eaten alive by mosquitoes while you ate cucumber sandwiches and drank tepid champagne wasn't my idea of fun. All the same, I wish now I'd gone . . . There we all were in the mess, some of us pretty drunk – no, I have to say, somewhat paralytic. I was not. In fact I was fed up with the rest of them. I didn't like the Greys officers and they didn't like me. They'd adopted the terrible practice of not speaking to junior officers and not expecting junior officers to speak unless spoken to. A lot of regiments used to be like that and cavalry regiments especially. I got fed up with them. "Snobbish, conceited, ill-mannered louts," I said to myself at the advanced age of eighteen! I went off to have a pee to get away from them and looking out of the window I saw, for God's sake, that the bloody place was on fire. Was anyone taking any notice? Not as far as I could see. Drawing a deep breath, I went back and told them. While they were drinking themselves senseless, the cantonment had caught fire. What were they going to do about it?

'Well, you can believe it or not but what they were intending to do about it was absolutely bugger all! Oh, sorry, Nancy! Ticked me off for mentioning it! Junior officers were not expected to rush in announcing a fire apparently. They were interested enough to walk on to the verandah and ascertain that the rumpus – by that time there were shots to be heard too – was coming from Prentice's bungalow. That made them laugh. They all hated him, I think, for one reason or another, and they just stood there and watched the spectacle. One of them actually called for a brandy and stood sipping it while the bungalow went up. That was Simms-Warburton. He was really blotto . . . "Ladybird, ladybird, fly away home," I remember he said. "Your house is on fire, your children are gone. Except that they aren't – took his wife and daughter with him, I suppose. He usually does."

'Carmichael was the senior officer present. And he'd drunk more than any of us. Could hardly move.'

'Five glasses of port,' said Joe.

'Was it? Hmm . . . And you can add the claret he'd drunk earlier. He loathed Prentice and couldn't see any reason for rushing to save his bungalow. "Stay where you are," he said. "It's not our job to go running around after a fire. Leave it to the Queen's – they're on duty. This is the army, you know.

And to be more precise, the Indian army. Not the bloody
Boy Scouts! So, stay where you are! I'll make that an order
if you like."

'And so we stayed where we were, for precious minutes –
perhaps for as long as a quarter of an hour – and finally I
could bear it no longer and Philip Forbes, the regimental doctor, backed me up and we went down there. The rest trailed
down after us. I wouldn't be surprised if, over all, we had
wasted half an hour.'

Suddenly his tone changed and, haunted afresh by the
memory, his face stiffened as he resumed, 'You asked if I
remembered. Of course. I shall never forget. And when we got
there, the dacoits had got away and Dolly Prentice was dead.
And Prentice's bearer was dead, apparently going to the rescue, brave chap that he was. And it was only by the mercy of
Providence and the brilliant improvisation of Midge's ayah
that she wasn't killed too! Those buggers were high on hash.
They'd have put anything white – man, woman or child – on
the bonfire if they could. And . . .'

He stared vacantly around the company for a moment.
'. . . it might so easily have been Midge. She was on the menu
all right!'

There was a silence which Nancy broke. 'But you were
there. You saved her. That's what's important.'

Dickie looked gratefully up. 'That may be,' he said, 'but
perhaps I could have done more. I could have got them going
earlier! I could have shouted at them! God knows, for a long
time after it happened, I could think of nothing else. And now
all that you've told me brings it back again.'

'I must ask you, Dickie,' said Joe, 'if Prentice was aware of
your – the group's – negligence? Because negligence it would
seem to have been.'

'He knew. Oh yes, he knew. He went a bit barmy when he
got back from Calcutta and they told him the news. He just sat
about and wouldn't speak to anybody. Cut himself off

completely and wouldn't be doing with words of sympathy from anyone. Then he pulled himself together and started making enquiries and we were all waiting for the wrath to descend on us. But it never did. He decided apparently to take it out on the people who were really responsible and set off on a punitive raid after the dacoits. He knew who they were – he'd been rousting them out of village after village for months. His information was always of the very best. This time he made a thorough job of it and cleared out the whole rats' nest. But I could tell from the way he looked at us – he knew. Hard to pin down and it could just be my conscience enlarging on it, of course, but I thought I caught his eye on each of us at one time or another . . . Ever looked a cobra in the face, Commander, eye to eye?'

Joe shook his head.

'I have. Chills you to the bone. But I can tell you this – I'd rather outface a cobra than Giles Prentice.'

Andrew voiced the thought they were each turning over. 'It took some courage to appear last night and meet him again after all these years. Especially when you knew you were about to ask if he would kindly allow you to relieve him of his only daughter.'

'Courage?' said Dickie. 'I don't know about courage. Awkward, perhaps, but for me not more than that. After all, I'm not the beardless, unattached youth I was in those days. I've been on the frontier off and on for ten years. You might say I'm, to an extent, the same type as Prentice. And I knew what I wanted.'

Nancy looked from Dickie to Joe and back again. 'There are things you should know, Dickie,' she said. 'Tell him, Joe. He has to be told.'

'Do you know why I'm here in Panikhat, Dickie?' Joe asked.

'Of course. Nancy was telling me you're on secondment from the Met and she shanghaied you over here to look into the murder of her friend Peggy . . . Peggy Somersham.'

'I'm enquiring into the murders of four women and their names are Carmichael, Forbes, Simms-Warburton and Somersham . . .'

Dickie leapt to his feet. 'Christ!' he said. 'The mess dinner! On the night of the fire! Are you telling me that each of those men has lost his wife? That she's been murdered? Can you be certain?'

'Naurung and I have looked into each death and we are convinced that they were not accidental . . .' He turned for confirmation to Naurung who nodded his agreement.

And so, in turn, and with frequent interruptions from Nancy, Joe and Naurung outlined for him the investigations they had carried out and Dickie listened in silence. When their account drew to a close, he muttered, 'This is the most devilish thing! I won't say I don't believe you – I do. I have to. But it is the most appalling thing . . .'

'It's quite incomprehensible. I've never heard of anything so evil,' said Nancy.

'Haven't you?' said Dickie dully. 'Then you know nothing about Waziristan! It's badal, Sandilands, isn't it? It's badal that we're dealing with?'

'I'm afraid that it is. A terrible mixture of revenge and conviction. Our murderer feels he has a God-given right – no, an obligation – to exact revenge. Not only from those who actually killed his wife but from those who failed through their drunken incompetence to save her.'

'Let's say it!' Nancy almost shouted. 'This clever chap . . . our murderer . . . person or persons unknown . . . It's *Giles Prentice* we're talking about! Giles Prentice killed Peggy and Joan and Sheila and Alicia!'

'But I don't understand,' said Andrew. 'Why, if he felt so strongly, didn't he – excuse me, Dickie – just kill off the five officers he considered responsible?'

Dickie gave a bleak smile. 'His mind doesn't work in the blunt, straightforward English way that yours or mine or the

Commander's does, Andrew. You say that Dolly suffered from a phobia – a phobia about fire? So – his much-loved wife dies in the worst conceivable way for her – by fire, her nightmare. And he is left for the rest of his life to deal not only with her loss – he's left with the tormenting thought that her last moments must have been not just agony for her but utter terror. And his revenge – which he is compelled to seek if he considers himself bound by the Pathan code, as you say he does – is to deal out exactly the same treatment to the men he hates. They are not to lose their lives – he wants them to live on in order to suffer, as he's suffered, a lifetime's loss and a lifetime's anguish thinking of the way their wives died.'

Joe watched Dickie finding his way along the track he had so unwillingly taken himself.

'And, from what we have seen of the bereaved husbands,' said Nancy, 'he has been successful. They are each as unhappy as Prentice is himself. And that, I suppose, is what put us completely off his track – we were counting him always as the first *victim* in a series of victims. The first of five to lose his wife in a hideous way. But Dolly was never part of that. She was the reason for it. She died in March. The other four died in March. Why do I keep saying "died"? – I mean were murdered! And on or around the anniversary of her death. Ritual. It was important to him. He was marking out the time of her death with other deaths.' She shuddered.

'And the roses,' said Joe. 'Prentice put roses on the graves of the women he'd killed in March each year.'

'Do you think that could show a more human side to his nature?' Andrew asked. 'I find it hard to enter into the mind of such a man but do you suppose that could be his way of – well, apologising – to his innocent victims? His way of acknowledging that they were not his real target, and honouring their memory? Mad, I know – but let's admit it, that's what we're trying to understand – madness.'

'Excuse me, sahib,' said Naurung, 'but I do not believe that there is a more human side to this man. The roses are not a mark of honour and regret as they would be when placed there by a normal person. I think he must be an evil spirit who takes delight in signalling what he has done. The victims may have been innocent and no more than a way of being revenged on their husbands but you will not be forgetting the horror of what he did. He did not need to cut Memsahib Somersham's wrists to the bone! I think he enjoyed killing these memsahibs. I think he puts roses – blood red roses, remember – on their graves to remind himself of the pleasure he took in killing.'

A chilled silence followed Naurung's confident statement.

'This man must be caught,' said Andrew in anguish. 'What can you do, Joe? It's outside everyone's experience here. What would you do if this were happening in London? What do investigators do when they're brought face to face with a multiple murderer or an evil spirit – and it's one and the same as far as I'm concerned.'

Joe had been expecting this question. It was a question he perpetually put to himself and he was not satisfied with the answer. 'I'm afraid,' he said slowly, 'that with all the might of Scotland Yard behind them, to say nothing of contacts with other police forces, what they do in these circumstances is wait.'

'Wait?' said Naurung urgently. 'Wait? Is that all we can do? And do you mean wait for the next tragedy to happen? Wait until our man strikes again?'

'I don't like it either,' said Joe. 'We could charge him and lay the facts as we know them before him – scare him, if you like, though he's not a man who scares easily but with what result? He'd either laugh in our faces or perhaps worse – disappear. Oh, he could disappear, all right. Like an eel into the mud. And then where would we be? No. I want him where I can see him. And . . .' His face suddenly distorted with loathing. '. . . let him overplay his hand and we will have a better chance of taking him. Think for a moment – what evidence have we got that would stand up against him? Andrew – you are the man who would have to deal with this, the ultimate authority in Panikhat. Would you feel able, on the strength of what we have so far, to issue a warrant for his arrest?'

Andrew shook his head.

'Wait until he strikes again, you say?' said Dickie. 'Look, I know what you're all thinking and I can quite see why no one wants to put the thought into words so I'll do it myself. I think we all know who the next – and last – victim is, don't we? According to the grisly schedule he's set himself, come next March it's whichever lady has made Dickie Templar the happiest of men.'

'Oh, no!' Nancy was horrified. 'I hadn't thought of that. But no. Certainly not! You're not suggesting that Midge, his own daughter . . .? No. Not even Giles is that mad. But I can quite see why he looked as though he'd seen a ghost when Midge greeted you last night.'

'No. I think he won't turn his anger on Midge but we are dealing, as you say, Drummond, either with madness or evil and I'm taking no chances. I'm certainly going to marry her but I won't marry her until he's under lock and key. I was thinking out loud, trying to guess how he'll react now that I've ruined his equation. How is he going to deal with an enforced change in his plans? I think he'll work out his revenge *before* she is able to marry me. He must know by now that I'm planning to leave for Calcutta and then on to Peshawar to rejoin my regiment the day after tomorrow . . .'

'I'd come to the same conclusion,' said Joe. 'He'll try to kill you, Dickie.'

Dickie gave a sharp laugh. 'So I'm to be the tethered goat? I can see that and I agree to it. But, tell me, which of you fellows is going to stand by with a rifle when the tiger comes for me?'

Looking round at their stricken faces, he banged his fist on the table, rattling the coffee cups. 'Ayo Gurkhali!' he said. 'It means, "The Gurkhas are here!" It's what we shout when we go into battle!'

'Ayo Gurkhali!' repeated Naurung.

Chapter Twenty-Two

DICKIE LOOKED AT each in turn resentfully. 'This is all quite unnecessary. I'm perfectly capable of looking after myself and I can't see any reason why any of you should risk your necks for me.'

Andrew took no notice of his protest but calmly went over the arrangements they had just made. 'From eight until five to midnight, I will be on watch. From midnight to five to four, Joe, and from five to four until relieved, Naurung. Is that agreed and understood? Dickie, you can be as proud and independent as you like but remember who we are dealing with – an obsessed and revengeful killer. I am not a Pathan but I am well aware of melmastia – you'll know what I mean. You are my guest, Dickie, and you will spend as many hours of the day as you can bear here and all hours of the night with someone by you on a rota. I don't mean that someone should shadow you every moment but one of us should be within hail at all times. As Joe has pointed out, nothing should change in my domestic arrangements – any door or window that is normally open will stay open, no special orders will be given to the servants. Same for Joe. We will not discuss the matter again unless we're absolutely sure we can't be overheard. We each have a firearm, it should be kept ready for use at all times.'

Dickie shrugged in a gesture of surrender. 'Oh, all right, Andrew,' he said. 'All right, you've said your piece.'

'I haven't said my piece,' said Andrew. 'I've issued an order.'

And so the day had developed. It had been an ordinary day in Panikhat. Midge and Nancy rode out together, Dickie, mounted by the Bengal Greys, played a leisurely chukka or two of polo. It was hard to tell how Naurung had spent the day, though he seemed never to be in the way or out of it. Joe, acutely conscious of many requests from Uncle George for a situation report, sat himself down to collect his thoughts.

'I'll have to send this handwritten,' he thought. 'It's too hot to have it typed here!'

And he began:

> *Dear Sir,*
> *Pursuant to your instructions, I duly proceeded on the*
> *10th inst. by train to Panikhat, accompanied by . . .'*

The standard police phrases rolled from his pen. He forced himself to concentrate, he forced himself to write neatly, well aware that an ambiguous phrase could be replayed by a Bengali typist in florid and inappropriate prose. Towards the afternoon he decided that he could do no more; he suddenly needed the calm company of Kitty and walked across to her bungalow. As he walked up her drive he heard the cheerful voice of Midge.

Rounding the corner, he saw them sitting together over a tea table. Midge was doing the talking. Joe listened. What, he wondered, would she find to say? 'I'm engaged to be married but my father is a multiple murderer. It's probable that my affianced will be murdered during the course of the day.' Something of that sort? But no. He overheard a highly coloured account from Midge of her adventures at her finishing school in Switzerland. She was even describing what she'd worn at an end-of-term dance, how much it had cost and confessing that she hadn't yet paid for it.

Kitty listened with affection, obviously enjoying herself, prompting Midge by shrewd questions to further and indiscreet revelations.

He made himself known and joined them both on the verandah. After a while and to Joe's acute embarrassment, Prentice rode up the drive. He was dirty and sweaty. He'd obviously been working.

'Morning, Kitty. Morning, Sandilands. There you are, Midge. Looking for your young man. Any idea where he is?'

'On the polo ground,' said Joe, having just seen him there. 'Knocking a ball about with the Greys. I'll ride down with you.'

'If you find him, Daddy, you're to be nice to him,' said Midge. 'Not like you were last night!'

She turned to Kitty. 'Daddy doesn't quite approve of Dickie.'

'I don't disapprove of Dickie especially,' said Prentice equably. 'If I disapprove of anybody – I disapprove of you!'

It was affectionately said.

'Who,' asked Kitty, 'could disapprove of Midge Prentice, I'd like to know?'

'Daddy can,' said Midge.

'I wanted to see Templar,' Prentice confided as they rode down together. 'Midge is right. I was a bit brusque with him last night. I don't approve of this engagement. I expect you've heard all about it? Minette's far too young – and young for her age. But I came the heavy father. Some excuse, of course, but I said more than I meant. No call for a row.'

In the face of such normality, it was difficult – it was almost impossible – to believe in the existence of the dark current. And the encounter between Dickie Templar and Prentice had – so far as such a thing could be in the circumstances – been entirely normal. Prentice, on the one hand, reserved but friendly, Dickie polite but determined.

Joe heard Prentice say, 'We should talk. Now, you're off the day after tomorrow – correct? Today's a bit full already but there's nothing wrong with tomorrow. Why don't we make an appointment as it were? Come and lunch with me at the Club. There are rather a lot of women about the place here, what with Midge, and Nancy. And, indeed, the all-seeing Kitty. I feel a bit – scrutinised. Let's have a moment or two when we're not being scrutinised. Eh?'

The long afternoon wore on.

With no hope of sleep that night and mindful that he would have to be on duty at midnight, Joe lay down on his bed, dressed in trousers and shirt, his Browning automatic pistol with a full magazine in its holster, and linked his hands behind his head. He gazed at the ceiling. His thoughts chased him down dark corridors and he longed to put on a light, to read a book, or check for the tenth time that his gun was properly loaded and ready but, they had agreed, nothing unusual. So – no light at this hour. The police detective, if anyone were watching, was fast asleep as normal.

He went over in his mind the road he would have to follow in the dark to reach Nancy's bungalow to relieve Andrew's watch. He had looked it over, even paced it carefully in the daylight when he was sure that Prentice was at work, exercising on the maidan a good mile away. He had borrowed a pair of gym shoes from Andrew and was confident that he could arrive unannounced by betraying noises.

But now, with his watch held up to the moonlight saying thirty minutes to go before he relieved Andrew, Joe was tense. He was not deceived by the softening conversation between Dickie and Prentice. In fact, the more he thought of it, the more contrived it seemed.

* * *

Prentice was sending a signal which read, 'Nothing to worry about. Nothing to worry about at all.' He was more than ever convinced that Prentice would strike that night. He was a military man after all, like Joe, and Joe reasoned that any soldier with two nights to carry out a vital offensive would not leave it until the second night. If he was unsuccessful on the first occasion he would have another one available to him.

Twenty minutes to go. He calculated that it would take him seven minutes walking carefully along the shadowed route he had picked out to reach the bungalow and another minute to slip in through the back door and take his place on the verandah outside Dickie's room. It was vital that he appear at exactly five minutes to midnight as he had arranged with Andrew. Any earlier or later and he might find himself taken for an intruder and have his head blown off. He swung silently out of bed and padded to the window to judge the strength of the moonlight. The moon and the stars combined to create an illusion of daylight, a clarity so intense Joe felt he could have read a book by their gleam. He slipped a concealing dark jacket over his white shirt and waited.

He looked down in the direction of the Drummond bungalow, wondering whether Dickie, exhausted by his practice on the polo field, had managed to snatch any sleep at all. He knew, in the circumstances, he would never have been able to sleep himself. All was quiet.

Prentice looked in the other direction towards the military lines and Curzon Street.

'Prentice! You bastard! What are you thinking tonight?'

He was aware of Dickie's imminent departure, was perhaps obsessed by it. He had to move and he had to move soon. Tonight? Tomorrow night? Waiting!

'If we were hunting, I'd say that we'd stopped the earth, stopped the fox. That's what I am! I am the earth-stopper!'

Again, his mind weary from this exercise, he went over their arrangements. Three watchers watching the earth, thinking round the problem, thinking through it, thinking of all angles, relevant or irrelevant.

'Dickie, are you all right? Midge, are you all right?'

He smiled to himself at the thought that, imperceptibly, in his mind, the two lovers had become one. Impossible to think of one without the other.

He gazed through the window and looked up at the yellow moon, the March moon, and a thought so chilling, a thought so devastating, hit him with an intensity that for a moment threatened to loosen his bowels.

'We've stopped the wrong earth!'

Chapter Twenty-Three

'PRENTICE HAS ALL the murderous patience of a Pathan in pursuit of a blood feud. Prentice is a man of method. He is not going to abandon his established pattern. His ritual. For Christ's sake! – he doesn't want Dickie dead! He wants him alive and suffering! Like all the others! He wants him deprived of the love of his life with the rest of his life to live in that knowledge. And marriage doesn't come into it! That's our own Western way of thinking. It's enough for him that Dickie loves her and Prentice reasons like a Pathan. An eye for an eye, a loss for a loss. Appropriateness. Fittingness. Dickie has never been in any physical danger himself.'

And a second thought to agitate him – 'March! We're still in the month of March! He doesn't need to wait for another year.'

Kitty's voice came back to him, scathing, acerbic, amused, '. . . and leathery old villains are known to have killed their own offspring if they thought the code demanded it . . .'

'We've been wrong! Wrong! Wrong!'

The horror of his conclusion froze his muscles. He was unable to move. Unable to make a decision. Run to the Drummonds for help?

Yes!

No! That would be to add a mile to his journey. It was probably too late anyway! His mouth was dry, his eyes staring, ears straining for any sound.

The paralysis passed away and he found himself without further thought outside his bungalow and running on silent feet in the moonlight. Running to Curzon Street. Running to the Prentice bungalow.

He stopped at the drive gate and moved forward on tiptoe. The house was in total silence. There was no light. The front door, as was Prentice's custom, stood open. Glancing down the garden, for a moment Joe could fancy he caught a gleam of light from the garden house but it was gone. The servants' quarters likewise lay in silence. The silence, it seemed to Joe, of complete desertion. Not even a tickle of smoke from kitchen fires. The silence was ominous, the desertion complete.

With stealth he ran up the verandah steps and stood by the open door. After only a moment's hesitation he stepped inside, waiting for a second for his eyes to grow accustomed to the deeper shadows of the house.

All internal doors were open. All, in fact, except one. And surely that one was Midge's bedroom? He remembered the room. He remembered the light, brittle, cane furniture and the pretty wall hangings that Prentice had thought appropriate to welcome his daughter home. He even remembered the layout of the room and, without hesitation, pushed the door open.

Sick with relief, on the charpoy under a mosquito net, he saw the recumbent figure of Midge. A second glance was less reassuring. She was lying on her back, an unnatural pose. Her hands were folded on her breast in an almost ritual stillness. He took a pace forward and then another. He bumped into a chair and bent to move it aside. As he picked it up he realised that it was broken. Broken, in fact, into small pieces. Looking again he saw that all the furniture in the room had been broken – smashed. All the hangings had been torn down and the debris had been piled about Midge's bed. Stepping forward again his foot hit a hard object. A tin of kerosene.

With desperate hands he tore the mosquito net away and knelt beside the sleeping Midge. And then he saw the dark stain on her breast. With a groan he reached out and touched it. His hand recoiled in horror. It was a spray of red roses, placed between her limp hands. Automatically, he took one of her folded hands and felt for her pulse. Automatically, he lowered his face to hers and breathed. What was that smell? His years in London had not prepared him for much that he found in India but at least he was able to recognise the smell of hashish. He brushed her forehead with his lips. Slightly damp. Midge was alive. Midge was drugged. Midge, it seemed, was intended to suffer the death her mother had suffered twelve years ago. The death on a funeral pyre which had haunted her through the years.

He extended hands that shook to lift her but a sound behind him caused him to turn.

Pale in the moonlight and insubstantial, a tall figure stood silent in the doorway watching him.

Every hair on his head, every muscle in his back signalling terror, Joe breathed, 'Chedi Khan.'

Nancy stirred uncomfortably and looked at her clock again. Five minutes past midnight. Andrew had not joined her in their room. Every sense was alert and crying out that all was not well. She had never expected to be able to sleep through the night and had settled down in a chair fully dressed in trousers, an old shirt of Andrew's and a pair of soft riding boots. She made her way silently on to the verandah.

'Andrew! Something's wrong,' she hissed. 'Joe's not here, is he? And if he's not here – that means the danger's not here . . . It's somewhere else. I'm going down to his bungalow.'

'Stay here, Nancy, I'll get Dickie to go . . .'

But Nancy was already running.

She covered the half-mile to the dak bungalow and paused at the end of the drive to catch her breath. No sounds. The front door hung wide open. She crept quietly up, stood to one side and listened. Only the sound of her own laboured breathing. She moved into the hall and made towards Joe's bedroom. In the doorway she bumped into a turbaned figure and opened her mouth to scream in uncontrollable reaction. An Indian hand closed around her mouth forcing it shut, killing all sound. Almost stopping her heart. The nightmares of Joan, of Sheila, Alicia and Peggy came starkly before her own eyes. Their last sight had been a vision of terror, an Indian with a snake in his hand, an Indian with hands grasping to throw his victim screaming over the cliff edge, an Indian using his strength to keep a mouth gasping for air under water, an Indian slashing with a razor.

Nancy struggled and caught her elbow on a uniform belt buckle. A voice spoke urgently in her ear. 'Memsahib! It is I, Naurung! Please be quiet!'

'Chedi Khan!'

Unbelieving, Joe stared at the tall figure of a Pathan warrior standing motionless, silhouetted in the moonlit doorway. Long fringed waistcoat, baggy white trousers and shirt, pagri twisted into a turban, embroidered slippers, curved knife thrust through a belt. But then he saw in the apparition's right hand the gleam of a slim dark barrel and Joe shrank from the menace of a Luger P'08.

His hand shot to the holster of his own pistol.

'Don't be stupid, Sandilands!' The dry drawl of Prentice's voice stopped him short.

Helplessly, Joe tried to speak and gestured towards Midge.

'Leave it! Leave it!' said Prentice. 'She's asleep. There's nothing you can do. In fact everyone in our little circle is asleep except for you and me. Old Andrew can sleep the sleep of senility, Nancy can sleep the sleep of surrendered innocence, and Templar, of course, can sleep the sleep – I imagine – of powerful sexual excitement and happy anticipation.' He paused. 'The only difference between him and Minette is that he will wake in the morning. But in the meantime, come with me.'

He gestured with his left hand. The right held the pistol pointed unwaveringly at Joe's stomach. 'Come with me, Sandilands,' he said. 'And perhaps it would be convenient if you raised your hands. Although you would be dead long before you had succeeded in drawing your cumbersome firearm. Just go ahead of me. We'll go in here.'

He indicated the door of his office. 'You'll see a box of matches on the table. Part of my evening's preparations, as you can probably imagine. Be kind enough to light the lamp and pray take a seat. We might as well be comfortable. Time passes so agreeably in your company.'

Painfully Joe found his voice. 'Prentice!' he said desperately and, hating himself for the clich´es that poured from him, 'There is no way in the world that you'll get away with this! Proceed with this and you're a dead man! George Jardine has a report. He knows all that we've discovered and all that we've guessed. By your actions tonight you have put the keystone on our enquiry. It's no part of my job to give you advice but I'll give you some – run! Get out of it. Hide yourself. If you don't there's no escape for you. Wherever you go, whatever you do, you'll be hunted down. Others will pick up the trail.'

'Escape?' said Prentice. 'Of course I escape. I'd be a poor schemer if I hadn't made appropriate arrangements.'

'And,' said Joe, unable to keep the quaver out of his voice, 'you would kill your daughter, the daughter of your wife?'

'The circle has to be closed.' Suddenly it seemed he was in the grip of a passionate intensity as he said, 'I've worked for this moment for twelve years. Since the year 1910. Blunderer though you are, you probably don't need to be told that.'

'I know very little of your wife,' said Joe, 'though many have spoken of her to me. She sounds to have been a free and beautiful spirit. I don't wonder – no one wonders – that you loved her so deeply. But, Prentice, can you imagine that the four women who've died and now your daughter to be added to the toll of death will comfort that bright spirit? You've made blood sacrifices enough to quench the thirst of Kali herself! Dolly would never have demanded such retribution!'

For a moment Prentice looked at him with genuine surprise. 'My wife? You speak of my wife's death?' He laughed bitterly. 'My wife! Oh, dear! Sandilands – for all the veneer of sophistication, for all the clever pontificating about police methods, for all the questions and answers, you remain at the last a plodding London bobby with about as much imagination in this situation as a cocker spaniel – or a Bulstrode! I ask myself what do you know about life? Life, that is, outside the boundaries of Wimbledon, outside Belgravia, outside the hunting counties of England? Nothing whatever!

'Commander, I have to tell you – you are pathetic! I can't easily believe you supposed my target was Dickie Templar. I can't any more easily suppose that you imagined my grief was for Dolly!'

Chapter Twenty-Four

ABRUPTLY JOE SAT down in a chair and they gazed at each other across the desk in silence until Prentice resumed, 'How often I've heard the phrase used – "The night of the tragedy" . . . "The death of your wife". No one, English or Indian, has ever noticed or registered the fact if they did notice that Dolly did not die alone.'

'Chedi Khan,' Joe whispered.

'Yes,' said Prentice roughly, 'Chedi Khan. Are you beginning to understand?'

'What of him?' said Joe. 'He died, by all I hear, trying to save your wife and God bless him. What is this you're trying to say?'

'I'm not trying to say anything,' said Prentice in sudden anger. 'I am saying, if you have ears to hear, that Dolly was nothing. Nothing! At best she was a promiscuous little trollop and she deserved to die. She died as she had so often lived – drunk! I wouldn't sacrifice a dog to save her and wouldn't lose a wink of sleep to avenge her. But . . .' He said the names slowly as though reciting a litany, 'Carmichael, Forbes, Simms-Warburton, Somersham and Templar on that night – "the night of the tragedy", if you care to call it that – where were they? Drunk and indifferent! They were a few minutes' ride away. Their appearance, merely the sound of their arrival, would have scared off the dacoits before they'd had a chance to do much damage. If they'd moved when the alarm was

given, had they any manhood, any honour – honour, that is, as
we would understand it in the north – they would have spent
their blood to save him. But they let him die! They didn't, I
suppose, even know that they'd let him die. But, as the years
have lengthened and the grass has grown, each has paid. Each
has been condemned to a lifetime of bereavement. And now
Templar! The Ghurka hero! Now Templar pays his bill.'

'You're mad,' said Joe. 'You *are* mad. This is madness!
Dementia!'

'Mad? You may say mad, you may believe mad but – Chedi
Khan was the love of my life. He was clear and he was clean.
He was beautiful. He loved me and I loved him. I would have
done anything for him. I could think of nothing that would
more fulfil my life than to have been allowed to die for him.
He filled me with joy, he filled me with hope, he filled me with
promise for a life that would have opened before us, but, as it
is, and through their neglect, he died with a drunken woman
in his arms, alone and in anguish! How should I forgive those
who took this away from me? He made my heart sing! It was
many months before I could bring myself to believe that he
was gone and the years have not softened my loss.'

Joe listened, aghast.

'More Pathan than the Pathan.' Again it was Kitty's voice he
heard. And here before him was a tribesman, ruthless,
inflexible, convinced of the rightness of his conduct. His aqui-
line profile, his dark eyes hooded and watchful, made a nonsense of the cultured English accent.

'And you learned to think like this – like a Pathan – in your
infancy?' said Joe. 'As they say: "As the twig is bent, so will the
tree grow." Distorted. Forever distorted.'

'Still the policeman! Minutes from death, Sandilands, and
you're still trying to understand.' He smiled pityingly. 'And
again failing utterly!'

He paused, wondering, Joe feared, whether to shoot him
dead out of boredom and have done with it or to succumb to

the urge he had seen so often in killers, an urge to explain themselves. To make someone, even the arresting officer, aware of their compulsions. They work in solitude, they cannot confide in anyone, cannot justify their actions and, the moment they are discovered, they have an uncontrollable need to pour out their story. He gambled on this same need in Prentice.

'No wonder people took you for an Indian,' he said. 'You're very familiar to me – we've had several conversations – but even I would find it hard to distinguish you from a real native . . .'

Prentice gave a short bark of derision. 'Clod!' he spat out. 'You don't see it, do you? You're as perceptive as that crass Superintendent Andrew keeps in office. The unseeing idiot interviewed me twice and each time he could see no further than a brown skin, a layer of saffron and ash, a caste mark and a turban. I *am* Indian! Half Indian to be precise. My father was English and my mother, my real mother, was Pathan, a Pahari from the mountains.'

Joe gaped at him in astonishment. What had Naurung senior said about his interview with the ferryman? 'He was Indian, sahib, to the soles of his feet.'

With an impatient gesture, Prentice shook one sleeve of his baggy shirt down to his armpit, revealing a muscular brown arm. 'No need for dye! I can appear naked before any Englishman and all he sees is an Indian. It was easy to get close to those stupid, unseeing Englishwomen. For them a brown man is a sight to make them avert their eyes, less important than a piece of furniture.'

The tone was bitter and Joe instantly seized on this. 'You have no liking, I think, for memsahibs? You showed your victims no pity, in fact I would say that you took considerable satisfaction in killing them.'

'No liking? I loathe them. You probably know that it is the charming English tradition for a gentleman to put aside his Indian mistress when he at length marries? When my father married a woman fresh from England, he cast my mother off though he continued to visit her. The Englishwoman, fulfilling his requirements in all other respects, did not have the children he wanted her to have. I was born to my Pathan mother and my father had the cruel notion of making his wife acknowledge me as her own. We were stationed at a very remote outpost of the far north-west and there were few to know and none to tell about his deception. My real mother was made to appear as my ayah and I grew up at her side, loving her and loving the Pathan way of life. My English mother hated me, naturally, and went out of her way to make my life uncomfortable. Indeed, she was most ingenious in her cruelties.'

'"Give me a child for the first seven years of his life and he is mine for ever."' Joe quoted. 'Who said that? The Jesuits, was it? And, equally, hatreds and fears acquired during those tender years would affect your life ever after.'

'Who are you quoting? Freud? Jung? Sandilands? Spare me the psychology! I will simply say that Englishwomen with their white faces, their sharp tongues and their idle ways became anathema to me.'

'But you married Dolly?'

'I took a wife to further my career, Sandilands.'

'And Midge?' Joe hardly dare ask.

'Oh, I think . . . no, I'm quite sure . . . that she is my daughter if that's where you're leading. But the child Dolly was carrying when she died . . . well, who knows?'

'But the women that you killed,' said Joe, desperately, 'each in a different way and each in a manner that would be most terrifying to her . . .?'

'And, again, you forget Chedi Khan! We pulled him out of a blazing village and the fear of fire remained with him to the end of his days . . .'

A picture came into Joe's mind of the rows of fire buckets lining the corridor of the burned bungalow. Not to calm Dolly's fears but Chedi Khan's.

'. . . and, at the last, it was fire that caught him. I think every day of what it must have cost him, the terror he must have felt as he turned back and fought his way through the flames to try to save – what? – a drunken, worthless Englishwoman!'

'But Midge – Prentice, you must know that from that night twelve years ago, the fear of fire has been strong in Midge's heart! You have pity for Chedi Khan and his terror, can't you feel the same emotion for Midge?'

'I close the circle,' said Prentice again. 'It is just. It has to be. She won't be alone. My work is done and I will go with her.'

At this last chilling declaration Joe gave up all hope. At last he understood. There was no reason he could use, no persuasion, no bargaining with a fanatic who had decided to kill himself.

For some time he had been aware of slight sounds in the house behind him. Joe had raised his own voice in an attempt to cover them. Could Midge have regained consciousness? Was she listening? If so she would understand what was going on and run for help. Perhaps she would come into the room? Even that might provide just the distraction Joe needed. Such was the intensity of his thought, Prentice had been unaware of the sounds. But now he fell silent, the silence which precedes violent action. '"The dreary, doubtful hours before the brazen frenzy starts",' thought Joe but in this case not hours so much as seconds. To cover any further sounds, Joe leapt to his feet as though in acute distress, and began to yell wildly at Prentice.

'You bastard!' he screamed. 'You'd murder your daughter, and carry that as a curse through all eternity?'

The muzzle of the Luger followed Joe's movement, trained on his abdomen.

'You may call it murder . . .'

A figure appeared in the doorway. A figure holding a .22 Smith and Wesson target pistol.

Nancy rested the barrel across her left forearm and fired.

The bullet hit Prentice in the shoulder and spun him round. His gun jerked from his grip, slid across the desk and clattered to the floor on the far side. She fired again but the bullet went wide. She fired a third time, hitting him squarely in the chest. A gout of blood spewed from his mouth and trickled down his white shirt.

Joe kicked the Luger to the far side of the room, drew his own pistol covering Prentice and began, 'Giles Prentice, I arrest . . .'

His words were cut short by a cry of impatience and another shot from Nancy's gun. She hit Prentice a second time in the chest and began to move carefully into the room, covering him every inch of the way.

Pale and haggard, Nancy gazed unwinkingly into Prentice's eyes. Harshly she spoke to him, 'Look at me, Prentice! Look! What are you seeing? You know so much about fear, don't you! Are you face to face at last with *your* worst fear? A white-faced, sharp-tongued Englishwoman? A memsahib who hates you? A memsahib who's just put three bullets into you and who's about to put a fourth one in your neck?'

She raised her pistol to his neck.

Prentice rocked on his heels and seemed about to collapse. A dribble of blood flowed from each corner of his mouth. He lurched forward and groped at the desk for support, his eyes never leaving Nancy's face. But he did not fall. With sudden convulsive strength, he reeled towards the open door. Half staggering, half running, he fled clumsily down the passage and towards the back door and the servants' quarters, leaving bloody hand prints on the wall, leaving a trail of blood on the floor.

With a curse, Nancy fired at his back and made to run after him.

Joe put out a restraining hand. 'No! Leave him, Nancy! Care for the living. Midge! She's in her room. Go and look after her. She's drugged, unconscious, in danger!'

'It's all right,' said Nancy. 'We found her. Dickie's with her. She's unconscious but she's alive. When you didn't turn up to do your shift I checked your bungalow. Naurung had had the same thought and we guessed you'd have come here.'

'Dickie's here? Then – between you – get her out of here, for God's sake! She mustn't see this. She mustn't wake to this!'

There was a confusion of voices and hurried footsteps in the hall. Dickie emerged from the shattered bedroom with Midge in his arms while Andrew, leaning on Naurung's arm, limped awkwardly into the house. He stopped and looked aghast at the bloodstains, sniffing the smell of cordite, the sound of the shots still ringing in his ears.

'Nancy!' he said. His voice was almost a groan. 'Nancy! Say you're all right!'

Clumsily he took her in his arms while tears ran down his face.

'I heard shooting. Oh, God! I thought you were another victim! That devil! Where is Prentice?'

'Come with me,' said Joe. 'We're going to find out. He's gone off with four of Nancy's bullets in him. And Nancy – go with Dickie.'

'Yes,' said Naurung with sudden informality, 'do, Bibi-ji, as the Commander says.'

'And you, Naurung – you're in charge here now. Let no one in. Do what you have to do.'

'Sahib,' said Naurung, 'be careful. The cobra has slid into his hole.'

In a voice of cold resolution Andrew replied to him. 'I'm armed.'

They set off down the passage following the trail of blood.

'I can guess where he's going.' said Andrew. 'At the bottom of this garden there's the river and he usually has a boat moored down there. A few hundred yards away and you're into the Indian town. If he gets as far as that we've lost him for good.'

'He's not going to the Indian town,' said Joe.

They walked carefully out into the moonlit garden, through the hedge and into the unkempt garden of Prentice's old house. Here, perpetually torn by trailing rose briars and picking their way with difficulty through the undergrowth, they found at last a little path and followed it together. In his clumsy haste, Andrew cannoned into a mohwa tree bringing down a cascade of heavily scented waxy blossoms.

'Be careful,' said Joe, 'he may yet be armed.'

They moved silently on.

The Mogul garden house was now in plain sight and, in spite of his foreboding, Joe paused for a moment, struck by its beauty. Pale and serene in the moonlight it seemed deliberately to set itself apart from the bloody doings of that night. Its Islamic dome rose to the starlit sky; fretted shutters closed its windows and a cascade of small fragrant red roses trailed and climbed. Joe pointed silently at the open door.

Andrew took out his gun and one on either side of the door they stood and listened for any sounds. There were none. Joe nodded and they entered. At first they could see nothing but after a while they became aware of Prentice, who seemed to be kneeling across the foot of a charpoy, his head buried in his arms.

Joe dropped on one knee beside him, parted his drapery and felt for his heart. Holding up a bloodstained hand he said, 'Dead. At last.'

'What was he doing?' said Andrew in wonderment. 'Why did he come here?'

Joe took a match from his pocket and struck it. Seeing a small lamp on a table, he lit it and held it up. The room was lined with patterned cupboards, each painted in glowing colours in the manner of the Mogul empire with lovingly depicted, and no less lovingly restored, scenes from Mogul mythology. On a table there were set out paints and brushes. The room had something of the quality of a shrine.

With surprising tenderness, Andrew reached forward and took Prentice by the shoulder, turning him over on his back. The dead hands clutched – of all incongruous things – a pressed flower which might once have been red and a battered school exercise book from which, as Andrew disturbed him, a sheaf of papers and photographs fell to the floor. Joe picked one up and saw a strikingly beautiful young man. Smiling, he stood by a river naked to the waist in a pair of cotton drawers. The next photograph showed the same figure a few years earlier mounted on a pony. The third Joe recognised. He had seen the same photograph in the Prentice family album, a laughing, handsome man in whose glossy dark hair was twined a spray of roses. The photographs told the story of Chedi Khan's youth and young manhood. Happy to the last. Beautiful to the last.

'Who's this?' said Andrew. 'Who could this possibly be?'

'It's Chedi Khan,' said Joe. 'Eternally the love of Prentice's life.' And he explained.

They turned from the photographs to the exercise book across the front of which was stamped 'ST LUKE'S MISSION AND SCHOOL. ARMZAN KHEL.' The pages were stained with Prentice's blood and they opened them one by one.

'A child's exercise book,' said Andrew. 'A child learning to write in English, it seems.'

'Chedi Khan,' said Joe. 'Prentice sent him to school. St Luke's Mission. Anglican Fathers but he ran away twice and each time went back to him.'

They turned the pages over and searched on, coming at last to a page of clear writing – evidently an exercise.

'How's your Hindustani?' asked Joe. 'Can you read this?'

'Ought to be able to,' said Andrew, tracing the writing with his forefinger. 'Let me see . . . Well, it says, "To G.P. from C.K." No puzzle about that. Now, what's this? Er . . . "Don't stop me

following you" . . . I think that's right . . . "because wherever
you are . . . I will follow you . . ." Here, wait a minute,' said
Andrew. 'I know this! Dammit, this is a translation from the
Bible! Just the sort of thing, I suppose, the Fathers would have
set as a writing exercise or a translation into Hindustani.'

He half closed his eyes in an effort to remember the text
and slowly recited:

'"Entreat me not to leave thee, or to return from following
after thee: for wherever thou goest, I will go, and wherever
thou lodgest, I will lodge: my people shall be thy people and
thy God my God.

'"Where thou diest, will I die, and there will I be buried: the
Lord do so unto me, and more also, if aught but death part
thee and me."'

They looked at each other.

'From the Book of Ruth,' said Andrew, marvelling.

'It's a love letter,' said Joe. 'It's Chedi Khan's declaration to
Prentice when he sent him away to school. ". . . if aught but
death part thee and me . . ." That's it. That's what it was all
about. And Prentice saw it as the most beautiful thing in his
life. The only thing in his life. Andrew, we can only touch the
fringe of this!'

Joe sat back on his heels and Andrew sat on the floor.

'Well,' said Andrew, 'as you say, that says it all.'

'Not quite all,' Joe said. He held up the bloodstained exercise book and opened it at the last page. 'This does say it all
though.'

The writing was Prentice's, cursive and carelessly sloping.

'"And the king was much moved, and went up to the cham-
ber over the gate, and wept and as he went thus he said, 'Oh,
Absalom, my son, my son. Would God I had died for thee.'
G.P. 1910"'

Chapter Twenty-Five

ANDREW CLOSED HIS eyes in exhaustion and pity. He leant back against the charpoy and after a while reached out and took Joe's hand. 'Well done!' he said. 'You did it.'

'Did it?' said Joe bitterly. 'God! What a mess!'

'No one could have done more. I can think of no one who could have done as much.'

'Prentice?' said Joe. 'What about Prentice? What can I think of him?'

'Think this – that he was an evil man, a cruel and a deadly man and he's gone to his reward. And as for Nancy – my wife! – well, by God, Joe, I'm proud of her! And think of something else – Midge is alive in this bloodstained house and that was where it was all tending.'

'I didn't do *anything*,' said Joe. 'Nothing whatever. I just let events unroll. And Prentice's death – that was no doing of mine. And Midge is alive and that was no doing of mine either.'

'Rubbish, man,' said Andrew firmly. 'You did everything! You got to her just in time. You worked it out. I saw that room – the bonfire. A few more minutes and he'd have applied the match.'

'But what the hell do we do now? How can we find words to explain all this to Midge?'

'We can't leave Prentice here,' said Andrew with sudden decision, attempting to get to his feet. Joe hauled him up and balanced him. Once he was steady on his feet Andrew took command. 'Get hold of Naurung. We'll carry the body back up to the house.' He added with embarrassment, 'I'll make that an order, Joe. Carry him up to the house!'

'We're disturbing the evidence,' said Joe. 'He should lie where he was killed.'

'For whose inspection, Joe? Yours and mine. You are the police representative appointed by the Governor to handle this and you are immediately responsible to me. I am the Collector of Panikhat. I am the Law Officer. Do I have to tell the world that the commander of a famous and distinguished cavalry regiment heartlessly killed four women – wives of his fellow officers – over a period, that he attempted to murder his own daughter and that he was shot to death by the Collector's wife? How does it sound?'

'Not the world,' said Joe. 'No, the world, perhaps, need not know but there is one person at least who must hear the truth.'

Leaving Andrew to watch over the body, Joe made his way back up the track to the bungalow and called Naurung. They set off down the garden together. With difficulty they carried Prentice and laid him on his bed. They looked down on him, on that bitter, vengeful face softened in death.

'It's a noble face,' said Joe consideringly.

'It's the face of a devil!' said Naurung hotly. 'He deserved to die. Over and over again. Would that I could make him suffer as he made others suffer! God will not forgive him and I, Naurung Singh, will never forgive him! But now I understand what must be done.'

He took a box of matches from his pocket and lit a small lamp, setting it on the table beside Prentice's head. By its flickering light, it seemed for a moment that, in death, that violent man was smiling.

Naurung turned with surprising authority to Andrew.

'Now, sahib, I beg – go back to the memsahib and to Missy Sahib and take the Commander with you. Leave me here. I am in charge of the crime scene. I will go and sit on the verandah and wait for the morning. Perhaps I may go to sleep. People are notoriously careless when they are asleep. Especially after what has happened.'

'Andrew!' said Joe urgently. 'Just reflect what you're doing! The suppression of evidence . . .'

'Oh, Joe,' said Andrew with affection, 'you're eternally the Good Centurion! You know I'm right. Naurung – am I right?'

'Yes, indeed, sahib.' He turned to Joe. 'Think of Missy. She will wake to a tragic accident. She will not wake to the bonfire, the bloodstains, the knowledge that her father is many times a murderer. I think for her, I think not for police procedures.'

Kitty's prophetic remark replayed in his head: 'There are the living to consider and to me they are more important than the dead. Perhaps even more important than the truth.' A view so opposed to his own, so at variance with his training and beliefs he could not accept it. What could be more important than the truth? But perhaps he was asking the wrong question. Shouldn't he be asking *who* could be more important than the truth? And the answer was clear and immediate. Midge was. Nancy was. Andrew was.

Without further question, Joe offered Andrew his arm and they set off up the dark street together.

'Getting a bit old for this sort of thing! Long past my bedtime. Shan't be sorry when we can get back to normal life,' Andrew murmured between clenched teeth as he laboured on beside Joe. 'See Bulstrode in the morning. Not now. Give Naurung a chance to tidy up.'

'Things as they are at the moment, I think even Bulstrode might notice something out of the ordinary had happened!' said Joe.

They paused at the end of the drive to the Drummond bungalow to give Andrew time to get his breath and both men looked up at the sky. It was the still moment before dawn.

'Good Lord, we'll be hearing Reveille soon,' said Andrew. 'There's a lot to arrange. Funeral for a start. I'll talk to Neddy about it. The Greys are very good at that sort of thing. Have to notify George Jardine, I suppose . . . Press announcement . . . I take it Midge is his next of kin. This is all up to me as her trustee and Giles' executor . . .'

His voice muttered on. Already his official personality was taking over from the desperate participant in the bloody doings of the night. But Joe could not yet fight his way clear. He turned and looked back down towards Curzon Street. A white mist from the river was rising, curling its way through the garden wilderness and reaching out to the bungalow. 'The Churel,' thought Joe. 'She's come to gather him in. She will have her revenge for those innocent souls. God, I'm tired!'

They stood together for a moment, lost in thought. Finally Andrew said, 'Come on, only a few more steps! Let's get off the street. Too embarrassing to be seen out here together, covered in blood and gaping at the moon.'

Chapter Twenty-Six

SAFFRON SKY TO the east was announcing dawn as Joe reached the stables. Running a hand over his face, he realised that he was both bloodstained and unshaven and to any passer-by would look disreputable and suspicious. He did the best he could; quickly plunging his head into a stable bucket and taking a towel from a nail nearby, he cleaned himself up and revived himself. He had not misjudged his man. Walking rapidly, William Somersham, punctual to the minute, came in view.

He stopped dead at the sight of Joe.

'Sandilands!' he said. 'You get earlier and earlier! What brings you here? I'm riding out. Won't you join me?' And, looking more carefully at Joe and taking in the bloodstains, 'What's happened? What's happened to you?'

'Somersham,' said Joe, taking him by the elbow, 'William, there's something you have to know.'

At once the horses began to stir uneasily and sniff the air. A moment later the smell of smoke borne on the wind off the river reached Joe's nostrils. 'Come with me,' he said and led Somersham to the door. The stars were dimming, the moon hung on the horizon ahead of them. Joe pointed down towards Curzon Street.

'Look there!'

The river mist was now swirling, shroudlike, about the bungalow. As they watched, silenced by the eeriness of the scene, a denser whiteness began to flow from the open doors and windows.

'Good God!' said Somersham. 'What is this? What are you showing me? It's fire! Is that Prentice's house? On fire? Again? What the hell's happening, Sandilands? I can't believe this!'

Transfixed, they gazed on as sparks began to shoot from the roof and a yellow flame began to lick its way along the edge of the thatch. The yellow flames turned to shooting sheets of orange leaping upwards and, with an exclamation of dismay, they watched as a blood red fireball burst out from the roof and hung momentarily over the house.

'Christ! You know I've seen this before, twelve years ago,' said Somersham. 'Surely not again!'

The rapid clamour of a bugle shattered the silence of the morning.

'We must go down there,' said Somersham urgently. 'We must run!'

'No! No, William, please listen to me. I know there's no one alive in there. There's something you have to know.'

As they watched, with commendable speed a horse-drawn fire engine galloped up from the infantry lines, furiously driven by a bearded Sikh and followed by the Shropshire fire picket at the double.

'Stay, William,' said Joe, 'and listen to me. The last time we spoke you asked if I was getting any nearer a solution.'

'Yes, I remember,' said Somersham. 'You gave me hope.'

'I can give you more than hope now. I have the murderer.'

'Peg's murderer?'

'Not only your wife – Joan Carmichael, Sheila Forbes, Alicia Simms-Warburton and – but for the mercy of God – his own daughter. It was Giles Prentice.'

'Prentice, you say? Prentice did these foul things? And he's still alive?'

'No,' said Joe. 'Dead. He's dead. He admitted his crimes. He would have murdered his daughter. He was shot in the act.'

Dazed, Somersham turned around and went to sit down heavily on the straw bale.

'Prentice!' he said. 'But how? And why?'

'I'll do my best to explain,' said Joe, patting his pockets in vain. He held out his hand. 'Give me a cigarette, shove over and I'll tell you.' He joined him on the straw bale.

Carefully he laid out the whole tale of Prentice's iniquity concluding with the words, 'Andrew Drummond said to me, "Find him. You find him and I'll shoot him." I found him, though perhaps more accurately he declared himself as such people often do, unable to believe that anyone could frustrate their purpose, but it was Nancy who shot him.'

'Nancy! And what now?' said William. 'Nancy – is she – er – all right? Is she safe? What would this be? Justifiable homicide? I hope she's not in trouble with the law . . .'

'There would be formalities to be gone through, of course, but no, I don't think she's in trouble with the law. My concern is not for Nancy but for Midge.'

'Midge?'

'Prentice's daughter, Minette.'

'Of course, Midge. Poor child. But look here, I say, Sandilands, Prentice's house is on fire. The evidence will be destroyed, won't it? Does she have to know what happened? Does she have to know her father was many times a murderer? Wouldn't it be possible to keep this knowledge from her?'

Joe hesitated a long time before replying. 'William, you're the only person in the world who could say that. I can't bring your wife's murderer to justice *and* keep the facts from Midge.'

'Justice!' said Somersham explosively. 'If Prentice were alive, I'd find the means to bring him to judgement. Silly Billy Somersham would have found the strength! But as it is, Joe, for God's sake – spare that child and for the rest, let pass the judgement of God.'

Chapter Twenty-Seven

THE ECHO OF the volley discharged by a Shropshire Light Infantry firing party over the grave of Giles Prentice died away and with it the rumble of wheels from the gun carriage which had carried him from his house to the cantonment cemetery. The clatter of hooves from the six grey troop-horses of Bateman's Horse was silent at last and the serried ranks of Greys sowars – black mourning bands wound about their turbans – had tearfully dispersed to their barracks to grieve in private for the man who had brought them safely back from France. There were, at the last, some to weep for him, thought Joe. He watched as Prentice's horse with muffled hooves and Prentice's boots reversed and suspended on either side of the saddle was led away to the stable.

George Jardine's Daimler with liveried chauffeur and footman waited outside Nancy's bungalow. 'I suppose I must go and talk to Uncle George,' said Joe, 'but not yet.'

But at that moment, 'Joe!' called George Jardine. 'There you are! I have to go but just walk a few paces with me, will you?'

He put his arm through Joe's and they turned aside from the crowd of mourners at the churchyard gate. 'Don't say anything, Joe,' he said. 'Don't tell me anything. There are certain things I don't want to know. "Death by misadventure" – that's all I needed to hear.'

'I was going to spend the day writing a report to you,' said Joe.

'I don't want it,' said George. 'Let the dead bury their dead. And I'll tell you – you've lifted a weight from this place. I feel it. All feel it. What more can I say? Congratulations, I suppose. So – congratulations!'

'It was a mess,' said Joe morosely.

'Nothing like the mess it would have been if you hadn't been here – never forget that!'

He started off back up the road to Nancy's house but turned and said, 'Oh, by the way, Joe – that box-wallah you and Naurung tracked down – the witness Bulstrode let go in the Peggy Somersham case – police finally caught up with him in Bombay. Wonderful invention, the telegraph! You were quite right, of course – March was the month he always visited Panikhat on his itinerary. Well spotted! Religious maniac apparently. And you spotted that too! I should think that by next week we'll be announcing that we've got a confession. Wouldn't be surprised to find he's been responsible for more mayhem around the country. If anyone were to enquire. Eh? What? Wrap the case up and no need for panic next March. Should think there's a promotion coming Naurung's way, wouldn't you?'

So cheerful, sincere and delighted was his large pink face that, for a moment, Joe believed him.

'Well?' said Kitty, taking the Governor's place at Joe's side.

'"The captains and the kings depart, The tumult and the shouting dies . . ."'

'And I suppose you'll be gone too. Gone from the Land of Regrets. Without regret, I wonder? Leaving some part of your heart behind?'

'Oh, yes,' said Joe, 'certainly that.'

Kitty gave him a steely and searching look. 'Leaving anything else behind? It's all right – you don't have to answer. Everybody thinks I'm the most irresponsible tell-tale in Bengal but such is not the case. Your secret – if secret there be – is safe with me!'

'Well, Nancy?' said Joe.

'Well, Joe?' said Nancy. 'Here we are.'

'I didn't want to stay and now, when it comes to it, I don't want to go.'

'Go you must, Joe. You see it, I'm sure. But, as for me, I've lived on a tightrope for days. It's been difficult sometimes, bloody difficult, but it would become impossible. It could only work if you didn't give a damn about me and I flatter myself . . .'

'You don't have to flatter yourself,' said Joe. 'I care more than I can say.'

'Go and say a fond goodbye to Andrew, will you? And – fond is right – he thinks the world of you! I like that.'

'He's very fine,' said Joe. 'He led us all that night.'

'You're right. He is fine. I noticed it from the first all those years ago at St Omer.'

And then, after a pause, 'Did I deceive you, Joe? Were you deceived?'

'For a moment, perhaps.'

'And did you mind?'

Joe hesitated, wondering whether to speak the truth. In the end, 'No,' he said. 'I was touched and perhaps even flattered and now – what on earth can I say? Something silly like – I hope it all works out.'

'Do you want to know what happens?'

'I've thought about that. The answer really is no. I'd be distressed for you if I knew it hadn't worked and distressed for me if I knew that it had. I'm not made of marble, you know!'

Making sure that he was not followed and hoping that he wasn't seen, he slipped away, returning to the grave-side. He held a spray of small red roses in his hand.

'The last Kashmiri rose,' he said as he laid it across the grave mound.

'I saw you go and thought I'd follow you,' came a familiar voice from behind him, and Midge came and stood at his side. Her pallor and slight figure were emphasised by the funeral dress she wore, a black silk outfit of Nancy's, hurriedly adapted to her size, and a long string of borrowed pearls. She looked so insubstantial that Joe automatically put out an arm to steady her.

'Funny,' she said. 'We had the same idea. I wanted to do something. I've brought him some flowers too. He always liked these little red ones so I'll put mine with yours. What were you saying? "The last Kashmiri rose?" Is that what they are? Well, there they are, side by side.'

Joe was overcome with pity and a tear stung his eye. He held out his arms and gathered Midge to him. She rested her head on his shoulder. 'I'm sad,' she said. 'Very sad. It's funny – I can't cry.'

'Brave girl,' said Joe. 'Colonel's daughter.'

Midge began to cry at last. 'I don't feel like a Colonel's daughter,' she said, through her tears. 'Now my mother's dead, my father's dead and there's only me left.'

'Dickie?' Joe ventured.

'Oh yes, there's Dickie,' she said, drying her tears on Joe's shoulder. 'Dickie of course. He's only gone to Peshawar and now – it seems an awful thing to say, I suppose – but as soon as Nancy can arrange it we can get married.' She looked thoughtfully down at the grave.

'I expect he would have approved in the end,' said Joe comfortably.

'I wish I could think so,' said Midge, surprisingly. 'Joe?' She hesitated for a moment. 'What everybody's saying – that it was all a hideous accident . . . overturning his bedside lamp and all that . . . it's just not true. Is it? You must tell me the truth, Joe.'

With a calm he didn't feel Joe said, 'What do you mean, Midge? It was an accident.'

Midge shook her head. 'I'm not such a fool, Joe, and I know why you and Nancy and – yes, Dickie too, he's in it with you – have been trying to keep the truth from me. But I've worked it out. I woke up at Nancy's feeling very ill and they tried to tell me it was something I'd eaten. It wasn't. It was something I'd drunk. Something Daddy gave me in a glass before bedtime. It made me sleep. Now why would he want me to sleep through the night and not wake up? I'll tell you . . .'

Joe could only let her talk on while his blood froze.

'It was because he . . . oh, it was all my fault . . . Joe, he was going to commit suicide. He'd planned it. We'd had another terrible row and I'd told him I was going to run away with Dickie – go away with him when he left. I didn't mean it! But I think he couldn't bear it. He'd lost my mother and now he was to lose me. I don't think he had anything left to live for. I killed him, Joe, didn't I?'

'Now listen, Midge,' said Joe softly, stroking her hair, 'listen to an experienced London bobby, will you – the finest Scotland Yard has to offer. We know about the drugs and yes, Nancy did invent the story of the food poisoning, though now I think perhaps we should have told you the truth there and then. Giles thought you really might try to run away and to stop you jumping out of a window at midnight into Dickie's arms, he gave you a sleeping draught. Not a very strong one, according to Nancy. We think he tried to stay awake reading his book, on watch, until almost dawn. He must have nodded off at the last and knocked his lamp over. In fact, Nancy thinks he could well have had a heart attack and overturned the lamp when he died. Otherwise, of course, the flames and the heat would have wakened him. Lucky for you, Midge, that Naurung Singh was passing on his way to work and managed to pull you out. He went back for Giles but it was too late.'

Midge looked at him with large eyes, eagerly reading his face. 'Joe! Is this true? Is this really the truth you're telling me?'

Joe considered for a moment. 'Well, I might conceivably lie to you – though I can't imagine the circumstances. Dickie I know would lie if he thought he was protecting you from something but – Naurung Singh? He will tell you that Giles was in bed with an overturned lamp on the floor when he died. If your father had been intending to commit suicide he'd have simply gone into the garden and shot himself. You know your father! An old warrior like Giles wouldn't have put his pyjamas on and gone to bed with a good book!'

Midge, smiling and weeping at the same time, stood on tiptoe and kissed him.

'May I be forgiven!' said Joe but he didn't say it out loud.

Turn the page for a sneak preview of

The Blood Royal

the latest mystery starring
JOE SANDILANDS

Prologue

LONDON, OCTOBER 1920

'ARE YOU SURE this is the place, cabby? It looks rather grand...'

'St Katharine's Square, number 1, Guv'nor, just like you said. They're all grand in this neck of the woods. This *is* a Royal Borough, sir. But if you don't fancy it, we can always move on.'

'No. Wait here. I'm in no hurry.'

The passenger in naval uniform peered again through the gloom of an October evening, taking in the magnificence of the four-storey mansion.

'Well *I* may be in a hurry,' the cab driver objected. 'Fog's coming up.'

'A pea-souper, eh? I've been away for years. I've forgotten what they look like.'

'Pea-souper – nothing! This one's going to be a brown windsor, judging by the smell of it. Straight up off the river,' the grumbling went on. 'It's to be hoped they've got the acetylene flares alight round Trafalgar Square or I'll never get you back to the station, Guv.'

The naval man was barely listening, all his attention on the stuccoed, balconied façade. Electric lights penetrated the growing darkness, offering a welcoming orange glow behind drawn curtains. In the upper floors, lamps or candles were moving between rooms as staff came off or went on duty.

'Well at least there's someone at home,' he said, awkwardly throwing a pebble into the silence ponding between him and the young woman by his side.

She made no reply.

He took her hand and gave it an encouraging squeeze. 'Nearly there, Miss Petrovna! Three thousand miles and three years – but you've made it!' He spoke with a cheerfulness he couldn't feel.

Sensitive as he'd become to his companion's moods, the captain interpreted the barely audible response as a mew of distress and his resolve began to crack. He'd avoided saying farewell - he was embarrassed by emotional leave-takings, especially those made in public - and there was nothing more to add.

Even so, he launched into one last speech. 'Look... Miss... um... Anna... There's still time to change your mind. You don't have to do this yet. Come home with me.' After the slightest pause, he resumed: 'My wife would make you very welcome. Joan is a fine woman – she'd care for you. Get you properly on your feet. Our family doctor is no slouch and he'd rally round, I know. It needn't be for long. Just as long as you choose.'

She turned reproachful eyes on him and shook her head in regret.

The captain realised with a shock that he'd experienced the same devastating rejection years before. How many? Well over twenty. He'd been no more than a boy in short trousers. He'd been tramping the moors with his father when they'd come across an injured otter. A very young female. His indulgent old pa had allowed him to carry the animal home in his jacket. He'd cared for her, fed her, watched her grow strong and mischievous. And always closing his ears to the concerned parental advice: 'Wild creatures, otters! Never think you can house-train 'em! Taking little things, of course, but you shouldn't get fond of 'em.'

The day came when she escaped from her pen, invaded his mother's kitchen and wrecked it.

He hadn't waited for his parents to tell him his duty. It was clear. He'd taken her back into the wild himself, choosing a spot where he knew the fishing was good and there was a thriving otter colony. On the river bank he'd whispered goodbye, never really thinking she would leave him.

Pain had gathered and lodged in his young throat like a ball of india-rubber, threatening to suffocate him, as he watched her leap with delight into the water, dive, surface, dive again, swimming away from him. He'd turned, swiping at the tears in his eyes with the sleeve of his rough sweater and he'd begun to blunder back home across the meadow.

A piercing chirp made him stop and turn and there she was behind him, on the bank again, wet fur comically spiked, staring at him with intelligent black eyes. Black eyes he could have sworn were asking where on earth he thought *he* was sloping off to. The moment he started back towards her, calling her name, she turned, yipped in satisfaction and dived into the water.

He never saw her again.

In a busy and danger-filled life, he'd scarcely thought about her until this moment of parting raised the same choking pain.

'Very well. Message received, cabby! Look, wait here with the young lady, will you, while I go and announce us. I'll be a few minutes.'

The door was opened by a butler as he approached.

'Captain Swinburne? Good evening, sir. Her Highness is expecting you. Will you come up to the drawing room?'

He followed the butler down the spacious hallway and up the stairs. They made towards an open door through which filtered smoky, autumnal music – a Chopin nocturne, he thought. When they entered, the pianist abandoned her piece and came smiling to greet him. A striking-looking Russian woman in her fifties, dark hair streaked with grey, she made a reassuring impression on him: friendly and, yes, he would have said – motherly. Somehow, he hadn't expected – motherly. Or small.

Sherry was offered and politely refused. He declined to take a seat by the fire.

Facing him across the rug in front of the fireplace, the princess came straight to the point. 'You have her, Captain? Our Anna?'

'Miss Petrovna is waiting in the taxi, Your Highness, and eager to see you. I wanted to have a word with you in private before I leave her in your hands.'

She listened intently as he moved through his account. He confirmed that the girl had been found collapsed and almost dead on the doorstep of the British consul in Murmansk in Northern Russia. On recovering sufficiently, she had begged to be given a passage to Britain where she knew members of her family were living. The consul had contacted Swinburne aboard his ship which was patrolling the Arctic seas off shore. He'd agreed to take her on board and bring her back to Portsmouth where he was due to call in for a refit in the autumn.

He was quite certain that none of this was fresh news to the Russian lady but she listened intently to every word, seeming to value his first-hand report.

He told her how pleased the ship's doctor had been with the patient's progress. The best food the boat could provide, fresh air, exercise and the stimulation of a late summer's cruise along the coast of Norway had almost restored her to full physical health. The captain was careful to explain that the ship had been conveying back home a consular family who had gladly lent one of their maids as nurse cum chaperone so all the proprieties had been observed.

The Russian acknowledged this with a tilt of the head and an understanding smile.

But it was the girl's mental state that he needed to lay out for her future guardian, he stressed. 'She has suffered unbelievable hardship... loss... torture would not be too strong a word... unremitting squalor for three years. Anyone less strong and tenacious of life would not have survived. But the work is not yet finished - it will be some time before she's fully recovered. It's possible that the services of an alienist might be called upon with advantage.' A radical suggestion but the lady seemed not to be offended. She even nodded in acceptance and Swinburne felt emboldened to press his point. 'There are physicians in London with certain skills acquired in the war... Anna's condition is in some ways similar to those I have witnessed for myself in men experiencing the prolonged terrors of the battlefield. And, survivor that she is, she deserves the appropriate treatment. I would like you to be aware of this. I will not leave her in any situation that I do not judge to be congenial and capable of responding to her condition.'

He knew he was going too far. His stewardship was officially at an end; he had to recognise the superior authority of the noble lady to whom he was daring to dish out advice and demands. But Captain Swinburne was not a man to retreat from a position he'd taken up, whether his feet were on the deck of a gunboat or on a silken rug in a douce London drawing room.

She looked up at him sharply, scanning his weather-beaten features and standing firm before the challenge in his very English blue eyes.

He steeled himself to receive the set-down he'd merited.

But the princess's response when it came was thoughtful: 'Captain, it occurs to me that losing *your* support could constitute yet another blow to Anna's well-being.'

'I did what I could. Believe me, ma'am, it was her choice to break the bond we have established.' The words stretched between them, vibrating with a resentment he had not intended. He hurried to add: 'But an encouraging sign, I'm sure you'll agree. She's ready to move forward. She recognises now that she has a future and I do believe she is making plans for it.' He broke off, unwilling to say more and indicated that he was ready to bring her in.

As he passed the grand piano, Swinburne's attention was caught by a photograph, the one at the forefront of a cluster of silver-framed portraits arranged on the shining surface. He exclaimed and went to examine more closely a group of five or six earnest-looking young women dressed in nurse's uniform, a flutter of angels gathered in a semiformal pose around a bed in a hospital ward. The wounded soldier at the centre of their attention looked suitably overawed.

'There she is! That's Anna! Good Lord! She actually *was* a nurse! So much she didn't tell me...'

Responding to the invitation in the Russian's expression, he smiled, eyes on the photograph. 'One of my crew was careless enough to cut his leg to the bone on a day when our doctor was ashore in Trondheim. They brought him to me, dripping blood and swooning and Anna, who was with me on deck, snapped out of her torpid state and had the chap sedated, stitched up and bandaged with all the skill of a medic in no time. Saved the leg, I reckon.'

The lady chuckled. 'She was always a fine needlewoman! But none of these girls was truly a nurse, you know. Amateurs all, some more capable than others. Some with decorative merit only. You're looking, Captain, at the contents of the topmost drawer of the Russian aristocracy doing their bit in wartime for their country. The Empress Alexandra herself led by example and floated through the wards in cape and wimple dispensing comfort. Though I ought not to disparage their efforts – they meant well and, in Anna's case, acquired a genuine skill they say. But, Captain... you do well to pick her out amongst so many beauties and all wearing an unflattering starched head-dress...?'

The question was lightly put but Swinburne was a man sensitive to the slightest change in wind and current. He picked up an underlying tension. Was he being quizzed in some way? Had the photograph, prominently placed as it was, been set there deliberately as some kind of test? He didn't doubt it. The captain was straightforward. He couldn't be doing with traps and subtleties. And he could understand the lady's deeper concerns. His reply came at once.

'Be assured, Ma'am. I'd know her face anywhere. It's the line of the nose – like a Greek statue... and the dark eyebrows – they have the sweep of a gull's wing. She's the one on the far left. I'd no idea this was her world.'

The Russian who had been tugging at the pearls at her throat in some suspense, sighed with relief at his identification and stopped her fidgeting. She came to stand at his side, looking at the photograph with him, relaxed now and companionable. Whatever test she'd just administered – he seemed to have passed it and, puzzled, he listened as she made further confidences. 'Yes, Captain. That is indeed our Anna. My poor dead cousin Peter's daughter. I held her in my arms the day she was born.'

He was pleased to note in her voice the tremble of an emotion she could no longer hold back, the tears gathering in her eyes, the furtive hunting in her sleeve for a handkerchief. She accepted the crisp square of linen he had instantly to hand and put it to use with grace and murmured thanks. After a moment, she spoke again more brightly. 'As a child, Anna spent many a summer with us in the Crimea... she will feel at home here with me now. But I share your dismay and wonder at a world so abruptly and tragically torn from us. Well connected as she was, Anna would have made a good marriage. She could have had her pick of the finest young men of Europe. Probably not royalty but a count at the very least... a duke perhaps? Sadly now all dead or dispersed and she herself ruined beyond any hope of...'

She suppressed the alarming thought and her tone became crisp. 'But then... that is all past and we must look, as you say, to her future. You may leave her with us in total confidence. I have heard your words and understood the deeper concerns on which you are tactfully silent. I say again – I will provide the care she needs.'

Swinburne had heard the same tone from admirals and generals. There was only one acceptable answer: 'Yes, sir. Of course, sir.' This tiny, decisive woman he had no knowledge of and no reason to trust, had, unaccountably, got under his defences. He nodded his superfluous agreement. 'Yes, ma'am. Of course, ma'am,' he said and he smiled as he spoke.

Swinburne bowed and made to leave.

'Wait, Captain!' She hesitated for a moment then picked up the photograph and handed it to him. 'If you will keep it for your eyes alone you may have this – some slight reward for your care. But be discreet! We aristocrats all have a price on our heads still and are pursued. London is full of ruthless men. Not a few of them, our enemies.'

As he took it from her, mumbling his thanks, he caught a flash of indulgence and pity in her eyes. She'd guessed his secret in minutes. Time he was gone.

∽

The two women ran into each other's arms exclaiming softly in delighted recognition. Swinburne skirted silently around them in the hallway, glad enough to hear:

'Aunt Tizzi!'...

'Anna! My dear girl! At last! We have you safe!'

In the outburst of tears and sobs that followed, they didn't hear him leaving.

∽

He was blameless. As innocent as the obliging bird that gob-bles down the inky, sweet berry of the deadly nightshade then flies off unwittingly to disperse the seed, Captain Swinburne had just dropped off a deadly cargo in a fertile corner of London.

He prepared to move on.

'We're finished here, cabby. Back to Piccadilly while you can still see the road.'

He shouldn't have looked back.

A last glance through the window showed him Anna. She'd come outside again and was standing motionless, neither wav-ing away nor beckoning back, watching him leave. The fog was coming down and he couldn't make out her face but, in his imagination, he saw her dark otter's eyes following him as the taxi drew away.

OTHER TITLES IN THE SOHO CRIME SERIES